Critical acclaim for Tami Hoag

'[Tami Hoag] confirms that she can turn out a police procedural as gritty, grimy and engrossing as the best of them . . . Hoag is in a crowded procedural market but the quality of the writing makes *Dust to Dust* a standout novel'
Observer

'Grisly tension is not the only commodity on offer here – the internal politics of the police investigations are handled with genuine panache . . . Hoag has demonstrated . . . an effortless command of the thriller technique, adroitly juggling the twin demands of character and plot. The set-piece confrontations will ensure that it will take quite a lot to distract the reader from Hoag's narrative' *Crime Time*

'A top-class follow-up to Hoag's bestseller *Ashes to Ashes*'
Publishing News

'Her books are cleverly plotted, feature strong female protagonists and are extremely – often emetically – violent . . . Hoag has the bestselling writer's way with a punchy sentence and keeps the surprises coming right up to the very last page'
The Times

'First-rate procedural detail with credible crew of homicide cops, spectacularly foul-mouthed and fending off the horrors with dirty jokes. Some ornate plotting . . . worth your while, though, if not for the faint-hearted'
Literary Review

'Lock the doors and windows, and turn on all the lights – Hoag has crafted a knuckle-whitening, spine-chilling thriller'
New Woman

'Accomplished and scary'
Cosmopolitan

Since the publication of her first book in 1988, Tami Hoag's novels have appeared regularly on the bestseller lists, including seven consecutive *New York Times* bestsellers. She lives in California. Visit her website at www.tamihoag.com.

By Tami Hoag

DUST TO DUST

TAMI HOAG

An Orion paperback

First published in Great Britain in 2000
by Orion
This paperback edition published in 2001
by Orion Books Ltd,
Orion House, 5 Upper St Martin's Lane,
London WC2H 9EA

Reissued 2007

A CIP catalogue record for this book is available
from the British Library.

Typeset at Deltatype Ltd, Birkenhead, Merseyside
Printed and bound in Great Britain by

The Orion Publishing Group's policy is to use papers that
are natural, renewable and recyclable products and
made from wood grown in sustainable forests. The logging
and manufacturing processes are expected to conform to
the environmental regulations of the country of origin.

www.orionbooks.co.uk

To the very good friends who
helped me through a very bad time:
Bob, Betsy, Jessie
and, as always, the Divas

Acknowledgements

The author wishes to thank the following people for their help and support in the making of this book:

Special Agent Larry Brubaker, FBI (retired); Sergeant Mark Lenzen, Homicide unit, Minneapolis Police Department; Sergeant Mike Carlson, Homicide unit, Minneapolis Police Department; Commander Thomas Reding, Internal Affairs, St Paul Police Department; Robert Crais; Eileen Dreyer; Nita Taublib; Beth de Guzman; and Andrea Cirillo.

PROLOGUE

It is stunning how quickly it happens. How little time it takes to go from trouble to tragedy. Seconds. Mere seconds without air and the brain begins to shut down. No time to struggle. No time to panic even.

Like a boa constrictor choking the life from its prey, the noose tightens and tightens. It makes no difference what thoughts explode in the brain. *Move! Grab the rope! Get air!* The commands don't make it down the neural pathways to the muscles of the arms. Coordination is gone.

The sturdy rope makes a tearing sound as the weight of his body stretches it. The beam creaks.

His body turns slightly this way and that. The arms pull upward in hideous, slow-motion spasms. A macabre marionette's dance – arms moving up and down; hands twitching, twisting, bending; fingers curling. The knees try to draw upward, then straighten again. Posturing: a sign of brain damage.

The eerie contortions go on and on. The seconds stretch as the death dance continues. A minute. Two. Four. The rope and beam creak in the otherwise silent room. The eyes are open but vacant. Mouth moves in a final, futile gasp for air. The most acute, exquisite split second of life: the final heartbeat before death.

And then it is over.

At last.

The flash explodes in a brilliant burst of white light and the scene is frozen in time.

I

'They oughta hang the son of a bitch came up with this shit,' Sam Kovac groused, digging a piece of nicotine gum out of a crumpled foil pack.

'The gum or the wrapper?'

'Both. I can't open the damn package and I'd rather chew on a cat turd.'

'And that would taste different from a cigarette how?' Nikki Liska asked.

They moved through a small throng of people in the wide white hall. Cops heading out onto the steps of the Minneapolis city hall for a cigarette, cops coming back in from having a cigarette, and the odd citizen looking for something for their tax dollar.

Kovac scowled down at her from the corner of one eye. Liska made five-five by sheer dint of will. He always figured God made her short because if she had the size of Janet Reno she'd take over the world. She had that kind of energy – and attitude out the wazoo.

'What do you know about it?' he challenged.

'My ex smoked. Lick an ashtray sometime. That's why we got divorced, you know. I wouldn't stick my tongue in his mouth.'

'Jesus, Tinks, like I wanted to know that.'

He'd given her the nickname – Tinker Bell on Steroids. Nordic blond hair cut in a shaggy Peter Pan style, eyes as blue as a lake on a sunny day. Feminine but unmistakably athletic. She'd kicked more ass in her years on the force than half the guys he knew. She'd come onto homicide – Christ, what was it now? – five or six years ago? He lost track. He'd been there himself almost longer than he could

3

remember. All of his forty-four years, it seemed. The better part of a twenty-three-year career, for certain. Seven to go. He'd get his thirty and take the pension. Catch up on his sleep for the next ten years. He sometimes wondered why he hadn't taken his twenty and moved on. But he didn't have anything to move on to, so he stayed.

Liska slipped between a pair of nervous-looking uniforms blocking the way in front of the door to Room 126 – Internal Affairs.

'Hey, that was the least of it,' she said. 'I was more upset about where he wanted to put his dick.'

Kovac made a sound of pain and disgust, his face twisting.

Liska grinned, mischievous and triumphant. 'Her name was Brandi.'

The Criminal Investigative Division offices had been newly refurbished. The walls were the color of dried blood. Kovac wondered if that had been intentional or just trendy. Probably the latter. Nothing else in the place had been designed with cops in mind. The narrow, gray, two-person cubicles could just as well have housed a bunch of accountants.

He preferred the temporary digs they'd had during the remodeling: a dirty, beat-up room full of dirty, beat-up desks, and beat-up cops getting migraines under harsh white fluorescent lights. Homicide crammed into one room, robbery down the way, half the sex crimes guys wedged into a broom closet. That was atmosphere.

'What's the status on the Nixon assault?'

The voice stopped Kovac in his tracks as effectively as a hook to the collar. He bit a little harder on the Nicorette. Liska kept moving.

New offices, new lieutenant, new pain in the ass. The homicide lieutenant's office had a figurative revolving door. It was a stop on the way for upwardly mobile management types. At least this new one – Leonard – had them back working partners instead of like the last guy, who'd tortured them with some bullshit high-concept team crap with rotating sleep-deprivation schedules.

Of course, that didn't mean he wasn't an asshole.

'We'll see,' Kovac said. 'Elwood just brought in a guy he thinks is good for the Truman murder.'

Leonard flushed pink. He had that kind of complexion, and short, white-gray hair like duck fuzz all over his head. 'What the hell are you doing working the Truman murder? That's what? A week ago? You're up to your ass in assaults since then.'

Liska came back then, wearing her cop face. 'We think this guy's a two-fer, Lou. He was maybe in on Nixon *and* Truman. I guess the Nation wants to start calling the Bloods the Dead Presidents.'

Kovac laughed at that – a cross between a bark and a snort. 'Like these dickheads would know a president if he pissed on them.'

Liska looked up at him. 'Elwood's got him in the guest room. Let's go before he uses the L word.'

Leonard stepped back, frowning. He had no lips, and ears that stuck out perpendicular to his head like a chimpanzee's. Kovac had nicknamed him the Brass Monkey. He was looking as if solving a murder would ruin his day.

'Don't worry,' Kovac said. 'There's more assaults where that one came from.'

He turned away before Leonard could react, and headed for the interview room with Liska.

'So this guy was in on Nixon too?'

'Beats me. Leonard liked it.'

'Brass asshole,' Kovac grumbled. 'Someone should take him out and show him the fucking sign on the door. It still says "Homicide," doesn't it?'

'Last I looked.'

'All he wants is to clear assaults.'

'Assaults are the homicides of tomorrow.'

'Yeah, that'd make a great tattoo. I know just where he can put it.'

'But you'd need a miner's hat to read it. I'll get you one for Christmas. Give you something to hope for.'

Liska opened the door and Kovac preceded her into the room, which was about the size of a spacious coat closet. The architect would have described it as 'intimate.' In keeping with the latest theories on how to interview scumbags, the table was small and round. No dominant side. Everybody equal. Pals. Confidants.

No one was sitting at it.

Elwood Knutson stood in the near corner, looking like a Disney cartoon bear in a black felt bowler. Jamal Jackson had the opposite corner, near the totally useless and empty built-in bookcase, and beneath the wall-mounted video camera, which was required by Minnesota law to prove they weren't beating confessions out of suspects.

Jackson's attitude hung on him as badly as his clothes. Jeans that would have fit Elwood were slipping off his skinny ass. A huge down coat in Nation black and red colors puffed up around his upper body. He had a lower lip as thick as a garden hose, and he stuck it out at Kovac.

'Man, this is bogus. I din' off no-body.'

Kovac lifted his brows. 'No? Gee, there must be some mistake.' He turned to Elwood and spread his hands. 'I thought you said he was the guy, Elwood. He says he's not the guy.'

'I must have been mistaken,' Elwood said. 'My profuse apologies, Mr Jackson.'

'We'll have a radio car take you back home,' Kovac said. 'Maybe have them announce over the bullhorn to your 'hood that we didn't mean to bring you in. That it was all a big mistake.'

Jackson stared at him, the lip moving up and down.

'We can have them announce specifically that we know you weren't really involved in the murder of Deon

6

Truman. Just so there's no mistake what we had you in for. We don't want a lot of bad rumors going around about you on account of us.'

'Fuck you, man!' Jackson shouted, his voice jumping an octave. 'You trying to get me killed?'

Kovac laughed. 'Hey. You said you didn't do it. Fine. I'll send you home.'

'An' the brothers think I talk to you. Next thing, my ass is horizontal. Fuck that!'

Jackson paced a little, pulling at the short braids that stuck up in all directions on his head. His hands were cuffed together in front of him. He gave Kovac the eye.

'You put me in jail, motherfucker.'

'Can't do it. And here you asked so nice. Sorry.'

'I am *under arrest*,' Jamal insisted.

'Not if you didn't do anything.'

'I done plenty.'

'So now you're confessing?' Liska said.

Jackson looked at her, incredulous. 'Who the hell is she? Your girlfriend?'

'Don't insult the lady,' Kovac said. 'You're telling us you capped Deon Truman.'

'The fuck I am.'

'Then who did?'

'Fuck you, man. I ain't telling you jack.'

'Elwood, see that the man gets home in style.'

'But I'm *under arrest!*' Jackson wailed. 'Put me in jail!'

'Fuck you,' Kovac said. 'Jail's overcrowded. It's not a goddamn hotel. What'd you pick him up on, Elwood?'

'I believe it was loitering.'

'Petty misdemeanor.'

'The fuck!' Jackson shouted, outraged. He pointed at Elwood with both index fingers. 'You saw me selling crack! Right there on the corner of Chicago and Twenty-sixth.'

'He have crack on him when you arrested him?' Kovac asked.

7

'No, sir. He did have a pipe.'

'I ditched the goods!'

'Possession of drug paraphernalia,' Liska said, unimpressed. 'Big deal. Cut him loose. He's not worth our time.'

'Fuck you, bitch!' Jamal said, swaggering toward her. 'I wouldn't let you suck my cock.'

'I'd rather gouge my eyes out with a rusty nail.' Liska advanced on him, blue glare boring into him like a pair of cold lasers. 'Keep it in your pants, Jamal. If you live long enough, maybe you'll find some nice guy in prison to do it for you.'

'He's not going to prison today,' Kovac announced impatiently. 'Let's wrap this up. I got a party to go to.'

Jackson made his move as Kovac started to turn for the door. He pulled one of the loose shelves out of the bookcase and rushed Kovac from behind. Caught back on his heels, Elwood shouted an obscenity and jumped too late. Kovac swung around in time to catch the corner of the shelf, the board slicing a gash above his left eyebrow.

'Shit!'

'Dammit!'

Kovac went down on his knees, his vision lacy with a spiderweb of black. The floor felt like rubber beneath him.

Elwood grabbed Jackson's wrists and jammed his arms upward, and the board went flying, a corner of it gouging the new wall.

Then Jackson screamed and went down suddenly, his left knee buckling beneath him. Halfway down he screamed again, back arching. Elwood jumped back, wide-eyed.

Liska rode Jackson down from behind, her knee in the middle of his back as his face hit the floor.

The door opened and half a dozen detectives stood with guns drawn. Liska raised a short black ASP tactical baton, looking surprised and innocent.

'Gosh, look what I found in my coat pocket!'

She leaned down over Jamal Jackson's ear and murmured

8

seductively, 'Looks like I'll get to fulfill one of your wishes, Jamal. You're under arrest.'

'Looks kind of faggy.'

'Is that the voice of authority, Tippen?'

'Fuck you, Tinks.'

'Is that a no or wishful thinking?'

Laughter erupted around the table, the kind of raw, hard laughter that came from people who saw too much ugliness on a day-to-day basis. Cop humor was rude and biting because the world they lived in was a crude and savage place. They had no time or patience for Noel Coward repartee.

The group had snagged a coveted corner table at Patrick's, an Irish-named bar owned and run by Swedes. On an ordinary day the pub – strategically located equidistant between the Minneapolis Police Department and the Hennepin County Sheriff's Office – was packed belly to butt with cops this time of day. Day-shift cops gearing down and loading up for life off the job. Retired cops who'd found they couldn't socialize with regular humans once they'd left the job. Dog-watch guys grabbing dinner and camaraderie, killing time before they were up for their tour.

This was not an ordinary day. The usual crowd had been augmented by PD brass, city politicos, and newsies. Unwelcome additions that put an extra layer of tension in the air that was already blue with smoke and language. A news crew from one of the local stations was setting up near the front window.

'You should've insisted on real stitches. The old-fashioned kind,' Tippen went on.

He tapped the ash off his cigarette and raised it to his lips for a long drag, his attention narrowed on the camera crew. He had a face like an Irish wolfhound: long and homely with a bristly gray mustache and fiercely intelligent dark eyes. A detective with the Sheriff's Office, he had been a member of the task force that had worked the Cremator murders a little more than a year before. Some of the task force members had become the kind of friends who did this – met in a bar to drink and talk shop and insult one another.

'Then he ends up with a big ugly Frankenstein scar,' Liska said. 'With the butterfly clamp, he gets a neat, thin scar – the kind women find sexy.'

'Sadistic women,' Elwood commented.

Tippen curled his lip. 'Is there another kind?'

'Sure. The kind who go out with you,' Liska said. 'Masochists.'

Tippen flicked a corn chip at her.

Kovac regarded himself critically in the mirror of Liska's compact. The split in his forehead had been cleaned and patched by an overworked resident in the Hennepin County Medical Center ER, where gangbangers were regularly patched up or zipped into body bags. He'd been embarrassed to go there with anything less than a gunshot wound, and the young woman had given him the attitude that treating anything less was beneath her. Sexual attraction hadn't been a part of the picture.

He assessed the damage with a critical eye. His face was a quadrangle punctuated with stress lines, a couple of scars, and a hawkish, crooked nose that made a nice accompaniment to the crooked, sardonic mouth lurking beneath the requisite cop mustache. The hair was more gray than brown. Once a month he paid an old Norwegian barber ten bucks to cut it, which probably accounted for the fact that it tended to stand up.

He'd never been handsome in the GQ sense of the word, but he'd never sent women running either – at least not because of his looks. One more scar wasn't going to matter.

Liska studied him as she sipped her beer. 'It gives you character, Sam.'

'It gives me a headache,' he groused, handing the compact back to her. 'I already had all the character I needed.'

'Well, I'd kiss it and make it better for you. But I already kneecapped the guy who did it. I think I've done my part.'

'And you wonder why you're single,' Tippen remarked.

Liska blew him a kiss. 'Hey, love me, love my ASP. Or in your case, Tip, kiss my ASP.'

The front door swung open and a gust of cold air swept in, along with a new pack of patrons. Every cop's eye in the place went instantly flat, and the tension level cranked a notch. The cop collective guarding against outsiders.

'The man of the hour,' Elwood said, as recognition rippled through the crowd and a cheer went up. 'Come to hobnob with the unwashed masses before his ascension.'

Kovac said nothing. Ace Wyatt stood in the doorway in a double-breasted camel-hair topcoat, looking like Captain America, master of all he surveyed. Square jaw, white smile, groomed like a fucking game-show host. He probably tipped his hairstylist ten bucks and got a complimentary blowjob from the shampoo girl.

'Is he wearing makeup?' Tippen asked under his breath. 'I heard he gets his eyelashes dyed.'

'That's what happens when you go Hollywood,' Elwood said.

'I'd be willing to suffer the indignity,' Liska said sarcastically. 'Did you hear the kind of money he's getting for that show?'

Tippen took a long pull on his cigarette and exhaled. Kovac looked at Captain Ace Wyatt through the cloud. They'd worked on the same squad for a time. It seemed a hundred years ago. He'd just made the move from robbery to homicide. Wyatt was the top dog, already a legend, and angling to become a star on the brass side of things. He'd succeeded handsomely within the department, then branched out into television – maintaining his office as a

CID captain and starring in a Minneapolis cross between *America's Most Wanted* and a motivational infomercial. The show, *Crime Time*, was going national.

'I hate that guy.'

He reached for the Jack he wasn't supposed to mix with his painkillers and tossed back what was left of it.

'Jealous?' Liska needled.

'Of what? Being a prick?'

'Don't sell yourself short, Kojak. You're as big a prick as any man here.'

Kovac made a growl at the back of his throat, suddenly wanting to be anywhere but here. Why in hell had he come? He had three parts of a concussion, and a perfect excuse to beg off and go home. So there was nothing to go home to – an empty house with an empty aquarium in the living room. The fish had all died of neglect while he'd pulled nearly seventy-two hours straight on the Cremator case. He hadn't bothered to replace them.

Sitting at a party for Ace Wyatt, he was as big a masochist as any woman Tippen had ever dated. He'd finished his drink. As soon as Wyatt's posse cleared the door, he could make his way through the crowd and slip out. Maybe go down to the bar where the Fifth Precinct cops hung out. They could give a shit about Ace Wyatt.

In the instant he made the decision, Wyatt spotted him and zeroed in with a blinding grin, a quartet of minions trailing after him. He wove through the crowd, touching hands and shoulders like the Pope giving cursory blessings.

'Kojak, you old warhorse!' he shouted above the din. He took hold of Sam's hand in a powerful grasp.

Kovac came up out of his chair, the floor seeming to shift beneath his feet. The aftereffects of his close encounter with the board, or the mix of drugs and booze. It sure as hell wasn't his thrill at Wyatt's attention. The asshole, calling him Kojak. He hated the nickname. People who knew him well mostly used it to grind him.

One of the minions came in close with a Polaroid and the flash damn near blinded him.

'One for the scrapbook,' the minion said, a thirty-something cover-boy type with shiny black hair and cobalt-blue eyes. He had the looks for a part in a low-end prime-time drama.

'I heard you took another one for the cause!' Wyatt bellowed, grinning. 'Jesus, quit while you're ahead. Quit while you still *have* a head!'

'Seven to go, Slick,' Kovac said. 'Hollywood's not beating my door down. Congratulations, by the way.'

'Thanks. Taking the show national is a chance to make a big difference.'

To the Ace Wyatt bank account, Kovac thought, but he didn't say it. What the hell. He'd never had a taste for designer suits or a weekly manicure. He was just a cop. That was all he'd ever wanted to be. Ace Wyatt had always set his sights on bigger, better, brighter, faster; reaching for the brass rings of life – and catching every goddamn one of them.

'Glad you could make it to the party, Sam.'

'Hey, I'm a cop. Free food, free booze – I'm there.'

Wyatt's gaze was already roaming for a more important hand to shake. The pretty-boy minion caught his attention and directed it toward the television camera. The Wyatt grin brightened by a couple hundred watts.

Liska popped up out of her chair like a jack-in-the-box and stuck her hand out before Wyatt could move on. 'Captain Wyatt. Nikki Liska, homicide. It's a pleasure. I enjoy your show.'

Kovac cocked a brow at her. 'My partner. Blond ambition.'

'You lucky old dog,' Wyatt said with good-natured chauvinism.

The muscles flexed in Liska's jaws as if she was swallowing something unpleasant. 'I think your idea of strengthening the link between communities and their police forces through the show and the Internet is a brilliant innovation.'

Wyatt soaked up the praise. 'America is a multimedia culture,' he said loudly, as the TV reporter – a brunette in a bright red blazer – edged in close with a microphone. Wyatt turned fully toward the camera, bending down to hear the woman's question.

Kovac looked to Liska with disapproval.

'Hey, maybe he'll give me a job as a technical consultant. I could be a technical consultant,' she said with a mischievous quirk to her lips. 'That could be my stepping-stone to working on Mel Gibson movies.'

'I'll be in the john.'

Kovac made his way through the mob that had come in to drink Ace Wyatt's booze and chow down on spicy chicken wings and deep-fried cheese. Half the people here had never met Wyatt, let alone worked with him, but they would gladly celebrate his retirement. They would have celebrated the devil's birthday for an open bar.

He stood at the back of the main room and surveyed the scene, made all the more surreal by the Christmas decorations reflecting the glare of the television lights. A sea of people – a lot of the faces familiar – yet he felt acutely alone. Empty. Time to get seriously hammered or leave.

Liska was hovering around Wyatt's people, trying to make nice with the main minion. Wyatt had moved to shake the hand of an attractive, serious-looking blonde who seemed vaguely familiar. He put his left hand on her shoulder and bent to say something in her ear. Elwood was cutting a swath through the buffet. Tippen was trying to flirt with a waitress who was looking at him as if she'd just stepped in something.

It'd be last call before they missed him. And then missing him would be just a fleeting thought.

Where's Kovac? Gone? Pass the beer nuts.

He started for the door.

'You were the best fuckin' badge on the job!' a drunken voice bellowed. 'The man who don't think so can talk to me! Come on! Come on! I'd give Ace Wyatt my goddamn legs!' he shouted.

The drunk sat in a wheelchair that teetered on the top of three shallow steps leading down to the main bar, where Wyatt stood. The drunk had no legs to give. His had been useless for twenty years. There was nothing left of them but spindly bone and atrophied muscle. In contrast, his face was full and red, his upper body a barrel.

Kovac shook his head and took a step toward the wheelchair, trying to catch the old man's attention.

'Hey, Mikey! No one's arguing,' he said.

Mike Fallon looked at him without recognition, his eyes glassy with tears. 'He's a fucking hero! Don't try to say different!' he said angrily. He swung an arm in Wyatt's direction. 'I love that man! I love that man like a son!'

The old man's voice broke on the last word, his face contorting with an inner pain that had nothing to do with the amount of Old Crow he'd put away in the past few hours.

Wyatt lost his glamour grin and started toward Mike Fallon just as Fallon's left hand landed on the wheel of his chair. Kovac leapt forward, crashing into another drunk.

The chair pitched down the steps and spilled its occupant. Mike Fallon hit the floor like a sack of potatoes.

Kovac pushed the drunk aside and hustled down the steps. The crowd had cleared back in surprise. Wyatt stood frozen ten feet away, frowning as he stared down at Mike Fallon.

Kovac dropped down to one knee. 'Hey, Mikey, let's get you off your face. You've got it confused with your ass again.'

Someone righted the wheelchair. The old man rolled over onto his back and made a pathetic attempt to sit up, flopping on the floor like a beached seal, tears pouring down the sides of his face. A guy Kovac knew from robbery took one side while Kovac took the other, and together they hoisted Fallon back into his chair.

The people standing nearby turned away, embarrassed for the old man. Fallon hung his head in abject humiliation – a sight Kovac had never wished to see.

He'd known Mike Fallon since day one on the job. Back then, every patrol cop in Minneapolis had known Iron Mike. They had followed his example and his orders. And a good lot of them had cried like babies when Mike Fallon was gunned down. But to see him like this – broken in every way – was a heartbreak.

Kovac knelt beside the wheelchair and put a hand on Fallon's shoulder. 'Come on, Mike. Let's call it a night, huh? I'll drive you home.'

'You all right, Mike?' Ace Wyatt asked woodenly, stepping up at last.

Fallon held a shaking hand out to him but couldn't bring himself to look up, even when Wyatt took hold. His voice was tight and raw. 'I love you like a brother, Ace. Like a son. More. You know, I can't say –'

'You don't have to say, Mike. Don't.'

'I'm sorry. I'm sorry,' the old man mumbled over and over, bringing his other hand up to cover his face. Snot ran in an elastic string from his nose to his lap. He had wet his pants.

In his peripheral vision, Kovac could see the newsies creeping in like vultures.

'I'll see he gets home,' he said to Wyatt as he rose.

Wyatt stared down at Mike Fallon. 'Thanks, Sam,' he murmured. 'You're a good man.'

'I'm a fucking sap. But what else have I got to do with my time?'

The blond had vanished, but the brunette from TV

16

sidled up to Wyatt again. 'Is this Mike Fallon? Officer Fallon from the Thorne murder back in the seventies?'

The black-haired minion appeared like the devil's familiar and pried the woman away with a serious something whispered in her ear.

Wyatt collected himself and turned away, waving off the reporters with a look of disapproval. 'Just a little accident, folks. Let's move on.'

Kovac looked down at the man sobbing in the wheel-chair.

Let's move on.

2

'Yeah, this is why I hired a sitter tonight,' Liska said. 'So I could cart a drunk home. I got enough of that when I was a uniform.'

'Quit bitching,' Kovac ordered. 'You could have said no, *partner*.'

'Sure. And look bad in front of Mr Community Service. I just hope he took note of my selflessness and remembers when I hit him up for a job on his program,' she said, teasing.

'Looked to me like you were trying to hit up the assistant for something else.'

Liska reached across and slugged his arm, trying not to laugh. 'I was not! What do you take me for?'

'What would *he* take you for? There's the real question.'

'He wouldn't.'

'He didn't. There's a difference.'

Liska pretended to pout. 'He's obviously gay.'

'Obviously.'

They drove in silence for a few blocks as the windshield wipers swiped at the snow coming down. Mike Fallon was propped up in a corner of the backseat, smelling of urine, snoring.

'You worked with him, huh?' Liska said, nodding to their passenger.

'Everybody worked with Iron Mike when I came on. He was the original warhorse. Always above and beyond the call. 'Cause it was right, he'd say. That's what being a cop is supposed to be about. And he's the one takes a slug in the spine. It's never some lazy shit just putting in his hours till the pension comes.'

'There's no such thing as fair.'

'There's a news flash. At least he nailed the mutt who shot him.'

'That was the Thorne murder.'

'You remember it?'

'I was a child at the time, Methuselah.'

'Twenty years ago?' he scoffed. 'You were probably busy making out with the captain of the football team.'

'Wide receiver,' she countered. 'And let me tell you, they didn't call him Hands for nothing.'

'Jeez,' Kovac grumbled, the corner of his mouth twitching against a chuckle. 'Tinks, you're something else.'

'Someone has to break your moods. You're too content to wallow in them.'

'Look who's talking –'

'So what was the story with Thorne?'

'Bill Thorne was a cop. Rode patrol for years. I didn't know him. I was new on the job at the time. He lived in a neighborhood over by the old West High School, where a bunch of cops lived back then. So Mike's patrolling the neighborhood, sees something doesn't look right at Thorne's place. He calls it in, then goes up to the house himself.'

'He should have waited for backup.'

'Yeah, he should have. Major mistake. But Thorne's car was there. It was a neighborhood full of cops. Anyway, there was a handyman who'd been working in the neighborhood. A drifter. Thorne had tried to run him off a couple of times, but the wife felt sorry for him and paid him to wash windows. Turned out Thorne was right – the guy was bad news. He broke into the house and raped the wife.

'Thorne had been scheduled to work that night, but he stopped back at the house for something. The mutt had found a gun and he used it on Thorne. Killed him.

'Then Mike showed up and went in. The bad guy shot. Mike shot back. Nailed the guy, but he went down. Ace

Wyatt lived across the street at the time. At some point Thorne's wife called him, hysterical. He kept Mike alive until the ambulance got there.'

'That explains tonight.'

'Yeah,' Kovac said, pensive again. 'Part of it, anyway.'

There was a lot of story between Iron Mike Fallon, fallen hero, and old Mike Fallon, pathetic alcoholic. The profession was too full of sad stories and sadder drunks.

The one in the backseat tipped over and puked on the floor as Kovac pulled up in front of Fallon's house.

Kovac groaned and hit his forehead on the steering wheel.

Liska opened her door and looked at him. 'No good deed goes unpunished. I'm not cleaning that up, *partner*.'

From the outside, the house was small and tidy in a neighborhood of small, tidy houses. Inside was a different story. Fallon's wife had died years before. Cancer. He lived here alone. The place smelled of old man and fried onions.

The rooms were spare, the furnishings kept to a minimum to make way for Mike's wheelchair. An odd mix of worn junk and state-of-the-art. A high-end massage recliner sat front and center in the living room, pointed at a thirty-one-inch color television. The couch was a relic from the seventies. The dining room looked as if it hadn't been used in two decades, and was probably exactly as Mrs Fallon had left it, with the exception of the booze bottles on the table.

Twin beds nearly filled the little bedroom – one stacked with piles of clothes, the other a tangle of sheets. Dirty laundry had been thrown in the general vicinity of an overflowing hamper. A bottle of Maker's Mark bourbon sat on the nightstand beside a jelly-jar glass sporting the likeness of Barney the Dinosaur. On the other end of the room, the dead wife's dresser was lined with family photos, half a dozen of them turned facedown.

'I'm sorry. I'm so sorry,' Mike muttered as Kovac went about the job of putting him in bed.

Liska found a laundry basket and took the discarded clothes away, nose wrinkled, but not complaining.

'Forget it, Mike. It's nothing we all haven't done once in a while,' Kovac said.

'Christ, I pissed myself.'

'Don't worry about it.'

'I'm sorry. Where ya workin', Sam?'

'Homicide.'

Fallon gave a weak, derisive, drunken laugh. 'Fuckin' big shot. Too good for a uniform.'

Kovac heaved a sigh and straightened, his gaze landing on the photographs across the room. Fallon had two sons. The younger – Andy – was a cop. He'd worked robbery for a while. His were the photos turned down on the dresser, Kovac discovered as he turned them up.

Good-looking kid. Athletic, handsome. There was a shot of him in a baseball uniform. He was built like a shortstop: compact, cat-like. Another photo showed him in his police uniform, graduating from the academy. Mike Fallon's pride and joy, carrying on the family tradition.

'How's Andy doing?'

'He's dead,' Fallon mumbled.

Kovac turned abruptly. 'What?'

Fallon turned his face away. He looked frail in the lamplight, his skin as pale and wrinkled as old parchment. 'He's dead to me,' he said softly. Then he closed his eyes and passed out.

The sadness and finality of Mike Fallon's words haunted Kovac all the way back to Patrick's, where he left Liska to catch the last of the party. He dropped her at the curb and drove on through empty side streets filling with snow, away from downtown to his own slightly shabby neighborhood.

Old trees dominated the boulevard, their roots buckling

the sidewalks like an LA freeway after an earthquake. The houses were crammed shoulder to shoulder, some big and square and cut up into apartments, some smaller. One side of the street was lined with a motley assortment of cars, the other side clear for snow removal.

The house just east of Kovac's was decorated for Christmas to within an inch of its life. It appeared to sag beneath the burden of colored lights. A plastic Santa and reindeer were mounted on the roof. Another Santa was crawling down the chimney. A third stood on the lawn, contemplating the others, while two feet away the wise men were about to visit the Christ child in a manger. The entire yard was spotlit.

Kovac trudged up the sidewalk to his house and went inside, not bothering to turn on lights. Plenty spilled in from next door. His home was not so different from Mike Fallon's in that it was short on furniture. The last divorce had left him with the castoffs, which he had never bothered to replace or add to. He was himself a castoff, so it seemed only fitting. His biggest indulgence in the last five years had been the aquarium. A sorry attempt to bring other living creatures into his home.

There were no photographs of children or family. Two failed marriages seemed nothing to brag about. He had a lot of bad memories and a daughter he hadn't seen since her infancy. She was dead to him in a way, he supposed. But it was more as if she had never existed. After the divorce, her mother had remarried with embarrassing haste, and the new family had moved to Seattle. Kovac hadn't watched his daughter grow up or play sports or follow him into law enforcement. He had trained himself not to think about the lost opportunities . . . most of the time.

He went upstairs to his bedroom, but the bed didn't interest him. His head was throbbing. He sat down in the chair by the window and looked out at the garish light show next door.

He's dead to me, Mike Fallon had said about his son.

What would prompt a man to say such a thing about a child who had clearly been the pride of his life? Why would he cut that tie when he had so little else?

Kovac dug his Nicorette gum out of his pocket and tossed it in the wastebasket, reached into the nightstand drawer for a half-empty pack of Salems, and lit one up.

Who was gonna tell him not to?

3

The photograph has a fake quality to it. Most people would have glanced at it, felt an immediate burst of horror, then quickly decided it was some kind of sick joke.

The photographer is not most people.

As the artist considers the portrait, there is an initial sense of shock, but what follows immediately on its heels is a strange, complicated mix of emotions: horror, fascination, relief, guilt. And beneath that layer, another darker dimension of feeling: a certain sense of excitement . . . a sense of control . . . a sense of power. Feelings that are frightening, sickening.

There is tremendous power in taking a life. To take a life: the phrase implies to take the energy of another living creature and add it to one's own life force. The idea is seductive in a sinister way. Addictive to a certain type of individual: the kind who kills for sport.

I'm not that. I could never be that.

Even as the pledge is made, memories of another death flash frame by frame through the memory: violence, movement, blood, white noise roaring in the ears, a deafening internal scream that can't be heard. Then silence and the stillness, and the terrible realization: *I did that.*

And the sense of excitement . . . and power . . .

The dark feelings move through the soul like a snake, sinuous and shiny. The conscience shudders in its wake. Fear rises like a flood tide.

The photographer stares at the captured image of a corpse dancing on the end of a rope, the image reflected in a mirror, the mirror scrawled with the single word. *Sorry.*

So sorry.

4

'Andy Fallon is dead.'

Liska met Kovac with the news at the door into the CID offices.

The breath went out of him. 'What?'

'Andy Fallon is dead. A friend found him this morning. It looks like suicide.'

'Jesus,' Kovac muttered, feeling as disoriented as he had this morning when he'd rolled out of bed too fast for his throbbing head. In the back of his mind he saw Mike Fallon, frail and white; heard him say the words. *He's dead to me.* 'Jesus.'

Liska stared up at him, expectant.

He shook himself mentally. 'Who's up?'

'Springer and Copeland,' she said, glancing sideways for eavesdroppers. '*Were* up. Past tense. I figured you'd want it, so I grabbed it.'

'I don't know if I should thank you or wish your parents had practiced better birth control,' Kovac grumbled, heading toward their cubicle.

'Did you know Andy?'

'No. Not really. I met him a couple of times. Suicide. Man, I don't want to be the one to tell Mike.'

'You'd rather some uniform do it? Or someone from the ME's office?' Liska said with disapproval.

Kovac blew out a breath and closed his eyes for a second as the burden settled on his shoulders. 'No.'

Fate had tied him to Iron Mike years ago, and again last night. The least he could do was maintain some continuity for the old man. Let the news come from a familiar face.

'Don't you think we should jump on it?' Liska said,

glancing around for Copeland and Springer. 'Try to keep a lid on things. Andy being on the job and all.'

'Yeah,' Kovac said, glancing at the blinking light on his phone. 'Let's blow this joint before Leonard saddles us with another "murder of tomorrow".'

Andy Fallon lived in a one-and-a-half-story house just north of the trendy district known as Uptown. Home to the upwardly mobile and the stylishly hip, Uptown was, in fact, south of downtown, which had never made any sense to Kovac. 'Uptown' in the sense of being too chic for the likes of him, he supposed. The business center was an area of reclamations and renovations – coffee bars, yuppie restaurants, and art house movie theaters. Homes on the west side, near Lake of the Isles and Lake Calhoun, went for a premium. Fallon's was just far enough north and east to be affordable on a single cop's salary.

Two radio cars sat at the curb out front. Liska marched ahead up the sidewalk, always eager for a new case. Kovac trailed behind, dreading this one.

'Wait'll you get a load of this,' said the uniform who met them at the door. 'It's one for the scrapbook.'

His tone was almost snide. He'd been at it too long, had grown numb to the sight of dead people to the point where they were no longer people to him – they were bodies. All cops got that way or they got off the street before they could lose their minds. Death simply couldn't affect them in a personal way every time they encountered it. Kovac knew he was surely no exception. But this time would be different. It already was.

Liska gave the cop the flat look all detectives mastered early on in their career. 'Where's the body?'

'Bedroom. Upstairs.'

'Who found him?'

'A "friend," ' the uniform said, again with the snide tone,

making the quotation marks with his fingers. 'He's in the kitchen, crying.'

Kovac looked at the name tag, leaning in, crowding him. 'Burgess?'

'Yeah,' he said, visibly resisting the urge to step back.

Liska scribbled his name and badge number in her notebook.

'You were first on the scene?' Kovac said.

'Yeah.'

'You used that mouth to talk to the guy found the body?'

Burgess frowned, suspicious. 'Yeah . . .'

Kovac took another small step into the cop's space. 'Burgess, are you always such a fucking asshole or is today special?'

The cop colored, his features growing taut.

'Keep the mouth in check,' Kovac ordered. 'The vic was a cop, and so's his old man. Show some respect.'

Burgess pressed his lips together and took a step back, eyes cold. 'Yes, sir.'

'I don't want anyone coming in here unless they've got a badge or they're from the ME. Got that?'

'Yes, sir.'

'And I want a log of every name, badge number, and the time they walk in the door and walk back out. Can you manage that?'

'Yes. Sir.'

'Ooh, he didn't like that,' Liska whispered gleefully as they left Burgess at the door and headed toward the back of the house.

'Yeah? Fuck him.' Kovac glanced down at her. 'Andy Fallon was queer?'

'Gay,' she corrected. 'How would I know? I don't hang out with IA rats. What do you take me for?'

'You really want to know?' Kovac asked, then, 'He worked IA? No wonder Mike said the kid was dead to him.'

The kitchen was hunter green with pristine white woodwork and had everything in its place. It was the kitchen of someone who knew how to do more than run the microwave – commercial range, pots hanging from the iron rack above a granite-topped island loaded with big-ass knives in a wood block.

On the far side of the room, at a round table nestled into a bay window, sat the 'friend,' head in hands. A good-looking guy in a dark suit. Red hair, stylishly cut. A rectangular face full of sharp angles and freckles. The freckles stood out against skin washed ashen by stress and by the cold gray light spilling in the windows. He barely glanced up as they walked into the room.

Liska flashed her ID and introduced them. 'We understand you found the body, Mr –'

'Pierce,' he said hoarsely, and sniffed. 'Steve Pierce. Yes. I . . . found him.'

'We know this is terribly upsetting for you, Mr Pierce, but we'll need to talk to you when we finish. Do you understand?'

'No,' he said, shaking his head. 'I don't understand any of this. I can't believe it. I just can't believe it.'

'We're sorry for your loss,' Liska said automatically.

'He wouldn't do this,' he mumbled, staring at the tabletop. 'He wouldn't do this. It's just not possible.'

Kovac said nothing. A sense of dread built in his chest as they climbed the stairs.

'I've got a bad feeling about this, Tinks,' he muttered, pulling on latex gloves. 'Or maybe I'm having a heart attack. That'd be my luck. I finally quit smoking and I have a heart attack.'

'Well, don't die at the scene,' Liska said. 'The paperwork would be a big pain in the ass.'

'You're full of sympathy.'

'Better than what you're full of. You're not having a heart attack.'

The second floor of the house had probably been open attic space at one time, but had been nicely converted to a master suite. Joist beams had been left exposed, creating a loft effect. A lovely, private place to die, Kovac thought, taking in the scene at a glance.

The body hung from a traditional rope noose just a few feet beyond the four-poster bed. The rope looped over a ceiling beam and was tied off somewhere at the head of the bed frame, that end of it hidden by the bedding. The bed was neatly made, hadn't been slept in or even sat upon. Kovac noted these things in the back of his mind, his concentration on the victim. He flashed on the photographs he'd turned over on the dresser in Mike Fallon's bedroom the night before: the handsome young man, the star athlete, the fresh-faced new cop with Mike beaming proudly beside him. He could see that same academy graduation photograph sitting on Andy Fallon's dresser. *Good-looking kid*, he remembered thinking.

Now the handsome face was discolored, distorted, purple and bloated, the mouth frozen in a kind of sneer. The eyes were half-open and cloudy. He'd been there a while. A day or so, Kovac guessed from the apparent lack of rigor, the tautness of the skin, the smell. The sickly sweet aroma of beginning decay commingled with stale urine and feces. In death, the muscles had relaxed, bladder and bowel discharging on the floor.

The body was nude. His arms hung at his sides, hands curled into fists held slightly forward of the hips. Dark spots dotted the knuckles – lividity, the blood settling in the lowest levels of the extremities. The feet, no more than a few inches off the floor, were swollen and deep purple as well.

Kovac squatted down, took hold of an ankle, and pressed his thumb against the flesh for a moment, then let go. He watched for the skin to blanch, but nothing happened. The blood had clotted long before. The leg was cold to the touch.

An oak-framed full-length mirror was propped against the wall some ten feet in front of the corpse. The body was reflected fully, the reflection distorted by the angle of the mirror. The word *Sorry* had been written on the glass with something dark.

'I always figured these IA guys for kinky.'

Kovac looked to the two uniforms standing ten feet away, smirking at the mirror. The cops were a pair of buzz-cut no-necks, the bigger one having a head as square as a concrete block. Their name tags read 'Rubel' and 'Ogden.'

'Hey, Dumb and Dumber,' Kovac snapped. 'Get the hell outta my death scene. What the fuck's the matter with you? Tromping all over the place.'

'It's a suicide,' the uglier one said, as if that mattered.

Kovac felt his face flush. 'Don't tell me what's what, Moose. You don't know dick. Maybe in twenty years you'll have a right to an opinion. Now get the fuck outta here. Go downstairs and secure the zone. I don't want anyone coming closer than the street. And keep your big fat yaps shut. Where there's a corpse, there's newsies. I read one word about this,' he said, pointing to the reflection in the mirror, 'I'll know who gets reamed new ones. You got me?'

The officers glanced at each other sullenly, then headed for the stairs.

'IA rat offs himself,' the ugly one said under his breath. 'So what's the crime? Looks like a service to everyone, you ask me.'

Kovac stared at the body. He could see Liska snooping around, making notes of every detail, sketching the room, the placement of the furniture and of anything that might be deemed significant. They took turns at that job – keeping the notes at the scene. It was his turn to shoot the preliminary Polaroids.

He started with the room itself, then slowly moved in on the body, photographing it from all angles. Each flash burned an imprint on his memory – the dead thing that had been Mike Fallon's son; the beam from which the noose hung; the Reebok exercise steps that sat just behind the body, near enough to have been what Andy Fallon had used for his big dismount into the hereafter; the mirror. *Sorry*.

Sorry. Yes, it was.

Had Andy Fallon been sorry? About what? Or had someone else scrawled the word?

The furnace blower kicked on, and the corpse began to twist slightly like a giant rotting piñata. The reflection in the mirror was a macabre dance partner.

'I never understand people who get naked to commit suicide,' Liska said.

'It's symbolic. Shedding their earthly skin.'

'Nobody is finding me naked.'

'Maybe he didn't commit suicide,' Kovac said.

'You think someone could have done this to him? Or forced him to do it? Murder by hanging is rare.'

'What's with the mirror?' Kovac asked, though it wasn't a question to him.

Liska studied the naked corpse for a moment, then looked to the mirror, catching a slice of her own reflection with that of Andy Fallon.

'Oh, man,' she said quietly. 'Autoerotic misadventure? I've never had one before.'

Kovac said nothing, trying to imagine what he would tell Mike. Bad enough to have to explain autoerotic asphyxiation to strangers, which he had done a couple of times in his career. But how did you tell a tough, hard-line, old-time cop that his son had been trying to get himself off by cutting off his oxygen supply, and had strangled himself in the process?

'But why the message?' Liska wondered aloud. '*Sorry* says

suicide to me. Why would he write that if he was doing this just to get off?'

Kovac touched a hand to the top of his throbbing head and winced. 'You know, some days it just doesn't pay to get out of bed.'

'Yeah, well . . . Here's your option,' Liska said, nodding to the body. 'Doesn't look too sweet to me. I always figure a bad day living beats any day dead.'

'Fuck me,' Kovac muttered.

Liska squatted down in front of the mirror to examine the letters more closely. She looked at Kovac's reflection. 'Not in front of a corpse. I'm not that kind of girl.'

'You know what I mean.'

'I do.' She rose slowly, dropped the act, and touched his arm, looking up at him with earnest blue eyes. 'I'm sorry, Sam. Like ol' Iron Mike doesn't have it bad enough.'

Kovac stared at his partner for a moment, stared at the small hand on his coat sleeve and briefly considered taking hold of it. Just for the comfort of contact with another human. She wore no rings – so as not to confuse potential suitors, she said. Her fingernails were short and unpolished.

'Yeah,' he whispered.

Below them there was a shout, then a sudden loud crash, followed by more shouting. Liska ran down the stairs like a mountain goat. Kovac pounded down behind her.

Rubel was trying to haul Steve Pierce off Ogden's prone body. 'Off him!' Rubel shouted.

In a rage, Pierce shrugged him off and took a swing at Ogden, connecting, by the sound of the thump and the grunt. Rubel grabbed Pierce again, hooking a thick arm around his throat and dragging him up and back, screaming in his ear.

'I said, off him!'

Ogden, scrambling to get his legs under himself, slipped on the polished wood. Shards of broken glass and china crunched beneath his thick cop brogues. He grabbed the edge of the china cabinet they had crashed into and hauled himself up, rattling everything left in it. His face was mottled and his nose was bleeding. He swiped a hand under it, eyes widening in disbelief. He had to have forty pounds on Steve Pierce.

'You're under arrest, asshole!' he yelled, pointing a bloody finger at Pierce.

'Let him go!' Liska shouted at Rubel.

Pierce's face had gone purple above the choke hold. Rubel released him and Pierce dropped to his knees, wheezing. He gasped and looked up at Ogden with venom in his eyes. 'You son of a bitch!'

'Nobody's under arrest,' Kovac declared, stepping between them.

'I want them out of here!' Pierce demanded hoarsely, fighting his way to his feet. His eyes gleamed with tears and fury. 'Get them out of here!'

'You –' Ogden started.

Kovac hit him in the chest with the heel of his hand. It was like slapping a slab of granite. 'Shut up! Outta here!'

Rubel stalked past and Ogden fell in step, fuming. Kovac dogged their heels into the living room.

'What the hell did you say to him?'

'Nothing,' Rubel returned.

'I was talking to the other ox. You said something stupid, didn't you? Christ, what a question! I might as well ask if shit is brown,' Kovac said with disgust.

'He attacked me,' Ogden said indignantly. 'He assaulted an officer.'

'Yeah?' Kovac said tightly, getting in his face. 'You want to go there, Ogden? You want to make a report detailing this little fiasco? You want Mr Pierce there to give a statement? You want your supervisor reading what a dickhead you are?'

Sulking, the officer pulled a dingy handkerchief out of his pocket and dabbed it under his nose.

'You're gonna be lucky he doesn't call the citizens' commission and sue the department,' Kovac said. 'Now get outta here and go do your jobs.'

Rubel led the way out the front door, jaw set, eyes narrow. Ogden hustled up alongside him to the street, bloody rag held to his nose with one hand, the other gesticulating as he tried to impress something on his partner, who didn't want to hear.

The crime scene van pulled up behind the radio car at the curb. A pair of shitty compacts swarmed in from opposite directions like buzzards. Newsies. Kovac felt his lip start to curl. He stepped back into the house, catching Burgess reaching for a stack of videocassettes on a shelf beside the television.

'Don't touch anything!' Kovac snapped. 'Get out on the lawn and keep the reporters away. "No comment" – do you think you can manage that, or is it too many syllables?'

Burgess ducked his head.

'And I want every license plate on the block noted and run. Got that?'

'Yessir,' the cop said through his teeth as he went out.

'Where do they get these guys?' Kovac asked as he went back to the kitchen.

'They breed them up north as pack animals,' Liska said, meeting him at the archway into the room. 'Ogden made a crack about one less fag. Pierce lost it. Who can blame him?'

'Great,' Kovac muttered. 'Let's hope he doesn't decide to get vocal about it. Bad enough Andy Fallon's dead. We don't need to broadcast to the whole metropolitan area which way his willy waggled.'

The crime scene team came through then, toting their cases and cameras. The scene would be photographed again and videotaped. The area of the death scene would be dusted for prints. If there was any evidence to gather, it would be photographed, its exact position measured and noted; it would be logged and marked and packaged with great care taken to establish the chain of custody so that its every moment could be accounted for. And all the while Andy Fallon's body would hang there, waiting for the arrival of the ME's people.

Kovac briefed the senior criminalist and directed them upstairs.

Liska had herded Steve Pierce back to the kitchen table. He sat like a man who wanted to pace, one hand rubbing his throat. Ogden's blood stained his knuckles. He had pulled his tie loose and undone his collar. The black suit was limp and rumpled.

'Mind if we sit down, Steve?' Kovac asked.

Pierce made no reply. They sat anyway. Kovac produced a microcassette recorder from his pocket, turned it on, and placed it on the table.

'We'll make a recording of our conversation here, Steve,' he explained casually. 'So that we're sure we've got all the details straight when we get back to the station to write our reports. Is that all right with you?'

Pierce nodded wearily, dragging a hand back through his hair.

'I'll need you to answer out loud, Steve.'

'Yes. Sure. Fine.' He tried to clear his throat. Distress etched lines beside his mouth. 'Will they . . . take him down now?' he asked, his voice closing off on the last words.

'The medical examiner's people will do that,' Liska explained.

He looked at her as if it had only just dawned on him there would have to be an autopsy. His eyes filled again and he looked out the window at the snow in the backyard, trying to compose himself.

'What do you do for a living, Steve?' Kovac asked.

'Investments. I'm with Daring-Landis.'

'Do you live here? In this house?'

'No.'

'What brought you here this morning?'

'Andy was supposed to meet me for coffee at the Uptown Caribou yesterday. He wanted to talk to me about something. He didn't show. He didn't answer my calls. I was concerned so I came by.'

'What was your relationship with Andy Fallon?'

'We're friends,' he said. Present tense. 'From college. Buddies. You know.'

'Suppose you tell us,' Kovac said. 'What kind of buddies?'

Pierce's brow creased. 'You know, out for beer and pizza, the occasional basketball game. Get together for *Monday Night Football*. Guy stuff.'

'Nothing more . . . intimate?'

Kovac watched his face carefully. Pierce colored from the collar up.

'What are you suggesting, Detective?'

'I'm asking if the two of you had a sexual relationship,' Kovac said with calm bluntness.

Pierce looked as if his head might burst. 'I'm straight. Not that it's any of your business.'

'There's a dead body upstairs,' Kovac said. 'That makes everything my business. What about Mr Fallon?'

'Andy's gay,' Pierce said, resentment bitter in his eyes. 'Does that make it all right that he's dead?'

Kovac spread his hands. 'Hey, I don't care who plugs what in where. I just need a frame of reference for my investigation.'

'You have a real way with words, Detective.'

'You said Andy wanted to talk something over with you,' Liska prompted, diverting his attention to her. Allowing Kovac to watch every facial tic. 'Do you know what?'

'No. He didn't say.'

'When did you last speak with him?' Kovac asked.

Pierce cut him a sideways look, the resentment lingering.

'Um, Friday, I guess it was. My fiancée was busy that night so I swung by to see Andy. We hadn't seen much of each other lately. I came by to suggest we get together for coffee or something. Catch up.'

'So the two of you were supposed to meet yesterday, but Andy was a no-show.'

'I called a couple of times, got the machine. He never called back. I decided to swing by. See if everything was all right.'

'Why wouldn't you just think he was busy? Maybe he had to go to work early.'

Pierce glared at him. 'Pardon me for being concerned about my friends. I guess I should just be an asshole like you. I could be at my desk now. I could have saved myself the trouble of seeing –'

He cut himself off as the image rose in his memory again. His face was still red but with a waxy sheen to it now as he looked out the window, as if the sight of the snow, white and serene, might cool and soothe him.

'How'd you get into the house?' Kovac asked. 'You have a key?'

'The door wasn't locked.'

'Had he talked about suicide? Had he seemed depressed?' Liska asked.

'He had seemed . . . frustrated. A little down, yes, but not to the point that he'd kill himself. I just won't believe that. He wouldn't have done something like that without trying to reach out to someone first.'

That was what the survivors always wanted to think at first. Kovac knew from experience. They always wanted to believe the loved one would have asked for help before taking that fatal step. They never wanted to think they might have missed a sign. If it turned out Andy Fallon *had* committed suicide, at some point Steve Pierce would start wondering if there hadn't been a dozen signs and he'd missed them all because he was selfish or scared or blind.

'Down about what?'

Pierce made a helpless gesture. 'I don't know. Work. Or maybe his family. I know there'd been some strain between him and his dad.'

'What about other relationships?' Liska asked. 'Was he involved with anyone?'

'No.'

'How can you be sure?' Kovac asked. 'You weren't living here. You weren't seeing each other. You just got together for the occasional cup o' joe.'

'We were friends.'

'Yet you don't really know what was bothering him. You don't really know how depressed he might have been.'

'I knew Andy. He would *not* have killed himself,' Pierce insisted, his patience wearing thin.

'Aside from the door being unlocked,' Liska said, 'did anything seem to be missing or out of place?'

'Not that I noticed. I wasn't looking, though. I came to find Andy.'

'Steve, did you ever know Andy to practice any unusual sexual rituals?' Kovac asked.

Pierce shot up out of his chair, sending it skidding backward. 'You people are *unbelievable!*' He jerked around as if scanning the kitchen for a witness or a weapon.

Kovac remembered the knives on the island and the rage in Pierce's face as he'd pounded Ogden. He got up and put himself between Pierce and the knife block.

'This isn't personal, Steve. It's our job,' he said. 'We need the clearest picture we can get.'

'You're a bunch of fucking sadists!' Pierce shouted. 'My friend is *dead* and –'

'And I didn't know him from Adam,' Kovac said reasonably. 'And I don't know *you* from Adam. For all I know, you might have killed him yourself.'

'That's absurd!'

'And you know what?' Kovac went on. 'I find a dead guy hanging naked, watching himself in a mirror . . . Call me a prude, but that strikes me odd. You know, I gotta think maybe this guy was into something a little out of the ordinary. But maybe you're into that too. Maybe you don't bat an eye at shit like that. What do I know? Maybe you choke yourself to get off every other day. Maybe you play spank the monkey with a cattle prod. If you do, if you and Fallon were involved in something like that together, you're better off telling us now, Steve.'

Pierce was crying now, tears streaming, the muscles in his face straining as if he was fighting to hold in all the raw emotions ripping through him. 'No.'

'No, you weren't involved in that kind of thing, or no, you won't tell us?' Kovac prodded.

Pierce closed his eyes and hung his head. 'God, I can't believe this is happening.' The burden of it all suddenly too much, he sank down to the floor on his knees and curled forward, his head in his hands. 'Why is this happening?'

Kovac watched him, a feeling of weary, familiar remorse coming over him. He squatted down beside Steve Pierce and put a hand on his shoulder.

'That's what we want to find out, Steve,' he said softly. 'You may not always like the way we do it. And you may not like what we find. But in the end, that's all we want – the truth.'

Even as he said it, Kovac knew that when they found the truth, no one was going to want it. There simply wasn't going to be a good reason for Andy Fallon to be dead.

5

Mike Fallon's house looked somehow more alone in the cold gray light of day. Night had a way of enveloping a neighborhood; homes seemed to huddle together like a flock with only slips of velvet darkness between them. By day, they were separated and isolated by light and driveways and fences and snow.

Kovac looked up at the house and wondered if Mike already knew. People sometimes did. As if a shock wave had somehow rippled out from the death scene, reaching them faster than the speed of sound, or the speed of the messenger.

He's dead to me.

He doubted Mike Fallon would remember saying those words, but they still rang in Kovac's ears as he sat alone in the car. He had dropped Liska at the station to get a running start on the investigation. She would contact Andy Fallon's IA supervisor to find out what he'd been working on, what his attitude had been lately. She would get his jacket sent up from personnel, find out if he'd been making any use of the department shrink.

Kovac would've traded places with her in a heartbeat, except the sense of obligation was too strong. He cursed himself for a sap and got out of the car. Some days life just sucked when you were a decent human being.

He peered into the house through a narrow, rectangular window in the front door. The living room seemed shabbier than it had the night before. The walls needed paint. The sofa should have seen the back door of Goodwill years ago. A strange contrast to the massage chair and big-screen TV.

He rang the doorbell and knocked for good measure, then waited, impatient, trying not to wonder what a stranger would think of *his* living room with the empty fish tank. Someday he'd have to get around to getting a life outside the job.

His hands fidgeted at his coat pockets. He dug out a stick of Juicy Fruit, his nerves quivering at the base of his neck like ants just beneath his skin. He knocked again. Flashes of last night popped in his memory – Mike Fallon, the old cop, broken, discarded, depressed, drunk. . . . There was no sign of life within the house. No motion. No sound.

Sinking in snow halfway up his shins, he went around to the side of the house, looking for a bedroom window. Wouldn't that be a story for the six o'clock news? Father-son cop suicides. Paul Harvey would probably pick that one up to depress all of America over lunch tomorrow. Pointless death over chicken salad and Big Macs.

He found a ladder in the tiny garage that was bursting at the seams with the usual life's accumulation of barely used junk. A nearly new Subaru Outback tricked out for a handicapped driver took up most of the space. Some other cop must have returned it from Patrick's back lot after the party, or someone else had taken Mike to the bar, then melted into the woodwork when the trouble started. Someone who didn't want a drunk puking in his backseat.

The shade was up on Mike Fallon's bedroom window. Mike lay on his back on the bed, arms flung out, head turned to one side, mouth hanging open like a busted gate. Kovac held his breath and looked for some sign of Fallon's heart beating beneath his thin T-shirt.

'Hey, Mikey!' he shouted, knocking on the window.

Fallon didn't flinch.

'Mike Fallon!'

The old man jolted on the second round of pounding, eyes slitting open, resentful of the light. He made a raw sound of fear at the sight of the face pressed to his window.

'Mike, it's Sam Kovac!'

Fallon rocked himself up in the bed, hawking up a night's worth of phlegm.

'What the fuck are you doing?' he shouted. 'Are you out of your fucking head?'

Kovac cupped his hands around the sides of his face so he could see better. 'You gotta let me in, Mike. We need to talk.' His breath fogged the glass and he wiped the moisture away with his coat sleeve.

Fallon scowled and waved him off. 'Leave me alone. I don't need to hear it from you.'

'Hear what?'

'Last night. Bad enough I did it. I don't need my nose rubbed in it.'

He looked pathetic sitting there in his underwear like a derelict Humpty-Dumpty: the barrel body and the twig legs, beard stubble and bloodshot eyes. He brushed over the flattop, wincing, pressing gingerly.

'Just let me in, will you?' Kovac said. 'It's important.'

Fallon squinted at him, trying to size it up. No one hated a surprise more than a cop.

Finally, he lifted a hand in defeat. 'There's a key under the mat in back.'

'A key under the mat.' Kovac set it on the counter and cocked a look at the old man. 'Jeez, Mike. You used to be a cop. You oughta know better.'

Fallon ignored him. The kitchen smelled of bacon grease and fried onions. The curtains were stiff with age. The countertops were lined with cups and glasses and plates and cereal boxes, and a giant jar of Metamucil with prescription bottles clustered around it like white-capped toadstools. All the doors had been taken off the lower cupboards, exposing the contents: boxes of instant potatoes, canned vegetables, about a case of Campbell's soup.

Fallon hadn't bothered with pants. He rolled around the

small room in his chair, his hairy, atrophied legs pushed to one side, out of the way. He ferreted out a bottle of Tylenol from the pharmacy on the counter, and got himself a glass of water from the door of the refrigerator.

'What's so damned important?' he demanded gruffly, though Kovac could see the tension in Fallon's shoulders, as if he was bracing himself. 'I got a hangover could drop a cow.'

'Mike.' Kovac waited until Fallon turned and looked at him, then took a deep breath. 'Andy's dead. I'm sorry.'

Blunt. Just like that. People always thought they had to lead in to bad news with platitudes, but that wasn't the way. All that did was give the recipient a chance to panic at the many horrible possibilities. He had learned long ago to just say it and get it over with.

Fallon looked away, his jaw working.

'We don't know yet what happened.'

'What do you mean, you don't know what happened?' Fallon demanded. 'Was he shot? Was he stabbed? Was it a car accident?' He worked up a temper, anger being more comfortable, more familiar than grief. A flush began at the base of his throat and pushed upward. 'You're a detective. Somebody's dead. You can't tell me how they got that way? Jesus H.'

Kovac let it roll off. 'It might have been an accident. Or it might have been suicide, Mike. We found him hanging. I wish I didn't have to tell you, but there it is. I'm really sorry.'

Sorry. As Andy had been. He could see the word on the mirror over the reflection of Andy Fallon. Naked. Dead. Bloated. Rotting. *Sorry* didn't mean a whole lot in the face of that.

Mike seemed to deflate and shrivel. Tears filled his small red eyes and spilled down his cheeks like glass beads.

'Oh, Jesus,' he said. A plea, not a curse. 'Oh, dear Jesus.'

He brought a trembling hand to his mouth. It was the

43

size of a canned ham but looked fragile, the skin thin and spotted. A sound of terrific pain wrenched free of his soul.

Kovac looked away, wanting to allow the man at least that much privacy. This was the worst part of being the messenger: trespassing on those first acute moments of grief, moments that should not be witnessed by anyone.

That, and knowing he would have to intrude on the grief with questions.

Fallon abruptly spun his chair around and wheeled out of the room. Kovac let him go. The questions could wait. Andy was already dead, most likely by his own hand, purposely or not. What difference would ten minutes make?

He leaned against the counter and counted the bottles of pills. Seven brown prescription bottles for the treatment of everything from indigestion to arrhythmia to insomnia to pain. Prilosec, Darvocet, Ambien. At least Mike had plenty of chemicals to help him get through this.

'Damn you! Damn you!'

The shouts were accompanied by a crash and the sound of glass breaking. Kovac bolted out of the kitchen and down the short hall.

'Damn you!' Mike Fallon screamed, smashing a framed picture against the edge of the dresser. The cheap metal frame bent like modeling clay. Glass sprayed out across the dresser.

'Mike! Stop it!'

'Damn you!' the old man cried again, swinging his arms and the shattered frame, flinging broken glass across the room. 'Damn you!'

Kovac thought the curses might be for him at this point as he grabbed Mike Fallon's wrist. The picture frame flew across the room like a Frisbee, crashing against the wall and falling to the hardwood floor. Fallon continued to fight, the strength in his upper body amazing for a man his age. His free arm flailed across the top of the dresser, sending more picture frames to the floor. Kovac got behind the wheel-chair, bending at an awkward angle to try to restrain the man. Wailing, Fallon threw his head back and butted him hard on the bridge of the nose. Blood came in an instant gush.

'Dammit, Mike, stop it!' The blood ran down his chin and onto Fallon's shoulder, his ear, his hair.

Sobbing, the old man flung himself against the dresser top, then back. Back and forth, back and forth. The energy ran out of him little by little with each motion, until he laid his face on the dresser amid the shards of glass, and moved only his hands. Pounding, pounding, slapping, slapping, tapping, tapping.

Kovac stepped back, wiping his bloody nose on his coat sleeve as he fumbled for a handkerchief. He went over to where the first of the destroyed frames had landed and tried to nudge it over with his foot. His shoes and the bottoms of his pants legs were soaked from stomping through the snow, but the cold only began to register now that he'd seen the evidence. He couldn't feel his toes inside his shoes.

Handkerchief crammed against his nostrils to stem the flow of blood, he squatted down and picked up the picture with his free hand. Andy Fallon's academy graduation. Andy beaming, Mike beside him in the wheelchair, a jagged line now cutting between them like a lightning bolt.

He shook off the last of the glass and tried to bend the frame back into shape.

'Mike,' he said quietly. 'Last night you said Andy was dead to you. What did you mean by that?'

Fallon kept his head on the dresser, his gaze on nothing, empty. He didn't answer. Kovac had to stare at him a moment to be certain the old man hadn't just died on him. That would have been the cap on the damn day – and it wasn't even two o'clock yet.

'The two of you were having problems?' he prompted.

'I loved that kid,' Fallon said weakly, still not moving. 'I

45

loved him. He was my legs. He was my heart. He was everything I couldn't be.'

But . . .

The word hung in the air, unspoken. Kovac had a feeling he knew where it would lead. He looked around at the scattered photographs of Andy Fallon. Handsome and athletic. And gay.

A hard-ass old-timer like Mike wouldn't have taken it well. Hell, Kovac didn't know how well *he* would have taken it if it had been his kid.

'I loved him,' Mike murmured. 'He ruined everything. He's ruined everything.'

His face pinched tight as he looked inward, seeing the pain in its brightest light. He flushed red with the effort to hold the tears back – or maybe to push them out. Hard to say which would have been more difficult for a man like Iron Mike.

Kovac dabbed absently at his nose, then stuffed the handkerchief in his coat pocket. Quietly, he picked up all the photographs and stacked them on the dresser so they would be there when the anger subsided and the need for memories set in.

The questions were there, lined up in the front of his mind, automatic, orderly, routine. *When was the last time you spoke to Andy? Did he talk to you about what he was working on? What was his mental state the last time you saw him? Did he ever talk about suicide? Had he been depressed? Did you know his friends, his lovers?*

None of those questions made it to his lips. Later.

'Is there anyone you'd like me to call, Mike?'

Fallon didn't respond. The grief had surrounded him like a force field. He wasn't hearing anything but the voice of regret in his head, wasn't feeling any pain but that in the deepest part of his soul. He was oblivious to everything external, including the bits of glass that cut into his cheek.

Kovac let out a long, slow breath, his gaze falling on one

photograph that still lay on the floor, half under the dresser. He pulled it out and looked at a past that seemed as far away as Mars. The Fallons all together before one tragedy after another had torn them apart. Mike and his wife and their two boys.

'I'll call your other son, if you want,' he offered.

'I don't have another son,' Mike Fallon said. 'One shut me out years ago, and I shut out the other. Helluva deal, huh, Kojak?'

Kovac looked at the photograph for another moment, then set it on top of the others. Fallon's admission left him feeling hollow inside, an echo of the old man's emotions. Or maybe the emotions were his own. He was no less alone in his life than Mike Fallon.

'Yeah, Mikey. It's a helluva deal.'

Liska stood in the hall, staring at the door to Room 126. Internal Affairs. The name conjured up images of interrogation rooms with bare lightbulbs and SS officers with narrowed eyes and rubber truncheons.

The Rat Squad. She'd had little cause to associate with them in her career, had never been investigated by them. She knew the job of IA was to root out bad cops, not to persecute the good ones. But the fear and loathing were instinctive things for most cops. Cops hung together, protected one another. IA turned on their own. Like cannibals.

For Liska, the aversion went deeper.

In the Minneapolis PD, IA was for fast-track, brown-nose, brass types. People destined for management. People born to be hated by their peers. The kind who had regularly gotten pushed down on the playground as kids, and ran to the teacher every time. The kind of people who inspired neither admiration nor loyalty.

Liska thought of Andy Fallon hanging in his bedroom, and wondered who might have turned on him.

47

She went into the IA offices before she could balk again. There were no human heads mounted on pikes. No manacles bolted to the wall. At least not in the reception area.

'Liska, homicide,' she said, badging the receptionist. 'I'm here to see Lieutenant Savard.'

She made the receptionist for early fifties. Plump and unsmiling, the woman asked no questions, which was likely a requirement of the job. She buzzed the lieutenant.

There were three offices off the reception area – one dark, one closed and lit, one open and lit. Looking in the last one, she could see a thin suit-and-tie standing behind the desk and frowning, deep in conversation with a short guy with chopped platinum hair and a neon-green parka.

'. . . don't appreciate being passed around,' Neon whined, his voice just high enough to irritate. 'This has been a nightmare from the start. Now you're telling me the case is being reassigned.'

'In point of fact, the case is closed. I'll be your contact should you need one. That's purely out of courtesy on the part of the department. I'm afraid there's nothing I can do about the change in personnel,' the suit explained. 'The circumstances are beyond our control. Sergeant Fallon is no longer with us.'

The suit caught Liska's gaze then. He frowned harder, came around the desk, and closed the door.

'Lieutenant Savard is expecting you,' the receptionist said in the hushed tone of a funeral director.

Savard's office was immaculate. None of the usual cop clutter. A place for everything and everything in its place. The same could be said of the lieutenant. She stood behind her perfectly neat desk in a perfectly tailored black pantsuit. Forty or thereabouts, with perfectly symmetrical features and perfect porcelain skin. Her ash-blond hair was perfectly coiffed in chin-length waves ingeniously cut to appear careless, but likely requiring a cosmetology degree to style every day.

Liska resisted the self-conscious urge to reach up and touch her own boy-short crop.

'Liska, homicide,' she said by way of introduction, not offering her hand. 'I'm here about Andy Fallon.'

'Yes,' Savard murmured, almost as if she were talking to herself. 'Of course.'

She seemed too feminine to live up to her rep, Liska thought. Amanda Savard had been described as tough and smooth, sharp and cold as a tungsten steel blade.

Liska helped herself to a seat. Cool, casual, in control. A good front anyway. She pulled out her notebook and pen.

'It's a terrible tragedy,' Savard said, easing into her seat with care. As if she had a bad back but didn't want to show it. Her hand trembled slightly as she reached for her coffee cup. 'I liked Andy. He was a good kid.'

'What kind of cop was he?'

'Dedicated. Conscientious.'

'When did you last see him?'

'Sunday evening. We needed to talk some things over in relation to a case he'd been working. He hadn't been pleased with the outcome.'

'And where did you go?'

'His home.'

'Isn't that a little intimate?'

Savard didn't bat an eye. 'Andy was gay. I was in Uptown doing some Christmas shopping. I called and asked him if I could drop by.'

'What time was that?'

'Around eight. I left around nine-thirty.'

'Did he say anything about expecting someone else?'

'No.'

'And what was his frame of mind when you left?'

'He seemed fine. We had talked everything through.'

'But he didn't come in for work yesterday?'

'No. He had asked to take Monday as a personal day. Christmas shopping, he said. If I'd had any idea . . .' She looked away, taking a few seconds to tighten the straps on her composure.

'Had he given any indication of having emotional problems recently?'

Savard released a delicate sigh, seemingly lost in the stark beauty of a black–and–white winterscape photograph that hung on one wall.

'Yes. He'd been quiet. Down. He'd lost some weight. I knew he was having some problems with a case. And I knew he was dealing with some stress in his personal life. But I didn't think he was a risk to himself. Andy did a good job of internalizing.'

'Was he seeing the shrink?'

'Not that I was aware of. I wish now I had been stronger in suggesting that.'

'You *had* suggested it?'

'I make it clear to my people the department psychologist is there for a reason. Internal Affairs can be a tough row to hoe. There's a considerable amount of job stress.'

'Yeah, I guess ruining other cops could have its drawbacks,' Liska muttered, scribbling in her pad.

'Cops ruin themselves, Sergeant,' Savard said, a hint of the steel glinting now in her voice. 'We stop them from ruining other people's lives. We provide a necessary service here.'

'I didn't mean to imply that you didn't.'

'Of course you did.'

Liska shifted on her chair, her gaze sliding away from Savard's cold green eyes.

'I've lost a good investigator,' Savard said. 'And I've lost a young man I liked a lot. Do you think I don't feel that, Sergeant? Do you think IA rats have ice water in their veins?'

Liska stared down at her lap. 'No, ma'am. I'm sorry.'

50

'I'm sure you are. You're sitting there wondering if I'll complain to your lieutenant.'

Liska said nothing because Savard was exactly right. She was more concerned about how this screw-up would affect her career than how it might have upset Savard personally. Sad but true. She put her career first when she wasn't busy sticking her foot in her mouth. Habitual behavior – on both counts. Professional ambition was one part of the survivor mentality that had kept her head above water all her life. The other was an unfortunate tendency that had hindered her progress more than once.

'Don't worry, Sergeant,' Savard said wearily. 'My skin is thicker than that.'

After an uncomfortable moment, Liska said, 'Do you think Andy Fallon killed himself?'

Savard's brow furrowed delicately. 'Do you think something else? I was told Andy hung himself.'

'He was found hanging, yes.'

'My God, you don't think he was –' The lieutenant broke off before she could say the word. *Murdered.* She had a homicide detective sitting in front of her.

'It may have been an accident,' Liska said. 'We can't rule out autoerotic asphyxiation. At this point, we don't know what might have happened.'

'An accident,' Savard repeated, dropping her lashes. 'That would be terrible too, but it's certainly better than any of the alternatives. No matter what, hanging isn't an easy way to die.' Her hand settled briefly at the base of her throat, then moved away.

'I figure any way to die isn't fun,' Liska said. 'Hanging's quick at least. It doesn't take long before you lose consciousness. A couple of minutes.'

The thought of what those couple of minutes would be like struck them both at the same moment. Liska swallowed.

'What was he working on? This case you talked about Sunday night? What was that about?'

'I'm not at liberty to say.'

'I'm investigating a death, Lieutenant. What if Andy Fallon didn't kill himself? What if he's dead because of one of his cases?'

She waited for Savard to cave, seeing no sign that would happen before the end of the decade.

'Sergeant Liska, Andy had been depressed,' Savard pointed out calmly. 'He was found hanging. I'm assuming his home was undisturbed, right? People don't say "suspected suicide" if the door's been kicked in and the stereo is missing.

'I don't see a crime, Sergeant,' she went on. 'I see a tragedy.'

'It's that no matter what,' Liska said. 'The details are for me to sort out. I'm only trying to do my job, Lieutenant. I'd like to see Andy's case files and notes.'

'That's out of the question. We'll wait until we hear what the ME has to say.'

'It's Christmastime,' Liska pointed out. 'The suicides are stacking up like cordwood. It could be days before they get to Fallon.'

Savard didn't blink.

'An IA investigation is a serious thing, Sergeant. I don't want details getting out unless it's absolutely necessary. Someone's career could be damaged.'

'I thought that was your goal,' Liska said, getting to her feet.

She closed her notebook, stuck it in her jacket pocket, and made a little face. 'Shit. There goes that tone again. Sorry,' she said without remorse. 'Well, while you're telling my lieutenant how flip I am, toss in the fact that you don't want to cooperate with a death investigation, Lieutenant Savard. Maybe he'll have better luck persuading you than I have.'

She made a mock salute and walked out.

The receptionist didn't so much as look up. The door was still closed on the suit's office. Liska could hear the tone of an argument but not the content. Whatever Neon Man had come here for involved Andy Fallon. The case was being reassigned.

She went out into the hall and looked up and down. Deserted – for the moment at least. The building often gave that impression, even though the place was full of cops and criminals, city officials and citizens. She went to the water fountain across the hall from 126 and waited.

Maybe three minutes went by before the door opened and Neon came out. His face was a shade of red that clashed badly with his parka. He crossed to the water fountain, ran some water on his fingers, and pressed them delicately to his cheeks. He breathed deliberately through pursed lips, visibly working to calm down.

'Frustrating place, huh?' Liska said.

Neon's head snapped around. His green eyes were bright, clear and translucent, and suspicious.

'I didn't get what I went in there for either,' Liska confided, moving closer. 'Feel free to hate them. Everyone hates IA. I hate them, and I work here.'

'All the more reason, isn't it?' he said. 'It certainly is hateful from what I've seen.'

Liska squinted at him. 'You a cop? A narc? I'd know you otherwise.'

He was no more a cop than her paperboy, but she scored points asking. Up close, she was surprised to find that he was barely as tall as she was – and three inches of that were the soles of a very funky pair of shoes. *Petite* was the best word to describe him. He wore mascara and lip gloss, and had five earrings in one ear.

'Just a concerned citizen,' he said, glancing up and down the hall.

'And what is it you're concerned about?'

'Injustice.'

'You've come to the right place. Theoretically.' She dug a card out of her jacket pocket and handed it to him. 'Maybe you're just talking to the wrong people.'

Neon took the card. His manicure was better than hers. He looked at the card as if he were trying to memorize it.

'Maybe,' he said, and slipped it into his coat pocket and walked away.

6

Neil Fallon had forsaken not only his father but the city as well. Kovac drove west on the broad speedway multilanes of 394, which thinned down to four lanes, then two, then two with no shoulders, the last a narrow ribbon of road that wound around the fingers of Lake Minnetonka. On other tributaries of asphalt around this lake stood old mansions that had been built by lumber barons and industrialists, and new mansions built in recent years by professional athletes and rock stars. But here the strips of land were too meager for ostentation. Cabins perched on the banks, crouching beneath towering pines. Some were summer places, some fishing shacks that should have seen a wrecking ball a decade or two past, others were modest year-round homes.

Andy Fallon's brother owned a motley collection of cabins congregated on a wedge of land between the lake and a crossroads. Fallon's Bar and Bait Shop squatted nearest the road, a building not much bigger than a three-car garage, with green shingle siding and too-small windows that made the place look as if it were squinting. The windows were glowing with neon advertising Miller's and Coors and live bait.

The thought of a late lunch shriveled and died in Kovac's empty belly.

He wheeled the piece-of-shit Chevy Caprice into the small, frozen parking lot, turned off the engine, and listened to it rattle on. He'd been driving the same car out of the department fleet for more than a year. In that time, no mechanic had been able to cure its hiccups or make the heater give more than a token effort. He had requested a different vehicle, but the paperwork had gone into a bureaucratic black hole, and no one on that end would return his phone calls. His driving record might have had something to do with it, but he preferred to think he was getting fucked over. Gave him an excuse to be pissed off.

A pool table dominated much of the floor space in the bar. Walls paneled with old barn wood were hung with dozens of photographs of people – presumably customers – holding up fish. The television over the tiny bar was showing a soap. A lumpy woman with thin brown hair and a cigarette hanging from her mouth stood inside the horseshoe-shaped bar drying a beer mug with a dingy cloth. *Mental note to Kovac: Drink out of the bottle.* On the consumer side of the bar, an old lake rat with half his teeth sat on a stool, a filthy red ball cap at a jaunty angle on his head.

'Hope would never do that to Bo,' the woman scoffed. 'He's the love of her goddamned life.'

'Was,' the lake rat corrected. 'Ain't you been paying attention, Maureen? Stephano planted a microchip in her brain makes her fucking evil. Evil Gina, that's what they call her now.'

'That's crap,' Maureen proclaimed, half an inch of ash glowing red on the end of her cigarette.

Kovac cleared his throat. 'Neil Fallon?'

The woman gave him the head-to-toe. 'What are you selling?'

'Bad news.'

'He's out back.'

Some friend.

She nodded him toward the kitchen door.

The kitchen was as cramped as a carnival concession stand and stank of rancid grease and sour washrags. Or maybe that damp scent came from dead minnows. Kovac kept his hands in the pockets of his topcoat and the coat pulled tightly around him. He tried not to wonder where Neil kept the live bait.

Fallon stood in the open mouth of a big storage shed. He

looked like old Mike twenty-some years previous: built like a bull with a meaty, ruddy face and a bit of a downward hook to his mouth. He looked at Kovac coming across the yard, pulled a welder's mask down over his face, and went back to work on the runner of a snowmobile. Sparks arced away from the torch like a tiny fireworks display, bright against the gloom of the shed.

'Neil Fallon?' Kovac called above the roar. He pulled his shield out of his pocket and held it up, staying out of range of the sparks. 'Kovac. Minneapolis PD.'

Fallon stepped back, turned the torch off, and raised the mask. His face was blank. 'He's dead.'

Kovac stopped a yard from the snowmobile. 'Someone called you?'

'No. I just always knew they'd send a cop to tell me, that's all. You were more his family than I ever was.' He pulled a red bandanna out of his coveralls pocket and wiped sweat from his face, despite the fact that the afternoon temperature was in the low twenties. 'So what was it? His heart? Or did he get drunk and fall out of the goddamn chair?'

'I'm not here about your father,' Kovac said.

Neil looked at him as if he'd started speaking Greek.

'I'm here about Andy. He's dead. I'm sorry.'

'Andy.'

'Your brother.'

'Jesus Christ, I know he's my brother,' Fallon snapped.

He set the welding torch aside on a workbench, hands fumbling at the task, then at the thick, grimy welder's gloves. He jerked the mask off his head and threw it as if it burned him. It landed with a crash amid a stack of old gas cans.

'He's dead?' he said, short of breath. 'How is he dead? How can he be dead? He can't be.'

'It looks like suicide. Or an accident.'

'Suicide?' Fallon repeated. 'Fuck.' Breathing harder, he

went to a rusty metal locker beside the workbench, took out a half-empty bottle of Old Crow, and drank two good glugs of it. Then he put the bottle down and bent over with his hands on his knees, muttering a long string of curses. 'Andy.' He spat on the ground. 'Suicide.' He spat again. 'Jesus.' He took two steps out the door and puked in the snow.

Everyone reacted differently.

Kovac dug around in his coat pocket and came up with a piece of Nicorette. Shit.

'Jesus,' Fallon muttered. He came back and sat down on a stool fashioned from a tree trunk. He set the bottle of Old Crow between his feet. 'Andy.'

'Were you close?' Kovac asked, leaning back against the workbench.

Fallon shook his head and scraped his fingers back through thick hair the color of old rust. 'Once, I guess. Or maybe never. He spent a lot of time looking up to me when we were little kids 'cause I was older, tougher. 'Cause I stood up to the old man. But he was always Iron Mike's favorite. I wasted a lot of time hating him for that.'

He made it sound as if he had given up the hate long ago, but there was still a trace of bitterness in his voice, Kovac noted. In his experience, family resentments were seldom set aside entirely, if at all. Instead people tossed a cover over them and ignored them, like an ugly old piece of furniture.

'Looked like he was the all-American kid, all right,' he said, poking at the old wound. 'The star athlete. The good student. Followed in the old man's footsteps.'

Fallon looked down at the floor, his mouth a tight, hard line. 'He was everything the old man wanted in a son. That's what Mike thought anyway. I was none of it.'

He reached inside the open zipper of his coveralls and dug a cigarette and a lighter out of his shirt pocket. On the first long exhale he muttered, 'Fuck 'em.' Then he huffed a humorless laugh, picked up the Old Crow, and took another swig.

'Did you see much of each other?' Kovac asked.

Fallon wagged his head, though Kovac wasn't certain if he was answering in the negative or still trying to shake off the news.

'He came by now and then. He liked to fish a little. He keeps his gear here. Stores his boat in the winter. It's like a token sibling thing, I guess. Like he thinks it's his duty to patronize my business. Andy's big on duty.'

'When did you last speak with him?'

'He stopped by Sunday, but I didn't talk to him. I was busy. I had a guy here to buy a snowmobile.'

'When was the last time you had a serious conversation?'

'Serious? A month or so ago, I guess.'

'What about?'

Fallon's lips twisted. 'He wanted to tell me he was coming out of the closet. That he was a fag. Like I needed to hear that.'

'You didn't know he was gay?'

'Sure I did. I knew it years ago. High school. I just knew it. It wasn't something he had to tell me.' He took another snort of the Crow, then pulled on the cigarette. 'I told the old man so once. Way back when. Just because I was pissed off. Sick of it. Sick of "Why can't you be more like your brother?" '

He laughed loudly then, as if at a hilarious joke. 'Man. He damn near broke my jaw, he hit me so hard. I'd never seen him so mad. I could've said the Virgin Mary was a whore and he wouldn't have been half that mad. I sinned against the golden child. If he hadn't been in that chair, he'd have kicked my ass blue.'

'How did Andy seem when he told you?'

Fallon thought about it for a moment. 'Intense,' he said at last. 'I guess it was a trauma for him. He'd told Mike. That must've been a scene and a half. I would've gone back to see that. I couldn't believe the old man didn't stroke out.'

He sucked on the cigarette, dropped the butt on the floor, and crushed it out with the toe of his work boot. 'It was strange, though, you know? I felt sorry for Andy. I know all about disappointing the old man. He didn't.'

'Had you seen him since?'

'A couple of times. He came out to ice fish. I let him have one of my shacks. We had a drink one other time. I think he wanted us to be like brothers again, but, shit, what did we have in common besides the old man? Nothing.

'How'd Mike take this?' Fallon asked quietly, staring at the floor. 'Andy being dead.' He blew out a breath of smoke through flared nostrils. 'He sent you out here? He couldn't call me to tell me himself. Couldn't bring himself to admit the perfect son didn't turn out to be so fucking perfect after all. That's Mike. If he can't be right, he'll be an asshole.'

Taking the bottle of Old Crow by the throat, he pushed to his feet and headed out the door. 'Fuck 'em.'

Kovac followed, hunching into his coat. It was getting colder, a damp kind of cold that bit to the bone. His head hurt and his nose was throbbing.

Fallon stepped around the corner of the shed and stopped, staring between the shitty little fishing cabins he rented out in the summer. The buildings squatted near the shore of Minnetonka, but there was no shore to speak of this time of year. Snow drifted across land and ice, making one nearly indistinguishable from the other. The landscape was a sea of white stretching out toward an orange horizon.

'How'd he do it?'

'Hung himself.'

'Huh.'

Just that: *Huh*. Then he stood there some more while the wind blew a fine mist of white from one side of the lake to the other. No denial or disbelief. Perhaps he hadn't known his brother as well as Steve Pierce had. Or maybe he'd wished his brother dead in the past and so had less trouble accepting his death by any means.

'When we were kids, we played cowboys,' he said. 'I was always the one that got strung up. I was always the bad guy. Andy always played the sheriff. Funny how things turn out.'

They said nothing for another few moments. Kovac imagined Fallon was seeing those old memories play out before him. Two little boys, their whole lives ahead of them, in two-dollar cowboy hats, riding on broomsticks. Bright futures stained dark by the jealousies and strains and disappointments of growing up.

The images of childhood faded into the memory of Andy Fallon hanging naked from a rafter.

'Mind if I have a belt of that?' he asked, nodding toward the bottle.

Fallon handed it over. 'Aren't you on duty?'

'I'm always on duty. It's all I've got,' Kovac admitted. 'I won't tell the brass if you don't.'

Fallon turned back toward the lake. 'Hey, fuck 'em.'

The neighbor was in his yard harvesting burned-out Christmas bulbs when Kovac pulled up. Kovac stopped halfway up the walk to watch him as he unscrewed a light from the Virgin Mary's halo and stuffed it into a garbage bag.

'Half of them could burn out and it'd still be like living next door to the sun,' Kovac said.

The neighbor stared at him with a mix of offense and apprehension, clutching the garbage bag to his chest. He was a small man of about seventy with a hard-boiled look and small mean eyes. He wore a red plaid bomber cap with the flaps hanging down like hound's ears.

'Where's your Christmas spirit?' he demanded.

'I lost it about the fourth night I didn't get any sleep on

account of your fucking lights. Can't you put that shit on a timer?'

'Shows what you know,' the neighbor huffed.

'I know you're a lunatic.'

'You want me to cause a power surge? That's what would happen turning these lights on and off. Power surge. Could black out the whole block.'

'We should be so lucky,' Kovac said, and went up the sidewalk and into his house.

He turned the television on for company, radiated some left-over lasagna, sat on the couch, and picked at dinner. He wondered if Mike Fallon was sitting in front of his big-screen television tonight, trying to eat, trying to temporarily hide from his grief in the ruts of routine.

During the course of his career in homicide, Kovac had watched a lot of people straddle that awkward line between normalcy and the surreal reality of having violent crime disrupt their lives. He never thought much about it, as a rule. He wasn't a social worker. His job was to solve the crime and move on. But he thought about it tonight because Mike was a cop. And maybe for a few other reasons.

Abandoning the lasagna and *Dateline*, he went to his desk and rummaged around in a drawer, digging out an address book that hadn't seen the light of day in half a decade. His ex-wife was listed under her first name. He dialed the number and waited, then hung up when an answering machine picked up. A man's voice. The second husband.

What would he have said anyway? *I had a dead body today and it reminded me I have a kid.*

No. It reminded him he didn't have anyone.

He wandered back into the living room with the empty fish tank and Stone Phillips on the TV. Too much like old Iron Mike sitting in his massage chair in front of the big screen, alone in the world with nothing but bitter memories and soured hopes. And a dead son.

Most of the time Kovac believed he was happier without a real life. The job was a safe place. He knew what to expect. He knew who he was. He knew where he fit in. He knew what to do. He'd never been good at any of that without the badge.

There were worse fates than being a career cop. Most of the time he loved the work, if not the politics that went with it. He was good at it. Not fancy, not flashy. Not in the flamboyant way Ace Wyatt had been, grabbing headlines and sticking out his granite jaw for any passing camera. But good in the way that counted.

'Stick with what you do best,' he muttered, then turned his back on his dinner, grabbed his coat, and left.

Steve Pierce lived in a brick duplex on a drab street too close to the freeway in Lowry Hill. The neighborhood was full of yuppies and artsy types with money to renovate the old brownstones. But this portion had been chopped up into odd little angles when the major traffic arteries of Hennepin and Lyndale had been widened years ago, and it remained fragmented not only physically but psychologically as well.

Steve Pierce's neighbors had no gaudy Christmas displays draining the Northern States Power supply. Everything was tasteful and moderate. A wreath here. A swag there. As much as Kovac hated his neighbor, he thought he liked this even less. The street had the feel of a place where the inhabitants were not connected in any way, not even by animosity.

He fit right in tonight.

He sat in his car, parked across and down the street from Pierce's, waiting, thinking. Thinking Andy Fallon probably didn't leave his doors unlocked. Thinking Steve Pierce seemed to know a lot and yet nothing about his old buddy. Thinking there was more to that story and Steve Pierce didn't want to tell it.

People lied to the cops all the time. Not just bad guys or the guilty. Lying was an equal opportunity activity. Innocent people lied. Mothers of small children lied. Pencil-neck paper pushers lied. Blue-haired grannies lied. Everyone lied to the cops. It seemed to be embedded in the human genetic code.

Steve Pierce was lying. Kovac had no doubt about that. He just had to narrow the field of possible lies and decide if any of them were significant to Andy Fallon's death.

He pulled a pack of Salems out from under the passenger's seat, held it under his nose, and breathed deeply, then put the cigarettes back and got out of the car.

Pierce answered the door in sweatpants and a U of M hockey jersey, the smell of good scotch hovering around him like cologne, and a cigarette dangling from his lip. In the hours since his discovery of Andy Fallon's corpse, his physical appearance had degraded to the look of a man who had been battling a terminal illness for a very long time. Gaunt, ashen, red-eyed. One corner of his mouth curled up in a sneer as he pulled the cigarette and exhaled.

'Oh, look. It's the Ghost of Christmas Present. Did you bring your rubber truncheon this time? 'Cause, you know, I don't feel like I've been abused enough for one day. I find my best friend dead, get in a fight with Hulk Hogan in a cop uniform, and get harassed by a dickhead detective. The list just doesn't go on long enough. I could go for a little torture.'

He made his eyes and mouth round with feigned shock. 'Oops! My secret is out now! S and M. Shit!'

'Look,' Kovac said. 'This hasn't been my favorite day either. I got to go tell a man I used to look up to that his son probably killed himself.'

'Did he even listen?' Pierce asked.

'What?'

'Mike Fallon. Did he even listen when you told him about Andy?'

Kovac's brow creased. 'He didn't have much choice.'

Pierce stared past him at the dark street, as if some part of him still clung to a tattered scrap of fantasy that Andy Fallon would materialize from the gloom and come up the walk. The weight of reality defeated him. He flicked the cigarette butt out the door.

'I need a drink,' he said, and he turned and walked away from the open door.

Kovac followed him, taking the place in with a glance. Dramatic colors and oak furniture of some retro style he couldn't have named on a bet. What he knew about decorating wouldn't dot an *i*, but he recognized quality and big price tags. The walls of the hall were a patchwork of artsy photographs in white mats and thin black frames.

They went into a den with dark blue walls and fat leather armchairs the color of a fielder's glove. Pierce went to a small wet bar in one corner and freshened his glass from a bottle of Macallan. Fifty bucks a bottle. Kovac knew because he had been asked to kick in a few so the department could buy a bottle for the last lieutenant when he left. He'd personally never paid more than twenty dollars for a bottle of booze in his life.

'Andy's brother told me Andy stopped by about a month ago to come out of the closet,' Kovac said, leaning a hip against the bar. Pierce frowned at that and made a task of wiping imaginary condensation off the soapstone counter. 'I guess it didn't go well with the old man, huh?'

'What was the point of telling him?' Pierce's voice tightened with anger he was trying hard to camouflage. 'Sure, Dad, I'm still the same son who made you so proud in all those ball games,' he said with heavy sarcasm to the room at large. 'I just like it up the ass, that's all.'

He tipped back the scotch and drank it like apple juice. 'Jesus, what did he expect? He should have just let well enough alone. Let the old man see what he wanted to see. That's all people really want anyway.'

'How long had you known Andy was gay?'

'I don't know. I didn't mark it on the calendar,' Pierce said, walking away.

'A month? A year? Ten years?'

'A while.' Impatient. 'What difference does it make?'

'Coming out – was that something he'd saved for his family? Everyone else in his life knew? His friends, his coworkers?'

'It wasn't like he was a queen or something,' Pierce snapped. 'It wasn't anybody's business unless Andy wanted it to be. We roomed together in college. He told me then. I didn't care. It didn't matter. More chicks for me, right? Major competition out of the dating pool.'

'Why'd he tell them now?' Kovac asked. 'His father, his brother? What brought that on? People don't just up and spill their guts. Something pushes them to it.'

'Is there a point to this? Because if there's not, I'd sooner just sit here alone and drink myself into unconsciousness.'

'You don't strike me as someone wanting to sit down, Steve,' Kovac said. He pushed away from the bar to lean against one of the fat leather chairs. It smelled like a fielder's mitt too. That probably cost extra.

Pierce held himself stiff before Kovac's scrutiny. People even lied with their body language – or tried to. That was seldom as successful as the verbal variety.

'Your friend took a big step coming out,' Kovac said. 'And he landed on his chin, at least with his father. That kind of rejection might push a person. A person like Andy, close to his dad, wanting to please him –'

'No.'

'He wrote an apology on the mirror. Why would he do that if he was just playing around, just getting himself off?'

'I don't know. He just wouldn't have killed himself, that's all.'

'Or maybe the note on the mirror wasn't Andy's,' Kovac suggested. 'Maybe Andy had a boyfriend over. Maybe they were having a little game, something went wrong. . . . The boyfriend got scared. . . . Do you happen to know the names of any of his partners?'

'No.'

'None? You being best pals and all? That seems strange.'

'I wasn't interested in his sex life. It didn't have anything to do with me.' He took a drink of the scotch and stared sullenly at an electrical outlet on the other side of the room.

'This morning you told me he wasn't seeing anybody. Like maybe you *were* interested.'

'Which reminds me,' Pierce said. 'We've had this conversation before, Detective. I don't care to relive the experience.'

Kovac spread his hands. 'Hey, you seem like a man with something he wants to get off his chest, Steve. I'm just giving you an outlet here, you know what I mean?'

'I know that I don't have anything of value to tell you.'

Kovac smoothed a hand over his mustache and down his chin. 'You're sure?'

Keys rattled in the front door, giving Pierce the opportunity to escape. Kovac followed him to the front hall. A drop-dead blonde had let herself in and was stepping out of a pair of low boots even as she set take-out bags on the hall table.

Garlic chicken and Mongolian beef. Kovac's stomach growled, and he remembered the lasagna on his coffee table with a fondness it didn't deserve.

'I told you, I don't feel like eating, Joss.'

'You need to eat something, sweetie,' the blonde chided gently, slipping out of her coat. Her features were beautifully sculpted, eyes impossibly large. Her shoulder-length hair looked like pale gold silk. 'I was hoping the aroma might revive your appetite.'

She hung the coat on an oak hall tree, which looked a hundred years old and worth a small fortune. When she turned around, she caught sight of Kovac for the first time and stiffened her back. She looked as unhappy as a queen finding an uninvited peasant in her chambers. Regal in her bearing and her disdain. Even in her stocking feet, she was as tall as Pierce and looked athletic. She dressed with the conservative flair of someone born to money – expensive fabrics, traditional style; tawny wool slacks and a navy blue blazer, an ivory turtleneck sweater that looked incredibly soft.

Kovac flashed his badge at her. 'Kovac. Homicide. I'm here about Andy Fallon. Sorry to disrupt your evening, ma'am.'

'Homicide?' she said with wary surprise, her eyes going wider. They were brown, like Bambi's. 'But Andy wasn't murdered.'

'We need to be as sure of that as you, Miss . . .'

'Jocelyn Daring,' she said, but didn't offer her hand. 'I'm Steven's fiancée.'

'And the boss's daughter,' Kovac ventured.

'You're out of line, Kovac,' Pierce warned.

'Sorry,' Kovac said. 'You'll get that a lot with me. Inappropriate is my middle name. I guess I wasn't brought up right.'

The look Jocelyn Daring gave him could have freeze-dried coffee. Kovac didn't care. He was busy thinking that Steve Pierce was an up-and-comer for Daring-Landis, and that up-and-comers for Daring-Landis probably needed to be straight arrows with skeleton-free closets.

The fiancée put her hand on Steve Pierce's arm in a gesture that struck Kovac as both possessive and reassuring. She kept her eyes on Kovac. 'Is there really any reason for you to be here now, Detective? Steven's had a terrible shock today. We'd like to have some time alone to process the grief. Besides, it's hardly his fault Andy committed suicide.'

Pierce didn't even look at her. His stare was directed across the hall and through the open doorway of the den –

or into another dimension. It wasn't difficult to imagine what he was seeing. The question was what it meant to him, and whether the weight of the emotion pressing in on him had anything to do with guilt. If it did, what kind of guilt.

'I just had some questions, that's all,' Kovac said. 'Trying to get a clear picture of who Andy was, who his friends were, what might have pushed him to the edge – provided he stepped over it voluntarily. You know, trying to find out if he'd had any recent disappointments, ended relationships, personal setbacks of any kind.'

Jocelyn Daring opened the slim black purse she'd set on the table beside the food and extracted a business card. Her fingers were long and elegant, the nails gleamed like sheer pearl. The square-cut diamond on her left ring finger could've choked a goat.

'If you have any more questions, why don't you call first?' she suggested.

Kovac took the card in at a glance and raised a brow. 'A lawyer?'

'Steven told me about the way you treated him this morning, Detective. I won't allow that to happen again. Do you understand me?'

Pierce still wasn't looking at her. Kovac nodded. 'Yeah. I'm a little slow, but I think I'm beginning to see how things are.'

He moved past them to the door, then paused with his hand on the knob and looked back at them. Jocelyn Daring had moved in front of Steve Pierce again, putting herself between Kovac and her fiancé-client, protecting him.

'Did you know Andy Fallon, Ms Daring?' Kovac asked.

'Yes,' she said simply. No tears. No strain of grief.

'My condolences on your loss,' Kovac said, and let himself out into the cold.

7

Small and unremarkable, Liska's house sat shoulder to shoulder with half a dozen like it on a street in a neighborhood of St Paul that had no name. 'Near Grand Avenue' was what people who lived there liked to say, because Grand Avenue was just that: grand. Lined with beautiful restored mansions of former lumber barons. The governor's mansion was on Grand Avenue. Not even the fact that the governor was a former professional wrestler could bring the neighborhood down. St Paul's version of Uptown, the heart of the Grand Avenue area was a trendy stretch of boutiques and upscale restaurants.

Liska's neighborhood was a lot like Andy Fallon's – just far enough outside the chic radius to be affordable on a single income. Theoretically, Liska's ex paid child support, which was supposed to ease the financial burden of single motherhood. But what Speed Hatcher had been ordered by the court to pay and what he actually came across with were two very different figures.

That's what she got for marrying a narc. Narcs lived too close to the edge too much of the time; the line between who they were on the job and who they were in civilian life often blurred very badly. For Speed, the line no longer existed. He liked that edge too well.

In retrospect, Liska knew she had caught glimpses of that wildness in him from the first, when they'd both still been in uniform. She admitted it was part of what had attracted her to him. That and a dazzling smile and a great ass. But while wildness might have been a desirable trait in a lover, it was not in a father. The smile could make her take him back only so many times. The ass, it turned out, had been a serious liability. Too many other women wanted to get their hands on it.

She shuffled the Polaroids of Andy Fallon and wondered if his lovers had felt the same way. Fallon had been a knockout before rigor set in. The kind of looks that made women lament same-sex attraction.

She spread the photographs on her living room coffee table, with a copy of the *St Paul Pioneer Press* at the ready to cover them if one of the boys wandered in, though it was late and both Kyle and R.J. had been in bed for an hour. It wasn't unknown for one or the other to come out bleary-eyed in his pajamas and snuggle up to her on the couch while she tried to unwind with Letterman or a book.

A part of her wished that would happen now so she could put the pictures out of her head and try to be a normal human being for a while. She had a headache and her jaw throbbed from grinding her teeth. The cap on the day had been getting cornered by Lieutenant Leonard while she'd waited for Kovac to show – which he hadn't. Jamal Jackson was making noise about suing her for brutality. He didn't have a case, but that wouldn't stop him from hooking up with some slimy ACLU lawyer and making her life a misery until the case was thrown out of court. The report would go in her jacket whether the charges were substantiated or not. Next she'd have IA on her case while she tried to dig into theirs.

Great. If the incident had happened a week ago, she might have met Andy Fallon before he became a corpse.

She studied the photographs, not feeling the shock or revulsion an ordinary person would have. She had been toughened past that initial instinctive response long ago. She looked at them as a cop, searching for what they could tell her. Then the thought occurred that Andy Fallon had been twelve once, just like Kyle, her oldest.

A tremor of fear rattled through her, slipping past her guard because she was tired. The worry that she didn't spend enough quality time with the boys was always in her mind, chewing at the edge of her consciousness. Their lives seemed to be set at fast-forward. The boys were swamped with school and Scouts and hockey. She was overburdened with work and trying to keep the house and put food on the table and sign permission slips and show up for parent-teacher meetings and attend to the thousand other business details of motherhood. They were all so exhausted, there was little energy left for one another at the end of the day. How was she supposed to know if one of them might be slipping through the cracks?

She'd read that experimentation with autoerotic asphyxiation was not uncommon among adolescent boys. Every year a fair portion of teen deaths written off as suicides were in fact autoerotic accidents. At twelve, Kyle was still more interested in Nintendo than girls, but puberty was right around the corner. Liska wanted to sneak around that corner and beat the shit out of puberty with her ASP.

She tried not to think about it as she focused on Andy Fallon. If his death was an accident, then why the note on the mirror? If this kind of sexual practice was a habitual thing for him, would Steve Pierce have known about it? Probably not, if they were just buddies. If they were more than that . . . If Pierce was lying, was he lying to protect Fallon's memory or to protect himself?

The *Diagnostic and Statistical Manual of Mental Disorders, Fourth Edition* – aka the DSM-IV – was on the table, open to page 529 and the heading 'Sexual Masochism.' Amazing the things people learned to do to get themselves off. The fantasies ranged from rape to bondage to being spanked to being peed on to wearing a diaper. Halfway down the page she found what she was looking for.

> One particularly dangerous form of Sexual Masochism, called 'hypoxyphilia,' involves sexual arousal by oxygen deprivation. . . . Oxygen-depriving activities may be engaged in alone or with a partner. Because of equipment

72

malfunction, errors in placement of the noose or ligature, or other mistakes, accidental deaths sometimes occur. . . . Sexual Masochism is usually chronic, and the person tends to repeat the same masochistic act.

Alone or with a partner. Pierce's initial response to the question of Fallon's sexual habits had been indignation, but indignation could be used to cover any number of other emotions: embarrassment, fear, guilt. Steve Pierce professed to be straight. Maybe he was trying to hide the fact that he really wasn't, or that he had dabbled on the other side of that line. Or maybe he was telling the truth and Andy Fallon had other partners. Who?

They needed to find out more about Andy Fallon's private life. If he'd been lucky, there would be one to uncover. Anyone looking into Liska's private life would have had a short glance at nothing. She couldn't remember the last decent date she'd had. She never socialized with anyone but cops, and cops made lousy boyfriends as a rule. On the other hand, men with normal jobs found her a little too intimidating. The idea of a girlfriend who could handle a tactical baton and a nine-millimeter handgun was a bit much for the average Joe. So what was a girl to do? And when was a mother of two to do it?

She sensed the presence at her front door a split second before she heard the faint rattle of the lock being opened. Adrenaline surged through her. She came up off the couch in a heartbeat, eyes never leaving the door, hand reaching for the cordless phone. She wished it was her gun, but the gun remained locked in a cabinet when she was home – a necessary precaution for the safety of the boys and their friends. The ASP, however, was never far out of reach. Her right hand closed on the cushioned handle and she snapped her wrist in a well-practiced move to extend the steel rod to its full length.

She moved to the hinged side of the door as it began to ease open, and took a position with the baton.

A Cartman hand puppet popped into view, the *South Park* character craning its fat head around the door to look up at her.

'Hey, lady, you gonna shoot my ass?'

Relief and anger poured through Liska in a hot–cold mix that prickled her skin.

'Goddammit, Speed, I *ought* to shoot your ass! One of these days I'm going to plug you through that door and let you bleed out on the front step. It'd serve you right.'

'Is that any way to talk to the father of your children?' he asked, slipping inside and closing the door behind him. Not for the first time, Liska wished she didn't have to let him have a key. She didn't like him coming and going from her life and the boys' lives at will, but neither did she want a hostile relationship with him – for the sake of Kyle and R.J. Speed was an asshole, but he was their father and they needed him.

'The boys up?'

'It's eleven-thirty, Speed. No one should be up. Kyle and R.J. and I live in the real world, where people have to get up in the morning.'

He shrugged and tried to look innocent. Other women would have fallen for it. Liska was too familiar with the expression and the lack of sincerity behind it.

'What do you really want?'

He grinned the wicked grin of a romance-novel pirate. He must have been working a case, she thought. Though his blond hair was cropped almost military-short, he hadn't shaved in a few days. He wore a filthy old army field coat hanging open over faded, paint-spattered jeans and an old black sweatshirt. Despite all this, he looked sexy as hell. But she had long ago become immune.

'I could say I want you,' he said, moving toward her.

'Yeah,' Liska said, unimpressed. 'And I could still coldcock you. Give me a reason.'

The smile dropped off. Just like that.

'I can't drop by to leave a toy for my kids?' he said, pulling the puppet off his hand. 'What the hell's the matter with you, Nikki? You have to be such a bitch about everything?'

'You break into my house at eleven-thirty, scare the shit out of me, and expect me to be happy to see you? What's wrong with that picture?'

'I didn't break in. I have a key.'

'Yeah, you have a key. Do you have a fucking telephone? Could you use that once in a while instead of just blowing in like a tornado?'

Speed didn't bother to answer. He never answered questions he didn't like. He put the Cartman puppet down on the coffee table and picked up one of the Polaroids of Andy Fallon.

'This the kind of shit you leave around for my kids to see?'

'*Your* kids,' she muttered, snatching the photograph out of his hand. 'Like you did anything but provide the raw materials – and only half of that. How is it they're never *your* kids when they're sick or need new clothes or they're having trouble?'

'Do I need to hear this?' he asked, making a face.

'You came to my house. You hear whatever I want to say.'

'Dad!'

R.J. was across the room before the exclamation died. He flung himself at his father, wrapping his arms around Speed's legs. Liska scrambled to put down the ASP and pull the newspaper over it and the Fallon Polaroids, even though no one was paying the least attention to her.

'R.J., my man!' Speed grinned and high-fived his youngest, pulling free of the boy's embrace to squat down in front of him.

'I wanna be called Rocket now,' R.J. said, rubbing the sleep from one eye. His blond hair stood up in little tufts at the crown of his head. His Minnesota Vikings pajamas, inherited from Kyle, were too big for him. 'I wanna have a nickname like you, Dad.'

'Rocket. I like it,' Speed declared. 'Seriously cool, little man.'

The hand puppet was discovered and the two males went into a five-minute riff on *South Park*. Liska's fuse grew shorter and shorter.

'R.J., it's really late,' she said, hating to do it and hating Speed for making her into the bad guy with his mere presence. He breezed in and out of the boys' lives as he chose, all excitement and fun and adventure. As custodial parent, Liska felt she provided little of that and all of the discipline and drudgery. 'You have school tomorrow.'

Her son looked up at her with duplicates of her own blue eyes, angry and disappointed. 'But Dad just got here!'

'Then be mad at Dad. He's the one who thought it'd be a great idea to come over in the middle of the night when everyone's supposed to be sleeping.'

'*You're* not sleeping,' R.J. pointed out.

'I'm not ten either. When you get to be thirty-two you can stay up half the night working and taking Tagamet too. So you've got that to look forward to.'

'I'm gonna work undercover and be a narc like Dad.'

'You're gonna be undercover in bed in two minutes, mister.'

R.J. and Speed exchanged a look that locked Liska out of the loop. Speed shrugged. 'I'm outranked, Rocket. Better call it a night.'

'Can I take Cartman with me?'

'Sure.' He ruffled the boy's hair, his attention already shifting from his son to his ex.

Liska bent down to brush a kiss to R.J.'s cheek, but he ducked away and retreated down the hall, talking to the puppet in a cartoon voice and making farting noises. When he was out of sight and earshot, she glared at Speed.

76

'You are such a shit,' she hissed, straining to keep her voice down when she wanted to rail at him. 'You didn't come here to see R.J. –'

'Rocket.'

'– or Kyle. Now you've got R.J. all wound up. He won't sleep half the night.'

'Sorry.'

'No, you're not. You never are,' she said bitterly. 'What do you want, Speed? I'll bet it isn't to pay me the money you owe me.'

He pulled in a big breath. 'Next week. I promise,' he said with well-rehearsed contrition. 'I'm in the middle of something right now, but next week –'

'Save it. Pack up the act and make it a road show, why don't you,' Liska said, flipping the paper off the Polaroids. She gathered the pictures into a stack. 'It's been a very long day. I'd like to go to bed now, if you don't mind.'

Speed said nothing for a minute, then reached out and tapped a finger against the top photograph.

'Anyone I know?' he asked quietly. 'I heard one of yours offed himself. Is this him?'

'Looks that way. An IA guy. You wouldn't know him.'

They had both started out in uniforms in St Paul; Speed had stayed but she had gone across the river to Minneapolis. He knew a lot of Minneapolis cops – mainly the narcs and some of the homicide dicks – but he had no reason to know Andy Fallon. No one went out of their way to meet the people from Internal Affairs.

He slipped the picture out of her hand and examined it closely. 'Hell of a way to check out. I guess IA guys don't know how to shoot a gun, huh?'

'Who knows what goes on in people's heads,' Liska said.

There had been a time in their marriage when they had shared details of cases and helped each other work things through. She thought of those as the Golden Moments, that

77

brief period of time before infidelity and professional rivalry pulled apart the fabric of their relationship.

'Maybe it wasn't his choice,' she said.

'Jesus, you homicide dicks.' He tossed the picture back down on the coffee table. 'It's a no-brainer, Nikki. Why torment yourself looking at these? The guy did himself. Hanging is suicide or an accident, not murder. Write it off and move on.'

'When the ME says let it go, I'll let it go. Not before,' she said, as much to be stubborn as anything. 'That's my job. That's the way I am.'

'Yeah. Well, you don't need to bring it home with you.'

'Don't accuse me of corrupting *your* children,' she said sourly. 'You heard R.J. He wants to be a narc. Can't get much lower than that.'

'Sure he could. He could be IA. Look how they wind up.'

Liska didn't look at the photo as he held it up. She didn't have to. 'All right. Enough pleasant chitchat for one evening. It's been . . . the usual. You know where the door is.'

Speed didn't move. He put on his yes-I-can-be-an-adult face. Liska sighed.

'You know, I came over here to see how you were doing,' he confessed. 'I heard you caught this one, Nikki. I thought it might be tough – because he was a cop, because he was IA. Because of your old man and all.'

'My father didn't kill himself,' Liska said too quickly, too defensively. The mistake left her feeling vulnerable.

'I know that, but the whole IA thing . . .'

'This has nothing to do with that,' she said flatly.

Speed considered his options. She could see him thinking, trying to figure how to play it. How to play her.

He spread his hands. The friend, just offering a sugges-tion. 'Still . . . Well, you can dump it as soon as the ME says suicide. Or you could pass it off now. A case like this hardly needs two detectives. Dump it on Kojak.'

Wrong tack. Liska bristled at the implication that she wasn't tough enough to handle it. 'What's it to you? I caught the case and I'll work it till it's over.'

'Fine. I just . . .' He blew out a long-suffering sigh and dragged a hand back over his head. 'I still care about you, Nikki, that's all. We have a history. That means something . . . even to an asshole like me.'

Liska said nothing. She trusted neither her voice nor the tangle of emotions knotting together inside her. His concern was unexpected and she was unprepared for the way it made her feel – vulnerable, needy. Not words she wanted associated with herself.

Speed reached inside his jacket, dug out a cigarette, and dangled it from his lip.

'Well,' he said softly, lifting a hand to touch her cheek. 'Don't say I never tried to do anything for you.'

Liska stepped aside, turned her face away.

'Yeah,' he said, letting his hand fall. 'I know where the door is. See you around, Nikki.'

He had his hand on the doorknob before she could make herself speak.

'Uh . . . Speed . . . thanks for your concern. But I'm fine. I can handle it. It's just another case.'

'Sure. Whatever. You'll be off it in a day and a half.'

He gave her one last long look, and Liska had the feeling he wanted to say something more. But he didn't. And then he was gone.

She locked the dead bolt behind him and turned out the lights. She gathered up the photographs of Andy Fallon and went to her bedroom to secure them in her briefcase. Then she checked on the boys, who were both pretending to be asleep, brushed her teeth, changed into an oversize T-shirt from the FBI National Academy, and went to bed so she could stare at the ceiling and watch the past whirl around in her memory like a carousel.

The junior high father-daughter dance. She was thirteen and mortified. Embarrassed. Guilt sat in her stomach like a huge, jagged rock because of the other emotions. Her father stood stiffly beside her, eyes downcast, as ashamed as she was to have people see him. A stocky man with piercing blue eyes, the left side of his face slack and drooping, as if all the nerves had been snipped with scissors. People staring at them – not only because of her father's face but because of the stories they'd heard: the implications of corruption in the police department, cops stealing drug money, an Internal Affairs investigation . . .

None of it was true, Nikki knew. She seemed to believe that more strongly than her father did, which made her angry. He was innocent. Why wouldn't he fight harder to prove it? Why wouldn't he spit in their faces? Deny, defy, take action. Instead, he went around in public with his head down in order to shield both his shame and the Bell's palsy the stress had induced. Words like *weak* and *spineless* drifted through his daughter's mind like dirt in a dust-bowl breeze. As each one crossed her mind, the feeling of guilt deepened and the resentment sharpened.

The investigation had dragged on for nearly eighteen months, petering out to nothing in the end. No charges had been brought. Everyone was supposed to forget and forgive. By then, Thomas Liska's health had begun to seriously deteriorate. Two years later he died of pancreatic cancer.

It was a very long night.

8

The body has been discovered.

Suicide. Accident. Tragedy.

The word *murder* has not been mentioned.

Is it really murder if dictated by necessity, if accompanied by remorse?

Sorry . . .

There is a sense of unease from knowing other people are now aware, even though they don't suspect. As if strangers are invading what should have remained private. The intimacy of death had been shared by just the two of them. The aftermath would be a public event.

That somehow cheapens the experience.

Andy Fallon stares out from the photograph, the last spark of life dying in the half-opened eyes, tongue coming out through the parted lips. The expression seems to take on an accusatory quality.

Sorry . . .

The photograph, cradled in one hand, is raised to the lips, the image of the death mask kissed.

Sorry . . .

But even as the apology is offered, the excitement rises.

9

Liska stormed into the cubicle, her face pinched with temper, cheeks pink with cold. Kovac watched her with dread because he knew the look and what it meant for the quality of his day. Still, he didn't move as she bore down on him. She slugged his left upper arm as hard as she could. It was like being hit with a ball peen hammer.

'Ouch!'

'*That* was for ditching me last night,' she announced. 'I waited for you, and because I waited for you, Leonard cornered me and gave me the third degree about the Nixon assault and how Jamal Jackson couldn't be tied to it in any way. Now he's got it in his head that Jackson can somehow claim false arrest and use it in his suit against the department.'

'What suit?' he asked, rubbing the sore spot.

'The suit Jackson's threatening. Brutality. Against me.'

Kovac rolled his eyes. 'Oh, for Christ's sake. We've got the video of him beaning me. Let him try to sue. If Leonard thinks Jackson has a case, he's got his head so far up his ass we should call the people at Guinness. It's gotta be some kind of record.'

'I know,' Liska said, calming. She tossed her purse in a deep desk drawer and dropped her briefcase in her chair. 'I'm sorry I belted you. I had a rotten night. Speed came by. I didn't get much sleep.'

'Oh, jeez. I'm not gonna have to hear about sex, am I?'

Liska's face went dark again, and she lunged across the cubicle and popped him a second time in exactly the same spot.

'Ouch!'

Elwood stuck his huge head around the side of the half-wall. 'Do I need to call the police?'

'Why?' Liska demanded, shrugging out of her coat. 'Is being a knothead a crime now?'

Kovac rubbed his arm. 'I guess I said the wrong thing.'

'Again,' Elwood added. 'Did she do that to your nose?'

Kovac tried to catch his reflection in the dark screen of his computer monitor, though he already knew how it looked: puffy and red and lumpy as an old drunk's. At least it wasn't broken for the umpteenth time.

'Physical abuse of men by women,' Elwood said. 'One of society's great taboos. Victim Services can probably hook you up with a support group, Sam. Should I call Kate Conlan?'

Kovac threw a pen at him. 'Why don't you go take a flying leap?'

Liska settled into her chair and swiveled toward him, looking sullen and maybe just a little contrite. 'I didn't get any sleep because my brain preferred to remain awake, dwelling on what an asshole my ex is, among other fine topics. What happened to your nose? Iron Mike didn't want to hear his son was into kinky sex?'

'It was an accident,' Kovac said. 'He took the news hard. He and Andy had had a split, probably about a month ago when Andy decided to tell him he preferred DC to AC. That's not an easy thing for a father to face, I guess. What'd you get from IA?'

'The cold shoulder. Lieutenant Ice Bitch gave me a lot of attitude and no information. She claims she doesn't want to compromise an IA investigation. Someone's career might get damaged.'

'I thought that was their goal.'

Liska shrugged. 'She was at Fallon's home Sunday night between eight and nine-thirty, discussing a case he was unhappy about. She says he seemed fine when she left. She did tell me he'd been depressed. She hadn't ordered him to see the shrink, but she'd suggested he do it.'

'Do we know if he took her up on it?'

'Confidential information.'

'No one's gonna talk until the ME's done,' Kovac said. 'They're all holding out to hear *suicide*, and then they won't have to talk at all, and to hell with anyone who wants to know why this kid killed himself. If that's what he did.'

Liska picked up a fat pen with a plastic bloodshot eyeball glued to one end. One of many odd treasures in their cubicle. They bought them for each other as a running joke. Kovac's most prized possession was a very realistic fake finger that looked as if it had been separated from its hand with a hacksaw. He liked to surprise people with it, leaving it in file folders, booby-trapping desks with it. It was the strangest thing a woman had ever given him – and, oddly, it brought him the most simple enjoyment. Two failed marriages to 'normal' women, and he got the biggest kick out of a chick who gave him imitation severed body parts. What did that say?

'You going to the autopsy?' Liska asked.

'What's the point? Bad enough seeing the kid dead. I don't need to watch him get carved up for no good reason. His brother told me Andy came to see him about a month ago. He was coming out of the closet. He'd told Mike, and it hadn't gone well.'

'That timing would coincide with his apparent depression.'

'Yeah. It sure smells like suicide,' he said. 'The crime scene guys didn't come up with anything unusual that I've heard about.'

'No, they didn't, but the grapevine says otherwise,' Liska said. 'Tippen told me it was the hot gossip at Patrick's last night. That they came up with all kinds of sex toys and gay pornography. Now, where do you think a rumor like that might have started?'

Kovac scowled. 'With the Three Stooges in uniform. Where'd you see Tippen this early?'

'Caribou Coffee. He has a really ugly double espresso habit.'

'Real cops are supposed to drink the sludge in the break room pot. It's tradition.'

'Christmas is a tradition,' Liska corrected him. 'Bad coffee is avoidable.

'The thing that bothers me with the whole sex angle is this,' she went on. 'What if Andy Fallon *was* into S and M? Let's say he and a pal are playing around with erotic rope tricks and something goes wrong. Fallon dies. The partner panics and leaves the scene. That's a crime in my book. Man two: depraved indifference. At least.'

'I've been thinking about that too,' Kovac said. 'I went to see Steve Pierce last night. He seems like a man with something heavy on his chest.'

'What'd he have to say?'

'Nothing much. We were interrupted by his fiancée: the lovely Ms Jocelyn Daring, attorney-at-law.'

Liska's brows went up under her bangs. 'Daring as in Daring-Landis?'

'I made that assumption. No one corrected me.'

Liska gave a low whistle. 'There's an interesting twist. Anything back yet from latent prints?'

'No, but we can expect to find Pierce's prints. They were friends.'

Liska's phone rang and she turned to answer it.

Kovac turned back to his computer and hit the power switch. He figured he'd get a jump on the preliminary report on Andy Fallon's death. A week or so after the autopsy they would get the ME's reports. He would call the morgue sooner than that to hear about the tox screens and to try to speed the report process along.

Lieutenant Leonard appeared suddenly at the cubicle. 'Kovac. My office. Now.'

Liska kept her head down as she spoke on the phone, avoiding eye contact. Kovac bit back a big sigh and followed Leonard.

One wall of the lieutenant's office was dominated by a huge calendar dotted with round colored stickers. Red for open homicides, black for when the case cleared. Orange for open assaults, blue for when they closed. Color-coordinated crime fighting. Neat and tidy. The shit they taught these guys in management class.

Leonard went behind his desk and stood with his hands on his hips and a frown on his mug face. He was wearing a tweedy brown sweater over a shirt and tie. The sleeves of the sweater were too long. The overall picture made Kovac think of a sock monkey he'd had as a kid.

'You'll have a preliminary report from the ME on the Fallon kid later today.'

Kovac gave his head a little shake, as if he had water in his ear. 'What? I was told it could be four or five days before they even got to him.'

'Someone called in a favor. On account of Mike Fallon,' Leonard added. 'He's a department hero. No one wants him suffering more than he has to because of this. What with the circumstances surrounding the suicide . . .'

His lipless mouth squirmed like a worm. Distasteful business: naked suicide with kinky sexual overtones.

'Yeah,' Kovac said. 'Damned inconsiderate of the kid to off himself that way. If that's what happened. It's an embarrassment to the department.'

'That's a secondary consideration, but it's a valid one,' Leonard said defensively. 'The media is all too happy to make us look bad.'

'Well, this would do the trick. First it's downtown beat cops spending their shifts in strip clubs. Now this. We got us a regular Sodom and Gomorrah down here.'

'You can keep that comment to yourself, Sergeant. I don't want anyone talking to the media with regards to this case. I'll give the official statement later today. "Sergeant Fallon's untimely death was a tragic accident. We mourn his loss and our thoughts are with his family." ' He recited the lines he'd memorized, trying them out for size and impact.

'Dry, brief, to the point,' Kovac critiqued. 'Sounds good, as long as it's true.'

Leonard stared at him. 'Do you have any reason to believe it *isn't* true, Sergeant?'

'Not at the moment. It'd be nice to have a couple of days to tie up the loose ends. You know, like an investigation. What if it was a sex game gone wrong? There could be an issue of culpability.'

'Do you have any proof anyone else was at the scene?'

'No.'

'And you've been told he was having problems with depression, that he was seeing the department shrink?'

'Uh . . . yeah,' Kovac said, figuring it was a half-truth, at least.

'He had . . . *issues*,' Leonard said, uncomfortable with the topic.

'I know he was gay, if that's what you mean.'

'Then don't stir the pot,' Leonard snapped. Taking a sudden interest in the paperwork on his desk, he sat down and opened a file folder. 'There's nothing to be gained in it. Fallon killed himself either accidentally or on purpose. The sooner we all move on, the better. You've got cases open.'

'Oh, yeah,' Kovac said dryly. 'My murders of tomorrow.'

'Your what?'

'Nothing, sir.'

'Tie this up and get back on the Nixon assault. The county attorney is riding me like a jockey on that one. Gang violence is a priority.'

Yeah, Kovac thought, heading back toward the cubicle, *keep those gang stats down to placate the city council*. The odd, unexplained death of a cop could be shrugged off.

He told himself he should be happy. He didn't want the Fallon case dragging on any more than Leonard did, though for different reasons. Leonard could give a shit about Iron Mike. He'd probably never even met the man. Leonard's concern was the department. Kovac wanted it over for Mike's sake – same as whoever had called in the marker with the ME. Yet that fist of tension Kovac didn't want to acknowledge held firm in the pit of his belly, as familiar to him as a lover's touch. More so, considering how long it had been since he'd had a lover.

Liska shoved his coat at him. 'You need a cigarette, don't you, Sam?'

'Hello? I'm quitting. Big fucking help you are.'

'Then you should get a lot of fresh air. To clean the crud out of your lungs.'

She stepped in close and gave him a meaningful look. He followed when she turned for the door.

'Fallon's over,' he said, pulling on his topcoat as they left the office.

Liska looked at him the same way he'd looked at Leonard, only more so.

'The autopsy's a done deal.'

'What?'

'Everyone expects a suicide ruling. Only they'll call it accidental, just to go easy on Mike. We'll have a preliminary report today and a benediction from Leonard. No one upstairs wants Mike – or the department – to be further embarrassed by the sordid details.'

'Yeah, I bet not,' Liska said, suddenly looking pale.

She didn't speak again until they were outside. Kovac didn't ask for an explanation. They'd been together long enough that he could read her easily. A partnership on the job was an intimacy – not in the sexual sense, but psychologically, emotionally. The more in tune with each other, the better they could work a case. His partnership with Liska was as good as any he'd had. They understood each other, respected each other.

He walked beside her through a maze of halls and out a little-used door on the north side of the building. The sun was out, brilliant and blinding on the snow. The sky was the pale blue of a robin's egg. A deceptively pretty day with a windchill factor in the teens. There was no one else on this set of steps, which caught no sunlight and all the wind. People flocked instead to the south side like arctic birds searching for warmth.

Kovac winced as the cold slapped him in the face. He jammed his hands down in his coat pockets and turned a hunched shoulder to the wind.

'Leonard told you Fallon was over,' Liska said.

'Wrap it up and close it.'

'Who made that autopsy happen so fast?'

'Someone higher on the food chain.'

Liska looked up the street, the muscles in her jaw tensing. The wind fluttered through her short hair and brought moisture to her eyes. He could sense he wasn't going to like what she was working up to tell him.

'So what bug's up your ass?' he asked irritably. 'It's colder than my second wife's mother out here.'

'I just had a call from someone who claims to have known what Andy Fallon was working on.'

'Does this someone have a name?'

'Not yet. But I saw him yesterday in the IA offices. Another dissatisfied customer.'

The fist in Kovac's belly pressed knuckles-down and started to grind. 'And what does he claim Fallon was working?'

She looked up at him. 'A murder.'

'Murder?' Kovac said with disbelief. 'Since when does IA touch a murder? No way. A felony always goes to the division, on account of IA can't find their own asses in a dark room. How could Fallon be working a murder and us not know about it? That's bullshit.'

'He could have if we thought it was closed,' Liska said. 'Remember Eric Curtis?'

'*Curtis?* The off-duty patrol cop? The mutt that did him is sitting in jail. What was his name? Vermin?'

'Verma. Renaldo Verma.'

'A string of robbery-assaults. Gay victims. He did – what? Three or four in eighteen months.'

'Four. Two of the vics died. Curtis was last.'

'Same MO as the others, right? Bound, beaten, robbed.'

'Yes, but Eric Curtis was a cop,' Liska pointed out.

'So?'

'So he was a cop and he was gay. According to my mystery man, months before his death, Curtis had complained to IA about harassment on the job because of his sexual preference.'

'And you're saying maybe a cop killed him because of it?' Kovac said. 'Jesus, Tinks. You want to believe that, maybe you ought to apply for Fallon's job.'

'Fuck you, Kojak,' she snapped. 'I hate IA. I hate what they do to people. I hate them like you can't know. But Eric Curtis was a cop, and he was gay, and now he's dead. Andy Fallon was looking into it, he was gay, and now *he's* dead,' she said, not liking the sound of it herself by the scowl on her face. And still, she stood up to him, toe to toe, and pressed her point. That was Liska: no job too mean or too ugly. She stepped up to the plate and swung at whatever she had to.

'And I just got told the book is all but closed on Fallon,' Kovac said, looking out at the street.

'You don't like it either, Sam,' Liska said quietly. 'You can feel it in your gut, can't you?'

He didn't answer her right away. He let it all roll through his head like a movie while the carillon in the city hall clock tower began to mark the hour with 'White Christmas.'

'No,' he said at last. 'I don't like anything about this.'

They were both silent for a moment. Cars rolled by on Fourth Street. The wind howled down the tunnels created by the buildings, snapping the flags on the federal building across the street.

'Andy Fallon probably killed himself,' Liska said. 'There wasn't anything at the scene to say he didn't. This guy that just called me. Who's to say he gives a shit about Andy Fallon? Maybe the Curtis murder is just his ax to grind and he thinks we'll get into it through the back door. . . . But what if it's not, Sam? We're all Andy Fallon has. And Mike. You taught me that – who do we work for?'

'The victim,' he murmured, that bad feeling still heavy in the bottom of his stomach.

They worked for the victim. He'd grounded that into countless trainees. The victims couldn't speak for themselves. It was up to the detective to ask all pertinent questions, to dig and prod, and turn over rocks until he found the truth. Sometimes it was easy. And sometimes it wasn't.

'What's it gonna hurt to ask a few more questions?' he said, knowing it sounded too much like something for the Famous Final Words file.

'I'll take the morgue.' Liska hugged her coat around her as she turned back for the door. 'You take IA.'

'I've already spoken with your partner, Sergeant,' Lieutenant Savard said, barely glancing up at him as she sorted through a pile of reports on her desk. 'And, in case you haven't been informed, Andy Fallon's death is being ruled an accident.'

'In record time,' Kovac said.

The IA lieutenant gave him her undivided attention at that. The green of her eyes was almost startling. Clear and cold, staring out from beneath brows several shades darker than the ash blond of her hair. The contrast intensified the

91

sharp seriousness of her expression. He had to think she scared the shit out of a lot of cops with that look.

He'd been around too long to feel fear. He was numb to it. Or maybe he was just stupid.

He sat in the chair across the desk from her, ankles crossed. He'd done a brief stint in IA himself a hundred years ago, back when the department had been run by a real cop, not some brass-polisher looking to shine his way up the chain of command. He hadn't been ashamed to work the job. He had no love for bad cops. But he hadn't liked it either.

In those days there hadn't been any lieutenants on the force who looked like this one.

'Damn decent of them to do the slicing and dicing so quick, don't you think?' he said. 'Seeing how backed up they are at the morgue this time of year. They've got bodies stacked up like Yule logs, for Christ's sake.'

'Professional courtesy,' Savard said curtly.

Kovac caught himself watching her lips. They were the perfect shape of an archer's bow, with a sheer coat of lipstick.

'Yeah, well,' he said, 'I feel like I kinda owe old Mike the same courtesy, you know? Do you know him? Mike Fallon?'

The eyes went back to the papers. 'I know of him. I spoke with him on the phone today and gave him my condolences.'

'Yeah, you're too young. You wouldn't have been around in the days of Iron Mike. You must be — what? Thirty-seven, thirty-eight?'

She looked at him as if she had a mouthful of bitters. 'That would be none of your business, Sergeant. And just a word of advice. If you're going to try to guess a woman's age, err on the side of youth.'

Kovac winced. 'Was I that far off?'

'No. You were that close. I'm vain. Now, if you don't

mind . . .' She lifted some of the papers and rattled them. The subtle reminder to leave.

'I just have a couple of questions.'

'You don't need questions or answers to them. You have no case to investigate.'

'But I have Mike,' he reminded her. 'I'm just trying to piece some things together for him. It's a tough thing for a parent to lose a child. If it helps for me to fill him in on Andy's last days, then I'll do that. That doesn't seem too much to ask, do you think?'

'It is if you want confidential information from an Internal Affairs investigation,' Savard said, pushing her chair back from the desk.

She had tried the cool dismissal. Now she would try to herd him out. Kovac stayed seated for a moment, just to irk her, just to let her know he wouldn't give up that easily. She came around the desk to show him the door. He waited until she was near his chair, then he stood, making her hesitate. She took a half step back, frowning, retreating and not liking it.

'I know about the Curtis thing,' Kovac bluffed.

'Then you know you don't need to speak with me after all, don't you?'

A wry smile tugged at one corner of his mouth. 'You didn't ride in here on the equal rights bandwagon, did you, Lieutenant?'

'Believe me, I'm more than qualified for my job, Sergeant Kovac.'

There was something like amusement in her voice, but it was darker. Irony, maybe. He couldn't begin to imagine why, or where it came from, or why she would allow him to hear it. It wasn't important to him now, but he filed the curiosity in his brain, just in case he might need it later.

He crossed his arms and sat back against the edge of her desk as she made a move toward the door. Irritation flashed in the green eyes. Temper brought a tint of color to her cheeks. This, he thought, was what television wanted lady lieutenants to look like: classy, sleek, stylish in a steel-gray pantsuit. Cool, controlled, sexy in an understated way.

Too classy for you, Kovac, he thought. A lieutenant. Jesus. Why was he even looking?

'Did you know Andy Fallon was gay?' he asked.

'His personal life was none of my business.'

'That's not what I asked.'

'Yes, he told me he was gay.'

'Before you went to his house Sunday night?'

'You're pressing your luck here, Sergeant,' Savard said. 'I've already told you, I'm not going to answer your questions. Do you really want me to speak to your lieutenant about this?'

'You can call him, but he's busy practicing his it-was-a-tragic-accident-now-drop-it speech.'

'He should be practicing it on you.'

'I've already given him my critique – there's no beat and you can't dance to it. He should keep his day job as a petty bureaucrat and forget about politics.'

'I'm sure your opinion means a great deal to him.'

'Yeah. Exactly nothing,' he said. 'Yours will mean more, if you decide to go that way. He'll ask me in his office and tell me to do my job the way he says or get suspended. Thirty days without pay. And all because I'm trying to do something decent for another cop. Life sucks, some days harder than others. But what am I supposed to do? Hang myself?'

Savard's face darkened. 'That wasn't funny, Sergeant.'

'It wasn't meant to be. I'm sure you know it was meant to make you see Andy Fallon in your head again. I can show you the Polaroids if you want.' He pulled one out of his inside breast pocket and held it up like a magician doing a card trick. 'It's a hell of a thing to see, isn't it?'

The blood drained out of the lieutenant's face. She

looked as if she wanted to hit him with something. 'Put it away.'

Kovac flipped it over and looked at it with the dispassion of someone who had seen hundreds of such photographs. 'You knew him. You had a connection to him. You're sorry he's dead. Think how his old man feels.'

'Put it away,' she said again. There was the barest hint of a tremor in her voice as she added, 'Please.'

He slipped the Polaroid back into his coat pocket. 'Do you care enough to help lay a father's doubts to rest?'

'Does Mike Fallon have doubts about Andy's death being an accident?' she asked.

'Mike has doubts about who Andy was.'

She moved away from him, silent for a moment, thinking, considering. 'No one knows anyone. Not really. Most of us don't even know ourselves.'

Kovac watched her, intrigued by the sudden turn to philosophy. She seemed reflective rather than defensive.

'I know exactly who I am, Lieutenant,' he said.

'And who are you, Sergeant Kovac?'

'I'm exactly what you're looking at,' he answered, lifting his arms to the sides. 'I'm a flatfoot, a straight-line cop in a cheap suit from JC Penney. I'm a walking, talking stereotype. I eat bad food, drink too much, and smoke – though I'm trying to quit and think I should score character points for that. I don't run marathons or do tai chi or compose opera in my free time. If I have a question, I ask it. People don't always like that, but fuck 'em – pardon my language, another bad habit I won't be shed of. Oh, yeah – and I'm stubborn as hell.'

Savard arched a brow. 'Let me guess. You're divorced?'

'Twice, but that won't stop me from trying again. Under the cheap suit beats the heart of a hopeless romantic.'

'Is there any other kind?'

Kovac chose not to answer. The better part of valor.

'So, I want to do this for Mike,' he said. 'Ask around

about his kid, try to put together a picture he can live with. Will you help me with that?'

Savard thought about that for a moment, digested it, dissected it, weighed the pros and cons.

'Andy Fallon was a good investigator,' she said at last. 'He always tried hard. Sometimes he tried too hard.'

'What does that mean? Too hard?'

'Just that the job was everything to him. He worked too hard and took failures too much to heart.'

'Had he had a failure lately? The Curtis case?'

'Officer Curtis's killer is sitting in jail awaiting sentencing.'

'Renaldo Verma.'

'If you know that, then you should know there is no case ongoing in this department regarding Eric Curtis.'

'I guess not, what with your investigator being dead and all.'

'The case was dead before Andy.'

'Had Curtis complained about harassment?'

Savard said nothing.

Kovac felt his patience slip. 'Look, I can go to the gay and lesbian officers' liaison. Curtis would have told them before he came to IA. But then I'll come back here, and I gotta think you've already seen enough of me to last you.'

'Yes,' she said, letting the answer hang a moment. 'Officer Curtis had filed a complaint some time before his death. Because of that there was some IA interest when he was murdered. But the evidence pointed to no one but Verma, and the case ended with Verma's plea agreement.'

'And the names of the officers in question?'

'Will remain confidential.'

'I can dig them up.'

'You can dig all you want,' Savard said. 'But you won't do it here. The case is closed and I have no reason to reopen it.'

'Why was Fallon so upset if the killer is sitting in jail?'

'I don't know. Andy had a lot on his mind this last month or so. Only he could tell you what or why. He didn't confide in me. And I don't care to speculate. No one can know another person's heart. There are too many barriers.'

'Sure you can.' Kovac met her eyes with an even gaze that tried to see past her barriers. Without luck, he acknowledged. Those walls were thick. A woman didn't get where she was by letting weaknesses show.

'You just have to be willing to chip away the bullshit,' he said. 'Me, I'm knee-deep in it half the time. I don't even mind the smell anymore.'

The lieutenant said nothing, though Kovac had the impression she had much to say, that words were building up inside her like water behind a dam. He could sense the tension in her. But in the end she stepped away from him.

'Take your pickax and chip elsewhere, Sergeant Kovac.' She pulled the door open, offering him the view of the outer office. 'I've told you as much as I'm going to tell you.'

Kovac took his time going to the door. When he was even with Amanda Savard, he stopped – just a hair inside her comfort zone. Close enough to catch the subtle hint of her perfume. Close enough to see the pulse beat beneath the delicate skin in the hollow at the base of her throat. Close enough to feel something like electricity hum just under his skin.

'You know, somehow I don't think so, Lieutenant,' he said softly. 'Thank you for your time.'

IO

Renaldo Verma was an oily rat of a man. Slight of build, he had the sinewy, boiled-down look of a longtime crack addict, which he was. It was difficult to imagine him overpowering anyone, let alone a police officer. Yet he had pled guilty to murder in the second degree for beating a man to death with a baseball bat. His record ran the gamut from soliciting to drugs, from burglary to robbery. Assault and murder were recent additions to his repertoire, but he had shown a flair for both. He had fallen into a pattern of robbery and assault that shared traits beyond MO. The mindhunters liked to call it 'signature,' acts committed during the crime that were unnecessary to the completion of the crime but fulfilled some inner need. He might eventually have graduated to serial killer had he been better at eluding capture.

Verma came into the interrogation room with a swagger to his gait, as if he had something to be cocky about. He took his seat opposite Kovac and immediately reached for the pack of Salems on the table. His hands were long and bony, like the paws of a rodent, the skin marked with lesions that were likely a sign of AIDS.

'I hadn't ought to be speaking to you without my lawyer,' he said, and blew smoke out his nostrils. His nose was thin and long, with a pair of bumps along the bridge. A pencil-thin mustache rode his long upper lip like a dirty shadow. He had an affected, somewhat effeminate way of speaking, and an elaborate body language. His whole upper body swayed and bent and twisted as he spoke, as if he were listening to ballroom dance music in his head.

'So call your lawyer,' Kovac said, rising. 'But I don't

have time for that bullshit. By the time he gets here, I'll be long gone and you'll get stuck with the bill.'

'Taxpayers get stuck with that bill,' Verma said, snickering, his bony shoulders collapsing together as his chest caved in. 'What do I care?'

'Yeah, I can see you don't give a rat's ass about anything,' Kovac said. 'So you'll only feed me what you think I want to hear because you're looking for a trade. Only it's too late for a trade. You made your bed with the county attorney. It's in the pen in St Cloud.'

'No, it ain't,' Verma said with smug confidence, wagging a finger at Kovac. 'It's in Oak Park Heights. I ain't going to that slab of granite way the fuck north. That place is medieval. I'm going to the Heights. That's part of the deal. I got friends in the Heights.'

Kovac pulled a folded sheet of paper from the inside pocket of his suit coat, consulted it as if it were something more important than the receipt for his dry cleaning, put it back. 'Yeah, well, whatever you think.'

Verma narrowed his eyes in suspicion. 'What do you mean? We did the deal. The deal is done.'

Kovac shrugged, indifferent. 'Whatever. I want to talk to you about the Eric Curtis murder.'

'I didn't do it.'

'You know how many mutts say that?' Kovac countered. 'Every last frigging one of 'em. Do I need to point out this ain't the Ritz-Carlton we're sitting in?'

'I copped to the Franz murder. And I didn't mean to kill him.'

'Of course not. How were you to know the human head can take only so much beating?'

'I didn't *go there* to kill him,' Verma clarified, pouting.

'Oh, I see. It was his fault for being at home when you came by to rob him. He was clearly an idiot. You should be commended for taking him out of the gene pool.'

Verma stood up. 'Hey, I don't need you on my ass, Kovac.'

'Yeah, I'm sure you've got some big homey back in lockup to cover that for you. Think he'll go up to St Cloud too? Or will you have to get back in the dating game?'

Verma pointed the cigarette at him, ash raining down on the tabletop. 'I am *not* going to St. Cloud. You talk to my attorney.'

'Your attorney, the overworked, underpaid servant of Hennepin County? Yeah, I'll look him up. See if he remembers your name.' He stood up, went around the table, and put a hand on Verma's bony shoulder. 'Have a seat, Mr Vermin.'

Verma's butt hit the chair with a thud. He crushed out the cigarette on the tabletop and lit another.

'I didn't kill no cop.'

'Uh-huh. So the county attorney charged that out just for the hell of it? Just 'cause he wanted some poor grunt in his office to do more paperwork?' Kovac made a face as he slid back down on his own chair. 'Give me a break. He charged it out because it fit you to a *T*. Same MO as the others.'

'So? You never heard of a copycat?'

'You don't strike me as a role model.'

'Yeah? So how come I got the deal?' Verma asked smugly. 'They didn't have shit on me for that murder. No prints. No witnesses.'

'No? Well, you're the fucking Shadow, aren't you? So if you didn't do Curtis, how come you had his watch in your apartment?'

'It was a shock to me,' Verma insisted. 'I sure as hell didn't put it there. Fucking Timex. Why would I steal that?'

'Takes a lickin' and keeps on tickin',' Kovac said. 'That could come in handy where you're going. You knew Eric Curtis,' he went on. 'He ran you in for soliciting – twice.'

Verma shrugged, pursing his lips and lowering his lashes coyly. 'No hard feelings. Last time I offered him a freebie. He was cute. He said, "Maybe some other time." Wish he would have taken me up.'

'So you dropped by his place for the rain check. One thing led to another . . .'

'No,' Verma said firmly. He looked Kovac in the eye as he drew hard on the cigarette. The smoke came out in a forceful stream directed at Kovac's chest. 'Look, Kojak, those other cops tried to stick me with that Curtis murder, and they couldn't. The county attorney tried, and he couldn't.'

He leaned across the table, trying to look seductive. It made Kovac's skin crawl. 'I know you're hard for it,' he murmured, 'but you can't stick it in me either.'

'I'd rather stick it in a light socket.'

Verma threw himself back in the chair and laughed dementedly. 'Spoken like a man who doesn't know what he's missing.'

'Believe me, I'm not missing it.'

Verma snickered, then stuck his tongue out as far as he could and waggled it obscenely. 'You don't want me to suck you off, Kojak? Maybe stick my tongue in your ass?'

'Jesus Christ.' Kovac shoved his chair back from the table. He pulled a brown muffler from the pocket of the overcoat he had hung over the back of the chair, went across the room to the corner where the video camera hung, and draped the scarf over it.

Verma sat up straight, one hand fluttering at the base of his throat. 'Hey, man, what you do that for?'

'Uh-oh, Renaldo!' Kovac whispered, wide-eyed, as he came back toward the table. 'I don't think that video camera is working anymore!'

Verma tried to scuttle off the chair, but Kovac caught him by the back of the neck and held him firmly in place, leaning down over his shoulder from behind.

'The only thing I want to put up your ass is the toe of my shoe,' he said softly. 'Cut the crap, Vermin. You think I don't have people in St Cloud who owe me favors?'

'I'm not going to –' The pressure tightened on his neck, cutting him off. His shoulders came up to his ears.

'My sister's kid is a guard up there,' Kovac lied. 'He's a big dumb fuck straight off the dairy farm. Not too bright, but he's loyal as a dog. Too bad about his temper.'

'Okay! Okay!'

Kovac let him go and went back to his seat.

'Can't blame me for trying,' Verma pouted, reaching for the Salems. Kovac pulled them out of reach, shook one out, and lit up, telling himself it was a tactical move rather than caving in.

'You've got that rugged thing going on,' Verma said, playing coy. '*So* hot.'

'Vermin . . .'

'What?' he asked with a great show of exasperation. 'What d'you want from me, Kojak? You want me to cop to Curtis? Fuck you. The deal is done and I didn't do him. The county attorney didn't press it 'cause they got shit. But they'll let it hang on my rep. They'll say they got me cold for Franz and saved the state some money on a trial. And that's okay by me. Won't do me no harm to have the boys at the Heights think I did a cop. But I didn't do Curtis. You want to know who did Curtis, you ask your homicide sergeant Springer. He knows who did Curtis.'

Kovac let that hang in the air for a moment, as if maybe he hadn't even been paying attention. He looked off into the middle distance, smoking, wondering how sick it was to actually enjoy the feel of tar and nicotine settling in his lungs.

'Yeah?' he said at last, turning back to Verma. 'Then why didn't he nail the son of a bitch?'

'On account of the son of a bitch was another cop.'

'Says you.'

'Says that good-looking boy from Internal Affairs.'

'I don't know who you mean,' Kovac said, nerves tightening.

'Lean muscle, pretty, like a Versace model.' Verma closed his eyes and hummed to himself. 'Yummy.'

'Uh-huh. So this IA weasel comes around and talks to you. He tells you balls-out he thinks a cop whacked Curtis?'

Verma stuck out his lower lip and slouched. Kovac wanted to smack him.

'Yeah, I thought so,' he said. 'What'd he ask you about?'

Verma shrugged. 'This and that. Stuff about the murder. Stuff about after the murder. The investigation – I use the term loosely.'

'And you told him what?'

'Why don't you ask him?'

''Cause I'm asking you. You oughta be happy about that, Renaldo. You rank above IA. Then again, so does the clap.'

'I tell him I didn't kill Curtis and I don't care how many cops want me to say different. Not him. Not Springer. Not the uniform.'

'What uniform?'

'The one gave me this,' he said, pointing to the higher of the two bumps on the bridge of his nose. 'Said I was resisting.'

'I apologize on behalf of the department,' Kovac said without remorse. 'This uniform have a name?'

'Big dude,' Verma said. 'Studly Steroid, I called him. He didn't like it. His partner called him B.O. He didn't seem to mind *that*,' he complained, flinging up a hand in disgust. 'But I guess that was short for something besides the way he smelled. I read his name on his chest just before he knocked me out. Ogden.'

'Ogden,' Kovac repeated, the flashback coming so fast it damn near made his head swim: Steve Pierce wrestling on the floor of Andy Fallon's kitchen with a human moose. The moose stumbling to his feet with blood gushing from his nose.

Ogden.

'Verma got a deal because your people fucked up,' Chris Logan said bluntly as he dug through a drift of paperwork on his desk. 'Talk to Cal Springer about chain of evidence. Ask him if he knows dick about the specifics of a search warrant.'

'Something was funky about the evidence?' Kovac stayed on his feet near the door of Logan's small office, ready to bolt with the prosecutor, who was due in court in five minutes.

Logan swore under his breath, still staring down at the mess on his desk, hands on his hips. He was a tall, athletic type. Early thirties, with good looks and a big chip on his shoulder. A tough guy with a law degree and a quick temper.

He was a good prosecutor. Ted Sabin's sword arm, seeing as the county attorney rarely tried a case himself.

'Everything was wrong,' Logan mumbled.

He dove for the wastebasket sitting beside his desk, tearing through crumpled paper, discarded candy wrappers, mutilated bags from half a dozen take-out places in the skyway system that connected into the government center. He came up with a yellow wad the size of a softball, spread it out, and scanned the handwriting. After a moment he blew out a sigh of relief and rolled his eyes heavenward. He crammed the paper into the briefcase and headed for the door.

Kovac followed, then matched him stride for stride.

'I'm due in court,' Logan said, weaving his way through the population in the hall outside the county attorney's offices.

'I don't have a lot of time, myself,' Kovac said. He

wondered if Savard had followed through on her threat to call his boss. She was too tough a read to say for sure one way or the other. Who could say how long before Leonard yanked him in for the Big Talk.

They stepped into an empty elevator and Kovac badged the people trying to get on behind them.

'Police business, folks. Sorry,' he said, hitting the CLOSE DOOR button with his free hand.

Logan looked unhappy, but then, he looked that way a lot of the time.

'Everything we had was circumstantial,' he said. 'Prior association, motive, Verma's MO. But there were no witnesses placing Verma at or near the scene, and there was no forensic evidence. No prints. No fibers. No bodily fluids. Verma had jacked off at the other crime scenes. Not with Curtis. We don't know why. Maybe something made him leave the scene early. Maybe he couldn't get it up. Who knows? It could have been anything.'

'So, what was the deal with the watch?' Kovac asked as the elevator landed and the doors pulled back to reveal a human hive of activity.

The hall outside the courtrooms was perpetually packed with wheeler-dealers, shysters, losers, the frightened, the bewildered. All summoned to feed themselves into the machine of the Hennepin County justice system.

'So, some idiot uniform claimed he found it on Verma's dresser, but the whole deal stank to high heaven,' Logan said, angling for a courtroom door. 'It was O.J. and the fucking bloody glove all over again. No way we were getting it admitted. And in light of the last few lawsuits against your department, Sabin didn't even want to try.'

'Even though the vic was a cop,' Kovac said with disgust.

Logan shrugged, heading for the counsel table nearest the best air vent in the room. 'We couldn't have won the case. The city didn't want another lawsuit. What was the point of pressing for it? We got Verma to cop to Franz. He's going away.'

'On murder two.'

'Piggybacked on assault with intent, on felony robbery. It's no lightweight stretch. Besides, he killed Franz with Franz's own baseball bat. Weapon of opportunity. How could we argue premeditation?'

'Was there ever any feeling Verma didn't do Curtis? That maybe he really was being railroaded?'

'There were some rumors Curtis had been harassed by other patrol cops because he was gay. But it didn't add up to murder, and the circumstantial case spelled out VERMA in big fat caps.'

Kovac sighed and looked around the room. The bailiff was joking with the clerk. The defense attorney, a squat woman with a frizzy gray bun and huge clear-rimmed glasses, set her mega-briefcase on the defense counsel table and came over to Logan with a hopeless smirk on her face.

'Last chance for a deal, Chris.'

'In your dreams, Phyllis,' Logan said, hauling a file as thick as the Bible out of his case. 'No breaks on kiddie porn freaks.'

'Too bad you don't feel as strongly about murderers,' Kovac said, and walked away.

'Why'd you go to Verma?' Liska asked, plucking a french fry from the red plastic basket Kovac's food had come in. She was late. He'd ordered without her. 'Lying sack of shit,' she added.

'You've met him?'

'No.' She swiped a second fry through the puddle of ketchup on his plate. 'They're all lying sacks of shit. That's my sweeping generalization of the day.'

'You want something?' he asked, hailing the waitress.

'No. I'll just eat yours.'

'The hell you will. You owe me ninety-two thousand french fries as it is. You never get your own.'

'They're too fattening.'

'What? They're less fattening if I order them?'

She flashed him a grin. 'That's right. And besides, you're gonna gain weight 'cause you're quitting smoking. I'm doing you a favor. Why'd you go to Verma?'

Kovac sat back from the burger, his appetite souring. He'd chosen Patrick's out of habit, and regretted it. As always, the place was populated by cops. He had claimed a booth in the rear and put his back to the corner. He felt a little that way – cornered. He didn't like what Verma had told him or what Logan had alluded to; didn't like the knowledge that if he were to pursue this look into Andy Fallon's life, most of the other players would be cops, and there was a fair chance not all of them would be good.

'Because if IA was involved in the Curtis thing, I can't say why. Savard wouldn't tell me,' he said, keeping his voice in the low register of confidences. 'Maybe they were looking into the actual murder, like your guy said. Or maybe they were looking at the investigation. I wanted a feel for it before I went to Springer for answers.'

'Cal Springer couldn't find shit in a cow pasture,' Liska proclaimed, then ordered a Coke from a slouchy waitress. 'But I've never heard anyone say he's rotten.'

'He's an idiot,' Kovac declared. 'Pompous prick. He spends more time trying to organize union socials than he does on his caseload. Still, this Curtis thing looked like a slam-dunk. Even Springer shouldn't have been able to screw it up. But Verma says he didn't do it.'

Liska made her eyes and mouth round. 'No! An innocent man in jail!'

'Yeah, he's pure as the driven snow,' Kovac said with heavy sarcasm. 'But here's the deal. He claims a cop threw down Eric Curtis's watch in his place. Ogden.'

Liska's brow furrowed. 'Ogden? From yesterday?'

'The one and only. An allegation like that would bring IA in. Logan told me the situation smelled so bad, Sabin didn't want to touch it. And Ted Sabin doesn't smell blood in the water, then climb out of the pool. Especially considering Curtis was a cop.'

'Curtis was a *gay* cop,' Liska reminded him. 'Who was a victim of a criminal targeting openly gay men. You think the mayor and her stooges want a media spotlight on that?'

Kovac conceded the point with a shift of his eyebrows.

'Verma also claims it was a cop did Curtis.'

'So why didn't we ever hear about any of this?' Liska asked, clearly perturbed to have been left out of the loop.

'That's a good question. IA only got involved within the last month or so. Verma's been in the can at least two. Maybe no one knew IA was looking. Springer sure as hell wouldn't broadcast the news if he knew about it. The ass-pucker factor would be so extreme as to render him incapable of speech.' He actually found a chuckle for the thought. 'Ha! IA after Cal Springer. That's funny.'

Liska didn't join in the merriment, but Kovac didn't notice.

'Maybe no one knew until Andy Fallon told them,' she said.

'Can you set up a meeting with your mystery man and get us some details?'

Liska pulled a face. 'He has to call me. He wouldn't give me his number this morning. He seemed nervous.'

'They'd have his name and number in IA, by the sound of what you heard in there yesterday.'

'But IA won't give it to us. We can't even ask. Our case is officially closed.'

'It's closed when I sign off on it,' Kovac said, realizing with no great enthusiasm that he had gone territorial. The case was his. He didn't want anyone telling him how to run it or when to stop it or anything else. He ran a case until he was satisfied. He was a long way from being satisfied.

'It won't be that simple this time,' Liska said. 'Guess who made Andy Fallon's corpse leapfrog the line waiting at the morgue?'

Kovac scowled. 'I'm not gonna like this, am I?'

'Guaranteed.'

He heaved a sigh and shoved his plate across the table to her. 'Ah, shit. Who?'

Liska cut away the chewed-on part of the burger, then picked up the sandwich and took a big bite, ketchup oozing at the corner of her mouth. She wiped it away with a napkin and looked him in the eye.

'Ace Wyatt.'

Kovac growled. 'That cocksucker.'

'Doing a favor for Mike.'

'Yeah. Throwing his weight around. He sure as hell didn't do us a favor.'

He took a pull on his beer and looked around the room, remembering it as it had been the night of Ace Wyatt's retirement party: over-festive, crowded, hot, smoky. He saw Mike Fallon on the floor, the tight expression on Ace Wyatt's face.

He considered the burden of having a man owe you his life, and having that man never let you forget it. The obligation never ended. Ace Wyatt was still saving Mike Fallon, calling in favors. It was likely Wyatt's influence that had gotten Andy Fallon's death ruled accidental rather than a straight-out suicide, sparing Mike that burden and freeing up Andy's life insurance.

'Did you get the reports?' he asked. 'Did Stone have them done?'

'Stone didn't do the autopsy. Upshaw did.'

'Upshaw? Who the hell is Upshaw?'

'Some new guy. Kinda cute, if you go for the type who has his hands in a dead body all day. I'll pass, thanks,' Liska said, then polished off the last of the burger.

'Did you notice anything else about him? Like if he has half a brain?'

'At least half, I'd say. He wasn't drooling. Whether or not he knows his shit – too soon to tell.'

'Great.'

'The preliminary report says Fallon died of asphyxia. No other significant wounds to the body. No signs of a struggle.'

'Had he had sex?'

'Upshaw said he didn't find any seminal fluid where it shouldn't have been. So if it was a game gone wrong, they were practicing safe sex or saving the main event for last. Or it wasn't about sex at all.'

'Tox screens in?'

'No paperwork yet, but I called and talked to Barkin. He says Fallon had a low level of alcohol in his bloodstream: point oh-four. And a barbiturate, something called zolpidem, which is a sleeping pill also known by the brand name Ambien. That would be more consistent with suicide than a sex game, although the amounts were by no means lethal, even in combination. Plenty of people dope themselves up for the big deed. Now, if they'd found Rohypnol or something, that would be a different story. No one plans to date-rape themselves, except maybe a lonely masochist.'

Kovac frowned at a memory that wouldn't quite come clear. 'Did anyone check out what was in Andy Fallon's medicine cabinet?'

'No reason to at the time.'

'I want to know.'

'You won't get a warrant.'

'What do I need with a warrant? Who's going to object?'

Liska shrugged and sucked on the straw of her Coke, her gaze scanning the room. She sat back, face impassive, but eyes suddenly hard and sharp.

'What?' Kovac asked.

'Here comes Cal Springer. Looks like he ate too many jalapeños and can't fart.'

Springer moved through the crowd like a wooden figure, muscles taut with anger, face pink with temper or cold or both. He had a long, flat face with a long, hooked nose, the look crowned by a mop of unruly brown-gray curls. His gaze lit on Kovac and he rushed forward, barreling into the slouchy waitress. She spilled a beer and swore, and Springer ruined his entrance with awkward apologies.

Kovac shook his head. 'Hey, Cal, I heard you knock the ladies out. I didn't know they meant it literally.'

Springer jabbed a finger at him. 'What were you doing with Renaldo Verma?'

'We did the tango and had a cigarette.'

'His lawyer was all over me this afternoon. No one cleared that meeting with him. Or with me.'

'No one had to clear it with him. Verma agreed to see me. He could have called the lawyer if he wanted. And since when do I have to ask you for permission to wipe my ass?'

'That's my case.'

'And it's over. You're out. What's the big deal?'

Springer glanced around like a man about to disclose sensitive state secrets. 'It's not over.'

'Oh, on account of IA?' Kovac asked loudly.

Springer looked sick.

'They don't have a case against you, do they?' Liska asked. 'I mean, you're not the one who threw down the watch, are you, Cal?'

'I didn't do anything.'

'Consistent with your usual investigative techniques,' Kovac said. 'If that's a crime, you'd better bend over and kiss your ass good-bye.'

Springer glared at him. 'I ran a clean investigation. I

worked that case by the book. Verma has no call coming after me. IA neither.'

'Then why are you wasting your time trying to ream me a new one?' Kovac asked.

Springer took a breath and held it tight for a couple of seconds, like a man trying to force something from his body by straining. 'Stay out of it, Kovac. It's over. The case is closed and everything with it.'

'Well, make up your mind, Cal. Is it over or isn't it?' Kovac said, watching him, wondering. He could see Liska watching Springer too, though her expression held a certain tension, as if it caused her distress to watch Cal Springer battle his nerves.

'The IA lieutenant told me there's nothing ongoing with the Curtis murder,' Kovac said. 'Not today, anyway. Her investigator's dead.'

'I know,' Springer murmured, glancing away, the red draining from his face. 'I heard. Suicide. Too bad.'

'So they say.'

Springer looked at him again. 'What's that mean?'

Kovac shrugged. 'Nothing. Figure of speech.'

Springer weighed that for a moment, weighed his options. In the end, his shoulders sagged and the air leaked out of his lungs.

'Look,' he said. 'I can't have IA on my ass. I'm running for union delegate.'

'Having IA on you oughta make you a shoo-in.'

'Only if guys like you bothered to vote. I've got bigger plans for my life than you do, Kovac. I care about what goes in my jacket. Please don't fuck that up for me.'

Kovac watched him walk away, watched him bang into the same waitress he'd run into on his entrance, his mind clearly not in Patrick's bar.

'By the book,' Kovac scoffed. 'What book do you suppose that is? *Practical Homicide Investigation For Dummies*?'

Liska didn't answer him. She had turned sideways in the

booth to watch Springer go, but she seemed to be looking at something a whole lot farther away. *Maybe light-years*, he thought. He reached across the table and poked her shoulder.

'Hey, that was a good one,' he said. 'Deserving of recognition.'

'Lay off him, Sam,' she said, turning back around. 'Springer's square. He doesn't deserve what IA might do to him for no good reason.'

'If he knows something, I want it.'

'I'll get it.'

Kovac watched her. She dodged his gaze. She looked fourteen and in possession of a burdensome secret. Knowledge of the football captain drinking beer and smoking cigarettes. She reached tentatively for the last french fry and traced the end of it through the coagulating glob of ketchup.

'Is something up with you?' he asked quietly.

Her mouth twisted into a semblance of her smart-ass smirk. 'Sure,' she said. 'My hormones. Wanna do something about that?'

'If your hormones are up because of Cal Springer, I want to hose you down with ice water.'

'Please. I just ate,' she said with disgust. 'It's been a long day. On top of a long night. I should go home.'

'I thought you didn't want anything to do with IA.'

'I don't,' she said, busying herself gathering her things. 'How's that stop me from getting what Springer has? He doesn't want anything to do with them either.'

'Suit yourself.' Liska was entitled to a mystery or two, he supposed, though he didn't like the idea.

He got up and tossed some bills on the table, then grabbed his coat off the hook on the end of the booth. 'I'm going to go see what Andy Fallon kept in his medicine chest.'

'Sam Kovac, Round-the-Clock Detective.'

'What else have I got to do with my time?'

'Nothing, apparently. Don't you ever want something more?' she asked, sliding out of the booth.

'Naw.' He ignored the image of Amanda Savard that came to mind. That was too ludicrous to even consider as a fantasy. 'If you never want anything, then you can't be disappointed when you don't get it.'

11

The parking garage had been named for a cop who had been murdered in cold blood in a pizza place on Lake Street. This thought always came to Liska when it was late and she was going in alone to find her car, or when she was tired and looking at the future with a jaundiced eye. She scored on all counts tonight. Rush hour had passed, the ramp seemed deserted, and her mood was dark. Kovac had gone back to the office to get the key to Fallon's house. She had blown off his offer to walk her to her car.

The hair prickled on the back of her neck. She stopped abruptly and turned around, glaring into the gloom. Sound bounced around and echoed in the concrete labyrinth, making it difficult to identify the source. The slam of a car door could be a level above or below. The scrape of a foot could be at the end of the row. Or right behind you. Parking ramps were a favorite of muggers and rapists. Vagrants, most of them drunk or mentally ill, liked the ramps for shelter and to use as public toilets when they got kicked out of places like the downtown public library.

Liska's breath burned in her lungs as she waited and watched, turning slowly, one hand slipping inside her coat and finding the butt of her gun at her waist.

She saw no one, heard nothing of any significance. Maybe she was just being edgy, but she had just cause. She had spent her day inquiring about the deaths of two cops. She felt as if someone had put a pillow over her head and beat her with a tire iron. She wanted her home, her sweats, her boys, a few hours to ignore the fact that she had volunteered to dig around in an IA shitpile.

'That was a blond moment,' she muttered, releasing the gun and digging her keys out of her coat pocket.

Now she had to figure a way to sweet-talk information out of Cal Springer. Christ. Without barfing. Tall order.

It was hard to figure Springer for being in on anything dirty. He was seldom allowed in on lunch, let alone a conspiracy, but there was no denying the smell of fear on him. It was a scent memory that tumbled her all the way back to her father. She hated it.

'Why couldn't I have listened to my mother?' she muttered. 'Learn a trade, Nikki. Cosmetology. Food service. Aim high. Get a job you can wear a nice skirt for. Meet the man of your dreams.'

The dark blue Saturn that served as traveling office and taxi sat at the end of the row, next to the wall, in a spot too dark for her liking now that night had fallen. Nose out, poised for a quick getaway. She hit the button on the keyless remote and swore under her breath. Nothing happened. No click of locks releasing. No flash of lights. The thing had been on the fritz for weeks, sometimes working, sometimes not. Liska, on the other hand, seemed *always* to be working and never had the time to take it in. It seemed too small an inconvenience to bother with. Until she was alone in a dark parking ramp.

A thump and a scrape froze her in her tracks a second time. On another level of the ramp she could hear the squeal of protest from a steering column being cranked too far in one direction. On this level, she could feel a presence. Another human. The awareness vibrated in her nerve endings. She didn't go through the bullshit rationalization most women did in a situation where they felt unease. Instincts were to be trusted above the teachings of an allegedly polite society. If she felt something was wrong, then something was probably wrong.

'Hey! Who's there?' she demanded, turning slowly. The tough chick. The come-over-here-and-I'll-kick-your-ass voice. Her heart rate had picked up fifteen extra beats per minute.

She sidled toward the car, key in her left hand, the right one reaching again for the gun, slipping it from the belt holster. With the tip of the key, she felt for the lock, missing once, twice. Her gaze remained up, scanning left to right, right to left, catching – Something. Someone. The shadowed side of a concrete column that seemed a bit too thick, a little distorted.

Liska blinked and tried to refocus. Too dark. It might have been something or nothing.

The key found the lock. She eased down into the Saturn, shut the door, hit the power lock button, and got no response. She cursed the car and started the engine, hit the lock button again, and this time was rewarded by the thump of locks engaging. Her gaze was still on the column fifty feet away. She could detect no motion, but the feeling of another living creature being there, watching her, lingered.

Time to go.

She tossed her briefcase on the passenger side, amid the debris of working motherhood, a mess that looked even worse than usual and spilled from the seat to the floor. Junk mail, a Burger King bag, a couple of magazines, one of the boys' stray sneakers, some plastic action figures. And a whole lot of broken glass.

Nine more extra beats a minute.

The passenger's side window was gone, reduced to a thousand bits that lay scattered on the seat and floor, mixed in with the junk mail and the Burger King bag, and the magazines and R.J.'s stray sneaker and the plastic action figures. It was probably the work of some junkie, Liska told herself. Probably her phantom in the shadows, who was now hiding, waiting for her to go so he could knock in someone else's window in search of valuables to hock. That was the likely explanation.

She started the engine and put the car in gear. She would

drive down to street level and call for a radio car from the well-lit area near the attendant's booth.

A red dash light caught her eye, telling her to service the engine soon.

'Yeah. How about you service *my* engine soon?' she grumbled, easing the car out of the slot.

Her headlights hit the column. Nothing. No one. She tried to let go of the suspicion as she exhaled, but the tension wouldn't dissipate.

She looked to the rearview mirror as she passed the column and caught a glimpse of something. Half the figure of a man standing near a sedan three cars away, back toward where she had been parked.

Nothing strange about a person in a parking garage. Every car had one sooner or later. Usually they opened doors and turned on lights. This one didn't. He stepped out of sight. Liska abandoned the mirror and looked over her left shoulder. Her right hand rested on her gun on the seat beside her: a neat little Sig Sauer, sized to fit her small hand and still knock the shit out of a charging bull.

Where had he come from? She'd been watching and listening for another person to the point of straining her eyes and ears. No one had walked that far into the ramp after her without her knowing.

'Hey!'

The voice struck like a bullet. Liska snapped her head around to the right to see a man lunging toward the car, his head and upper body thrusting through the window frame.

'Hey!' he shouted again. His face was like something carved out of a stump with a penknife. Craggy, dirty. Yellow teeth. Filthy beard. Wild, dark eyes. 'Gimme five dollars!'

Liska gunned the engine. The tires shrieked against the concrete. The man screamed in rage, rough hands grabbing hold of the front passenger's seat by the stems of the headrest. Liska brought the Sig up and swung it toward his face.

'Get outta my car! I'm a cop!'

The man's mouth tore open and a sound of rage roared up out of him on a foul breath.

Liska stabbed the Sig at him, half an inch from his mouth. 'Let go, asshole!'

With one hand, she cranked the wheel left and hit the brakes, sending the Saturn into a skid. One of the back panels hit a minivan, and the drunk lost his grip on the headrest and was flung out the window.

Liska jammed the car into park, jumped out the door, and ran around the hood, leading with the Sig in a stiff-arm grip. The drunk lay crumpled near the back door of a filthy seventies Cadillac, still as death, eyes closed. Shit, that was all she needed — to have killed somebody. The parking ramp booth attendant ran up the ramp from the level below: a fat guy in a bad uniform with a too-small parka open to let his beer gut lead the way.

'Jeez, lady!' he exclaimed between gulps of air. It was twenty degrees and he was sweating like a racehorse, limp brown hair matted to his big head. His eyes bugged as he caught sight of the gun, and he raised his arms.

'I'm a cop,' Liska said. 'He's under arrest. Is there any security on duty?'

'Uh . . . he's on a break.'

'Great. At the strip joint down the block, right?'

The attendant opened and closed his mouth a couple of times. Liska checked the drunk for signs of life. His breathing was regular and he had a good pulse. There was no blood she could see. She pulled a pair of handcuffs out of her coat pocket and snagged one of his wrists.

'You got a cell phone on you?' she asked, glancing at the attendant.

'Yes, ma'am.'

'Call nine-one-one. We need police and an ambulance.'

He looked ready to dive for cover. 'Yes, ma'am. I thought you said *you're* a cop.'

'Just do it.'

The drunk cracked open a bloodshot eye and tried to focus on her. 'You're a boy,' he declared. 'Gimme five dollars.'

Liska glared at him. 'You have the right to remain silent. Use it.'

She snapped the other cuff to the back door handle of the Caddie. Then she went back to the Saturn and dug a huge Maglite patrolman's flashlight out of the glove compartment. The thing weighed three pounds and doubled as a club. The attendant was still standing with his hands up as she came out of the car.

Liska glared at him. 'Why aren't you calling?'

'I didn't want to make any sudden moves.'

'Oh, for God's sake.'

She snapped on the Maglite with her left hand, dug the Sig back out of her pocket, and started back up the ramp.

'Where are you going?' the attendant called.

'To look for the boogie man. Go make that call, Slick.'

It was nearly ten o'clock by the time Liska pulled into her own driveway, exhausted and disgusted. More so when she saw Speed's car blocking her way into the garage. It didn't matter that she couldn't actually get her car in the garage because of the accumulation of junk. It was a matter of principle.

She sat in the Saturn, freezing, the heater not able to compete against the cold rushing in the busted window. She'd found no trace of her phantom in the ramp. The uniforms had taken custody of the drunk – Edward Gedes – and followed the ambulance to HCMC, where they would kill time drinking coffee and flirting with the nurses in the ER as they waited for Edward to get checked out. There wasn't much to charge him with unless they could prove he was the one who broke the window, and Liska didn't see that happening. Her gut told her it *hadn't* happened. Maybe Gedes had busted the window, then waited for her to come so he could try to jump through it like a trick pony, but she didn't think so.

Nothing had been missing from the car, not that she kept anything of real value in it. No one had broken in to steal R.J.'s Jesse Ventura action figure. The glove compartment had not been ransacked. The stereo hadn't been touched. She almost wished it had been. The theft of something would have made the broken window make sense. The only thing in the car that had been disturbed had been her junk mail. Someone willing to break into a car in a public garage now had her home address.

The phantom in the shadows.

Why her car, of all the cars in the ramp?

She gathered her stuff and trudged to the house. No one noticed her entrance. A battle was being waged in her living room. In one corner a tent had been fashioned from a blanket. Dining room chairs had been dragged in and overturned to make a fort near the Christmas tree. Their faces streaked with camo paint, the boys were running around in their pajamas, waving plastic light sabers, making enough noise to wake the dead. Her ex-husband was crouched behind the recliner, wearing a bathrobe over his clothes, a black rag tied around his head, a glow-in-the-dark samurai sword in hand.

'Welcome home, Mom,' Liska said, slinging her purse onto the dining room table. 'Did you have a good day? Not really,' she answered herself. 'But thank you for asking. I'm just glad to be home where everything is peaceful and orderly, and I feel loved by all.'

Kyle reacted first, stopping in his tracks, the grin dropping off his face as he looked from his mother to his father and back. Two years older than R.J., he remembered the hostilities at the end of the marriage, and was sensitive to the tension that remained between his parents.

'Hi, Mom,' he said, glancing down at the toy in his hand and setting it aside, as if he were embarrassed to be caught having fun. He had his father's heartbreaker looks, but a seriousness lacking in Speed's genes.

'Hi, Big Guy.' Liska went to him, brushed his hair back, and kissed his forehead. Kyle looked at the floor.

R.J. squealed like a wild pig and ran around in circles, swinging his saber with reckless abandon, stubbornly refusing to acknowledge his mother's presence. Anger burned a familiar path through her as she turned her gaze on her ex.

'Hey, Speed, fancy meeting you here. Again. You're almost acting like you're a father or something. Where's Heather?'

'I sent her home,' he said, straightening out of his crouch. 'Why should you pay a sitter if you don't have to? I had some time tonight.'

'That's very considerate of you to think of my financial situation,' she said, wanting badly to add, *especially considering you never bother to contribute to the cause.* But she bit her tongue for the boys' sake.

'It's way past bedtime, boys,' she said, playing the bad guy again and resenting Speed for it. 'Go wash your faces and brush your teeth, please.'

Kyle started from the room. R.J. stared at her with big eyes, then gave a bloodcurdling shout and leapt in the air, twisting and flailing his arms and legs in his best Ninja impersonation.

Kyle went and grabbed his arm. 'Knock it off, Rockhead,' he said in his sternest voice. Liska didn't reprimand him.

'I realize you made a career of truancy,' she told Speed after the boys had left the room, 'but your sons actually attend school. They need a certain amount of sleep for that.'

'One late night won't kill them, Nikki.'

'No.'

But why did you have to pick tonight? she wanted to say, except she was afraid she might burst into tears if she did. She was too worn out for Speed tonight, and Kovac's burger was a long time past. She rubbed her face with her hands and walked away from him, back through the dining room and into the kitchen, where she began rummaging through one of the lower cupboards.

She could see Speed strike a pose in the doorway. He had shed the bathrobe, revealing a black Aerosmith T-shirt stretched taut across his chest and clinging to his flat belly. The short sleeves strained around upper arms thick with well-cut muscle. He looked as if he'd been pumping iron in a serious way. He pulled the rag off his head and ruffled his short hair, making it stand up in tufts.

'You want to talk about it?' he asked.

'Since when do we talk about anything?'

He shrugged. 'So we start tonight.'

'I don't want to start anything tonight.'

She pulled a box of translucent blue trash bags from the cupboard and scrutinized one for size and durability. 'It'll do for now.'

'Do for what?'

'Someone busted the side window out of my car tonight. Makes for a drafty ride doing sixty on the freeway.'

'Goddamn junkies,' he muttered. 'They steal anything?'

'Nope.'

'They just broke the window?'

'And rummaged through the junk mail on the front seat.'

'You're sure it was junk? No credit card statements? No cell phone bill? Nothing like that?'

'Nothing like that.'

'Didn't touch the stereo?'

'What's to touch? I drive a Saturn. It's got a radio. Who would want it?'

Speed frowned. 'I don't like that they didn't take anything.'

'Me neither.' She pulled the junk drawer open and dug around for a roll of duct tape. 'I wish they had taken the car. The engine light is coming on. With my luck, it has some terminal illness.'

'You working anything that someone might want to find you?' he asked, coming to the counter where she stood compulsively folding the trash bag into the smallest square possible.

Liska thought of Neon Man, and Cal Springer, and IA, and the uniform Ogden and two dead cops. She shook her head, looking down at the bag. 'Nothing special.'

He's standing too close, she thought. *I don't want him that close. Not tonight.*

'I hear the ME ruled on your IA guy,' he said. 'Accident, huh?'

Liska shrugged a little and fingered a frayed piece of tape. 'The insurance pays out that way.'

'You think something else?'

'Doesn't matter what I think. Leonard says it's closed.'

'It matters if you're going to keep digging on it. What are you thinking? That he bought it because of an investigation? You think some rotten cop lynched him? That's pretty fucking out there, Nikki. What could be going on in the Minneapolis PD that would push someone that far off the ledge?'

'I don't think anything,' she said impatiently. 'And I'm not in on what goes on in IA. It doesn't matter anyway. The lieutenant signed off on it.'

'So it's closed,' he said. 'You're out of it. That's gotta be a relief.'

'Sure,' she said without conviction. She could feel him watching her, waiting for what she wasn't saying.

'Nikki . . .'

There was frustration in his voice, and maybe a little

longing. Maybe more than a little. Or maybe she just wanted to think it. He touched her chin and she looked up at him, holding her breath. Many things about their relationship had turned sour in the last few years, but never the physical aspect. He had always – and to her eternal despair, probably would always – excited her physically. Chemistry didn't care about jealousies or rivalries or infidelities.

'Are you guys gonna kiss?'

'R.J.,' Liska said as Speed exhaled heavily. 'You don't ask people questions like that. It's rude.'

'So?'

He hadn't quite rubbed all the camo paint off his face. She bent down and kissed a smudge on his forehead.

'So I love you,' she said. 'Time for bed.'

'But Dad –'

'Was just leaving,' she said, giving Speed a pointed look. R.J. scowled. 'You *always* make him leave.'

'Come on, Rocket,' Speed said, scooping R.J. up and over his shoulder. 'I'll tuck you in and tell you about the time I busted Big Ass Baxter.'

Liska watched them leave the kitchen, part of her wanting to follow. Not because she wanted to give any impression they had a normal family life. She wanted to follow because she was jealous of the rapport Speed had with the boys. That didn't seem a healthy thing to indulge. No more than her need for her ex-husband's touch.

She picked up the duct tape and garbage bag and went out the kitchen door, glad for the slap of cold night air.

'How stylish,' she muttered as she taped the bag over the broken-out window. Nothing like a little duct tape to class up a car.

The neighborhood was quiet. The night was clear and crisp with a sky full of more stars than she could see from this spot in the city. Her neighbor on this side of her house worked for United Way. On the other side was a couple who'd been with 3M for a collective thirty-some years. None of them had ever seen a dead guy hanging from a rafter. Standing in the middle of the neighborhood, Liska felt suddenly alone, set apart from normal humans by the experiences she had had and would have. Set apart tonight by violence that had been directed at her.

Someone she didn't know and couldn't identify had her address.

She looked down the driveway to the street. Any car going by . . . Any pair of eyes watching from the dark . . . Any strange sound outside her bedroom window . . .

Vulnerability was not a familiar or welcome feeling. It went through her and over her like the chill of an illness. The anticipation of fear. A kind of weakness. A sense of powerlessness. A sense of isolation.

She wanted to kick someone.

'Alone at last.'

Liska startled and spun around, voice recognition coming a split second before she came face-to-face with the source. 'Dammit, Speed! How have you lived this long?'

'I don't know. I expected you to kill me a long time ago.' His grin lit up the dark.

'You're lucky I wasn't holding a gun,' she said.

'I'm probably still lucky you're not holding a gun.'

He stuffed his hands in the pockets of the old jacket he was wearing and dug out a pack of Marlboros and a lighter. He fired one up.

'I wouldn't shoot you now,' she said. 'I want this night to be over. If I shot you, I'd have to be up till dawn with the arrest and the booking and all of that. It's not worth it.'

'Gee, thanks.'

'I'm tired, Speed. Can you say goodnight now?'

He took a long pull on the cigarette and exhaled, looking down the driveway to the street as a dark nondescript sedan crept past and kept going. Liska watched it out of the corner of her eye and pulled her coat tighter around her.

'You'll call someone and get that window fixed tomorrow?' Speed said, flaking ash off his cigarette as he gestured toward her car.

'I'm on the phone mentally, even as we speak.'

''Cause that garbage bag just screams white trash.'

'Thanks for your concern over my safety.'

'You're the mother of my children.'

'That speaks volumes about my judgment, doesn't it?'

'Hey.' He looked straight at her and flicked the cigarette on the snow. 'Don't say you regret the boys.'

Liska met his gaze. 'I don't regret the boys. Not for half a heartbeat.'

'But you regret us.'

'Why are you doing this?' she asked wearily. 'It seems a little late for remorse and bargaining, Speed. Our marriage has been dead a very long time.'

Speed pulled his keys out of his pocket and sorted out the one he needed. 'Regret's a waste of time. Live for the moment. You never know which one will be your last.'

'And on that cheery note . . .' Liska turned toward the house.

He caught her by the arm as she went past. He was thinking he might try to kiss her. She could see it in his eyes, feel it in the tension of his body. But she didn't want it, and she supposed he could see and feel that too.

'Take care, Nikki,' he said softly. 'You're too brave for your own good.'

'I'm what I need to be,' she said.

He found a sad smile for that and let go of her. 'Yeah. Too bad I was never what you needed.'

'I wouldn't say never,' she said, but she didn't look at him. She kept her eyes on the ground.

She didn't watch him walk away, but she watched him back out the driveway and turn onto the street. She stood there until the red glow of his taillights was a faded memory. And then she was alone again, she thought as she stared at her patchwork car window. Or so she hoped.

She went up the back steps and into the house. She locked the door and turned out the light. And as she retreated to her bedroom, alone, a dark sedan rolled past on the street . . . for the second time.

12

Andy Fallon's house was a dark spot in the neighborhood, the only glow the reflection of the neighbor's porch lights off the yellow police line tape that crossed the front door.

Kovac detached the tape and let himself in with the key. There was always a lingering sense of violation about a house that had been gone through by a crime scene unit. The place had been probed and examined and trooped through by a dozen or more strangers, without the blessing of the homeowner. Personal items had been touched, the sanctity of privacy raped. Judgments had been passed, remarks made. All of that seemed to hang in the air like a sour smell. And yet Kovac tried to return to a home after the fact if it was possible, to walk the rooms and get a feel for who the victim had been before he or she had become a corpse.

He started with the living room, with the Christmas tree – a Fraser fir decorated with small clear lights and a red bead garland. It was a beautiful tree that had the smell of fake pine scent. Kneeling, he checked the tags on the few wrapped gifts, noting names. Most were from Andy Fallon, yet to be delivered to Kirk and Aaron and Jessica . . . He would cross-reference the first names against Fallon's address book and try to get a line on the friends. He would do the same with the Christmas cards that filled a basket on the coffee table.

Moving on to the entertainment center, he scanned the titles on the spines of the videotape cassettes. *Miracle on 34th Street. Holiday Inn. It's a Wonderful Life* – a movie that began with a man wanting to kill himself, but concluded with all the usual nauseating sap of a Hollywood happy ending. No angel named Clarence had saved Andy Fallon from his fate. In Kovac's experience, there was never an angel around when you needed one.

He passed through the dining room on his way to the stairs. The room appeared unused, as most dining rooms were.

The master bath at the head of the stairs was loaded with the usual assortment of stuff a man needed on a daily basis. There were no towels in the hamper. If there had been, the towels could have been checked for hairs and body fluids, the detritus sent off for DNA comparisons. If Fallon's death had been an obvious murder – or ruled a murder – he could have had the crime scene people clean the drain traps in the sinks, checking for hairs. In his experience, that kind of trace evidence never made a case, but it was always welcomed by the prosecutors as more rocks in their pile. But this case was officially closed, and no one would be fishing pubic hairs out of Andy Fallon's bathtub.

A brown prescription bottle of Zoloft sat on a shelf in the medicine cabinet. Antidepressant. Dr Seiros. Kovac noted all pertinent information and left the bottle on the shelf. Beside it was a bottle of Tylenol and one of melatonin. No Ambien.

The smell of death lingered in the bedroom over a layer of room freshener. The room had been dusted for latent prints, and a fine, ashy residue was left behind on the dresser and nightstands. Other than that, the room was as neat as a new hotel room. The blue spread was smoothed impeccably over the four-poster. Kovac peeled it back at one corner. Clean sheets. Unlike his father, Andy Fallon had no piles of soiled clothing, no jelly jars with half an inch of evaporating whiskey. His closet was neat. He folded his underwear and matched his socks in the dresser drawers.

On the nightstand beside the bed was a hardcover book about a young man's ill-fated trek into the Alaskan wilderness. Probably depressing enough to warrant an extra

Zoloft or two. In the drawer was a Walkman, half a dozen tapes for relaxation and meditation, a couple of honey-lemon cough drops. The table on the other side held an array of squat ivory candles in a hammered metal bowl. Matchboxes from various restaurants and bars were in the drawer with a bottle of K-Y personal lubricant.

Kovac closed the drawer and looked around the room and thought of Andy Fallon. The good son. Fastidious. No trouble. Always striving to excel. Keeping his secrets tucked away in metaphorical drawers and closets. On the dresser was the same photograph Mike had smashed in his fit of grief: Andy's graduation from the police academy. Tucked back in a corner, out of harm's way. A memory Andy Fallon had preserved and refreshed every day of his life, despite the strain between him and his old man.

Sadness ran down through Kovac like a slow rain, draining energy. Maybe this was why he'd never tried harder to be something beyond a cop. He'd seen too many families torn like rotten drapes. Ruined by unrealistic or unrealized expectations. No one could ever let well enough alone. It was human nature to want more, to want better, to want what was out of reach.

He filled his lungs with air and paused as he started to leave the room. The faint scent of stale cigarette smoke caught his nostrils. From his own clothes, he thought at first, then tested the air again. No. It was a scent beneath a masking scent. A woodsy air freshener over burnt tobacco. Faint but there.

There were no ashtrays in the room. No half-empty packs. He hadn't seen any evidence of a smoker in any other part of the house. The crime scene people weren't allowed to smoke at a scene.

Steve Pierce was a smoker. Kovac thought again of his impression that Pierce had something heavy sitting on his chest. He thought of the doe-eyed Ms Daring.

His attention turned back to the bed. Neatly made.

Clean sheets. Hadn't even been sat on. Didn't that seem strange? Fallon had been found hanging just a few feet from the bed with his back to it. It seemed to Kovac a man might prepare the scene for his suicide or for a sex game, then sit down to think it through before putting his head in a noose.

He went and stood in the spot where Fallon's body had been hanging and checked the distance to the bed. Only one or maybe two small steps apart. He scowled at his reflection in the full-length mirror. *Sorry.*

The word was still there. They had found the marker that had probably been used to write it. Nothing special. A black Sharpie permanent marker left lying on the dresser. Kovac made a mental note to call and ask about fingerprints on it.

They had made a ten card of Pierce's prints Tuesday in the kitchen downstairs – for elimination purposes. Standard op. Pierce hadn't been happy about it. Because he knew his prints could be found in this bedroom? On the front of the nightstand drawer with the K-Y lube in it? On a bedpost? On the mirror? On that black Sharpie?

It wasn't a tough scenario to put together: Pierce and Fallon were secret lovers who liked to play on the dark side. The game went wrong, Fallon died, Pierce panicked. Or maybe it wasn't as innocent as that. Maybe Fallon wanted Pierce to make a commitment and dump the fiancée. Maybe Steve Pierce had seen his cushy future at Daring-Landis circling the drain as Fallon threatened to expose him. Maybe Steve Pierce had come back Tuesday morning to check his tracks, then called the cops and put on the face of the shocked best friend.

He took one last look around the bedroom, then headed back downstairs. In the kitchen, he checked the cupboards for prescription bottles. None. Nor were there any used glasses on the counter. The dishwasher had been run with half a load: three plates, some silverware, an assortment of glasses and coffee mugs. Two wineglasses. Off the kitchen, a washer and dryer sat in an alcove behind a pair of louvered doors. Inside the washer: towels and sheets, molded to the sides of the tub.

Either Andy Fallon had wanted his house in order before he died or someone else had wanted it in order afterward. The second possibility made Kovac's nerves hum.

There were two bedrooms on the main floor, down the hall from the stairs to the second story. The smaller was a guest room that held nothing of interest. The larger had been converted into a home office with a modest desk, bookshelves, and a couple of filing cabinets. Kovac clicked on the desk lamp and went through the desk drawers, careful to see but not to disturb.

A lot of cops he knew kept old case files. He had a basement full himself. If there was a God, Andy Fallon would have kept a duplicate file on his investigation of the Curtis murder. If he had, chances were good he would have it filed under *C* like a good little anal retentive IA automaton.

The first of the file cabinets held personal financial information and tax returns. The second was the jackpot drawer. Neatly ordered manila folders, the tabs marked with last names printed in careful block letters followed by eight-digit case numbers. None bore the name Curtis. No Ogden. No Springer.

Kovac sat back in Andy Fallon's desk chair and let it swivel and dip. If the Curtis investigation had been Fallon's obsession, there should have been a file. The file cabinets hadn't been locked. Anyone could have pinched the thing and walked off with it. Ogden came to mind, though he didn't seem as though subterfuge would have been among his strengths. Busting concrete block with his forehead, yes. Clever sleight of hand, no. But then, there was no telling who might have been in and out of the house between Fallon's death and the discovery of his body. There was too much time unaccounted for, too many people in the neighborhood who minded their own business.

He played angles and odds in his mind, trying to scheme a way to get at the actual IA file, but nothing good came to mind. Every path was blocked by the lovely Lieutenant Savard. He couldn't get to the file without her, and she had no intention of letting him past her guard. In any respect.

He could see her plainly as she had looked standing beside the desk in her office. A face right off a Hollywood glossy from the days of black-and-white and Veronica Lake. And he somehow knew that what lay beneath those looks was a mystery worthy of any of the great detectives, real or fictional. That drew him in as much as the looks. He wanted to slip in the secret door and find out what made her tick.

'Like you got a shot, Kovac,' he mumbled, amazed by and embarrassed at himself. 'You and the IA lieutenant. Yeah, *that* could happen.'

It struck him then, as he wasted time with thoughts of a woman he couldn't have, that there was something missing from Andy Fallon's desktop. There was no computer. The printer cord with its wide, multi-pinned connector lay there like a flat-headed snake, its other end joined with an ink-jet printer. Kovac checked the drawers again, finding a box of blank diskettes. He pulled the drawer with the case files and found that each folder contained a diskette. He went to the bookcase and found, in the collection of instruction manuals for phone/fax, for printer, for stereo equipment, a manual for an IBM ThinkPad laptop computer.

'So where is it?' Kovac asked aloud.

As he considered possibilities, a sound pierced his consciousness – sharp, electronic, coming from another part of the house. A beep followed by the creak of a floorboard. He flicked off the desk lamp, plunging the room into darkness. His hand went automatically to the Glock in his belt holster as he moved to the door, waited for his eyes to adjust, then slipped into the hall.

Out of habit he had turned out the lights as he left each room during his search. Not wanting to attract attention from the neighbors. The only light now was muted and white, coming in through the glass panes in the front door. Enough to backlight the figure of a person.

Kovac pulled the Glock and leveled it in his right hand, located the hall light switch with his left.

The figure near the front door lifted a hand close to the face.

Kovac held his breath, waiting for the click of a trigger.

'Yes, it's me,' a man's voice. 'I'm at the house. I –'

'Freeze! Police!' Kovac yelled, hitting the switch.

The man started, letting out a cry, eyes going wide, then squinting against the light, free hand coming up as if to ward off bullets. A tinny voice squawked out of the cell phone in his hand.

'No, it's all right, Captain Wyatt,' he said, slowly lowering his free hand. The cell phone was still pressed to his ear. 'Just one of the city's finest, doing his job.'

Kovac took a good long look at the man before him, keeping the Glock out because he was pissed now and wanted to show it. He recognized the face from the party. Mr Too Handsome with the black hair and the smell of Ace Wyatt's ass on his breath.

'Hang up the phone,' Kovac ordered crossly.

Too Handsome stared at him. 'But it's –'

'Close the goddamn phone, Slick. What are you doing walking in here? This is a secure police scene.'

Wyatt's man clicked the little phone shut and slipped it into the inner breast pocket of an expensive charcoal topcoat. 'Captain Wyatt asked me to meet him here. You might think that would be reason enough –'

'You might think wrong, Slick,' Kovac snapped, coming

forward, gun still in hand. 'I could have blown your pretty head off. You never heard of a doorbell?'

'Why would I ring the bell at a dead man's house?'

'Why would you come here at all?'

'Captain Wyatt's on his way with Mike Fallon. Mr Fallon has to select burial attire for his son,' he explained, using the kind of tone one might use on ignorant hired help. 'I work for Captain Wyatt. Gavin Gaines is my name, in case you get tired of calling me Slick.'

The smile was a little too self-amused, Kovac thought. College-educated pricks were his least-favorite kind.

'Should I assume the position?' Gaines asked, hands out at his sides. Outside a car door slammed.

'Don't be a smartass.' Kovac slid the Glock back into its holster. 'Like you can help it. What exactly do you do for Captain America?'

'Personal assistant, public relations, media liaison. Whatever he needs.'

Translation: toady, gofer, suckup.

'He needs you to help get Mr Fallon in the house,' Kovac said, going to the door and opening it. 'Or will that muss the look?'

Gaines gritted the perfect teeth. 'Like I said, whatever he needs. I live to serve.'

It took the two of them to negotiate the steps with Fallon, Mike hanging on them, deadweight. Worse than when he had been drunk, Kovac thought. Grief had somehow increased his body mass; the desperation of it had sapped his strength. Ace Wyatt brought the wheelchair.

'Sam, I hear you nearly took out my right hand here,' Wyatt joked. Mr Congeniality.

'If you're paying him per brain cell, he probably owes you some change back,' Kovac said. 'He's a little short in the common-sense department.'

'What makes you say that? It's not as if Gavin was

136

walking into a crime scene. He had no reason to expect anyone to be here. Why *are* you here, by the way?'

'Just doing the usual walk-through,' Kovac said. 'Looking for pieces.'

'You know Andy's death has been ruled an accident,' Wyatt said in a hushed tone, his gaze on Mike Fallon sitting slumped in his wheelchair. Gaines stood farther into the room, waiting with his hands folded in front of him and a thousand-yard stare going off in the direction of the Christmas tree. A look he'd probably picked up watching actors play Secret Service agents in the movies.

'So I heard,' Kovac said. 'That was big of you, Ace, moving things along the way you did.'

Wyatt missed the bite in Kovac's voice. 'Well, what was the point of prolonging Mike's misery? Whose interest would be served calling it suicide?'

'The insurance company. Fuck 'em.'

'Mike gave the department everything,' Wyatt said. 'His legs. His son. The least they can do is pay out the benefits and put a better face on it.'

'So you've seen to it.'

'My last great act as captain.' He flashed a tired version of the famous smile. His skin looked a little jaundiced under the hall light, and the lines at the corners of his eyes seemed chiseled deeper than two nights ago. No makeup.

His last great act. Fitting, Kovac thought, considering the case that had launched Ace Wyatt's stardom within the department had been the one that had brought Mike Fallon down.

'Where's my boy?' Mike roared.

Wyatt looked away.

Kovac squatted beside the chair. 'He's gone, Mikey. Remember? I told you.'

Fallon stared at him, face slack, eyes vacant. But he knew. He knew his son was gone, knew he was going to have to

137

face it, deal with it, carry on. But if he could pretend for just a little while . . . An old man should be entitled to that.

'I can take care of selecting the clothes, if you'd like, Captain,' Gaines offered, moving toward the stairs.

'You want that, Mike?' Kovac asked. 'You want a stranger picking what your boy wears to the hereafter?'

'He won't go,' Fallon mumbled, bleak. 'He took his own life. That's a mortal sin.'

'You don't know that, Mikey. Might have been an accident, like the ME said.'

Fallon stared at him for several seconds. 'I know. I know what he was. I know what he did.'

His eyes filled and he started to shake. 'I can't forgive him, Sam,' he whispered, clutching Kovac's forearm. 'God help me. I can't forgive him. I hated him. I hated him for what he was doing!'

'Don't talk that way, Mike,' Wyatt said. 'You don't mean it.'

'Let him say what he needs to,' Kovac said shortly. 'He knows what he really means.'

'Why couldn't he just do like I said?' Fallon mumbled, talking to himself or his God – the one who kept a bouncer at heaven's gate to keep out gays and the suicidal and whoever else didn't fit within the confines of Mike Fallon's narrow mind. 'Why?'

Kovac touched the old man's head. A cop-to-cop benediction. 'Come on, Mikey. Let's go do it.'

They left the wheelchair at the foot of the stairs. Again, Kovac and Gaines carried Mike Fallon. Wyatt brought up the rear of the procession. They set the old man on the edge of the bed with his back to the mirror that bore the apology for his son's death. But there was nothing to do about the smell – a smell every cop knew too well.

Mike Fallon hung his head and began to cry silently, lost in the torment of wondering where it had all gone so wrong for his boy. Gaines went to the window and looked out. Wyatt stood at the foot of the bed and stared at the mirror, frowning.

Kovac went into the closet to pull out a couple of Andy Fallon's suits, and wondered who would do the chore for him when the time came.

'You like one of these, Mike?' he asked, coming out of the closet with a blue suit in one hand and a dark gray in the other.

Fallon didn't answer. He stared across the room at the photograph on the dresser. The one of Andy's graduation from the academy. A frozen split second of pride and joy.

'A man should never outlive his kids,' he said bleakly. 'He ought to die before they can break his heart.'

13

A man should never outlive his kids.

He shouldn't have.

He hadn't.

He can see the scene unfold before his eyes, as plainly as if two decades hadn't passed: The still night. The squeak of his shoes. The sound of his own breathing.

The house seems huge. A trick of the adrenaline rush. The back door stands ajar.

In the kitchen. White fluorescent under-counter lights humming like high-voltage wires. Pass through into darkness. Rooms dark, moon bright and beaming through windows. A silence that presses like fingers against his eardrums. Seconds that pass in slow motion.

He moves with athleticism. (The feeling is vivid, even though he hasn't been able to feel anything below his waist for twenty years. He remembers the tension in each and every muscle of his body – his legs, his back, the fingers of his left hand curled around the grip of his gun, the contractions of his heart.)

Then there it is. Surprise at the sight of something he can't quite remember. Death in a sudden blue-white flash. An explosion so loud. The power of it knocks him backward even as he shoots in reflex.

Officer down.

Blind. Deaf. Floating.

Disbelief. Panic. Release.

I'm dead.

He wishes he had stayed that way.

He stares in the darkness, listens to his own breathing, feels his own frailty, feels his own mortality, and wonders for the millionth time why he didn't check out that night. He has wished it often enough but has never done anything about it, has never found the nerve. Instead, he's stayed alive, steeping himself in bitterness and booze and drugs. Twenty years in purgatory. Never emerging because he won't look the demons in the face.

He faces one now. Even in his drugged state, he sees it clearly and recognizes it for what it is: the Demon of Truth. The Angel of Death.

It speaks to him calmly and quietly. He sees its mouth move, but the sound seems to come from within his own head.

Time to die, Mike. A man should never outlive his kids.

He stares at his old service revolver, a squat .38 with a big scar on the butt where the bullet that severed his spinal cord had cut deep on its way to his body. The gun they said he had killed his killer with that night, the last night of his career.

He hears a little cry of fear and guesses it must have come from his own body, though it sounds far away. His hands try to push at the wheels of his chair, as if his body were trying to escape the fate his mind has already accepted. Strange.

He wonders if it was this way for Andy – fear swelling as the noose tightened around his throat. God, the feelings that image sets loose inside him! Embarrassment, rage. Guilt and hate and love.

'I loved him,' he says, his speech slurred. Spittle runs down his chin from the corner of his mouth. 'I loved him, but I hated him! He did that. It was his own fault.'

Saying it is like plunging a knife into his chest over and over. Yet he can't stop saying it, thinking it, hating Andy, hating himself. What kind of man hates his own son? He cries again, a loud, agonized wail that rises and falls and rises and falls, like a siren's call. Only the demon hears him. He is alone in the world, alone in the night. Alone with his demon, the Angel of Death.

A man should never outlive his kids. He ought to die before they can break his heart. Or before he can break theirs. You killed him. You hated him. You killed him.

'But I loved him too. Don't you see?'

I saw what you did to him, how you broke his heart. He did everything for you, and you killed him.

'No. No,' he says, tasting tears. Panic and anguish swell like a tumor in the base of his throat. 'He wouldn't listen. I told him. I told him . . . Goddamn him,' he sobs. 'Goddamn fag.'

The pain tears out of him in a raw scream and he flails his arms at the demon, pawing like an animal.

You killed him.

'How could I do that?' he cried. 'My beautiful boy!'

You want free of it, Mike? End the pain.

End the pain. . . .

The voice is seductive, tempting. He cries out again, nearly choking on the fear as it thrusts up his throat.

End the pain.

It's a sin!

It's your redemption.

Do it, Mike.

End it.

The cold barrel of the service revolver kisses his cheek. His tears roll over the black steel.

End the pain.

After all these years.

Do it.

Sobbing, he opens his mouth and closes his eyes.

The flash is blinding. The explosion is deafening.

The deed is done.

Smoke drifts in sinuous strings in the silent air.

Time passes. A moment. Two. Respect for the dead.

Then another flash, and the whir of a motor drive.

The Angel of Death slips the photo in a pocket, turns and walks away.

14

She woke from a restless, dream-filled sleep and saw him. He stood beside her bed, backlit by the grainy light that seeped around the bathroom door: a huge, faceless silhouette with shoulders like mountain slopes.

Panic exploded like a bomb in her chest. Shards of it wedged in her throat, making her gasp for breath. It tore down through her stomach like shrapnel. The muscles in her arms and legs spasmed at the shock.

Run!

He raised both hands and let go of something as she started to come up off the mattress. She saw it coming as if in slow motion: the thick, twisting body of a snake. The colors of it were very clear to her: the creamy underside, the brown and black pattern on the back.

Arms flailing, she launched herself up and forward. For a split second, confusion tipped her brain this way and that. The world went pitch-black. She couldn't see. She couldn't feel. Her feet didn't seem to be under her, though she was running as hard as she could.

Something hit her on the side of her right eye and cheek. The force was like a sledgehammer connecting to her skull. Her neck snapped back and she thought she might have cried out. Then all motion stopped and she realized the thing that had hit her was the floor.

Oh, my God, I've broken my neck.

He's still in the room.

I can't move.

She felt consciousness ebb away like a slippery thing. She clawed at it with her will, forced her brain to continue functioning.

If she could move her legs . . . Yes.

If she could move her arms . . . Yes.

She pulled her arms in tight to her sides and slowly pushed up from the floor. Her head felt as heavy as a bowling ball, her neck as fragile as a broken toothpick. She sat back on her knees, cradling her face in her hands, pain coming like a pulse. Realization blinking on and off in her mind. Neon bright, then blackness. Neon bright, then blackness.

It wasn't real.

It didn't happen.

It hadn't been a dream, though, not really. More like a hallucination. She had been awake but not conscious. Night terrors, the experts called them. She was an expert by experience. Years and years of it.

Now came the familiar wave of despair. She wanted to cry but couldn't. The protective numbness had already begun to set in. She didn't welcome it, merely resigned herself to it, and slowly, unsteadily rose to her feet.

Still holding her head in one hand, she turned on the lamp on the dresser. There was no one in the room. The light reflected a warm glow off the creamy tone-on-tone striped wallpaper. The bed was empty, the curved upholstered headboard naked of its usual pile of pillows. She'd thrown the pillows to the floor on either side of the bed, and had knocked her water glass off the nightstand. A wet stain darkened the ivory rug. The alarm clock lay on the floor near the empty glass: 4:39 A.M.

Moving carefully, in pain, she went to the bed and pulled the covers off. There was no snake. In the logical part of her brain, she knew there had never been, yet her gaze scanned the floor. She half expected to see the dark, slender shape disappearing beneath the closet door.

She worked on regulating her respiration, the exercise nearly as familiar to her as breathing. Her head was pounding. Pain was like a knife in her neck. She felt sick to her stomach. She gradually became aware of a stickiness in the hand that cradled her head, and knew it was time to assess the damage.

Amanda Savard stared at herself in the bathroom mirror, dimly taking in the surroundings reflected around her image. Soft, elegant, feminine: the environment she had created for herself to give a sense of security and belonging. The same words generally described the image she presented the world, but now she looked as if she'd gone five rounds in a boxing ring. The area around her right eye was swollen from the impact of the fall, and bright red where skidding across the rug had burned her skin. The color blazed against the pallor of her face. She pressed two fingertips gently around the wounds, feeling for fractures, the pain making her breath hiss through her teeth.

How would she explain this? How could she hide it? Who would believe her?

She took a washcloth from the linen cupboard, wet it with cold tap water, and touched it to the raw spots, gritting against the urge to wince. She took three Tylenol and went back to the bedroom. Awkwardly she stripped off the nightshirt she'd sweat through, and pulled on an oversize sweatshirt and a pair of leggings.

The house was silent. Everything was normal according to the security system panel on the wall beside the bedroom door. She'd gone through her nightly ritual, checking locks before going up to bed. And still the sense of danger lingered. She knew from experience the only thing to do was to walk through the house and prove there was no intruder.

She took her gun from the drawer in the nightstand and went out into the hall, moving like a ninety-year-old woman. Room by room, every light in the house was turned on, every room checked, every window, every lock. All of the lights remained on. Light was a good thing. Light chased away the ghosts in the shadows. Those ghosts had been haunting her for so long, it was a wonder they still possessed the ability to frighten her. They were as familiar as family, and as deeply hated.

In her office, Kenny Loggins came on at the flick of a switch on the bookcase stereo system. A quiet, gentle song about the holidays and memories of home. The emotions it evoked in her were emptiness, loneliness, sadness, but she left the song on anyway.

She liked this small room at the back of her house. The space was cozy and felt safe, and looked out on her backyard, which was very private and dotted with bird-feeders. She lived in Plymouth, a suburb that bent and twisted around marshes and woods and Medicine Lake. It wasn't uncommon to see deer nosing around the feeders, though none was braving the security light tonight. Three photographs she'd taken of them through the window hung in small frames in the office. One held a ghost image, her own reflection in the glass superimposed over the animal as it stared at her.

She closed the blinds, too edgy to expose herself to the outside world. She needed to feel enclosed. Her bedroom was her sanctuary when she had to get away from work. The office was her sanctuary when she had to escape the shadows of her life.

There was no escape from anything tonight.

Her desk was neat, the shelves and cubbyholes above it well organized. Bills and papers properly filed, paper clips in a magnetic dish, pens in a cherrywood cup. There were no photographs and only a few mementos, including a badge kept in the far upper-right-hand nook of the shelves. Her constant reminder of why she had become a cop in the first place. She rarely looked at it, but she picked it out now and held it in her hand and stared at it for a long while, acid burning in her stomach.

Spread on the otherwise uncluttered surface of the desk was a copy of the *Minneapolis Star Tribune*, open to the pages most people skipped on their way to the sports. The piece that interested her was an inch long, stuck down near the bottom. DEATH RULED ACCIDENTAL. There wasn't even a photo.

That seemed a shame, she thought. He'd been so handsome. But to most of the metro area, he would never be anything more than a few lines of type, skimmed over and forgotten. Yesterday's news.

'I won't forget you, Andy,' she whispered.

How could I? I killed you.

Her hand closed tightly on the badge until the edges bit into her fingers.

Darkness still cloaked Minneapolis as Amanda Savard arrived at city hall. Most of the lights that shone in office windows facing the street were left on overnight. No one came in at this hour, which made it the perfect time for her to sequester herself in her office without being seen. The longer she could avoid that, the better. Though there would be no ducking the funeral in the afternoon. At least she would be able to get away with dark glasses for the occasion.

Even now, with little chance of running into another human, she wore black sunglasses with frames just large enough to cover the damage she'd done to herself. She had swathed her head in a wide black velvet scarf that wrapped around her neck and trailed dramatically back over her shoulders. Drama had not been her goal. Hiding was.

Her footfalls echoed in the empty hall, boot heels ringing against the old floor. The distance to Room 126 seemed to stretch out before her. Inside her gloves, her hands were sweating. She gripped her keys too hard. The adrenaline from the dream had never entirely burned off, the residue leaving her feeling both jittery and exhausted. Dizziness swam through her head at random moments. Her legs were weak and her head pounded. She couldn't turn her neck to the right, and she felt nauseated.

She put the key in the lock and pulled up short, the skin prickling on the back of her neck. But the hall was empty – what she could see of it. She passed through the Internal Affairs outer office without bothering to turn the light on, and went directly to her own office, where she'd left on the desk lamp.

Safe. For an hour or two. She hung the scarf and her coat on the wall-mounted rack near the door, and went around behind the desk. She slipped the sunglasses off to check her reflection in the mirror of her compact. As if there had been some chance of a miracle between home and here.

The burns around the right eye looked angry, red, shiny with antibiotic gel. There had been no hope of covering them with makeup, and no way to keep bandages in place. The area directly around the eye was puffy and bruised purple and black.

'That's a hell of a shiner.'

Savard bolted at the sound of the voice. She wanted to turn her back, but realized it was too late. Embarrassment and shame flooded her. Anger and resentment rushed in their wake. She grabbed the sunglasses and put them back on.

Kovac stood just inside her door looking like something out of a Raymond Chandler novel: long coat with the collar turned up, hands stuffed in the pockets, an old fedora slouching down over his forehead.

'I suppose getting popped in the face is a common hazard of working IA.'

'If you want to see me, Sergeant, make an appointment,' she said in the chilliest tone she could manage.

'I've already seen you.'

Something about the way he said it made her feel vulnerable. As if he had seen something more than just the physical evidence of what had happened to her, something deeper and more important.

'Did you go to a doctor for that?' he asked, coming closer. He pulled the fedora off and set it on her desk, then ran a hand back over his short hair. His gaze was narrow and zoomed in on the damage she'd done to herself. 'Nasty.'

'I'm fine,' she said, glad to have the desk as a buffer. She moved to the far end of it on the pretext of putting her compact away and stowing her purse in a drawer. The dizziness swirled through her and she kept one hand on the desktop to steady herself.

'And I should see the other guy, huh?' Kovac said.

'There was no other guy. I took a fall.'

'From what? A three-story building?'

'It's none of your business.'

'It is if someone did that to you.'

He was paid to protect and serve, as the saying went. It was nothing personal. She shouldn't have wanted it to be.

'I told you – I fell.'

He didn't believe her. She could see that. He was a cop, and a good one. She'd made it her business to find out. Sam Kovac had years of experience listening to the nuances of lies. And while she wasn't exactly lying, neither was she exactly telling the truth.

She watched Kovac's gaze slide to her left hand, in search of a ring. Wondering if there was an abusive husband. The only ring she wore was on her right hand. An emerald that had been passed down through the women in her mother's family for a hundred years.

'Believe me, Sergeant. I'm the last woman who would let a man get away with this,' she said.

He weighed the idea of saying something more, drew breath for it, then stopped himself.

'You didn't come here to see about my well-being.'

'I ran into Cal Springer last night,' Kovac said. 'You'll be proud to know he's still sweating bullets over your investigation.'

'I have no interest in Cal Springer. I told you, the Curtis case is closed. The investigation was full of mistakes, but none of the allegations of impropriety bore fruit. None that would stand up in court, at any rate.'

'Incompetency is Cal's forte, but he's too big a chicken-shit for impropriety. What about Ogden? I hear he threw down Curtis's watch at Verma's place.'

'Can you prove it?'

'I can't. Could Andy Fallon? Ogden was on the scene when my partner and I got to Fallon's house on Tuesday.'

'No, he couldn't prove it. We closed the case,' she said, struggling to keep her focus over another wave of unsteadiness. Pain pounded her head like a hammer. 'He was moving on to other assignments.'

Not by choice. By order. Her order.

'Did Ogden know that?'

'Yes, he did. What was he doing there – at Andy's?'

'Sightseeing.'

'That's ghoulish.'

'Stupid too, but I don't think he's the brightest bulb in the chandelier to begin with.'

'Have you questioned him about his presence at the scene?'

'I have no right to question anyone, Lieutenant,' Kovac reminded her. 'The case is closed. A tragic accident. Remember?'

'I'm not likely to forget.'

'I assumed Ogden and his partner responded to the radio call. I had no reason to think he'd have any other motive to be there. Silly question – was there bad blood between him and Fallon? Had Ogden threatened him?'

'Not that I'm aware of. No more animosity than the usual, I should say.'

'You're all used to having people hate you.'

'So are you, Sergeant.'

'Not my own kind.'

She let that pass. 'Resentment comes with the territory. People who do bad things don't like to suffer the consequences of their actions. Bad cops are worse than criminals in that respect. They have the idea they can hide behind the badge. When it turns out they can't . . .

'I can check the case file,' she said, letting out a long, carefully measured breath. She felt hot and clammy with sweat. She needed to sit down, but she didn't want to show weakness in front of him, nor did she want him to think she would pull the case up on the computer while he waited. 'I don't expect to find anything. At any rate, you and I both know in our hearts that – despite what the ME ruled – Andy probably committed suicide.'

'I don't let my heart get involved, Lieutenant. I let my gut do my feeling for me.'

'You know what I mean. He wasn't murdered.'

'I know he's dead,' Kovac conceded stubbornly. 'I know he shouldn't be.'

'The world is full of tragedy, Sergeant Kovac,' she said, breathing a little too quickly. 'This is our piece of it for the week. Maybe it would make more sense to us if it were a crime, but it wasn't. That means we deal with it and move on.'

'Is that what you're doing?' he asked, moving to the end of the desk where she stood. 'Dealing with it?'

Savard got the feeling he wasn't talking about Andy Fallon anymore. He seemed to be looking at the marks on her face – what he could see of them around the sunglasses. She started to take a step back, but the floor didn't quite seem to be under her foot. Blackness closed in around her, and the dizziness came in a rippling wave.

Kovac moved quickly, catching her by the upper arms. She brought her hands up to his chest to steady herself.

'You need to see a doctor,' he insisted.

'No. I'll be fine. I just need to sit for a minute.'

She pushed against him, wanting free. He didn't let go. Instead, he turned her, and this time when her knees gave out, her butt hit her chair. Kovac pulled the sunglasses off her face and looked into her eyes.

'How many of me do you see?' he asked.

'One is plenty.'

'Follow my finger,' he ordered, moving it back and forth, then up and down in front of her face. His expression was grim. His eyes were a smoky shade of brown, a hint of blue in the depths. More interesting up close than from a distance, she thought absently.

'Jesus,' he muttered, staring at the area around her right eye. One big hand came up and cradled that side of her face gently, thumb pressing experimentally against the bones. 'Ten bucks says that scars.'

'It won't be my first,' she said softly.

His hand stilled. His gaze found hers, searching. She turned away.

'You need to see someone,' he said again, sitting back against her desk. 'You might have a concussion. This is the voice of experience talking.' He pointed to a butterfly clip holding together a gash over his left eye. The area surrounding it was mottled purple with a yellow tint.

'Did you have a concussion?' Savard asked. 'That might explain some things.'

'Naw. My head's like granite. Maybe you and I have something in common after all,' he said, as if he'd given the subject some thought.

'I imagine you have a job to do, Sergeant,' she said, moving her chair toward the desk and hoping the motion wouldn't make her dizzy enough to fall off or to vomit. Kovac didn't move. She didn't like the proximity at all. He could have lifted his hand and touched her hair, touched her face the way he had a moment ago.

She didn't like him behind the desk. That was her space. He had breached a defense, and she imagined he knew it.

'You don't want to talk about Andy Fallon,' he said quietly. 'Why is that, Lieutenant?'

She closed her eyes in frustration, then opened them. 'Because he's dead and I feel responsible.'

'You think you should have seen it coming. Sometimes you can't,' he said. 'Sometimes you're watching for one thing, and life belts you with a sucker punch out of nowhere.' He pantomimed a slow left hook that pulled up just short of her injured eye.

Savard stared at him. 'You probably have an actual murder to investigate,' she said, reaching for the telephone. 'I suggest you get to it.'

He watched as she dialed to get her messages. He didn't look happy, but then, she'd never seen him happy. Perhaps he never was.

Something else we have in common, Sergeant, she thought.

He went back around the desk reluctantly and picked up his hat.

'It's not always smart to be brave, Amanda,' he said quietly.

'You may call me Lieutenant Savard.'

His mouth hooked up on one corner. 'Yeah. I know. I just wanted to hear how it sounded.' He paused. 'When you saw Andy Sunday night, did you have a glass of wine?'

'I don't drink. We had coffee.'

'Mmm. Did you know Andy changed his sheets and did his laundry before he killed himself?' he asked. 'Strange, huh?'

Savard said nothing.

'See you at the funeral,' he said, and walked out.

She watched him go, her messages playing to a deaf ear.

15

For forty years the uniforms had liked having breakfast at a place called Cheap Charlie's, which was located in the no-man's-land northeast of the Metrodome. Run-down, with a filthy fifties exterior, the place had spat in the face of progress, recession, gentrification, and everything else that might have changed it in the years it had existed. Cheap Charlie's had no need to change. Their clientele was cops. The decades could come and go, but cops would never change. Tradition was all.

Mike Fallon had probably eaten here as a rookie, Liska thought, looking at the place through the blue bag serving as her passenger's window. She had lucked out and caught a parking spot in the front just as a radio car was pulling out.

She had eaten here as a rookie. They had probably all been served by the same waitress, a woman called Cheeks. In her heyday, before modern photography, Cheeks had looked like a chipmunk with a full load of nuts in her mouth. All cheeks, no chin, and a button of a nose. In the intervening years, gravity had done its thing to the point that Jowls would have been a more appropriate nickname, but Cheeks had stuck.

She was working the counter this morning, a shrunken doll with slitted eyes and a leaning tower of dyed-black hair, pouring coffee and smoking a cigarette in defiance of all known health codes. Not one cop in the place would reprimand her, and the place was a sea of uniforms and mustaches. A lot of the detectives ate breakfast here as well. Kovac among them some days. Tradition.

She went to the counter and took a vacant stool beside Elwood Knutson, her gaze scanning the room.

'Elwood, I thought you were too enlightened to eat here.'

'I am,' he said, regarding a plate smeared with the remains of bacon and eggs. 'But I've decided to try the Protein Power diet, and I couldn't think of a better place for the required breakfast. See, it's so out, it's hip again. What's your excuse?'

'I haven't had a really good heartburn in a long time.'

'You're in for a treat.'

'Bingo,' she said to herself as she spotted Ogden. He had wedged himself into a booth at the back and had an expression on his face that suggested he hadn't had a proper bowel movement in too long. Because of the angles, she couldn't see his breakfast partner and the recipient of his sour scowl.

Elwood didn't turn, studying Liska instead. 'Something I should know about?'

'Something you might know about. Do you remember when that uniform Curtis was murdered off duty?'

'Yes. Part of a string of gay crimes. A serial killer in the making.'

'Supposedly. What do you know about gay-bashing in the department?'

Elwood nibbled thoughtfully on the end of a bacon strip. He wore a mouse-brown porkpie hat with the brim bent up in front.

'I know I find it deplorable to harass or discriminate on the basis of sexual preference,' he said. 'Who are we to choose for others? Love is rare –'

'Thank you. That's admirable. I'll send your mailing address to the ACLU,' Liska said dryly. 'We're not talking about you, Elwood.'

'Who are we talking about?'

She glanced around discreetly for eavesdroppers, hoping for a few. 'I'm talking about the uniforms. What's it like in the trenches? Department PC policy aside, what's the attitude among the rank and file? I heard Curtis had complained to IA about harassment. What was that about? Are they still letting Neanderthals into the club? I thought that went out with Rodney King and the LA riots.'

'Sadly, the job attracts them,' Elwood commented. 'It's the badge. It's like a shiny coin to a monkey.'

The uniform on the other side of Liska looked around her to give Elwood a dirty look.

'Might have been an orangutan in a past life,' Liska whispered. She took a sip of the coffee Cheeks had poured for her and was instantly reminded it was time to change the oil in the Saturn. 'Anyway, I know that Curtis investigation was a major cluster fuck.'

'That was Springer's. His conception was a cluster fuck.'

'That's true, but it was a uniform that screwed the pooch on that investigation, the way I hear it. Big dumb ox of a guy name of Ogden. You know him?'

'We don't travel in the same social circles, I'm afraid.'

'I'd be more afraid if you did,' Liska said, sliding from the stool.

She made her way toward the back of the diner, fielding greetings without looking, holding her gaze on Ogden. He still hadn't noticed her, and his conversation with the man she couldn't see was becoming more intense. She couldn't make out the words, but the anger was distinct. She wished she could have come in behind him and blindsided him, but the diner was too narrow. He finally saw her and straightened, nearly tipping over a glass of orange juice.

'I'd go with prune if I were you,' she said. 'I hear those steroids can stop a person up like concrete.'

'I don't know what you're talking about,' Ogden said. 'I'm no steroid juicer.'

A comeback stuck in Liska's mouth as she got her first look at Ogden's dining companion. Cal Springer. And he couldn't have looked more guilty if he had been caught with a hooker.

'Hey, Cal. Interesting company you keep. Is this how you don't look bad to IA? Hanging out with the guy they think screwed your case? Maybe people are wrong about you. Maybe you really are as dumb as you look.'

'Why don't you mind your own business, Liska?'

'I wouldn't be much of a detective, then, would I?' she pointed out. 'Look, Cal, I'm not on your ass here. I'm just saying it looks bad, that's all. You should think about these things if you want to be a political animal.'

He turned toward the window. No view there. The plate glass was fogged over with smoke and hot breath and airborne grease.

'Where's your partner these days, Cal?' Liska asked. 'I need to talk to him.'

'Vacation. Two weeks in Hawaii.'

'Lucky stiff.'

Springer looked as if he would have preferred two weeks in hell to this conversation.

Liska turned back to Ogden and asked him point-blank: 'How'd you and your partner come to be at the Fallon scene?'

Ogden scratched at his flattop. His scalp was fish-belly white between the fine, short hairs. 'Caught the call on the radio.'

'And you just happened to be in the neighborhood.'

'That's right.'

'Dumb luck. Well, that'd be the kind you'd have.'

Ogden's little eyes looked like BBs set in dough. He rolled the sloped shoulders back. 'I don't like your attitude, Liska.'

Liska laughed. '*You* don't like *my* attitude? Guess what, Ox,' she said, bending down to get in his face. 'You're a few evolutionary limbs below me in the cop tree. I can shit my attitude all over your head if I want and nobody will listen to you complain about it. Now, if *I* don't like *your* attitude – and I don't – *that's* a problem.

'Why were you there?' she asked again.

'I told you, we caught the call.'

'Burgess had the first response. Burgess was first on the scene.'

'We thought he might need help.'

'With a DB.'

'He was riding alone. He had to secure the scene.'

'So you and Rubel came and tromped all over it. And it was just a happy coincidence that the vic turned out to be the IA investigator that was on you for the Curtis screw-up.'

'That's right.'

Liska shook her head in amazement. 'Were you busting rocks with your head when they were passing out brains? What were you thinking? You want IA on you again?'

Ogden looked around, scowling at anyone he thought might be listening. 'We responded to a call. How were we supposed to know the DB was Fallon?'

'But when you found out, you stayed. You put your prints all over his house –'

'So? He offed himself. It wasn't like somebody did it for him.'

'You couldn't know that. You still don't know that. And it's *never* your call to make as long as you're in a uniform.'

'The ME ruled it,' he said. 'It wasn't a murder.'

'It wasn't a spectator sport either, but you couldn't resist, could you? Did you take a couple of Polaroids to share with the rest of the homophobes back in the locker room?'

Ogden slid out of the booth and stood up. Liska tried to hold her ground, but had to take a step back or be forced back. One big vein stood out in a zigzag on his forehead, like a lightning bolt. His eyes were cold and as flat as buttons. The chill of fear that went through her was instinctive, and that was frightening to her in and of itself. Fear was not a common companion.

'I don't answer to you, Liska,' he said in a tone that was both quiet and taut.

She met his glare with her own, knowing she was poking a stick at a bull. It might not have been the smartest tack, but it was the one she'd chosen and there was nothing to do now but ride it out. 'Fuck up another one of my crime scenes and you won't have to answer to anyone, Ogden. You won't be wearing a badge anymore.'

The vein pulsed like something in a horror movie, and color pushed up from his too-tight collar into his face.

'Hey, B.O., let's rock 'n' roll.'

Liska knew it had to be Ogden's partner, Rubel, coming toward them from the front of the diner. Still, she didn't turn away from Ogden. She sure as hell would never have turned her back on him. He couldn't seem to break his fixation on her. The rage within him swelled with every short breath. She could see it, feel it.

Liska's brain flashed on the crime scene photos from the Curtis murder. Rage. Overkill. A human skull smashed like a pumpkin.

People around them were staring now. Cal Springer got up from the booth and beat a path for the front door, narrowly missing banging shoulders with Rubel.

'B.O., come on. Let's do it,' Rubel ordered.

Ogden looked at him finally, and the tension snapped like a twig. Liska felt the air rush out of her lungs. Rubel gave her a once-over from behind a pair of mirrored shades.

He was definitely the better-looking of the two. Dark hair, square jaw, built like Michelangelo's *David* on steroids. He was the brains of the pair, she guessed, when he herded his partner toward the door. Hustling Ogden away from trouble, much as he had done that day at Fallon's.

She followed them out to the sidewalk. They were headed toward the corner parking lot across the street.

'Hey, Rubel!' she called. He turned and stared at her. 'I

need to speak with you too. Alone. Come to the CID offices at the end of your shift.'

He didn't answer. His expression didn't change. He and Ogden walked away, the collective width of their shoulders taking up the entire sidewalk.

If Andy Fallon's death had not been ruled an accident or suicide, Ogden would have been high on the list of suspects. Was he stupid to have shown up at the scene? Maybe not. Responding to the dead body call had given him ample opportunity to legitimately put his fingerprints all over Andy Fallon's house.

How did you force a man to hang himself?

A chill went through her, and Liska knew it had little to do with the temperature and everything to do with the fact that she was looking at another cop and trying to see what was rotten about him.

The little bell rang on Cheap Charlie's door as it swung open behind her.

'Call me a stickler for details,' Elwood said, 'but I was of the impression we don't investigate closed cases.'

Liska watched the uniforms get into a cruiser. Rubel was the driver. Ogden rode shotgun. The car dipped down on its springs as he got in on the passenger's side.

'Who do we work for, Elwood?'

'Technically or figuratively?'

'Who do we work for, Elwood?'

Kovac had raised them all on this.

'The victim.'

'My employer hasn't properly notified me to terminate my services,' she said without any of her usual humor.

Elwood gave a big sigh. 'Tinks, for someone so determined to get ahead, you devote a lot of time to putting your backside in a crack.'

'Yeah,' she said, digging her car keys out of her coat pocket. 'I'm an oxymoron. Emphasis on the moron.'

16

The world is full of tragedy, Sergeant Kovac.

Savard's voice stayed in his head as he drove toward Mike Fallon's. His mind played the trick of making her sound breathy in a sexy way. It made the play of light and shadow on her face dramatic and soft, the look in her eyes full of mystery.

That part was true enough. Amanda Savard was a puzzle, and he'd always found puzzles too tempting. He was usually pretty good at them, but he knew instinctively this one would be more difficult than most, and the odds of any kind of payoff weren't good. She wouldn't appreciate his trying, that was for damn sure.

You may call me Lieutenant Savard.

'Amanda,' he said, just to be defiant. She wouldn't like knowing he was saying her name while he was alone any more than she liked it in her presence. Maybe less. She couldn't boss him around if she wasn't there to hear him, and control was her big thing. He wondered why, wondered what events had shaped her into the woman she was. 'What's your tragedy, Amanda?'

She didn't wear a wedding ring. There were no pictures of a significant other in her office. She didn't seem the type to troll bars for the kind of guy who could have given her that shiner.

He didn't buy the explanation of a fall. The placement of the wounds was too suspicious. Who took a fall and broke it with her face? The natural reaction to falling was to bring the hands out to hit first and save doing the kind of damage that had been done to her. She hadn't had a mark on her hands.

The idea of someone striking a woman made him sick and furious. The idea of this particular woman allowing it baffled him.

He set the questions aside as he pulled into Mike Fallon's driveway. There were no cars at the curb or in the drive. No one answered the doorbell.

Kovac pulled out his cell phone and dialed Mike's number from the scrap of paper he'd scribbled it on. The phone rang unanswered. That Mike was asleep or unconscious from tranquilizers or booze seemed a good bet, and either possibility suited Kovac fine. All he really wanted was a few minutes alone in the house.

He went around the side and checked the garage. The car was there. He went around to the back and took the key out from under the mat.

The house was silent. No distant sound of a television or radio or a shower running. The old man was probably dead to the world. He could have another five or ten minutes before he had to face the day he would bury his son.

Kovac went to the kitchen counter cluttered with the pharmaceuticals that kept Mike Fallon functioning in one way or another, and sorted through the bottles. Prilosec, Darvocet, Ambien.

Ambien, aka zolpidem. The barbiturate found in Andy Fallon's blood. Kovac stared at the bottle, a tight feeling in his chest. He popped the childproof cap and looked inside. Empty. The prescription was for thirty tablets with instructions to take one at bedtime as needed. The refill date was November 7.

It was probably just a coincidence that father and son had been using the same stuff to knock themselves out. Ambien was a common prescription sleep aid. But there had been no Ambien at Andy Fallon's house, and that seemed strange. If he'd taken the drug the night of his death, then where was the bottle? Not in the medicine cabinet, not in the garbage, not in the nightstand. Mike's bottle was empty, but he could have taken all the pills himself in accordance with the instructions. On the other hand, if 'as needed' meant once or twice a week, then there were a hell of a lot of pills unaccounted for.

Kovac let possibilities run through his mind, unchecked, uncensored. None of them pleasant, but then, that was the nature of his work and the bent of his mind because of the work. He couldn't afford to trust, to discount, to filter possibilities through a screen of denial the way most people did. He didn't feel badly about that. It didn't depress him, the way it did others in his line of work. The simple truth of the world was that people, even otherwise decent people, regularly did rotten things to other people, even to their own children.

Still, he couldn't come up with a scenario in which Mike Fallon played a direct role in his son's death. The old man's physical limitations made it impossible. He supposed Andy could have taken the pills from his father's stash, but that didn't ring true for him either. Or he could have gotten them from a friend. He thought again of the sheets and towels in the washing machine, of the few clean dishes in Andy's dishwasher.

'Hey, Mike! You up?' he called. 'It's Kovac!'

No answer.

He set the prescription bottle back on the counter and went out of the cramped little kitchen. The house had a stillness to it he didn't like, a sense of being vacant. Maybe Neil had come and carted Mike away already, but the funeral was hours away. Maybe Mike had other relatives who were, even now, giving him comfort and coffee and saying all the right things, but Kovac didn't think so. He'd known Mike Fallon only in the context of being alone. Isolated first by his toughness, then by his bitterness. It was hard to imagine anyone loving him the way people in close families loved one another. Not that Kovac knew much about it. His own family was scattered to the four winds. He never saw any of them.

He looked at the empty rooms of Mike Fallon's house and wondered if he was looking at his own future.

'Mike? It's Kovac,' he called again, turning down the short hall to the bedrooms.

The smell hit him first. Not overpowering, but unmistakable. Dread fell like an anvil on his chest. His heart beat up against it like a fist hammering on a door.

He swore under his breath, pulling the Glock from its holster. With his foot, he pushed open the door to the spare bedroom. Nothing. No one. Just empty twin beds with white chenille spreads, and a sepia-toned portrait of Jesus in a cheap metal frame on the wall.

'Mike?'

He moved toward Fallon's bedroom door, already knowing. The images of what he would find on the other side were rolling through his head. Still, he stood to the side as he turned the knob. He filled his lungs with air and pushed the door open with his foot.

The room was in the same state of disarray as when he had last seen it. The framed photographs Fallon had smashed were still piled where Kovac had left them. The bed was still unmade. The jelly glass still sat on the nightstand with a splash of whiskey in it. Dirty clothes still littered the floor.

Kovac stared at the empty room, at a loss for a moment, trying to clear the images he'd had from his head. The smell was stronger here, where he was standing. Blood and excrement and urine. The biting, metallic scent of gunpowder. The bathroom door was directly across from him. Closed.

He stood to the side and knocked, said Fallon's name again, though barely loud enough to hear himself. He turned the knob and pushed the door open.

The shower curtain looked as if someone had given birth on it. Bloody chunks of tissue and hair clung to it.

Iron Mike Fallon sat in his wheelchair, in his underwear, his head and shoulders flung backward, arms hanging out to the sides. The spindly, hairy, useless legs were canted over to the left. His mouth hung open and his eyes were wide, as if he had realized in the final instant that the reality of death was surprisingly different from the way he had imagined it would be.

'Aw, Mikey,' Kovac said softly.

Out of long habit, he came into the room carefully, taking in the details automatically, even as another part of his brain considered his own loss in this. Mike Fallon had broken him in, set a standard, became a legend to live up to. Like a father in a lot of ways. Better than, he supposed, considering Mike's strained relationships with his own sons. It had been bad enough to see the old man soured and angry and pathetic. To see him dead in his underwear was the final indignity.

The back of his skull was gone, blown wide open. A flap of scalp clung to the crown of his head by a collection of bloody gray hairs. Brain matter and tiny bone fragments had splattered the floor. An old .38 service revolver lay on the floor to Fallon's right, flung there as his body had jerked in its death spasm.

Iron Mike Fallon, just another cop to end it all by his own hand with the gun he had carried to protect the public. God knew how many did it each year. Too many. They spent their careers as a part of a brotherhood but died alone – because none of them knew how to deal with the stress and every last one was afraid to tell anybody. It didn't matter if they'd turned in the badge. A cop was a cop until the day he died.

That day was today for Mike Fallon. The day his son would be buried.

A man should never outlive his kids, Kojak. He ought to die before they can break his heart.

Kovac touched two fingers to the old man's throat. A mere formality, though he'd known people who'd survived such wounds. Or rather, he'd known a few whose hearts had continued beating for a time because the damage had been done to some less useful part of the brain. It wasn't really survival.

Fallon was cool to the touch. Rigor was setting in in the face and throat, but not yet in the upper body. Based on that, Kovac put the time of death within the last five or six hours. Two or three in the morning. The loneliest hours of the night. The hours that seem to stretch endlessly when a man was lying awake, staring into the dark at the bleaker realities of his life.

Kovac went out of the room, out of the house, and stood on the back stoop, staring at nothing. He lit a cigarette and smoked it, his fingers stiffening in the cold. He had gloves in his pockets, but didn't bother to put them on. Sometimes it was good to hurt. Physical pain as an affirmation of life, as an acknowledgment of deeper suffering.

He wished for a glass of whiskey to toast the old man, but that would have to wait. He finished the cigarette and reached for his cell phone.

'This is Kovac, homicide. Send me the tag 'em and bag 'em boys. I've got a DB,' he said. 'And send the A team. He used to be one of ours.'

He had taken a seat on the front step, trench coat wrapped around his freezing ass, and was smoking a second cigarette by the time Liska rolled up.

'Jesus, Tinks, what're you trying to do? Bring down the neighborhood?' he called as she climbed out of the car. It was her own, the Saturn sporting a trash bag window.

'You think the neighborhood watch block commander will call the cops?' she asked, coming up the sidewalk.

'He'll probably gun you down in the street. Shoot first, ask questions later. America at the dawn of the new millennium.'

'If I'm lucky he'll hit the gas tank and toast the rotten thing. I could stand a break this week.'

'You and me both,' Kovac said. He nodded at the car as Liska came up the snow-packed steps, ignoring the clean wheelchair ramp. 'So what happened?'

She shrugged it off. 'Just another victim of the moral decline. In the Haaff ramp, no less.'

'World's going to hell on Rollerblades.'

'Keeps the paychecks coming.'

'Did they get anything?'

'Not that I could tell. There was nothing worth getting, except my address off some junk mail.'

Kovac frowned. 'I don't like that.'

'Yeah, well . . . Didn't your mother ever tell you you'll get hemorrhoids sitting on cold concrete?'

'Naw.' He got up slowly, stiffly. 'She told me I'd go blind beating off.'

'I didn't need that image in my head.'

'Beats what you'll see inside,' he said. He bent over to crush out the cigarette and dropped the butt off the side of the stoop, behind a juniper shrub.

Neither of them spoke for a moment as an awkward tension fell around them.

'I'm really sorry, Sam,' Liska said softly. 'I know he meant a lot to you.'

Kovac sighed. 'It's always the tough ones that eat their guns.'

Liska gave him a little shove. 'Hey, you do that to me, I'll revive you just so I can shoot you myself.'

He tried to smile but couldn't, so he looked away, to next door. Fallon's neighbor had plywood silhouettes of the three wise men on camels in front of their picture window, hot on the trail of the Christ child. A schnauzer was taking a whiz on one of the camels.

'I'm not that tough, Tinks,' he confessed. He felt as if all of that old armor had rusted and flaked away, layer by layer, leaving him exposed. Which was worse? Being too hard to feel, too remote to be touched, or being open to feel the touch of other people's lives and emotions, open to being hurt by that contact? Hell of a choice on a day like this. *Like trying to decide if you'd rather be stabbed or bludgeoned,* he thought.

'Good.' Liska put her hand on his back and leaned her head against his shoulder for a few seconds. The contact gave comfort, like something cool against a burn.

Better to be open, he decided, reflecting back on the original question. Even if it hurt more often than not. Sometimes it felt like this. He slipped his arm around his partner's shoulders and gave her a squeeze. 'Thanks.'

'Don't mention it. Really,' she teased, straight-faced, as she stepped away. 'I have a reputation to uphold. And speaking of people with reputations . . . Guess who was seen dining together this morning at that celebrity hot spot Chez Chuck.'

Kovac waited.

'Cal Springer and Bruce Ogden.'

'I'll be damned.'

'Strange bedfellows, huh?'

'Were they happy to see you?'

'Yeah, like they'd be happy to have head lice. My guess is it wasn't a planned meeting. Cal was sweating like a monk in a whorehouse. He bolted at the first chance.'

'He's pretty damn nervous for a man who's been cleared of any wrongdoing.'

'I'll say. And Ogden . . .' She looked out at the street as if she might find something there to compare him to. A garbage truck rumbled past. 'That guy's like a keg of nitro with a tricky detonator. I'd love a peek in his personnel jacket.'

'Savard told me she'll check Fallon's case file regarding the Curtis investigation. See what notes he might have made about Ogden, whether Ogden threatened him, that kind of thing.'

'But she wouldn't let you see the file.'

'No.'

'You're losing your touch, Sam.'

He huffed a laugh. 'What touch? I'm hoping she gets so sick of the sight of me she gives me what I want just to make me go away. Aversion therapy.'

'Well, I have to say, if I weren't such the tough cupcake, Ogden would have given me a little chill this morning,' Liska admitted. 'There we are, him getting in my face, and all I could think of was Curtis – beaten to death with a ball bat.'

Kovac turned it over in his head. 'You're thinking what if Ogden was the one harassing Curtis and went off on him for complaining to IA. But Ogden would never have been privy to the Curtis investigation if there'd been any beef about him harassing Curtis in the past. That shit only happens in the movies.'

'Yeah,' Liska said on a sigh. 'If you were Mel Gibson and I were Jodie Foster, that could happen.'

'Mel Gibson's short.'

'Okay. If you were . . . Bruce Willis.'

'He's short and bald.'

'Al Pacino?'

'Looks like someone dragged him down a gravel road behind a truck.'

Liska rolled her eyes. 'Jesus. Harrison Ford?'

'He's getting kind of old.'

'So are you,' Liska pointed out, then looked at the street again. 'Where's the CSU?' She bounced up and down a little on the balls of her feet. She wasn't wearing a hat, and the rims of her ears had turned bright pink in the cold.

'At a terminal domestic situation,' Kovac said. 'Get this. Common-law wife says she got fed up with the hubby raping her when she was passed out drunk – after nine years of it. She stabbed him in the chest, face, and groin with a busted vodka bottle.'

'Wow. Absolut homicide.'

'Good one. Anyway, they'll be a little while.'

'I'll do the Polaroids, then.' She held her hand out for his car keys so she could go get the camera.

By the book. Every violent death was processed like a homicide.

Kovac went back into the house with her and started making notes. There was a certain comfort in the routine, provided he didn't remind himself the victim had been his mentor once upon a lifetime ago. Liska made none of the usual dark jokes they used to take the edge off a horrific death scene. For a time the only sound was the click and whir of the camera as it spat out one gruesome photo after another. When he realized the sound had stopped, Kovac looked up from his notebook.

Liska was squatting down in front of Fallon, staring at him as if she expected him to answer some question she had asked telepathically.

'What?' Kovac asked.

She didn't answer, but stood and glanced from wall to wall in the narrow bathroom, then over her shoulder and back. Her brows puckered together and she made a little knot of her mouth. 'Why'd he back in?'

'Huh?'

'This room is narrow, besides the obstacles of the toilet and sink. Why'd he back in? That had to be tricky. Why bother?'

Kovac considered the old man and the question. 'He goes in frontwise, whoever opens the door opens it on the hamburger side of his head. Maybe he wanted to preserve a little dignity.'

'Then he might have had the consideration to put on some clothes, don't you think? Those skivvies don't exactly scream "Respect me".'

'Suicides don't always make sense. Someone's gonna take and eat a thirty-eight slug, he's not exactly in his right mind. And you know as well as I do – plenty of people off themselves in the can. You'd think they were gonna have to clean up the mess themselves.'

Liska said nothing. Her attention had gone to the floor, dingy vinyl that had been mostly white twenty years ago. Behind Fallon, the vinyl had taken a spray of blood flecked with bits of bone and chunks of brain matter that looked like overcooked macaroni. In front of him: nothing. The shower curtain was a mess; the door they had entered through was clean.

Anyone coming into – or going out of – the room had a clean path. No blood to step in or to mark fingerprints.

'If he'd been a billionaire with a young, pretty wife, I'd say you're on a hot scent, Tinks,' Kovac said. 'But he was a bitter old man in a wheelchair who just lost his favorite son. What'd he have left to live for? He was torn up about Andy, couldn't forgive himself for not forgiving the boy. So he rolled it in here, parked it, and capped himself. And he did it the way he did it to make a neat death scene – so none of us would come busting in here and step on his brain.'

Liska pointed the Polaroid at the .38 on the floor and snapped one last shot.

'That'll be his old service weapon,' Kovac said. 'When we look around, we'll find that he kept it in a shoe box in the back of his closet, 'cause that's where old cops always stash their guns.' He made a sharp, hard-edged smile. 'That's where I stash mine, if you want to come and take it away from me. We're pathetic creatures of pattern and habit.' He stared at Fallon. 'Some of us more pathetic than others.'

'You're sounding a little bitter yourself, Kojak,' Liska said, handing the snapshots to him.

He slipped them into the inside breast pocket of his topcoat. 'How can I look at this and not be?'

From another part of the house came the thump of an exterior door closing. Kovac gladly turned away from the corpse and started down the hall.

'It's about damn time,' he barked, then pulled up short at the same time Neil Fallon stopped dead in the archway between the living room and dining room.

He looked as if he'd been rolled. His hair stood up on one side, a purpling bruise crowned the crest of his right cheek, and his lip was split. The brown suit looked slept in. The cheap tie was askew and the top button of the white shirt undone. He couldn't have gotten the collar closed with a winch. He'd obviously bought the shirt a couple of neck sizes ago and hadn't had occasion to wear it since.

He gulped a couple of breaths, pumping himself up.

'Jesus Christ, he can't even leave *this* to me?' he said, his expression sliding from shock to anger. 'I can't even drive him to the goddamn funeral home? He's gotta have one of his own for that too? The son of a bitch –'

'He's dead, Neil,' Kovac said bluntly. 'Looks like he shot himself. I'm sorry.'

Fallon stared at him for a full minute, then shook his head in amazement. 'You're the regular Angel of Death, aren't you?'

'Just the messenger.'

Fallon turned around as if he might walk right back out the front door, but he just stood there with his hands on his hips, the bull shoulders rising and falling.

Kovac waited, thinking about another cigarette and that glass of whiskey he'd wanted earlier. He remembered the bottle of Old Crow Neil had had out in his shed the day he'd told him about his brother, and how they had stood out in the cold and shared it while they stared at the snow blowing across the frozen lake. It seemed a year ago.

'When did you last talk to Mike?' he asked, falling back on the routine, same as he always did.

'Last night. On the phone.'

'What time was that?'

Fallon started to laugh, a harsh, discordant sound. 'You're some piece of work, Kovac,' he said, starting to pace a small circle at the far end of the dining room table. 'My brother and my old man dead inside a week and you're giving me the fucking third degree. You're something. I hadn't seen the old man five times in the last ten years, and you think maybe I killed him. Why would I bother?'

'That's not why I asked, but as long as you've brought it up, I'll need to know for the record where you were this morning between midnight and four A.M.'

'Fuck you.'

'I think I'd remember that. Must have been someone else.'

'I was home in bed.'

'Got a wife or girlfriend to corroborate?'

'I've got a wife. We're separated.'

Fallon looked around as if searching for some neutral third party to witness what was happening to him now, but there was no one. He paced some more and shook his head, the anger and frustration building visibly.

He made a little lunge toward Kovac and bounced back, jabbing the air with a forefinger, a grimace contorting his face. 'I hated that old son of a bitch! I fucking hated him!'

Tears squeezed out of his tightly closed eyes and rolled over his cheeks. 'But he was my old man,' he said, and sucked in a quick breath. 'And now he's dead. I don't need any shit from you!'

He stopped pacing and bent over with his hands on his

knees, as if he'd taken a blow to the stomach. He groaned in the back of his throat. 'Christ, I'm gonna be sick.'

Kovac moved to block the path to the bathroom, but Fallon went for the kitchen instead and straight out the back door.

Kovac started to follow, then pulled up as the head of the crime scene unit walked in the front door. Just as well. By the time he was able to join Neil Fallon on the back steps, any gastrointestinal pyrotechnics had subsided. Fallon stood leaning against the railing, staring at the backyard, sipping out of a slim metal flask. His skin looked slightly gray, his eyes rimmed in red. He didn't acknowledge Kovac's presence, but pointed to a naked oak tree in the far corner of the yard.

'That was the hanging tree,' he said without emotion. 'When Andy and I were kids.'

'Playing cowboys.'

'And pirates, and Tarzan, and whatever. He should have come back here and done it. Andy hanging dead in the backyard, Iron Mike in the house with his head blown off. I could have come and parked my car in the garage and gassed myself.'

'How'd Mike sound last night on the phone?'

'Like an asshole, like always. "I wanna be at the goddamn funeral home by ten o'clock." ' The impersonation was less than flattering, but not less than accurate. ' "You can damn well be here on time." Fucking old prick,' he muttered, and swiped a gloved hand under his running nose.

'What time was that? I'm trying to get a frame for what happened when,' Kovac explained. 'We need it for the paperwork.'

Fallon stared at the tree and shrugged. 'I dunno. I wasn't paying attention. Maybe like nine or something.'

'Couldn't have been. I ran into him at your brother's house around nine.'

Fallon looked at him. 'What were you doing there?'

175

'Poking around. There's a couple of loose ends need tying up.'

'Like what? Andy hung himself. How can you have any doubts about that?'

'I like to know the why of things,' Kovac said. 'I'm funny that way. I want to look at what he was working on, what was going on in his personal life, things like that. Fill in the blanks, get the whole picture. You see?'

If Fallon saw, he didn't like it. He turned away and took another pull on the little flask.

'I'm used to people dying,' Kovac said. 'Drug dealers kill each other over money. Junkies kill each other over dope. Husbands and wives kill each other out of hate. There's a method to the madness. Someone like your brother buys it, a guy with everything going for him, I need to try to make some sense of it.'

'Good luck.'

'What'd you do to your face?'

Fallon tried to shake off the attention. He touched a hand to the bruise on his cheek as if to brush it away. 'Nothing. Mixed it up a little in the parking lot with a customer last night.'

'Over what?'

'He made a remark. I took exception and said something about his sexual preferences and a sheep. He took a swing and got lucky.'

'That's assault,' Kovac pointed out. 'You call the cops?'

Fallon gave a nervous laugh. 'That's a good one. He *was* a cop.'

'A cop? A city cop?'

'He wasn't in uniform.'

'How'd you know he was a cop?'

'Please. Like I can't spot one a mile off.'

'Did you get a name? A badge number?'

'Right. After he knocked me on my ass, I demanded his badge number. Anyway, I don't need the hassle of filing a report. He was just some asshole knew Andy. He made a crack. We took it outside.'

'What'd he look like?'

'Like half the cops in the world,' Fallon said impatiently. He slipped the flask into his coat pocket, pulled out a pack of cigarettes, and went about that ritual, fumbling with his gloves, fingers clumsy with cold – or with nerves. He swore to himself, got the thing lit, took a couple of hard puffs.

'Look, I wish I hadn't said anything. I don't want to do anything with it. I'd had a few myself. I got a mouth on me when I'm tanked.'

'Big guy? Little guy? White? Black? Old? Young?'

Fallon scowled and fidgeted. He looked as if his skin suddenly didn't fit him right. He wouldn't meet Kovac's gaze. 'I don't even know that I'd know him if I saw him again. It didn't mean anything. It's not important.'

'It could mean a hell of a lot,' Kovac said. 'Your brother worked Internal Affairs. He made enemies for a living.'

'But he killed himself,' Fallon insisted. 'That was what happened, right? He hung himself. The case is closed.'

'Everyone seems to want it to be.'

'But you don't?'

'I want the truth – whatever it might be.'

Neil Fallon laughed, then sobered, staring once again at the backyard – or back in time. 'Then you picked the wrong family, Kovac. The Fallons have never been very dedicated to the truth about anything. We lie to ourselves and about ourselves and about our lives. That's what we do best.'

'What's that supposed to mean?'

'Nothing. We're the all-American family, that's what. At least we were before two-thirds of us committed suicide this week.'

'Could anyone else at your place ID this guy from last night?' Kovac asked, more concerned for the moment with the notion of Ogden going way the hell out to Neil Fallon's bar and bait shop than he was with the crumbling dynamics of the Fallon family.

'I was working alone.'

'Other customers?'

'Maybe. Jesus,' Fallon muttered, 'I wish I'd told you I walked into a door.'

'You wouldn't be the first person to try it today,' Kovac said. 'So, was it before or after the donnybrook when you talked to Mike?'

Fallon blew smoke out his nose. Annoyed. 'After, I guess. What the hell difference does it make?'

'He was pretty out of it when I saw him. On sedatives or something. If you talked to him after that, I guess he had snapped out of it.'

'I guess. When it came to chewing my ass, he always rose to the occasion,' he said bitterly. 'Nothing was ever good enough. Nothing ever made up.'

'Made up for what?'

'That I wasn't him. That I wasn't Andy. You might have thought after he found out Andy was queer . . . Well, he's dead now, so what's the difference? It's over. Finally.'

He looked at the oak tree once more, then threw the cigarette into the snow and checked his watch. 'I have to get to the funeral home. Maybe I can get one in the ground before the other turns cold.'

He gave Kovac a sideways look as he went to open the door. 'Don't take it personal, but I hope I never see you again, Kovac.'

Kovac didn't say anything. He stood on the stoop and looked back at the Fallon brothers' hanging tree, imagining two young boys with their lives ahead of them, playing good guys and bad guys; the bonds of brotherhood twining the paths of their lives, shaping their strengths and weaknesses and resentments.

If there was one thing from which people never

recovered, it was childhood. If there was one tie that could never truly be broken, for good or for ill, it was to family.

He turned the thoughts over in his head like a bear turning over rocks to see what kind of grubs it might find. He thought about the Fallons and the jealousies and disappointments and anger among them. He thought about the faceless cop Neil Fallon had picked a fight with in the parking lot of the bar and bait shop.

Would Ogden have been stupid enough to go there? Why? Or maybe *stupid* was the wrong word. What would he stand to gain? Maybe that was the question.

Even as he pondered that, Kovac couldn't stop thinking that Neil Fallon hadn't even asked to see his father. The vic's family usually did. Most people would refuse to believe the bad news until they saw the body with their own eyes. Neil Fallon hadn't asked. And he hadn't taken a step toward the bathroom when he'd said he felt sick. He'd gone straight for the back door.

Maybe he'd wanted air. Maybe he hadn't asked to see his dead father because he wasn't the sort of person who needed the visual image to make the death real, or maybe because he couldn't stomach that kind of thing.

Or maybe they should be running tests for gunpowder residue on Neil Fallon's hands.

The back door opened and Liska stuck her head out. 'The vultures have landed.'

Kovac groaned. He'd bought some time calling in the request for the crime scene unit over his cell phone, but dispatch would have called the team over the radio, and every reporter in the metro area had a scanner. News of a dead body never failed to bring out the scavengers. According to the press, The People had a right to know about the tragedies of strangers.

'You want me to handle them?' Liska asked.

'No. I'll give them a statement,' he said, thinking about the life and times of Mike Fallon, the pain, the loss, the soured love and wasted chances. 'How's this? Life's a bitch and then you die.'

Liska arched a brow and spoke with heavy sarcasm. 'Yeah. There's a headline.'

She started to go back inside. Kovac stopped her with a question.

'Hey, Tinks, when you saw Ogden this morning, did he look like he'd been in a fight?'

'No. Why?'

'Next time you see him, ask him what the hell he was doing at Neil Fallon's bar last night. See if you get a rise.'

Liska looked unhappy. 'He was at Fallon's bar?'

'Maybe. Fallon claims some cop was out there making cracks, and they mixed it up in the parking lot.'

'Did he describe Ogden?'

'No. He dropped his little bomb, then clammed up. He acts like a man who's scared of something. Like retribution maybe.'

'Why would Ogden go all the way out there? What would be the point? Even if – God, *especially* if he had something to do with Andy Fallon or with the Curtis murder. Go out there and pick a fight with Neil Fallon? Not even Ogden is that stupid.'

'That's what I'm thinking. And the next logical question is, then why would Neil Fallon lie about it if it didn't happen?'

'Neil Fallon, whose father is sitting in the bathroom missing the back of his head?'

Neil Fallon, who was seething with long-held hard feelings. Neil Fallon, who had admitted to a quick, harsh temper. Neil Fallon, who resented his brother and hated his father, even after their deaths.

'Let's do a little digging on Mr Fallon,' Kovac said. 'Put Elwood on it, if he's not busy. I'll talk to some of Fallon's customers. See if anyone else saw this phantom cop.'

'Will do.'

Kovac took one last grim look at the hanging tree. 'Make sure the ME's people bag Mike's hands. We could be looking at a murder, after all.'

17

It wouldn't be a cop funeral like the ones shown on the six o'clock news. The church would not overflow with ranks of uniforms who had rolled in from all over the state. There would be no endless caravan of radio cars to the cemetery. No one was going to play 'Amazing Grace' on the bagpipes. Andy Fallon had not fallen in the line of duty. His death had not been heroic.

The place didn't even look like a church, Kovac thought as he left the car in the lot and walked toward the low brick building. Like most churches built in the seventies, it looked more like a municipal building. Only the thin, stylized iron cross on the front gave it away. That and the illuminated sign out near the boulevard.

ST MICHAEL'S
ADVENT: WAITING FOR A MIRACLE?
MASS WEEKDAYS: 7 A.M.
SATURDAY: 5 P.M.
SUNDAY: 9 A.M. & 11 A.M.

As if miracles were performed regularly at those scheduled hours. The hearse was sitting on the circle drive near the side entrance. No miracles for Andy Fallon. Maybe if he had come here Saturday at five . . .

The wind whipped Kovac's coat around his legs. He bent his head into it to keep his hat. The windchill was in the teens. Mourners moved toward the church from scattershot spots in the parking lot. Cop. Cop. Three civilians together – a man and two women in their late twenties. The cops were in plain clothes, and he didn't know them, but he could spot a cop as easily as Neil Fallon. It was in the carriage, in the demeanor, in the eyes, in the mustache.

The usual dirge was playing on the organ as they trailed one another into the building to loiter in the narthex. Kovac renewed his promise to himself not to have a funeral when he died. His pals could hoist a few for him at Patrick's, and maybe Liska could do something with his ashes. Toss them out on the steps of city hall to join the ashes of a thousand cigarettes smoked there by cops every day. Seemed fitting. He sure as hell wouldn't put people through this: standing around staring at one another, listening to god-awful organ music and choking on the smell of gladiolas.

He put his hat on the rack but kept his coat, and stood off to the side watching the civilians move as a trio to another small knot of their own kind. He would approach them later. Afterward. After they had all shared the experience of putting their friend in the ground. He wondered if any of them had been close enough to Andy Fallon to share a sexual paraphilia.

Impossible to tell. In his experience the most normal-seeming people could be involved in the weirdest shit. Andy Fallon's friends looked like the cream of their generation. Well dressed, clean-cut, their faces pale with grief beneath the fading red of wind-kissed cheeks. Couldn't say who was gay, who was straight, who was into S and M.

The doors opened again, and Steve Pierce held one back, letting Jocelyn Daring precede him in. They made a handsome couple in expensive black cashmere coats: Jocelyn a statuesque porcelain doll with every blond hair neatly swept back and held in place with a black velvet bow. She may not have felt the loss of her fiancé's best friend, but she knew how to dress the part. She appeared to be pouting. Pierce stood beside her near the coatrack with a thousand-yard stare. He didn't help her with her coat. She said something to him, and he snapped at her. Kovac couldn't make out the words, but his tone was sharp and her reaction was to intensify the pout. They didn't touch as they went into the church.

Not a happy couple.

Kovac went to the glass doors and looked in at the assembled mourners. The pews were chrome and black plastic chairs hooked one to the next. There were no kneelers, no creepy statues of the Virgin or the saints adorned with real human hair. There was nothing daunting about the place, no overriding sense of God glaring down on His terrified flock. Not like when Kovac had been a kid, when eating a burger on Friday during Lent was a sure pass to hell. He had feared and respected the church of his youth. This place was about as scary as going to a lecture at the public library.

Pierce and Daring had taken seats on the center aisle about halfway toward the front. Pierce rose abruptly and came back out, the girlfriend watching him all the way. He stared at the floor, digging a cigarette and a lighter from his coat pocket as he walked. Kovac moved away from the doors. Pierce didn't see him as he crossed the narthex and went outside.

Kovac followed and took a position three feet to Pierce's right on the broad concrete step. Pierce didn't look at him.

'I keep saying I'm quitting,' Kovac said, shaking one out of a pack of Salems. He hooked it with his lip and lit it with a Christmas Bic. Nothing says Christmas like lung cancer. 'But you know what? I never do. I like it. Everybody tries to make me feel guilty about it, and I buy into that. Like I think I deserve it or something. So then I say I'm quitting, but I never do.'

Pierce regarded him from the corner of his eye and lit his own cigarette with a slim brushed-chrome lighter that looked like a giant bullet. His hands were shaking. He returned his stare to the street and slowly exhaled.

'I guess that's just human nature,' Kovac went on, wishing he'd grabbed his hat on his way out. He could feel all his body heat rushing out the top of his head. 'Everybody carries around a load of shit they think they ought to feel guilty about. Like somehow that makes them a better person. Like there's some law against just being who you are.'

'There are plenty of laws against that,' Pierce said, still staring at the street. 'Depending on who you are.'

Kovac let that hang for a moment. Waited. Pierce had opened the door. Just a crack. 'Well, sure, if you're a prostitute or a drug dealer. Or did you mean something less obvious?'

Pierce blew out a stream of smoke.

'Like if you're gay,' Kovac suggested.

Pierce moved his shoulders and swallowed, Adam's apple bobbing. 'That would depend on who you ask.'

'I'm asking you. Do you think that's something a person should feel guilty about? Do you think it's something a person should hide?'

'Depends on the person. Depends on their circumstances.'

'Depends on whether he's engaged to the boss's daughter, for instance,' Kovac offered.

He watched as the missile hit the target square in the chest. Pierce actually took a step back.

'I believe I've already told you I'm not gay,' he said in a tight voice. His gaze darted from side to side, looking for eavesdroppers.

'You did.'

'Then you clearly didn't believe me.' Angrier.

Kovac took a slow pull on his smoke. All the time in the world.

'Would you care to ask my fiancée? Would you like us to videotape ourselves having sex?' Angrier. 'Any requests for positions?'

Kovac didn't answer.

'Would you like a list of my ex-girlfriends?'

Kovac just looked at him, letting the anger roll off him. And still it was visibly building in Pierce, a kind of frenetic excitement he was having difficulty containing.

'I've been a cop for a lot of years, Steve,' he said at last. 'I can tell when someone's holding something back on me. You're carrying a lot of extra weight.'

Pierce looked as if the blood vessels in his eyes might pop. 'I just lost my best friend since college. I found him dead. We were like brothers. You think one man can't grieve deeply for another without them being gay? Is that what your life is like, Sergeant? You wall yourself off for fear of what other people might think of you if they knew the truth?'

'I don't give a shit what anybody thinks of me,' Kovac said matter-of-factly. 'I got nothing riding on it. I'm not trying to impress anyone. I've seen too many people carry rocks around every day until the weight of it all drags them under and kills them one way or another. You've got a chance to unload one.'

'I don't need to.'

'He's going in the ground today. If you know something, it won't go in the ground with him, Steve. It'll hang around your neck until you take it off.'

'I don't know anything.' He gave a harsh laugh that came out on a cloud of smoke and warm breath in the cold air. 'I don't know a damn thing.'

'If you were there that night –'

'I don't know who Andy was fucking, Sergeant,' Pierce said bitterly, turning the heads of several people going into the church. 'But it wasn't me.'

The cords stood out in his neck. His face was as red as his hair. The blue eyes were narrow and filled with venom and tears. He threw his cigarette down and ground it out with

186

the toe of an expensive oxford. 'Now, if you'll excuse me, I'm a pallbearer. I have to go move my best friend's corpse.'

Kovac let him go and finished his own smoke, thinking that a lot of people would have called him cruel for what he'd just done. He didn't think of it that way. He thought of Andy Fallon hanging dead from a rafter. What he did, he did for the victim. The victim was dead – there weren't many things crueler than death.

He crushed out the cigarette, then picked up both butts and deposited them in a plant pot near the door. Through the glass he could see the casket had been rolled into the narthex from a side hall. The pallbearers were being given instructions by a portly man from the funeral home.

Neil Fallon stood off to one side, looking blank. Ace Wyatt put a hand on the funeral director's shoulder and said something to him in confidence. Gaines, the über-assistant, hovered nearby, ready to step, fetch, or kiss an ass.

'Are you going in, Sergeant? Or are you watching from the cheap seats?'

Kovac focused on the faint reflection that had appeared beside his in the glass. Amanda Savard in her Veronica Lake getup. The glam sunglasses, the velvet scarf swathing her head. Not a getup, he thought, a disguise. There was a big difference.

'How's the head?' he asked.

'Nothing hurt but my pride.'

'Yeah. What's a little concussion to a tough cookie like you?'

'Embarrassing,' she said. 'I'd sooner you let the subject go.'

He almost laughed. 'You don't know me very well, Lieutenant.'

'I don't know you at all,' she said, taking hold of the door handle with a small gloved hand. 'Let's keep it that way.'

She may as well have waved a red flag. He wondered if

she knew that – and if she did, then what game she was playing at.

You and the IA lieutenant. Yeah, right, Kovac.

'I don't let go,' he said, making her glance back at him over her shoulder. 'You might as well know that.'

Inscrutable behind the shades, she made no comment and went into the church. Kovac followed her. Glutton for punishment. The procession of casket and mourners had gone up the aisle. The organist was pounding out yet another depressing song of death.

Savard chose a seat in the back, in an otherwise empty row. She didn't so much as acknowledge Kovac as he slid in beside her. She didn't sing the required hymn, didn't join in the spoken prayers or responsories. She never took the sunglasses off or lowered the scarf or unbuttoned her coat. As if she were in a cocoon, the layers of clothing insulating her from the thoughts of the outside world. Wrapping her in her own thoughts about Andy Fallon.

Kovac watched her from the corner of his eye, thinking he had to be an asshole to tempt fate this way, to push her buttons. One word from her and he'd be suspended. On the other hand, it seemed not a bad idea to give the appearance of having aligned himself with IA for the moment. Not that anyone in this crowd seemed to care.

All focus – not simply that of Amanda Savard – seemed inward. No one really heard the priest, who hadn't known Andy Fallon at all, and could speak of him only because someone had filled him in. As with most funerals, it didn't matter what the presiding clergyman had to say anyway. What mattered was the panorama of memories playing through each person's head, the mental and emotional scrapbooks of experiences with the person lost.

As Kovac studied the faces, he wondered which, if any, hid memories of intimacies with Andy Fallon; memories of shared passions, of shared perversions. Which of these people might have helped Andy Fallon put a noose around his neck, then panicked when things went wrong? Which one knew that missing piece to the puzzle of Andy Fallon's state of mind: would he have killed himself?

Did any of them really care to know? The case had been closed. The priest was pretending the word *suicide* had never been mentioned in the same sentence with Andy Fallon's name. In another hour, Andy Fallon would be in the ground, buried, a fading memory.

The moment came for eulogies. Neil Fallon shifted in his seat, glancing furtively from side to side as if to see whether anyone was watching him not get up and speak at his only brother's funeral. Steve Pierce stared down at his feet, looking as if he was having trouble getting a deep breath. Kovac felt a similar pressure in his own chest as he waited. The mindhunters called emotionally charged situations such as this 'precipitating stressors,' triggers for actions, triggers for confessions, for testimonials. But this was Minnesota, a place where people were not naturally given to speaking openly about their emotions. The moment passed without drama.

Savard rose, slipped her coat off, and – sunglasses and scarf still in place – walked with all the elegance and import of a queen to the front of the church. The priest stepped aside for her to take the lectern.

'I'm Lieutenant Amanda Savard,' she said in a tone that was at once quiet and authoritative. 'Andy worked for me. He was a fine officer, a dedicated and talented investigator, and a wonderful person. We are all richer for having known him and we are poorer for his untimely loss. Thank you.'

Simple. Eloquent. She came back to the pew with her head bowed. Mysterious. Kovac rose and stepped into the aisle to allow her back to her seat. People were staring. Probably at Savard. Probably wondering how a guy like him came to be sitting with a woman like her.

Kovac stared back, silently challenging. Steve Pierce met

his gaze for just a moment, then looked away. Ace Wyatt rose and adjusted his shirt cuffs as he went to the lectern.

'Jesus Christ,' Kovac grumbled, then crossed himself as the woman sitting two rows ahead turned and gave him a dirty look. 'Can you believe this guy? Any excuse for a photo op.'

Savard lifted a brow at him.

'He'd hang his bare ass out a tenth-story window and fart the national anthem if he thought it'd get him publicity.'

One corner of Savard's perfect mouth curled in wry amusement. 'Captain Wyatt is a longtime acquaintance of mine.'

Kovac winced. 'Stepped right into that, didn't I?'

'Headfirst.'

'That's how I do most everything. That's why I look this way.'

'I knew Andy Fallon when he was a boy,' Wyatt began with all the dramatic talent of a community theater actor. The fact that he was about to become a star on national television was testimony to the declining standards of the American public. 'I didn't know Andy Fallon the man very well, but I know what he was made of. Courage and integrity and determination. I know this because I came up through the trenches with his old man, Iron Mike Fallon. We all knew Iron Mike. We all respected the man and his opinions, and feared his temper if we screwed up. A finer police officer I have never known.

'It is with deepest regret I have to announce Mike Fallon's passing late last night.'

A small gasp went through the crowd. Savard jerked as if she'd been hit with a cattle prod, her pale skin instantly turning paler. Her breathing turned quick and shallow.

Wyatt went on. 'Despondent over the death of his son . . .'

Kovac leaned down. 'Are you all right, Lieutenant?'

'Excuse me,' she said, standing abruptly.

Kovac rose to let her out. She pushed past him, nearly shoving him back into his chair. She wanted to run down the aisle and out of the church, and just keep on running. But she didn't. No one she passed gave her more than a passing glance, their collective attention on Wyatt at the lectern. No one else seemed to hear the pounding of her heart or the roaring of her blood in her veins.

She pushed open the glass door to the narthex and turned down the hall, seeking and finding the ladies' room. The light was dim and the room smelled of commercial air freshener. Ace Wyatt's voice was still in her head, bringing on a sense of panic. Then she realized it was coming from a speaker hung high on the wall.

She tore off the scarf and sunglasses, nearly crying out in pain as the earpiece dragged through the oozing rug burn. Eyes squeezed tight against the threatening flood of tears, she fumbled blindly for the faucets. The water exploded into the sink, splashing up on her. She didn't care. She scooped it with both hands and put her face in it.

Dizziness swirled through her brain, weakness drained her legs. She fell against the sink, clutching at the porcelain basin with one hand, reaching to brace against the wall with the other. She tried to will herself past the nausea, begged God to get her through it, ignored her convenient faith in a higher power she had ceased to believe in long ago.

'Please, please, please,' she chanted, doubled over, her head nearly in the sink. In her mind's eye she could see Andy Fallon staring at her with accusation and anger. He was dead. Now Mike Fallon.

Despondent over the death of his son . . .

'Lieutenant?' Kovac's voice sounded just outside the door. 'Amanda? You in there? Are you all right?'

Savard tried to push herself upright, tried to get a breath deep enough to speak with a steady voice. She couldn't quite manage either.

'Y-yes,' she said, wincing at the weakness of her tone. 'I'm fine. Thank you.'

The door swung open and Kovac came in without hesitation or regard for the modesty of any woman who might have been in the rest room. He looked fierce.

'I'm fine, Sergeant Kovac.'

'Yeah, I can see that,' he said, coming to her. 'Even better than when you were fine this morning, keeling over at your desk. Do you often feel the overwhelming urge to take a shower with your clothes on?' he asked, his gaze cutting from the wet tendrils of hair plastered to the sides of her face to the dark splotches of water on her suit.

'I was feeling a little dizzy,' she said, pressing a hand to her forehead. She took a slow breath through her mouth and closed her eyes for a second.

Kovac put a hand on her shoulder and she stiffened, telling herself she should bolt, telling herself not to. She looked at him via his reflection in the mirror and saw the concern in his dark eyes. She saw herself and was appalled by how vulnerable she appeared in that moment – pale and battered.

'Come on, LT,' he said softly, shortening her title to a nickname, 'let me take you to a doctor.'

'No.'

She should have told him to take his hand off her, but the weight of it was solid and strong and reassuring, even if she couldn't lean into it the way she wanted to, needed to. A shiver went through her. She shouldn't have wanted or needed anything, certainly not from this man.

She looked at the reflection of his hand on her shoulder. A big hand, wide, with blunt-tipped fingers. A working man's hands, she thought, regardless of the fact that Kovac's work was done with his mind and not his hands. His fingers tightened briefly.

'Well, at least let's get out of here,' he said. 'This damn air freshener is enough to choke a goat.'

'I can take care of myself,' Savard announced. 'Really. Thank you anyway.'

'Come on,' Kovac coaxed again, turning toward the door and neatly drawing her with him. Years of practice herding drunks and victims and people in various states of shock made it easy for him. 'I've got your coat in the hall.'

She pulled away, went back to the sink, and collected her sunglasses and carefully slid them on. The velvet scarf was wet in spots. She put it back on anyway, arranging it carefully, draping it just so. Kovac watched her.

'I thought you only knew Mike Fallon by reputation,' he said.

'That's right. I'd spoken to him, of course. About Andy.'

'Your reaction to the news of his death seems a little extreme, then.'

'I told you, I was feeling dizzy,' she said. 'The announcement of Mike Fallon's death didn't really have all that much to do with it. It's a tragedy, of course. . . .'

'The world's full of them, I hear.'

'Yes.'

Satisfied with the scarf, she walked past Kovac and out under her own steam. Show no weakness. Too late for that.

He had left her coat draped over a table piled with church bulletins. She picked it up and started to put it on, the pain in her neck and upper back grabbing hold and stopping her with only one arm in a sleeve. Kovac helped her on with it the rest of the way, standing a little too close behind her, trapping her between himself and the table.

'I know,' he said softly. 'You're fine. You could have done it yourself.'

Savard stepped sideways and ducked around him, heading across the narthex. The organ had started up again, and the acrid-sweet smell of incense burned the air.

'I'm not letting you drive away from here, Lieutenant,' Kovac said, falling into step beside her. 'If you're dizzy, you're not safe to be behind the wheel.'

'I'm fine. It's passed.'

'I'll give you a ride. I'm headed back to the station myself.'

'I'm going home.'

'Then I'll drop you off.'

'It's out of your way.'

He held the door for her. 'That's all right, the ride will give me the chance to ask you a couple of questions.'

'God, do you never stop?' she said through her teeth.

'No. Never. I told you – I don't let go. Not until I get what I want.'

His hand slipped around hers and she tried to jerk away, her heart jumping, eyes going wide behind the glasses. 'What do you think you're doing?'

He stared at her for a second, reading God knew what in her expression. Even with the scarf and glasses, she felt naked in front of him.

'Keys.'

As he said it, the muscles of her hand relaxed marginally and he slipped the key ring from her fingers. A major tactical error. She didn't want Kovac driving her home. She didn't want him in her house. She didn't want his interest. She was accustomed to a position of power, but even though she outranked him, Kovac had years and experience over her. Knowing that made her feel subordinate, like a little girl pretending at a job of great importance.

'If you have a question, ask it,' she said, folding her arms around herself. The wind was bitter and raw. The temperature had dropped in the hour they'd been in the church. The sun was already sagging in the winter-white sky. 'Then you'll give me my keys back, Sergeant.'

'Did Andy Fallon ever talk about his brother?'

'No.'

'Did he ever mention he was seeing someone – dating – or that he was having problems in his personal life?'

'I told you before – his personal life was none of my business. Why are you pursuing this, Sergeant?'

He tried to look innocent, but Savard doubted he had been able to pull that off even as an infant. There was a world-weariness to Kovac that surpassed his years by a thousand. 'I'm paid to investigate,' he said.

'To investigate *crimes*. There's been no crime I'm aware of.'

'Mike Fallon is minus half his head,' Kovac said. 'I'm gonna make damn sure somebody else didn't do that job for him before I walk away from it.'

Savard stared at him through the dark glasses. 'Why would you think anyone would murder Mike Fallon? Captain Wyatt said he took his own life.'

'Captain Wyatt was speaking prematurely. The investigation is ongoing. The body wasn't even stiff yet when I left the scene to come here.'

'It wouldn't make any sense for someone to murder Mike Fallon,' Savard argued.

'Who says it has to make any sense?' Kovac returned. 'Someone gets pissed off, loses their temper, strikes out. Boom, murder. Someone holds a grudge long enough, gets fed up on it, something strikes a spark. Bang, somebody's dead. I see it every damn day, Lieutenant.'

'Mr Fallon was in poor health. He'd just lost his son. I'm assuming the signs at the scene of his death pointed to suicide. Doesn't it seem more logical that he pulled the trigger himself than to think someone else might have done it?'

'Sure. But then, a clever killer might think that too,' Kovac pointed out.

'It must be slow in homicide these days,' Savard remarked, 'that one of their best detectives can spend all his time on non-cases.'

'The more I'm around the people involved with Andy and Mike Fallon, the less I consider these deaths "non-cases."

You knew Andy. You claim to have cared about him. You want me to walk away from this if I think there's a chance he didn't put that noose around his neck himself? You want me to shrug it off if it looks like maybe Mike didn't stick that thirty-eight in his mouth without help? What kind of cop would I be if I did that?'

Behind them, the doors of the church swung open and the mourners came out, bundled against the cold and hurrying toward the parking lot. Kovac spotted Steve Pierce and Jocelyn Daring, Daring trying to put her arm through her fiancé's, Pierce shrugging her off. Not far behind them came Ace Wyatt and his toady. Wyatt looked impervious to cold, shoulders back, jaw out. He drew a bead on Kovac like a laser-sight missile.

'Sam,' he said in his serious TV voice, 'I understand you found Mike. My God, what a tragedy.'

'His death, or me finding him?'

'Both, I suppose. Poor Mike. He just couldn't take the burden. I think he felt a tremendous guilt over Andy's death, over the unresolved issues between them. It's too bad. . . .'

He looked to Savard and nodded. 'Amanda, good to see you, despite the occasion.'

'Captain.' Even with the shades on, Kovac could tell she was looking past Wyatt, not at him. 'Terrible news about Mike Fallon,' she said. 'I'm sorry to hear it. I know you and he had a history.'

'Poor Mike,' he said in a thick voice, looking away. He let a beat of silence pass, as if out of respect, then pulled in a cleansing breath. 'I see you know Sam.'

'Better than I'd care to,' she said, and reached out and took her keys from Kovac's hand. 'If you gentlemen will excuse me . . .'

'I was just telling the lieutenant how it struck me odd Mike would be so upset last night about Andy killing himself, that being a mortal sin and all, then go home after

196

and eat his gun,' Kovac said, effectively holding Savard in place. 'Doesn't make sense, does it?'

'Who says it has to make sense?' Savard said sarcastically.

'Amanda's right,' Wyatt said. 'Mike wasn't in his right mind, was he?'

'He was barely coherent last I saw him,' Kovac said. 'How about you, Ace? You took him home. How'd he seem when you left him?'

Gaines looked pointedly at his watch. 'Captain . . .'

Wyatt made a face. 'I know, Gavin. The meeting with the PR-people.'

'And miss the interment?' Kovac said. *There goes a photo op.* Somehow, he managed to have the sense not to say that.

'It's been postponed,' Gaines informed him. 'Some kind of equipment problem.'

'Ah. TFC technical difficulty,' Kovac said. 'Too Fucking Cold to dig the hole. Excuse my language, Lieutenant,' he said sweetly.

'I don't think there is an excuse for you, Sergeant Kovac,' she said dryly. 'And on that note, gentlemen, I'll say good-bye.'

She raised a hand in farewell and made her escape across the snowpacked lot. Kovac let her go, sensing that to try to stop her now, with witnesses around, would be crossing a line he'd come too close to as it was. He allowed himself to watch her for a second.

'Sam, you can't seriously be thinking Mike was murdered,' Wyatt said.

'I'm a homicide cop.' Kovac settled his hat on his head. 'I think everyone's murdered. It's my natural mind-set. What time was it when you left Mike?'

Gaines interrupted. 'Captain, if you'd like to go on to the meeting, I'll take care of this.'

'Do you eat his food and wipe his ass too?' Kovac asked, earning a cold look from the assistant.

'You're holding the captain from a very important

meeting, Sergeant Kovac,' Gaines said curtly, subtly moving to put himself between them. 'I was there with Mr Fallon and the captain last night. I can answer your questions as well as Captain Wyatt.'

'There's no need, Gavin,' Wyatt said. 'By the time you bring the car around, Sam and I will be done.'

Kovac looked smug. 'Yeah, Slick, you run along and start the car. You and I can get together later and get your take on things over a latte. So you'll have that to look forward to.'

Gaines didn't like being bested, and didn't like being dismissed. The blue eyes were as cold as the concrete beneath their feet, the handsome jaw set. But he bowed to Wyatt's orders and hustled away toward a black Lincoln Continental.

'That's some elegant guard dog you've got yourself, Ace,' Kovac said.

'Gavin is my right hand. Ambitious, single-minded, fiercely loyal. I wouldn't be where I am without him. He's got a very bright future. He's a bit overzealous at times, but I could say the same about you, Sam. Unless I'm out of the loop – and I'm not – there wasn't anything about Mike's death to warrant suspicion of murder.'

Kovac stuffed his hands in his coat pockets and sighed. 'He was one of ours, Ace. Mike was special. Sure, maybe the legend was more special than the man, more important, but still . . . I feel like I owe him a good hard look. You know what I mean? You ought to, considering your own history with him.'

'It's hard to think the door's closing on that chapter of our lives. Hard to believe he's gone,' Wyatt said quietly, staring across the parking lot as exhaust billowed in a cold vapor cloud from the tailpipe of the Lincoln.

It had to be as much a relief to him as anything, Kovac thought. The night of the Thorne murder, all those years ago, had been the defining moment in the lives of Ace

Wyatt and Mike Fallon. That night their lives had turned on a dime, never to be the same again, always to be linked by that moment that had made Mike Fallon a cripple and Ace Wyatt a hero. With Mike gone, the weight of that burden must have lifted, a sensation that would both relieve and confuse. How could there be an Ace Wyatt if there was no Mike Fallon to counterbalance?

'It was around ten-thirty when we left Mike's house,' Wyatt said. 'He was quiet. Wrapped up in his grief. I had no idea what he was thinking or I would have tried to stop him.' His mouth twisted with irony as the car pulled up. 'Or maybe that would have been the greater tragedy. He suffered a lot of years. Now it's over. Let him go, Sam. He's at peace now.'

Gaines got out of the car and went around to open the passenger door. Wyatt got in without another word, and the Lincoln was off in a cloud of exhaust. The Lone Ranger and Tonto riding off into the sunset.

Kovac stood on the curb a moment longer, the only one left of the group who had come to see Andy Fallon off to the hereafter. Even the priest had disappeared.

'Lone Ranger,' he muttered, and started across the frozen parking lot with his hands in his pockets and his shoulders hunched into the wind.

18

'Neil Fallon has a record.'

Kovac paused with his coat half off. 'That was fast.'

'Service with a smile,' Elwood said, peering over the cubicle.

Liska sat on her chair, her maniacal pixie look lighting her face. She was something when she caught a scent on a case, he thought. It was like an addiction with her. The excitement was so intense, it was just a few steps to the right of sexual. Kovac couldn't remember ever being that hot for the job, and the job was the one great love of his life. Maybe he needed to consider hormone therapy.

'He has a juvie record – sealed, of course, though I've put through a request to have a peek,' Liska said. 'He spent seven years in the army. I've requested his service records. The year he got out, he went away for assault. Three to five. He did eighteen months.'

'What'd he do?'

'Got in a fight at a bar. He put the guy in a coma for a week.'

'Temper, temper, Neil.'

Kovac finished taking off his coat and hooked it on the rack, thinking. The office was the usual buzzing hive of constant low-level activity. Phones rang, someone laughed. A multiply-pierced twenty-something thug with bleached, spiked hair and pants hanging off his ass was led past in cuffs and ushered into an interview room. In the days of Mike Fallon, someone would have kicked his ass for his fashion choices alone.

'So how'd he get a liquor license with a felony

conviction on his sheet?' Kovac asked, sagging into his chair.

'He didn't,' Elwood said.

'Come around here, for chrissake,' Kovac groused. 'You're giving me a stiff neck.'

Liska grinned and pushed at his chair with the toe of her boot. 'You should be glad for the sensation.'

'Very funny.'

Elwood rounded the end of the cubicle, holding out a fax. 'The license on the bar was issued by the municipality of Excelsior in the name of Cheryl Brewster, who months later became Cheryl Fallon.'

'Ah, the estranged missus,' Kovac said.

'The soon to be ex-missus,' Liska corrected. 'I called her at home. She's a nurse. She works nights at Fairview Ridgedale. She says she's divorcing him, and it can't happen a moment too soon to suit her. Drunken, mean son of a bitch – just a sampling of the terms of endearment.'

'Gee, and I found him such an agreeable fellow,' Kovac said. 'So, the wife holds the liquor license. What happens when she dumps him?'

'Neil's shit-out-of-luck, that's what,' Liska said. 'They can sell the bar with the license, pending approval of the new owner by the powers that be in Excelsior. Neil could get himself a new front man, but that hasn't happened yet. Cheryl says he's trying to buy the rest of the business out and forget the liquor license, but he can't seem to get the cash together for that either. Even if he could, she says he can't make a living off the place without the bar, so . . .

'I asked her if she thought he'd try to borrow money from his family. She laughed and said that Mike wouldn't give Neil change for a dime, let alone enough money to buy out the business – even though she says she knows Mike had plenty.'

'We call that motive in the detective business,' Elwood pointed out.

'I wonder if he put the touch on Andy,' Kovac mused.

'He had told Cheryl he was going to see if Andy wanted to invest, but she didn't know what ever happened with that,' Liska said. 'We can ask Pierce. It's safe to think he might have advised Andy on his financial stuff.'

'But if Pierce thought Andy's brother might have had something to do with his death, why wouldn't he have said so?' Elwood asked.

Kovac nodded. 'Why not point the finger instead of acting like the weight's on his shoulders?

'Let's check through the notes on the canvass of Fallon's neighbors. See who we missed, make some follow-up calls. Maybe someone might recognize a car, or know he'd been seeing someone. Elwood, do you have time to run through Fallon's address book and check with the friends?'

'Will do.'

'We've got to redo part of the neighborhood canvass anyway,' Liska said.

'Why?'

'First time around, two of our little elves were Ogden and Rubel.'

Kovac groaned. 'Great. That's what we need, Ogden telling people they didn't see anything.'

'If a wit saw someone other than him or Rubel – like Neil Fallon or Pierce – even Ogden would have brains enough to bring it to our attention,' Liska said.

'So we have to hope the uniforms missed that someone.'

'Who missed who?' Leonard demanded, coming to an abrupt halt at the cubicle.

Kovac pretended to search for a file on his desk, covering the notes he'd made regarding Andy Fallon's death.

'The guy that beat up Nixon,' he said. 'Deene Combs's henchman. We have to hope his people missed scaring the shit out of someone who knows something about it.'

'Have you talked to that woman again? The one the cab driver saw going inside that building as the perp ran away.'

'Five times.'

'Talk to her again. She's the key. We know she knows something.'

'That's a dead end,' Kovac said. 'She'll take it to her grave.'

'If Nixon isn't going to rat the guy out himself, Chamiqua Jones isn't gonna do it for him,' Liska pointed out.

Leonard frowned at her. 'Talk to her again. Go to where she works. Today. I don't want these gangbangers thinking they can run wild.'

Kovac glanced at Liska, who looked down at the floor and crossed her eyes. The common logic regarding the Nixon assault was that Wyan Nixon had shorted his boss, Deene Combs, on a small-time drug deal and had been made an example by said boss, but no one was talking, including Nixon. The county attorney, who wanted to take a more publicly visible hard line against drug dealers, had pledged the county would press the charges if Nixon wouldn't. But without a witness, there was no case, and the cab driver hadn't seen enough to give a detailed description of the assailant.

'It's a black hole,' Kovac said. 'No one's going to testify to anything. What's the point?'

Leonard made his monkey frown. 'The point is, it's your job, Kovac.'

'I know my job.'

'Do you? It sounds to me that you've been redefining the parameters.'

'I don't know what you're talking about.'

'Fallon is closed. Leave it alone.'

'You heard about Mike?' Kovac said. The deliberate curveball, even as he wondered who had ratted him out to Leonard. His money was on Savard. She didn't want him hanging around, getting too close to her, threatening to breach the security of the walls she had so carefully erected around herself. Wyatt didn't give a shit what went on in Kovac's little world. All he cared about was getting to his next PR event.

Leonard looked confused. 'That he killed himself?'

'I'm not so sure that's what happened.'

'He ate his gun.'

'Looked that way.'

'There are a couple of red flags, Lieutenant,' Liska said. 'The positioning of the body, for instance.'

'You're saying the scene was staged?'

'Not staged, but a little too convenient. And there's no suicide note.'

'That doesn't mean anything. A lot of suicides don't leave notes.'

'The older son has some issues – and a record.'

'I want to dig a little,' Kovac said. 'Maybe Mike did whack himself, but what if he didn't? We owe him better than to let it slide because suicide was the easy answer.'

'Let's see what the ME has to say,' Leonard said grudgingly, unhappy with the idea of a slam dunk turning into a whodunit – especially this case, with Wyatt and the rest of the brass monkeys looking on. 'In the meantime, go see Chamiqua Jones. Today. I want the county attorney's office off my ass about Nixon.'

'I'd rather stick myself with needles than go to the Mall of America during the Christmas season.'

Kovac glanced over at Liska as he piloted the Caprice through rush-hour traffic going east on 494. 'Where's your consumer spirit?'

'Dying from lack of oxygen down at the bottom of my bank account. Do you have any idea what kids want for Christmas nowadays?'

'Semiautomatic weapons?'

'R.J. gave me a list that looks like the inventory for Toys 'R' Us.'

'Look on the bright side, Tinks. He didn't send it to you from a juvenile detention center.'

'Whoever said it cost a million bucks to raise a kid through college did not take Christmas into account.'

Kovac negotiated a lane change around a snot-green Geo doing fifty with a white-knuckled balding guy at the wheel. Iowa plates.

'I-wegian farmers,' he growled. 'They don't know how to drive without a cornfield on either side of them.'

He cut across two lanes to catch the exit he wanted. His driving usually spurred remarks from Liska, but she said nothing, seeming lost in her thoughts of the holiday bearing down on them.

Kovac remembered the Christmas the year after his first wife had left. He'd sent gifts to their daughter. Stuffed animals. A rag doll. Shit like that. Things he'd hoped a little girl might like. The boxes had been returned unopened. He'd hauled the stuff to a Toys for Tots drop, then gone out and drunk himself into a stupor. He wound up in a fistfight with a Salvation Army Santa out in front of the government center, and got suspended for thirty days without pay.

'He's your kid,' he said. 'Get him something he really wants and quit your bitching. It's only money.'

Liska stared at him.

'What's he really want?' he asked, uncomfortable with her scrutiny.

'He wants me and Speed to get back together.'

'Jesus H. Any danger of that happening?'

She was silent half a beat too long as they drove into the mall's west-side ramp. Kovac looked over at her again.

'Has hell frozen over yet?' she asked defensively. 'Did I miss that on the news?'

'He's an asshole.'

'I don't need you to tell me that.'

'I'm just saying.'

Kovac parked and memorized the level and row number. One of 12,750 parking spaces on mall property. This was not the place to get lost.

The Mall of America was like a giant, elegant, four-tiered rat maze, the wide hallways teeming with frantic humans scurrying from one store to the next. The biggest mall in the United States – five hundred stores, two and a half million square feet of commercial space – and still there weren't enough retail outlets for those searching for the perfect item to wrap and have returned two days after Christmas. Human nature.

The noise from the Camp Snoopy amusement park at the mall's center was constant; the dull roar of roller coasters and the water flume ride, punctuated by shrieks of customers. A high school choir was assembling on risers in front of the entrance to Macy's, boys cutting up and girls wandering toward the windows of Lerner's as their director barked at them ineffectually.

They passed the three-story Lego Imagination Center with its twenty-five-foot Lego clock tower, huge Lego dinosaur, Lego space station, and a Lego blimp made from 138,240 Lego blocks hanging suspended above it all.

Kovac turned in at Old Navy with a jaundiced eye on a display of track pants and T-shirts and ugly quilted vests.

'Look at this shit.'

'Retro-seventies,' Liska said. 'Shirts in the all-my-clothes-shrunk-in-the-wash-but-I-wear-them-anyway style.'

'I thought it was ugly the first time around. Looking at this is like having a bad flashback on high school.'

The clerk Kovac badged was a girl with a lip ring, cat-eye glasses, and maroon hair that looked as if a five-year-old had hacked at it with a pinking shears. 'Is your manager around?'

'I'm the manager. Is this about that guy who's always hiding in the racks and flashing his thing at women?'

'No.'

'You ought to do something about him.'

'I'll put him on my list. Is Chamiqua Jones working?'

'Yes.' The girl's eyes looked big behind the glasses. 'What'd she do? She's never flashed a penis at anyone.'

'We've just got a couple questions,' Liska said. 'She's not in any trouble.'

Cat Eyes looked skeptical but made no comment as she led them toward the dressing rooms.

Chamiqua Jones was twenty-something, looked forty-something, and was built like a fifty-five-gallon drum with a rusty Brillo pad hairdo. She stood guard near the dressing rooms, directing would-be consumers and shoplifters.

'That door over there, honey.' She pointed a customer down the row, then shook her head and muttered under her breath as the customer walked away, 'Like you gonna get your fat white ass in them pants.'

She glanced at Kovac and Liska, then let herself into one of the dressing rooms to pick up a tangled pile of discarded jeans.

'You again.'

'Hey, Chamiqua.'

'I don't need this hassle on my job, Kovac.'

'Here I was missing you, and that's the greeting I get? I feel like we're getting to be old pals.'

Jones didn't smile. 'You gonna get my ass killed, that's what.'

'You still don't have anything to say about Nixon?' Liska said.

'The president? Nope. Nothing. I wasn't born yet. I hear he was a crook, but ain't they all?'

'Witnesses put you at the scene of the assault, Chamiqua.'

'That rag-head cab driver?' she said, carrying the jeans to a table. 'He lying. I never seen no assault. I told y'all before.'

'You didn't see a man jump Wyan Nixon and beat him with a tire iron.'

'No, ma'am. All I know 'bout Wyan Nixon is he is *bad* news. Especially for me.'

She folded the jeans with quick, practiced movements. Her hands were chubby, with short fingers and taut skin. They made Kovac think of small balloon animals. Her gaze darted twenty feet away to a stocky young man with a tight white spandex cap that looked like a condom for the skull. Kovac had never seen him before, but there was no mistaking what he was: muscle. A hundred eighty pounds of sociopathic meanness. He might have been sixteen or seventeen, but he was no kid. He stood near a rounder of polar fleece vests, turning it without looking, his flat, cold gaze on Chamiqua Jones.

'I'm very busy here,' she said, and went to unlock a dressing room with a key hanging from a neon-green plastic coil around her wrist.

Kovac turned his back to the muscle. 'We can offer you protection, Chamiqua. The county attorney wants Deene Combs behind bars.'

'Protection,' she snorted. 'What? You gonna send me on a bus to some flea-trap motel in Gary, Indiana? Hide me out?' She shook her head as she returned to the table with another pile of clothing. 'I'm a decent person, Kovac. I work two jobs. I'm raising three good kids. I want to live to see them through school, thank you very much. Wyan Nixon can look out for his own black ass. I'm looking out for mine.'

'If he wants to be a hard-ass, the county attorney can charge you as accessory after the fact,' Liska said, fishing. 'Obstruction of justice, failure to cooperate . . .'

Jones held her hands out in front of her, darting a glance at Condom Cap. 'Then you put the cuffs on me and take me away. I got nothing to say about Wyan Nixon or Deene Combs. I didn't see nothing.'

Kovac shook his head. 'Not today. See you around, Chamiqua.'

'I hope not.'

'Nobody loves me today,' Kovac complained.

Liska pulled out a business card and put it down on the stack of folded jeans. 'Call if you change your mind.'

Jones tore the card in two as they walked away.

'Who can blame her?' Kovac said under his breath, giving the skunk eye to Condom Cap as they passed.

'She's looking out for her kids,' Liska said. 'I'd do the same. It's not like she could take Deene Combs off the street, anyway. You know he didn't do Nixon himself. She could give up some piece of meat like that guy watching her and still get herself killed for her trouble, and for what? There's a thousand more where he came from.'

'Yeah. Let it go. One scumbag beats the shit out of another scumbag. That's one less scumbag on the street for a while. Who cares? Nobody cares.'

'Somebody has to care,' Liska corrected him. 'We have to care.'

Kovac looked at her. 'Because we're all that's standing between society and anarchy?'

Liska made a face. 'Please. Because our clearance rates count big-time toward promotion. Screw society. I have kids to put through college.'

Kovac laughed. 'Tinks, you never fail to put things in their proper perspective.'

'Someone has to keep you from getting morose.'

'I'm never morose.'

'You're always morose.'

'I'm not morose, I'm bitter,' he corrected her as they passed the Rainforest Cafe, where sounds of thunder and rain were playing over the speaker system, and one of the live parrots on display was screaming like a banshee. People lined up for that.

'There's a difference,' he said. 'Morose is passive. Bitter is active. Being bitter is like having a hobby.'

'Everyone needs a hobby,' Liska agreed. 'Mine is the mercenary pursuit of easy money.'

She veered to the entrance of Sam Goody, where a near-life-size cutout of Ace Wyatt stood with its arm protectively around a box full of videotapes titled *Pro-Active: A Police Professional's Tips on How Not to Become a Victim*. She put her sunglasses on and struck a pose beside the display.

'What do you think? Don't we look good together?' she said, grinning. 'Don't you think he needs a younger female partner to broaden his demographics? I'd wear a bikini if I had to.'

Kovac scowled at the cardboard Wyatt. 'Why don't you just go up to the third floor here and get a job at Hooters? Or you could walk Hennepin Avenue.'

'I'm a mercenary, not a prostitute. There's a difference.'

'No, there isn't.'

'Yes, there is. A mercenary doesn't use a vagina.'

'Jesus.' Kovac felt heat creep up his face. 'Don't you ever embarrass yourself?'

Liska laughed. 'With what? My mouth or my seemingly shameless quest for advancement?'

'I was raised not to talk about . . . those . . .' He flushed an even darker shade of red as they started back down the hall.

'Vaginas?'

Kovac gave her a furious look as passing shoppers turned to stare at them.

'That might help explain why you don't have one at your disposal,' Liska speculated. 'You need to open up, Sam. You need to get in touch with your feminine side.'

'If I could touch my own feminine side, I wouldn't need . . . one of those . . . at my disposal.'

'Good point. And you could have your own TV show – Hermaphrodite Homicide Detective. Think of the following that would have. You could stop being jealous of Ace Wyatt.'

'I'm not jealous of Ace Wyatt.'

'Yeah, right. And I'm Heather Locklear.'

'You're just hot for his assistant. That's what you're after,' Kovac said.

Liska rolled her eyes. 'Gaines? Please. He's gay.'

'Gay or not interested?'

'Same difference.'

Kovac laughed. 'Tinks, you're too much woman for him, either way. The guy's a prick. And Wyatt's a big asshole. They deserve each other.'

'Yeah, all that community service, helping people, working with victims . . . What a jerk.'

Kovac scowled darkly. 'All that publicity, all those promotions, all that Hollywood money. Ace Wyatt never did anything that didn't benefit Ace Wyatt.'

'He saved Mike Fallon's life.'

'And became a legend.'

'Yeah, I'm sure that was premeditated.'

Kovac made a face at the bad taste in his mouth.

'All right. He did one decent, selfless thing in his life,' he conceded as they pushed through the doors and were hit with cold air and exhaust. 'That doesn't mean he's not an asshole.'

'People are complex.'

'Yeah,' Kovac agreed. 'That's why I hate them. At least with a psychopath, you know where you stand.'

19

The shift had changed and Leonard had gone by the time they returned to the office, saving them from having to report their lack of success with Chamiqua Jones. Liska considered and discarded the idea of making phone calls from her desk. She couldn't shake the feeling that everyone around her was watching her, listening, straining to hear – all because the questions she needed to ask were about other cops.

She had always thought of herself as tough, able to take whatever the job dished out, but she would have preferred any kind of case to this, with the exception of a child killing. Nothing was worse than working a child's murder. As she gathered her stuff and left the office, she wondered what she would do if the road to advancement led through IA. Make another road.

The walk to the Haaff ramp was cold, the wind biting her cheeks and ears. The drive home wouldn't be much better. She hadn't been able to get an appointment with the glass replacement shop. Too bad the busted window diminished the chances of the car's being stolen. Her insurance would at least have paid for a loaner then.

The same fat attendant manned the booth. He recognized her and ducked his head, afraid to attract her attention. Liska rolled her eyes and felt in her pocket for the reassuring weight of her ASP. She had briefly considered parking elsewhere, but in the end had made herself go back to the scene of the crime. Climbing back on the horse – with an eye peeled for her perpetrator at the same time. If she was lucky, she could conquer her fear and make a collar all in one fell swoop, though it seemed unlikely her mystery man would still be hanging around. Unless he had chosen her specifically as his target.

Nothing stolen. Nothing disturbed but her mail . . .

Patrol had been instructed to take tours through the concrete maze of the ramp today. The show of a police presence in the form of the occasional radio car was meant to scare off the vagrants, who all had likely moved across the street to piss in the corners of the Gateway Municipal ramp and try all the car doors there in search of spare change.

The Saturn sat a third of the way down a mostly empty row, parked nose out. The plastic window was still intact. No one had broken any of the others. Liska walked past it, checking, scanning the area. This level of the ramp was quiet, half deserted. She went back to her car and let herself in. She locked the doors, started the engine and the heater, and dug her cell phone out of her purse. She punched in the number for the gay and lesbian officers' liaison and stared at the CHECK ENGINE light glowing red on her dash as the phone rang on the other end.

Rotten car. She was going to have to think about trading. Maybe in January, provided her finances survived Christmas. Maybe bite the bullet and trade up to an SUV. The extra room would be good for hauling the boys with their buddies and all their hockey gear. If she could squeeze Speed for the money he owed her . . .

'Hello?'

'Is this David Dungen?'

'Yes, it is.'

'David, this is Sergeant Liska, homicide. If this is a good time for you, I have a couple of questions you might be able to help me with.'

A cautious pause. 'Regarding what?'

'Eric Curtis.'

'About the murder? That case is closed.'

'I realize that. I'm looking into a related matter.'

'Have you spoken with Internal Affairs?'

'You know how they are. They don't want to untie the nice, neat bow, and they're not inclined to share anyway.'

'There's a reason for that,' Dungen said. 'These matters are sensitive. I can't just volunteer information to anyone who asks.'

'I'm not just anyone. I'm homicide. I'm not asking because I have some kind of morbid curiosity.'

'This has something to do with another case?'

'I'll be honest with you, David.' Use the first name. You're my pal. You can tell me anything. 'It's a fishing expedition at this point. If I get something I can take to my lieutenant . . .'

Dungen said nothing for a moment, then finally, 'I'll need to take your badge number.'

'I'll give it to you, but I don't want any paperwork on this. You understand?'

Again the pregnant pause. 'Why is that?'

'Because some people would sooner let sleeping dogs lie, if you know what I mean. I'm checking out some things regarding Curtis because someone asked me personally. I don't know that anything will come of it. I can't go to my boss with hunches and funny feelings. I need something real.'

He was silent for so long this time, Liska began to think she'd lost the connection.

'What's your number?' he asked at last.

Liska breathed deeply, silently letting go a sigh of relief. The smell of exhaust was strong. She cracked the window but left the engine running. It was too damn cold to shut it off. She gave Dungen her shield number, along with her phone number, and hoped to God he wouldn't call Leonard to check it out.

'All right,' he said, satisfied. 'What would you like to know?'

'I know Curtis had complained to IA he was being

harassed by someone on the job. What do you know about that?'

'I know he'd gotten some hate letters. In the ransom-note style with letters cut out of magazines. "All faggots must die. That's why God invented AIDS." That was the gist of it. The usual homophobic vitriol with bad grammar and bad spelling.'

'Had to be a cop,' Liska said dryly.

'Oh, it was a cop. No question. Two of the letters were slipped into his locker. One was found in his car after his shift. The mailman smashed out the passenger's window to deliver it.'

Liska looked to her blue plastic window, a chill running through her. 'Did he have any idea who it was?'

'He said no. He'd ended a relationship several months prior, but he swore it wasn't the ex.'

'And the ex was someone in the department?'

'Yes, but the boyfriend wasn't out. That's one of the reasons he was an ex. Curtis wanted him to be honest about who he was.'

'Curtis was out.'

'Yes, but in a quiet way. He wasn't some flaming militant. He was just tired of living a lie. He wanted the world to be a place where people could be who they are without having to fear for their lives. Ironic that he was killed by a gay man.'

'Do you know who the ex was?'

'No. I know Curtis had changed patrol partners a couple of times, but that doesn't necessarily mean anything. He didn't suspect any of them. At any rate, it wasn't my business. I'm not an investigator. My business was to lodge his complaint and work as a liaison with Internal Affairs and with his supervisor.'

'Do you remember the names of his patrol partners?'

'He was riding with a guy named Ben Engle at the time. As for the others, I don't remember off the top of my head.

He had no complaints with Engle. They seemed to get along well.'

'When he was found murdered, did you think it was the person who had sent the letters?'

'Well, yes, of course that was my first fear. It was terrible. I mean, we – that is to say, gay officers – we've all experienced harassment and prejudice to one degree or another. There are plenty of guys on the job with small brains and thick red necks. That whole weightlifting crowd comes readily to mind. But murder would have taken everything to a whole new, very ugly level. It was frightening to think. But that's not how it turned out, thank God.'

'You believe Curtis was killed by Renaldo Verma?'

'Yes. Don't you?'

'Some people aren't convinced.'

'Ah . . .' he said as if the lightbulb of awareness had just gone on. 'You've been talking to Ken Ibsen.'

The name meant nothing to her, but Liska put it to Neon Man's face. Dungen took her silence for agreement.

'There hasn't been a bigger conspiracy theorist since Oliver Stone,' he said.

'You think he's a kook?'

'I think he's a drama queen. He doesn't get enough stage time at the club he works. He has a history of filing lawsuits for sex discrimination and sexual harassment. He knew Eric Curtis – or claims to have known him – and so that gave him a reason to draw a bead on the department. And now he's come to you because Internal Affairs got tired of listening to his theories,' Dungen added.

'Actually, he came to me because the Internal Affairs officer he was working with was found dead.'

'Andy Fallon. Yes. That was too bad.'

'Did you know Fallon?'

'I spoke with him regarding his investigation. I didn't know him personally.'

'He was gay.'

'It's not a club, Sergeant. We don't all play together,' Dungen said. 'I suppose Mr Ibsen has found a way to incorporate Fallon's death into his latest theory. It's all a part of the larger conspiracy to cover up the menace of AIDS in the police department.'

'Curtis had AIDS?'

'He was HIV-positive. You didn't know that?'

'I'm new to the game. I've got some catching up to do,' Liska said, a part of her brain already reconfiguring the playing field, taking this new bomb into consideration. 'He was HIV-positive and he was still working the streets?'

'He hadn't told his supervisor. He came to me first. He was afraid he'd lose his job. I told him that couldn't happen. The department can't discriminate against an officer because of a medical condition. So says the Americans With Disabilities Act. Curtis would have been taken off the street and reassigned. Obviously, there's too great a risk – not the least of which is to the department in the form of potential lawsuits – having an HIV-positive officer on the street, having to deal with accident and injury situations, situations where the officer himself or herself might become injured and run the risk of infecting someone.'

'At the time he was being harassed, who else knew Curtis was HIV-positive? Would other uniforms have known?'

'To my knowledge, he hadn't told anyone. I told him he was obligated to inform everyone he'd been intimate with. I don't know if he did,' Dungen said. 'The killer couldn't have known. Who would be stupid enough to go after someone who was HIV-positive with a baseball bat?'

Liska could see the crime scene in her head. Blood everywhere, splattering the walls, the ceiling, lampshades; spraying everywhere as the killer struck Eric Curtis again and again with the baseball bat.

Who would knowingly expose himself to contact with contaminated blood?

Someone ignorant about the transmission of the disease or someone who didn't care. Someone arrogant enough to believe in his own immortality. Someone who was already infected.

'When was the last time Fallon spoke with you about the case?' she asked, rubbing a thumb against her right temple, where a headache was taking root. She buzzed her window back up, thinking it was letting in more fumes than oxygen. 'Recently?'

'No. The case was closed. The guy cut a deal. What's this about, Sergeant?' Dungen asked, suspicious. 'I thought Andy Fallon committed suicide.'

'Yeah,' Liska said. 'Just trying to find out why, that's all. Thank you for your time, David.'

One of the great tricks of interviewing people: know when to quit. Liska bailed on the phone call, and wondered again if it would come back around to bite her in the ass with Leonard. The idea made her feel nauseated. Or maybe that was the carbon monoxide, she thought, only half joking. She felt a little dizzy.

She turned off the engine and got out of the car, taking a big breath of cold air as she leaned against the roof of the Saturn.

'Sergeant Liska.'

The voice went through her like a blade. She turned abruptly to see Rubel twenty feet away. She hadn't heard the elevator, hadn't heard footfalls coming up the stairwell. It seemed as if he had simply materialized.

'I tried to catch you at your office,' he said. 'You'd already gone.'

'It's a little past the end of your shift, isn't it?'

He came steadily forward, looming larger and larger. Even without the mirrored shades he seemed to have no expression. 'Paperwork.'

'And you found me here . . . how?'

He gestured to a black Ford Explorer across and down from the Saturn. 'Coincidence.'

My ass, Liska thought. Of all the parking spots in all the parking ramps in downtown Minneapolis . . .

'Small world,' she said flatly. She leaned back against the car to offset the watery feeling in her legs, and slipped her hands into her coat pockets, curling her fingers around the handle of her ASP.

'What was it you wanted to talk to me about?' Rubel asked. He stopped just a few feet from her. A foot closer than she would have liked, which he probably knew.

'Like your pal B.O. didn't fill you in. Please.'

Rubel said nothing.

'You knew IA was looking at Ogden for fucking with evidence in the Curtis investigation –'

'That's over.'

'But you went to the investigator's house on a DB call anyway. Whose bright idea was that?'

'The call came over the radio. We were in the vicinity.'

'You're a regular magnet for coincidence.'

'We had no way of knowing the dead body was Fallon.'

'You knew it as soon as you got there. You should have hauled Ogden out of there. You seem to make a habit of saving his ass. Why didn't you do it when you got to Fallon's house?'

Rubel stared at her for a long, unnerving time. Liska's head pounded with the beat of her pulse. The nausea swirled in her stomach.

'If you suspect some impropriety on our part,' he said at last, 'why aren't you talking to IA about it?'

'Is that what you want me to do?'

'You won't because your case is closed. Fallon killed himself.'

'That doesn't mean it's over. It doesn't mean I won't still talk to your supervisor –'

'Go ahead.'

'How long have you been riding with Ogden?' Liska asked.

'Three months.'

'Who was he riding with before you?'

'Larry Porter. He left the department. Hired on with the Plymouth PD. You could get all this from our supervisor. If you wanted to talk to him.'

There was a hint of smugness in his tone, as if he knew she wouldn't go to his supervisor for fear it would get back to Leonard.

'You know, I'm trying to cut you a break here, Rubel,' she said irritably. 'I don't want bad blood with the uniforms. We need you guys. But we need you not to fuck up at a scene. A case can be made or broken on what happens at the scene. What if it turned out someone murdered Andy Fallon? You think a defense attorney isn't going to make us all look like assholes when he hears Ogden, of all people, was there stomping around?'

'You've made your point,' Rubel said calmly. 'It won't happen again.'

He started to walk away toward his truck.

'Your partner is a loose cannon, Rubel,' Liska said. 'If he has the kind of problems I think he has, you'd be smart to get yourself clear of that.'

Rubel looked at her over his shoulder. 'I know what I need to know, Sergeant.' He looked at her car and said, 'You'd better get that window fixed. I'd have to pull you over for that.'

Liska watched him walk away and get in his truck. Gooseflesh pebbled the skin of her arms and raised the fine hairs on the back of her neck. The Explorer started with a rumble, exhaust billowing out the tailpipe. He backed out and drove away, leaving her alone again.

She couldn't decide who was scarier: Ogden with his steroid-pumped temper, or Rubel with his eerie calm. What a pair they made.

Breathing deeply for the first time since Rubel had startled her, she moved away from the Saturn and made herself walk, hoping to shake off the weird weakness that trickled down the muscles of her arms and legs. She looked at her garbage-bag window and wondered if she was being paranoid reading into Rubel's crack about getting it fixed. He wouldn't have to break into her car to get her address off her junk mail. Cops had any number of ways to easily come by that information.

But then, someone might have broken the window for another reason. Out of anger. To frighten her. As a setup to cast suspicion regarding any future crime against her on someone like the old drunk who had tried to jump in the car with her. None of the options was good.

As she stared at the window, she slowly became aware of something hanging down from the back end of the Saturn. A chunk of grungy snow, she thought. Another reason to hate winter: the filthy snow boogers that built up behind the tires and would freeze to the density of granite if not quickly removed.

But as Liska went back to kick the thing off, she realized that wasn't what she'd seen at all. What had caught her eye wasn't hanging behind the tire. It was hanging from the tailpipe.

The nausea surged up her esophagus as she bent down. The pain in her temples intensified. Dizzy, she had to brace a hand against the trunk as she squatted behind the car.

A filthy white rag had been stuffed into the tailpipe.

A cold sweat misted her skin.

For all intents and purposes, someone had just tried to kill her.

The cell phone in her pocket began to bleat. Shaking, Liska rose and leaned against the car as she dug the thing out and answered it.

'Liska, homicide.'

'Sergeant Liska, we need to meet.'

The voice was familiar. She put a name to it this time: Ken Ibsen.

'Where and when?'

20

'Hey, Red, I have a couple of questions about autoerotic asphyxiation.'

Kate Conlan stared at Kovac. Rene Russo might be this good-looking on her best day, he thought. She combed an errant strand of hair behind her ear. A wry smile pulled up one corner of her sexy mouth.

'I'm so flattered you thought of me, Sam. Come on in,' she said, stepping back from the door. 'John and I were just talking about indulging in some weird sex games.'

'I didn't need to know that.'

'You rang the doorbell. Let me take your coat.'

He stepped into the entry hall, scrubbing his shoes on the mat. 'The house looks great.'

'Thanks. I'm liking it out here in the 'burbs. It's nice having space,' Kate said. 'And there's the added benefit that no one's tried to murder me here, or died a hideous death in the basement.'

She tossed that out as if she were saying it was great not to have carpenter ants. *Oh, those pesky serial killers.* The truth was that she had come too damn close to becoming a victim herself instead of an advocate for victims, which was her job. Kovac had been on the scene that day, along with John Quinn. Kovac ended up with smoke inhalation. Quinn ended up with the girl.

The story of my life.

'You're something, Red.'

'Follow me to the inner sanctum,' she said, leading the way down a wide hall with a polished wood floor and red oriental rugs. An enormous hairy cat sat on the hall table. It reached out and tapped Kovac with a paw as he started past.

'Hey, Thor.'

The cat made a sound like a squeaky toy, jumped to the floor with a thump, and dashed down the hall ahead of them with his huge plume tail straight up in the air.

They went into a den with lots of light-stained pinewood paneling and dark green paint on the walls. A Christmas tree stood near a set of French doors that led outside. A fire crackled in a fieldstone fireplace. A big yellow Lab puppy slept heavily on a pillow near the hearth. Thor the cat went to the puppy and stared at him with suspicion and disdain.

A pair of desks sat back-to-back on one side of the room, each fully equipped with computer, phone-fax machine, and the usual clerical clutter. John Quinn sat at one, intent on the computer screen.

'Look what the cat dragged in,' Kate said.

Quinn did, and grinned, pulling off a pair of reading glasses. 'Sam. Good to see you.'

'Don't be too thankful,' Kate said dryly. 'He wants to talk about his sex life. The joys of autoerotic adventures.'

Kovac blushed. 'I'm not *that* desperate.'

Quinn walked to him and shook his hand. Rugged and athletic, he looked younger now than when they had met during the Cremator case, more than a year past. There was an ease about Quinn he had not possessed then, and the haunted look was gone from the dark eyes. That was apparently what love and contentment could do for a person.

After the Cremator, Quinn had left the FBI, where he had been top gun among the mindhunters. Too many cases, too much death, too much stress had taken a toll on him. The Bureau had a history of running its best horses into the ground, and so they had done with Quinn – with Quinn's willing participation. But nearly losing Kate to a killer had been the wake-up call. Quinn had traded the Bureau for private consulting and teaching – and life with Kate. A sweet deal all the way around.

'Have a seat,' he offered, gesturing to a pair of fat couches in front of the fire. 'What are you working on, Sam?'

'An apparent suicide that was ruled an accident that might be something else.'

'The Internal Affairs guy?' Kate asked, handing Kovac a neat scotch. She sat down on the couch too close to Quinn, and put her stocking feet up on the coffee table.

'That's the animal.'

'He was found hanging, right?' Quinn asked. 'Was he nude?'

'Yes.'

'Any evidence of masturbatory activity?'

'No.'

'Fantasy, role-playing, bondage?'

'No, but there was a full-length mirror there so he could see his reflection,' Kovac said. 'Someone had written the word *Sorry* on the glass with a marker.'

Quinn's brow furrowed.

'Did he have any kind of protective padding positioned between the rope and his throat?' Kate asked. She herself had worked for the FBI in the old Behavioral Sciences unit – in a past life, as she said.

'No.'

Kate frowned. Quinn got up from the couch and went to a set of bookshelves on the far side of his desk.

'Most practitioners of autoerotic asphyxiophilia – the more sophisticated and experienced ones – won't risk the rope leaving a mark on their throat,' Kate said. 'How would they explain it to coworkers, family members, friends, et cetera.'

Kovac reached into the breast pocket of his suit coat. 'I've got some of the Polaroids.'

He laid them out on the coffee table. Kate looked at them without reaction, sipping at a gin and tonic from time to time.

'Did you find any videotapes with sexual subject matter?'

Quinn asked, coming back to the couch with a couple of books and a videocassette.

'*Holiday Inn*,' Kovac said. 'I suppose some people could argue it's full of latent homosexual subtext or some such bullshit.'

'That's a little more subtle than I was thinking.' Quinn went to the television, punched on the VCR and the set, and loaded the tape.

'No porn – gay, straight, or otherwise. The vic was gay, by the way, if that matters.'

'It doesn't. There's no data suggesting this paraphilia is more a gay hobby than a straight one,' Quinn said. 'The reason I asked about videotapes is that a lot of people who indulge in this kind of thing will videotape themselves, so they can relive the fun later on.'

He came back to the couch, settled in next to Kate, and hit the play button on the remote. Kovac leaned forward with his forearms on his thighs and his eyes on the screen, studiously avoiding looking at Kate's hand, which settled casually on her husband's stomach.

The show that rolled across the screen was sordid and sad and pathetic. A man's home video of his own accidental death. A pudgy, balding guy with too much body hair, dressed in a black leather S and M harness. He set the stage carefully, checking the elaborate rigging of the rope, which hung in what looked to be a garage or storage shed. He had draped the background with white drop cloths and strategically placed a couple of female mannequins dressed in dominatrix garb. He spent three minutes taping a riding crop into the hand of one of his silent witnesses. INXS played in the background: 'Need You Tonight.'

When he was satisfied with the set, he walked to a full-length mirror and went through his own little play, complete with dialogue. He sentenced himself to punishment, pulled a black discipline mask over his head, and wrapped a long black silk scarf around his throat several times. Then he danced his way from the mirror toward his makeshift gallows, fondling himself, presenting himself to the mannequins. He mounted the step stool and put the noose around his neck. He stroked his erection and eased one foot and then the other off the step.

His toes were just touching the floor, a position he couldn't maintain for long. The noose tightened. He didn't realize he was in trouble yet. He was still playing out the fantasy. Then he began to struggle with his balance. He extended one foot back to step onto the stool. The stool skidded backward and the noose tightened as he tried to reach behind and hook the thing with his foot. He let go of his penis to grab for his safety rope, but he had twisted to one side in an effort to catch the stool and he couldn't quite reach the rope.

And then it was too late. That fast. Seconds, and his dance became something from a horror movie.

'See how quickly it all goes wrong?' Quinn said. 'A couple seconds too long, a slight miscalculation – it's all over.'

'Jesus,' Kovac muttered. 'You don't want to accidentally return this one to Blockbuster.'

Though Kovac knew this was from Quinn's tape library. His specialty was sexual homicide.

They sat there and watched a man die the way other people would sit through their neighbor's vacation video. When the guy stopped kicking and his arms pulled up and went back down for the last time, Quinn clicked the tape off. From start to finish, the hanging had taken less than four minutes.

'There's not always this much ceremony involved,' Quinn said. 'But it's not uncommon. Not that any of this is *common*. Rough estimate, you're probably looking at a confirmed thousand autoerotic deaths in this country every year, with maybe two or three times that that are missed calls, labeled suicide or something else.'

'But those are just the people who miscalculate and don't escape whatever contraption they've devised,' Kate said. 'Who knows how many actually practice the paraphilia and don't screw up. You haven't found any family or friends who suggested he was into this kind of thing?'

'The brother says they used to play hangman when they were kids. You know, cowboy stuff, war games, like that. Nothing kinky. But what about that angle? Have you ever seen family members involved in this kind of thing together?'

'There's not much I haven't seen, Sam,' Quinn said. 'I haven't seen that, but it could certainly happen. I never say never, 'cause just when I think I can't be shocked, someone comes up with something worse than I ever imagined. What's your read on the brother?'

'He's a redneck type. I don't make him for kinky sex, but I could be wrong. There was a lot of resentment for the younger brother.'

'What about friends?' Kate asked.

'The best friend says no, Fallon wasn't into kink, but the best friend is hiding something.'

'The best friend – a man or a woman?' Kate asked.

'Male, allegedly straight, engaged to someone prominent. The vic, like I said, was gay. He'd just come out to his family.'

'You think they might have been partners,' Quinn said.

'I think they could have been. That might explain the word on the mirror. Things got out of hand, went wrong, the friend panicked . . .'

Kate shook her head as she studied the Polaroids. 'I don't see this as a game. I still say he would have taken some precautions with his neck. It looks more like suicide.'

'Then why the mirror?' Quinn challenged.

'Self-humiliation.'

While they argued over details Kovac had wrestled with again and again, he flipped through the books Quinn had brought out: The *DSM-IV*, *Abnormal Psychology and Modern Life*, *The Handbook of Forensic Sexology*, *Autoerotic Fatalities*. A little light reading. He had already studied the photographs in the 'Modes of Death' chapter of *Practical Homicide Investigation*, which showed photo after photo of one dumb schmuck after another, dead in some elaborate invention of ropes and pulleys and vacuum cleaner hoses and plastic garbage bags – contraptions designed for bigger, better orgasms. Floaters on the shallow end of the gene pool. People surrounded with bizarre sex toys and sick pornography. People living in crappy basement apartments with no windows. Losers.

'He doesn't seem to fit in with this crowd,' Kovac said.

'You never see Rockefellers and Kennedys in these books,' Kate said. 'That doesn't mean they can't be just as sick or worse. It just means they're rich.'

Quinn agreed. 'The studies show this behavior crosses all socioeconomic lines. But you're right too, Sam. The scene strikes me as being wrong for AEA. It's too neat and tidy. And the absence of sexual paraphernalia . . . The scene we're looking at doesn't fit. Any reason to believe it's not suicide?'

'Motives and suspects coming out my ears.'

'Murder by hanging is rare,' Quinn said. 'And damn hard to pull off without leaving tracks. Any defense wounds on the hands or arms?'

'Nope.'

'Contusions to the head?'

'No. I don't have the full report on the autopsy, but the doc who cut him didn't mention anything to Liska about a head wound,' Kovac said. 'Toxicology is back. He'd had a drink and taken a prescription sleeping pill – not an overdose, just a couple of pills.'

'That's sounding like suicide.'

'But there's no trace of a prescription bottle anywhere in

his house. If he had a scrip, he didn't fill it at his usual pharmacy, nor was it written by his shrink.'

'He was seeing a psychiatrist?'

'Minor depression. He had a bottle of Zoloft in his medicine cabinet. I talked to the doc this afternoon.'

'Did the doctor consider him a candidate for suicide?' Kate asked.

'No, but he wasn't surprised either.'

'So you've got yourself a genuine whodunit,' Quinn said.

'Unfortunately, no one wants to hear about it. The case is closed. I'm hanging my ass out on a limb for a victim everyone wants buried. He'd be in the ground right now if it hadn't turned so fucking cold.'

He scooped the Polaroids up, returned them to his coat pocket, and pasted on a sorry smile for the couple sitting across from him. 'But, hey, what else have I got to do with my time? It's not like I have a life or anything.'

'I recommend getting one,' Quinn said, winking at Kate, who smiled at him with warmth and love.

Kovac stood up. 'All right. I'm out of here before the two of you embarrass yourselves.'

'I think we're embarrassing you, Sam,' Kate said, getting up from the couch.

'There's that too.'

Quinn and Kate saw him out together. His last image before the front door closed was the pair turning to walk back into their lovely home, each with an arm around the other. And damn if that didn't hurt, he thought as he started the car.

He hated admitting it, wished he could have lied to himself, but there it was: he'd been half in love with Kate Conlan for the better part of five years and had never done a damn thing about it. Because he wouldn't allow himself to try. Nothing ventured, nothing lost. What would a woman like her see in a guy like him?

He would never find out now. Facing that reality left a

hollow feeling in the deepest part of his soul. There was no escape from it, sitting there in the dark. He'd never felt more alone.

Unbidden, Amanda Savard's face came to mind. Beautiful, battered, haunted by something he couldn't even guess at. He wanted to tell himself she was just a part of the puzzle, that that was his entire interest in her. But there were no lies in him tonight. The truth was right there, just under the surface. He wanted her.

Night was wrapped closer to the earth here than in the city. Kate and Quinn's house was technically in Plymouth, but it was more in the country than in a suburb. The drive was off a secluded side road. There was a small lake practically in their backyard. Few lights, less traffic. No distractions to keep him from looking too closely at what he was feeling tonight as he sat in his car on the side of the road.

Maybe there was an advantage to having a neighbor who lit up his yard like a cheap Vegas hotel after all.

21

Ken Ibsen couldn't shake the feeling someone was watching him, but then, that was nothing new. Ever since the start of this mess, he'd felt as if some giant malevolent eye had hovered above him, tracking his every move. And the worst of it was, it all seemed for nothing on his part. He had done his best to be a conscientious citizen and a good friend, and all he'd gotten for his trouble was ridicule and harassment. Eric was just as dead. The wrong man was sitting in jail for his murder, and no one cared he hadn't done it – apparently, including the convict. The world had gone stark raving mad.

Andy Fallon had been the only one interested in getting to the truth of what had happened to Eric, and now Fallon was dead. Ken counted himself lucky to be alive. Maybe it wasn't such a terrible thing having people think he was a flaming conspiracy nut.

But Liska seemed genuinely interested in the truth.

So where the hell was she?

She had agreed to meet him at 10:30. After his first show. He was due back onstage at 11:30. He checked the delicate watch he wore over his white kid glove, and sighed out a delicate stream of cigarette smoke. 10:55. It was a cold five-minute walk in heels back to the club, and he would have to touch up his lipstick. . . .

He wished now he'd told her to meet him backstage, but he hadn't wanted certain extra ears listening in. And the parking lot behind *Boys Will Be Girls* did too brisk a business in clandestine trysts, even in this cold. He didn't want Liska hearing the guy in the next car getting a blowjob while Ken tried to tell her about the organized hatred of gays in the Minneapolis Police Department. Credibility was a major issue. Bad enough that he would be meeting her in full costume.

He hoped she would see past the makeup and mascara, but then, that was the problem with people, wasn't it? Judgments were most often based on face value and stereotypes. Most of the people in this coffeehouse would have looked at him sitting here dressed as a woman and decided he was a transvestite/transsexual, the terms being interchangeable to the average heterosexual. He was neither. They would have a neat package of preconceived ideas about the way he would walk, the way he would talk, his likes, dislikes, talents. Some of their ideas would be right, but most would not.

What he was was a gay man with an exceptional voice and a talent for mimicry. He was a serious actor working at a ridiculous job because it paid well. He liked to shoot pool and wear jeans. He owned a Weimaraner dog, which he never dressed up in costumes. He preferred steak over quiche, and he couldn't stand Bette Midler.

Most people are more than their stereotypes.

He sipped his coffee and crossed his legs, staring back at the older man who was watching him from across the room. Just to be a jerk, he pursed his lips and sent the old fart an air kiss.

Instead of feeling conspicuous dressed as Marilyn Monroe, he felt safe hidden beneath the platinum wig and behind the thick stage makeup. He had slipped into the coffeehouse the back way and taken a back corner table to avoid the notice of the other customers. There weren't many. It was too cold to bother to go out on a weeknight. That suited Ken's plan – a public place without much of the public present.

Now all he needed was Liska.

He sipped his coffee and watched the door.

Liska swore a blue streak under her breath as she idled at yet another red light. She was late. She was shaken. She was angry. Tonight of all nights she hadn't been able to find a sitter who could stay late. She'd spent an hour and a half on the phone, calling everyone she could think of while Kyle complained that she'd promised to help him with his math, and R.J. expressed his displeasure in her by covering the dining room table with action figures, then dramatically sweeping them onto the floor.

In the end she'd called Speed. Grudgingly. Hating it. There was nothing worse to her than having to rely on him openly for anything. Especially when it came to the boys. She was supposed to be self-reliant, *had to be* self-reliant, *was* self-reliant. But instead, she felt inadequate, and a failure, and a poor mother. It frustrated her no end that had the circumstances been reversed, Speed would have done exactly the same thing and never batted an eye. He wouldn't have even bothered to go through the endless calls to the sitters, and he wouldn't have felt inadequate.

A huge, hot ball of emotion wedged in her throat, and tears burned her eyes. She'd caught him on his cell phone at the gym with every other ironhead in the department, and he had whined about having his workout interrupted. Liska doubted he had cut it short or skipped his shower. It had taken him for-fucking-ever to get to the house. Asshole. Now she was late.

The light changed and she gunned the Saturn around a Cadillac, cut him off, and took the next right fast. She didn't know how long Ibsen would wait. Drama queen that he was, he was playing the skittish informant to the hilt, refusing to tell her his tale over the phone, insisting on a face-to-face. She wanted to believe he had something valid to tell her. But given the mood she was in, she was more inclined to believe he'd turn out to be everything Dungen had said, and she would have put herself through this evening and risked her career, only to be proved a big idiot.

Still, beneath the simmering cynicism, Liska believed she was poking at a live hornet's nest rather than a dead case, and Ken Ibsen – kook or no kook – was a part of that. If he would wait five minutes more, she might find out just what his role in the drama could be.

She wasn't coming. He'd said it in his mind every two minutes for the last ten. In between, he'd distracted himself by doodling on a napkin, drawing a caricature of himself in costume, writing random notes.

Maybe she didn't believe him. Maybe she had spoken with that viper David Dungen, and he had poisoned her mind against him. Dungen, the traitor. Dungen, the puppet of the department higher-ups. He was nothing but a shill, a warm gay body willing to fill the token post of liaison. The Minneapolis Police Department cared nothing for the concerns of its gay officers.

Of course, Ken didn't know this from firsthand experience, but he was certain of it nevertheless. Eric had alluded to as much. The liaison post had been created to pay lip service to gay issues. Therefore, the department hadn't *really* cared about the harassment Eric had suffered. Therefore, the department had fostered the environment of hatred that had led to Eric's death. *Therefore*, Ken wrote on his napkin, underlining the word, the department should be held accountable in a wrongful death suit.

If only the court would recognize his right to file the suit. He was no blood relation to Eric Curtis. They hadn't been married – same-sex marriage was (unconstitutionally, to his way of thinking) against the law. Therefore, the court would hear nothing from him.

Sure, it was fine for Neanderthal cops to bludgeon people for their private preferences, but allow caring individuals to express their love . . . Not that he and Eric had been in love. They had been friends. Well . . .

acquaintances, with the potential to be friends. Who knew what they might have become.

The bell above the coffeehouse door rang and Ken looked up from his doodling, hopeful, only to have his heart sink. The newest patron was a scruffy-looking guy in an old army fatigue jacket.

She wasn't coming.

Eleven-eighteen.

He put out his smoldering cigarette, stuffed the napkin he had written on into the pocket of his full-length faux leopard coat, and went out the back way.

Not that he liked going by way of the alleys. Drunks and drug addicts and the homeless traveled this maze of back routes, avoiding the cops. That was his reason as well. He'd been harassed by the police more than once for walking down the street in costume. Like any common street whore could do the kind of job he did. Idiots. And, naturally, they assumed any man in a blond wig and a dress was a prostitute. Then there was the fact that he hadn't exactly made a lot of friends among the patrol cops with his diligent pursuit of the truth in Eric's death.

It was awfully dark and creepy in this alley. The buildings created a sinister canyon of concrete. The darkness was broken only intermittently by weak bulbs over the back doors of dubious businesses. Every Dumpster, every empty box was a potential hiding place for a predator or a scavenger.

As if his thoughts had called up the devil, a shape suddenly loomed up at the end of a trash bin thirty feet down the alley. The end of a cigarette glowed red, an evil eye in the dark.

Ken's step faltered and he slipped on the rutted ice and had to catch himself against the side of a building. He swore as he felt a false nail tip give way. He would have to keep his gloves on for the next set. There wouldn't be any time to fix the fingernail. Damn Liska.

The figure down the alley didn't move. The business behind the specter was a tattoo parlor. The kind of place where the patrons got AIDS and hepatitis from dirty needles.

Ken dug around in the pocket of his coat for his pepper spray and kept walking, staying as far on the other side of the alley as possible. The club was two blocks away.

He held his breath with each step. He ran every day to stay in shape, and he was better than most women in the heels, but he didn't want to have to try sprinting in them.

He could feel the specter's gaze on him. He waited for the eyes to glow red, like a wolf's.

He drew even with the back door of the tattoo parlor, ready to bolt, hand sweating around the canister of pepper spray even in this cold. His heart seemed to be quivering in his chest behind the falsies.

God, he did not want to die in drag. In his mind's eye he could already see the crime scene photographs being passed around. He could hear the cops snickering. Maybe, if he wasn't killed tonight, he would go get a tattoo of his own: I Am Not A Transvestite.

The specter tossed the cigarette, the glowing ember an arc of light in the gloom, and lurched forward suddenly. Ken bolted. Hoarse laughter followed him as he slipped and skidded. His right ankle buckled beneath him and he fell, sprawling gracelessly. Pain hit him like so many hammers — both knees, one elbow, one hipbone, his chin. A cry wrenched out of him, sounding desperate and weak, dying against the brick and concrete.

He scrambled to get back on his feet, clawing at anything to pull himself up. He grabbed hold of the edge of a Dumpster and hauled himself up, slipping, banging against it. His nylons were ruined. He could feel cold and wet against bare skin. He heard stitching pop as his legs splayed and strained the seams of his dress.

He jerked his head around to look behind him. Still

laughing, the specter turned and went back into the tattoo parlor. *Asshole.*

Ken leaned against the Dumpster, breathing hard, the air feeling like dry ice rasping down his throat.

Damn Liska. He had half a mind to send her his dry cleaning bill.

Limping, he started down the alley again. One shoe was missing a heel, and his ankle felt sprained. He touched a hand to his mouth and chin, and brought it away; the white glove was smeared with blood and dirt. Damn. If he needed stitches, his boss was going to have a hissy fit. Two blocks was looking a lot farther than it had in the beginning of the evening. And with the repairs he was going to have to make, there was no way he was making the last set.

The end of the alley was near. There was no traffic on the side street. A single dark car sat parked along the near curb. He could see the trunk and no more. He thought nothing of it until just a split second before the large, dark shadow of a man fell across the mouth of the alley, when the cold wash of a horrible premonition swept over him.

I'm going to die tonight.

The trunk of the car opened, the light illuminating a face in a dark ski mask. The man reached into the trunk and came out with a tire iron.

Ken Ibsen stopped and stood still, the moment seeming both real and surreal. Then he turned slowly, thinking to go back the way he'd come, after all. The better part of valor. The lesser of evils. But there was no going back. And there was no lesser evil. Another dark, faceless figure blocked the escape route behind him. A hulking silhouette with something in its hand.

He could feel evil emanating from them as they closed the distance from either side. Fear hit him like a bolt of lightning, and he screamed and pulled the pepper spray from his pocket, fumbling with the trigger. The attacker with the tire iron made one quick move, and Ken's arm flung out to the side, broken and useless. The canister clattered to the ground like a piece of trash.

He thought to run as the iron hit the side of his knee, and bone shattered like glass.

He thought to cry out for help, and felt his jaw crumble and his teeth spill like Chiclets from his mouth.

He thought, *I don't want to die in drag,* and everything went black.

Liska slid the Saturn to the curb in a no-parking zone a quarter of a block from the coffeehouse Ibsen had chosen for their meet. She was way late. Damn Speed for taking so long.

The few customers sat in knots of two or three, scattered as far away from each other as possible, wrapped up in their own conversations. No one looked up as Liska came in. She went directly to the bar, where the only visible employee was engrossed in a textbook as thick as the Yellow Pages.

'What are you learning?' she asked as she pulled her badge out of her purse.

The bartender looked up at her through a pair of trendy glasses. He had soulful brown eyes and the kind of thin, elegant face painters attributed to Jesus Christ. 'I'm learning that my father is spending a lot of money to send me through school so I can learn to make a great cappuccino.' He glanced at her badge. 'Are you here to arrest me for impersonating a med student?'

'Naw. I was supposed to meet someone here a little while ago. Short, slim guy with platinum hair.'

The med student shook his head. 'Haven't seen anyone like that. There was a transvestite dressed as Marilyn Monroe. He seemed like he was waiting for someone, but he left. Not a blind date, I hope.'

'No. How long ago did Marilyn leave?'

'Ten, fifteen minutes. Went out the back way. He works down at *Boys Will Be Girls*. They come in between sets sometimes. Otherwise I wouldn't know anything about that,' he hurried to add.

'A transvestite,' Liska muttered to herself, turning away. 'This night just gets better and better.'

Her big informant went around dressed up as Marilyn Monroe. Preachers and bankers seldom ended up as informants to crimes, she reminded herself. And when they did, it was because they were secretly perverts or thieves.

And her mother wondered why she didn't date more.

She went down the hall, past the bathrooms, to the back door of the coffeehouse. Med Student followed like a puppy.

'Do you know anyone at the county morgue?' he asked. ''Cause the way things are going, I'm thinking pathology might be best for me. No malpractice.'

'Sure, I know people,' Liska said. 'It's not a bad job if you can stand the smell.'

She pushed the door open and looked out. The alley was dark and wet and filthy. There should have been some rats and ragged orphans to complete the picture, she thought, and just then noticed a scavenger bent over something thirty feet down the way. He stood in a little puddle of light coming from over the back door of some other business. He started and stared back at her, like a coyote caught going through the garbage – wanting to run, but loath to give up the treasure. He moved just enough to allow the pale light to fall on his find, and the details of the scene began to register in Liska's brain: a woman's shoe, a bare leg, a glimpse of pale hair.

'Hey, you!' she shouted, drawing her weapon, moving so that the Dumpster gave her cover. 'Police! Step away from the body!'

'Call nine-one-one,' she said to Med Student. 'Request police and an ambulance. Tell them there's been an assault. Hurry.'

Coyote bolted. Liska was in gear instantly, running,

shouting, leading with her weapon, wondering if he had a gun, if he would turn and use it. He tripped and staggered, lost precious seconds trying to get his feet back under him. Liska hit him running and rode him down to the ground, driving her knee into his back, grabbing a handful of coat collar and greasy hair in her left hand as she put her weapon on him with her right.

'You're under arrest, motherfucker! Don't move!'

'I didn't do nothing!'

The smell of cheap bourbon and diarrhea wafted from him in a noxious cloud. He tried to rise up and Liska banged him hard on the back of his skull with the butt of her Sig. 'I said don't move!'

'But I didn't do nothing!'

'If I had a dollar for every talking asshole who said that, I'd have a mansion and pool boy named Raoul.'

'Ask Beano! It was them other guys!'

'Shut up!'

Other guys.

She glanced back over her shoulder at the victim. She couldn't make out features, couldn't tell if the person was breathing. She cuffed Coyote's hands behind his back.

'Stay right here. Don't get up. Don't move.'

'But I didn't do it,' he whined.

'Say that again and I'll fucking shoot you. *Shut up!*'

He started to cry as she turned away and went back to the victim.

'Ma'am, are you all right?' she asked. A stupid question meant simply to elicit a response. A moan, a groan, something, anything.

She squatted down beside the body and reached under the matted mess of white-blond hair to try to find a pulse in the throat. At first, she thought what she was looking at was the back of the skull – a bloody mess of caved-in bone without features. Then the victim drew a shallow, shuddering breath; a horrible, wet, sucking sound; and she saw bubbles in the blood coming from what must have been a mouth.

'Oh, Jesus,' she whispered, finding the weak, thready pulse with shaking fingertips. With her other hand, she carefully brushed the hair back. It was a wig, and it pulled free with little pressure, revealing short platinum hair streaked with blood leaking from a skull fracture. Ken Ibsen.

He lay on the ground like a discarded rag doll, limbs bent at odd angles. In one hand he clutched a scrap of paper – a napkin. Liska slipped it from his twitching fingers and held it so that the faint light fell across it. Doodling. Probably what he'd done while he'd waited for her to show up. Random words and little drawings. One phrase caught her eye: *wrongful death*.

Med Student ran up, panting. 'They're on the way.'

Even as he said it, a siren sounded not too far in the distance.

'I brought a flashlight,' he said, and directed the beam on the face of the victim.

The flashlight hit the ground and bounced. Med Student turned and vomited, and began to reconsider medicine as a career.

242

22

She felt him behind her before she looked. Awareness rose inside her like a floodtide, lapping at the back of her throat, threatening to spill out of her mouth in a scream. Fear stiffened the muscles of her back, making it difficult to turn around. She felt as if she were wearing a straitjacket.

He stood in the shadows of the living room, the moonlight coming through the windows making his form clear, yet she couldn't make out his features at all. He didn't speak. He didn't move as long as she watched him. She wondered if he thought he could make himself invisible by being still. She had thought that when she was a child: *If I can be still, they won't see me.*

Conversely, she wondered whether if she pretended not to see him, he might disappear.

She walked away, trying not to hurry, and went into the dining room. She didn't hear him follow. She should have heard his shoes on the hardwood floor, but she heard nothing. Still, when she looked over her shoulder, he was there. He stood in the shadows of the hall, looking in.

She held her breath until it felt as if someone was strangling her. Then she realized with a jolt of raw panic that someone *was*. His large hands closed around her throat from behind, fingers pressing against the small, vital bones. She clawed at his hands and tried to jerk free. He pulled her back against him and tried to push her down to the floor. Adrenaline surged through her, and she broke his grip suddenly, gasping air into her lungs. She looked over her shoulder then, as she started to run, and saw him clearly: Andy Fallon, his face purple and bloated, eyes dull, tongue coming out of his mouth.

And then she was awake. She had leapt up off the couch, becoming conscious as her feet hit the floor. She stumbled, crashing into the antique steamer trunk that served as a coffee table. She clawed at her throat, scratching herself as her fingers tore at the high zippered neck of the sweater she wore. The soft cotton sweater she had put on because it made her feel cocooned and safe. She had sweat through it.

The tears came then, as she realized what had happened, as she thought of how many times she had gone through this, and wondered if it would ever end. She sank down to the floor on her knees and started to put her face in her hands, gasping as she touched the raw spots.

She was so tired. Physically, mentally, emotionally. Tired from the lack of sleep, and from the stress, and from the nightmares, and the guilt. God, all of it.

For just a moment, she wondered what it might be like to have someone there to hold her up as she shouldered the burdens of her life. Foolish fantasy. She was meant to be alone whether or not that was what she wanted. That was the thing about fate: it didn't ask for your opinion, didn't consider what you might want or need. And so she sat alone in the night, shaking from the strain and from the sweat now chilling on her skin. Trying not to cry because there was no point in it. Crying was just a waste of energy she couldn't afford – one of the few useful lessons her father had taught her.

She closed her eyes and started the breathing exercise to slow her heart rate and calm her nerves. Unbidden came the memory of a strong hand on her shoulder, solid strength beside her. She could see Sam Kovac's dark eyes looking at her reflection in the ladies' room mirror. She could feel his concern, hear it in his voice. For just a second she let herself imagine what it might have been like to turn toward him and rest her head on his chest, and have him put his arms around her.

Kovac was a rock, an anchor. He seemed so grounded,

she doubted anything could knock him off balance. Not that she would ever find out. He was the last man she would allow to see inside her and try to tame the snakes in her head. She was destined to fight them alone, and she would. She had done so for a very long time. It was just that tonight . . . tonight she felt so tired, and so alone. . . .

She breathed a sigh and forced herself to her feet. She made the obligatory search of the downstairs rooms, walking through the silent house like a zombie, not really seeing anything, dimly aware that she was searching for something that couldn't be seen. She ended the search back in the living room, standing for a long time just staring at the wall of photographs she had taken over the years. Black-and-white, landscapes and still lifes. Beautiful, empty, bleak, stark. A projection of the photographer's inner self, a therapist would say.

Time slipped by unnoticed. She might have been standing there five minutes or an hour when the doorbell rang. The sound startled her so, she wondered if she had gone back under into that place of waking dreams and was now being shocked back out of it, or if this was part of the next nightmare and she wasn't really awake at all.

The bell rang again. Heart pounding, she went to the door and looked out through the peephole. Kovac stood on her front step. Not sure that her mind hadn't conjured the image, she pulled the door open.

'Your lights were on,' he said by way of explanation for being there.

Savard stared at him.

'I assumed you were up,' he said. 'Was I wrong about that?'

She touched her hair self-consciously, started to shield the wound around her eye, but stopped. She glanced down to see that she was actually wearing clothes. 'I . . . ah . . . fell asleep on the couch.'

'I'm sorry, then, if I got you up.'

'What do you want, Sergeant?'

He shifted from foot to foot, his hands in his coat pockets, his shoulders hunched. 'Getting in out of this cold would be a good start.'

Hugging herself against the night air, Savard went back into the hall, leaving him to follow. She checked her reflection in the mirror above the hall table and was appalled. Dark circles, pale skin, hair limp and messy. She looked battered and lost. Haunted. She would rather he *had* caught her naked, at least then he wouldn't have been paying enough attention to her face to wonder at her mental state.

'I'm not keeping you from anything – like a significant other?' he asked bluntly.

Not unless inner demons count, she thought. 'What are you doing here?'

'I was in the neighborhood.'

She caught his reflection in the mirror. He was looking at her, studying her, and she jerked around, the pain in her neck and shoulder making her wince. 'Plymouth is out of your jurisdiction.'

'I'm off duty. I have friends out here. John Quinn. You know him?'

'I know of him.'

'I had a couple of questions for him regarding your boy Andy. I'm still not convinced he died alone or by choice. Could have been an accident,' he conceded. 'But if it was an accident and he wasn't alone, then someone left the scene of a death, and I'd wanna know who, 'cause they got something to answer for, you know?'

Savard smoothed one hand over the wrinkles sleep had pressed into her top. She couldn't quite keep her other hand from touching her hair again. She hated him seeing her like this. *Vulnerable* – the word pulsed in her brain like a nerve that had been struck with a hammer.

'What did Mr Quinn have to say?' She couldn't seem to

make herself look directly at him. As if he couldn't really see what a mess she was if they had no direct eye contact. *If I can be still, they won't see me. . . .*

'He had some thoughts,' Kovac said, moving to stay in front of her. 'I don't always take a lot of stock in that mindhunter stuff. You know, sometimes people do things just on account of they're rotten. Then again, sometimes a person's past can haunt him – or her – to the point of driving him to do things.'

'Profiling is a tool for hunting serial criminals,' Savard said. 'You're not dealing with a serial criminal. You're not dealing with a criminal at all.'

'The Fallon family might beg to differ, two of them being dead inside a week,' Kovac said. 'Anyway, as I was leaving his house, I remembered you, Lieutenant.'

'With regards to?'

'At the funeral, I forgot to ask if you'd looked up that case file. Fallon's investigation into the Curtis-Ogden thing.'

'Are you now going to try to tell me Ogden was Andy's secret gay lover, and that he's a potential serial killer? You're losing me, Sergeant.'

'I'm just trying to take in all the facts so I have as clear a picture as possible. I learned a long time ago, if an investigator gets tunnel vision on one aspect of a case, he runs the risk of missing crucial pieces of the puzzle. How can you know where everything fits if you can't see the big picture? So, did you look it up?'

She looked past the living room to her office, wanting to go in there and shut the door behind her. 'No. I didn't have a chance.'

Kovac moved into her line of vision again. 'Could we sit down? You look like you need to, Lieutenant. No offense.'

'Asking you to sit down would imply I don't mind you staying for an indefinite period of time,' Savard pointed out. 'I do mind.'

He shrugged off the insult. 'Then you sit. I'll stand. You look a little rocky.'

For the – what? – third time that day, he put his hands on her, and she allowed it. He guided her by the shoulders to the Windsor settee along the wall. She felt as small as a child, and fragile, and ineffectual. She could have just told him to leave, but there was that part of her that didn't want him to. Anger and frustration and shame coiled inside her with needs she rarely acknowledged having.

'You know, I looked for it at Andy's place,' Kovac said. 'I looked in his office there for a duplicate file on the Curtis–Ogden thing. I wanted to see what he was investigating, what his take on things might be, see if he'd been threatened, anything like that, anything that could give me some idea of his life, his state of mind. But there was no file, and his computer was gone. An IBM ThinkPad. You know anything about that? Did he leave it in his office downtown?'

'I don't know. I don't think so. Maybe he left it in his car. Maybe he'd lost it. Maybe it's in the shop. Maybe it had been stolen.'

'Maybe it was stolen by someone who didn't want something in it to be seen by someone like me.' He picked up a small carved Santa figurine from the hall table and studied it.

Savard sighed. 'I'll check the file in the morning. Is that all, Sergeant?'

'No.'

He set the figurine aside and came toward her, leaning down. He tipped her chin up and looked in her eyes. 'How are you feeling?'

I'm feeling my pulse in my throat. I'm feeling light-headed. I'm feeling vulnerable. God, there was that word again.

'I'm fine. I'm tired. I'd like to go to bed.'

He traced a forefinger slowly in front of her eyes, the

248

same as he had done in her office that morning. Across and back. Up and down. His left hand still cupped her chin.

'No offense, LT,' he said softly, 'but for a beautiful woman, you look like hell.'

Savard arched a brow. 'Gee, why would I take offense at that?'

He didn't answer her. He was looking at the rug burn, taking in the lines of her face . . . still touching her chin. . . . His gaze lingered on her mouth. Her breath caught in her throat.

'You are, you know,' he whispered. 'Beautiful.'

She turned her face away, the air shuddering from her lungs. 'You should go now, Sergeant.'

'I should,' he admitted. 'Before you see to it I get suspended for paying you a compliment. But I want one thing first.'

Scraping together what was left of her strength, Savard managed to put on the imperious mask that was her everyday game face. It didn't make Kovac back off an inch.

'Call me Sam,' he said, one corner of his mouth crooking upward. 'Just to hear how it sounds.'

I can't want this, she thought, fear tightening in a knot in her stomach. *I can't want him. I can't need him.*

'You should go now . . . Sergeant Kovac.'

He did nothing for a moment, and she held her breath and tried without success to read his mind. Finally, his hand dropped away from her face. He stepped back and straightened.

'Call me,' he said. 'If you come up with anything from that case file.'

She rose to her feet, feeling unsteady, and banded her arms across her chest. Kovac paused at the door.

'Goodnight . . . Amanda.' He shrugged, the slight smile still pulling at his lips. 'What's another suspension to an old horse like me?'

Cold air rushed into the hall as he let himself out. Savard

locked the door behind him and leaned against it, thinking of the warmth of his fingers against her skin. Tears stung her eyes.

She climbed the stairs slowly. The table lamp was already on in her bedroom, and would remain on all night. She changed into a nightgown and crawled into bed, took a drink from the glass on the nightstand, and washed down a sleeping pill. Then she lay down carefully on her left side, hugging the spare pillow to her, and waited for sleep, eyes wide open, feeling so alone it was an ache in the very center of her being.

Goodnight . . . Sam. . . .

23

Liska wished it was all a nightmare. All of it: that her informant was a transvestite in a coma, that she'd spent half the night freezing to the bone in a filthy alley, that Speed's car was in her drive and he was in the house, waiting.

She parked at the curb, trying to remember the snow emergency rules, fatalistically certain her car would be mowed down by a city snowplow and she would be fined, to add insult to injury. *Screw it*, she thought, climbing out of the car and trudging to the front door. At least she'd collect insurance and get a new vehicle. A used Chevette, perhaps, considering where her career would be headed in the near future.

The table lamp was on low and the television was showing an infomercial for Tae-Bo. Billy Blanks offering self-esteem and spiritual enlightenment through kickboxing. Speed and R.J. were asleep, side by side, in the recliner, unmistakably father and son. Their hair even stood up in the same places. R.J. was in Spiderman pajamas with feet. The Cartman hand puppet was tucked under one arm.

Liska stood looking at them, hating the emotions the sight awakened in her. Longing, regret, need. How unfair to be hit with that tonight, on the heels of everything else that had happened. She pressed a hand to her mouth and fought the feelings as if they were demons.

Damn you. She didn't know if she had spoken the words or just thought them, didn't know if she was cursing her ex-husband or herself.

Speed cracked an eye open and looked at her, then checked his son. Slowly and carefully, he eased himself from the chair and covered R.J. with a throw from the couch.

'Is it that bad?' he asked softly as he came toward her.

He was asking about the moment, about the way she was looking at him, the way she felt about him being here. But taking a page from his book, Liska chose to interpret the question the way she wanted, and applied it to the case. 'My drag queen informant is lying in ICU with a face only Picasso could love. According to two witnesses – one of whom was caught trying to steal valuables off the guy's body – he was attacked by ninjas with lead pipes.'

'Ninjas don't use lead pipes. Nunchuks, maybe.'

'Please don't be cute, Speed. I can't deal with it right now.'

'I thought you liked me cute. It's one of my better qualities.'

Liska just looked away.

'Hey, come on. It can't be all that bad, you're still standing.'

'It's worse than bad,' she whispered.

'You want to talk about it?'

Translation: Do you want to lean on me, confide in me, let me help carry the load?

Yes, but I won't let myself.

'Nikki,' he murmured, stepping too close. He touched her cheek with a warm hand, slid his fingers back through her short hair, and gathered her to him with his other arm. 'You don't always have to be the tough one.'

'Yes, I do.'

'You don't tonight,' he murmured, his lips brushing her temple.

A shudder rippled through her as she fought the urge to melt against him, to let him hold her up.

'What's the worst part of it?' he asked.

Knowing you'll let me down in the end. Fearing that maybe I'm wrong and you wouldn't, but I won't give you the chance to prove it because I'm tired of you hurting me.

She sniffed back tears and said, 'Thinking he ended up that way because I wasn't there in time.'

'The guy's a snitch, Nik. He got beat up because of that, not because of you.'

'But if I had been there –'

'He would have got it some other time.'

'I don't know if he'll live. I don't know if he'll want to,' she said. 'You should have seen what they did to him, Speed. It was horrible.'

'Don't do that to yourself, Nikki. You know better.'

A cop learned early on not to allow that kind of emotion. The road to madness was paved with guilt. Kovac had reminded her of the same when she had called him from the scene with news of Ibsen's assault. Still, it was hard not to place the blame at her own feet. Ibsen had been there waiting for her.

'They must have shattered every bone in his face,' she said. 'Broke his arm, his collarbone, ribs, one knee. They assaulted him anally with a pipe.'

'Jesus.'

She took a deep breath and made the confession that lay at the heart of it for her: 'And the worst part of it is, I think they were cops.'

Speed went still. She could feel his heart beat beneath her hand. 'God, Nikki, what are you into? Looking at other cops . . .'

'I don't want it to be true,' she said. 'I don't want any part of it. We're supposed to be the good guys. I don't want to be the one to prove otherwise.'

The idea was so abhorrent to her, it felt like a virus in her blood, and she shuddered against the intrusion. Speed tightened his arms around her. She allowed it. Because it was the middle of the night, and she felt very alone. Because it would be only for a moment. Because the feel and the smell of him were familiar. Because when he left, she would have to carry all the weight herself.

'I hate it,' she whispered, knowing she meant more than the case. That she hated feeling needy, that she hated always having to be tough, that she hated the contradictions, that she hated the tears that were burning her eyes and the conflicts she felt at being in the arms of her ex-husband.

'Why do you think they were cops?' he asked as softly as a lover whispering endearments.

'That's why he was meeting me – to talk about a rotten cop.'

'Maybe it was a random hate crime. Drag queens are unpopular in certain circles.'

She pulled away and gave him a look. 'Yeah, I believe in that kind of coincidence, and in Santa Claus and the Easter Bunny.'

She walked away from him to rearrange the blanket over her son, then went to the television and turned it off.

'Is this still about the dead IA guy?' Speed asked.

'Partly.' She almost laughed. 'It's about a closed murder with a convicted killer, and a closed suicide–slash–accident. Strange that someone should be beaten nearly to death over that, don't you think?'

'Who are you looking at?'

'A uniform. No one you know,' she said, then turned and looked at him with the scrutiny of a cop. He was in his stocking feet, in jeans that hung low on a flat belly, and a T-shirt that showed off an enviable physique. The cop in her resurfaced. 'Or maybe you do. You look like you've been pumping some iron lately. This guy's a serious lifter.'

'Does he come to the St Paul station house to do it?'

'You're working out at the station like a common cop?'

'It's free. I have enough obligations for my paycheck.'

'Can't imagine what they are,' Liska muttered. 'I never see any evidence of it.'

Speed opened his mouth to fire a retort, but Liska held up a hand to fend him off. R.J. was right there. Asleep, but who was to say how deeply or what sounds might penetrate his subconscious. She tried not to fight with Speed in front of the boys. She failed a lot, but she tried.

'Sorry,' she said. 'That was out of bounds. The fuse is a little short tonight, you know. What I meant to say was, I know a lot of the cops from both departments lift at that gym on University – Steele's. I thought you might have seen this guy there.'

He just stood there for a moment, working up his hurt feelings. She could see it in his face. R.J. did the same thing when he felt he'd been wronged. She could see him mentally reliving each slight, each sharp remark in order to reinforce his sense of affront.

'I said I'm sorry,' she reminded him.

'You know, I'm trying here, Nikki,' he said, the wounded martyr. 'I'm trying to help when I can with the boys. I told you I'd come up with some cash soon –'

'I know –'

'But you just have to keep at it with the digs, don't you? Why is that, Nikki? Is it that you really hate me that much? Or is it because maybe you're afraid you still have feelings for me?'

Bull's-eye, she thought. 'It's just habit.'

'Break it,' he said softly, his eyes locked on hers. He went to her, lifted a hand, and touched her cheek. 'I care about you, Nikki. I'm not afraid to say it, even if you are.'

He bent his head and touched his lips to hers, a soft kiss that lingered but didn't press for more. Liska's heart seemed to press up against the base of her throat.

'Be careful, Nikki,' he said as he stepped back.

Of the case or of you? she wanted to ask. Then she thought, *Both.*

'You make serious enemies when you turn on your own kind.'

'If this guy is what I think he is, he's not "my kind." '

That was how she had to look at it, she thought, as Speed went to the front entry, stepped into his hiking boots, and pulled on his coat. If Ogden was a killer, if he was the kind of animal who could beat a man, rape a man with a piece of pipe, then the fact that he carried a badge was the worst kind of offense.

'What do you have on him? Anything solid?'

She shook her head. 'Hunches, feelings. This drag queen was supposed to have something to fill me in. I think the cop's a juicer. If nothing else, maybe I can give him to the narcs,' she said, giving him a lopsided excuse for a smile as she went to the door.

'If the guy's doing steroids, his temper will be unpredictable,' he said. 'He's dangerous.'

'That's not exactly news to me. Anyway, thanks for watching the boys. And thanks for caring.'

'Thanks isn't what I'm after,' he said, catching her off guard. She barely had time to register the look in his eyes before his arms were around her and his mouth was on hers. Not soft this time. Hot, hungry, demanding. Her lips felt bruised when he pulled away.

He was out the door the next moment. She listened to the slam of a car door, the growl of a motor turning over. Only then did she touch two fingers to her lips.

'I need this like I need the plague,' she muttered.

She put a second throw over R.J., choosing not to disrupt his sleep, left the light on low, and went to bed herself, with no real hopes of sleep or dreams.

The clock was glowing 3:19 when the phone rang.

'Hello?'

The silence on the other end had the quality of a held breath. Or maybe the held breath was hers.

And then came a whisper that raised all the fine hairs on her arms. 'Let sleeping dogs lie.'

24

The photographs are lying on a narrow worktable, a cone
of yellow light shining down on them from the desk lamp.
The room is otherwise in darkness. The room is silent.

The photographs are in a neat row. Life exploding.
Blood spray. Bone splinters. Still life. Lifeless. A study in
destruction. A testimony to the fragility of the human body.
Abstract. Violent. Sad and pathetic.

Too easily accomplished.

A necessary evil, but still . . . it should have been
impossible. The concept should have so gone against the
moral grain that execution would simply not have been
possible.

Execution.

The word brings a rush of remembered emotions.
Regret, loathing, relief, excitement. Fear. Fear of what had
been done, of the rush of excitement in that final instant.
Fear that something human, something civilized, something
vulnerable could be replaced . . . or had been replaced long
ago.

But then if that were true, sleep would have come easily
instead of not at all.

25

Observation: an autopsy is not a good way to begin the day.

The thought rolled around in Kovac's head as he settled into his desk chair, a cup of bad coffee in hand. Liska was nowhere to be seen. The office was momentarily quiet. He had managed to slip in more or less unnoticed, and was glad for it. He needed a few minutes to reflect, to regroup. He pulled out Mike Fallon's death-scene Polaroids and spread them out on top of the paperwork he had been neglecting the last few days.

A nagging unease moved around the edges of his awareness, undefined, barely formed, a shadow. He could have called the case a slam-dunk suicide, and it would have been over, pending the paperwork from the ME. Except for that feeling, and the fact that Neil Fallon was starting to show as many rotten layers as a bad onion.

Kovac let his gaze wash over the pictures almost without focusing, hoping to see something he'd been missing. At the same time, hoping he would see nothing. The idea that Iron Mike had chosen to check himself out was definitely preferable to the alternative.

Viewed that way, he could almost think of the photographs as abstract art instead of pictures of a man he had known for twenty years. It was certainly easier to look at the pictures than it had been to stand in on the autopsy and see a personal acquaintance sliced and diced.

Maggie Stone, the Hennepin County ME, had performed the autopsy herself. Despite such eccentricities as carrying concealed weapons and changing hair color every six months, Stone was the best. When she said it was so, it was so. Kovac had known her for years. They had the kind of rapport that allowed him to ask for favors, such as standing in on an old friend's autopsy at the crack of dawn. Stone hadn't blinked an eye. To someone who spent her life cutting open the dead to extract their internal organs and their secrets, nothing much came as a shock.

And so Kovac had stood there in the autopsy suite, just out of the way as Stone and her assistant, Lars, moved around the stainless steel table, doing their thing. A hell of a way to kick off the morning.

Liska came into the cubicle looking grim, no color in her cheeks, despite the fact she had come in from outside, where the temperature was struggling toward the mid-teens. She said nothing as she put her purse in a drawer and slipped out of her coat.

'How's your snitch?'

'Looks like he'll live. Sort of. I just came from the hospital.'

'Is he conscious?'

'No. But he hasn't curled up like a fetus, so they're hopeful there's no serious brain injury. Broken bones will heal, and hey, who would mind having a colostomy, really?' she said sarcastically. 'And looking like the Elephant Man? A minor trade-off for not biting the big dirt sandwich.'

'You didn't do it to him, Tinks,' Kovac said evenly.

Liska didn't meet his eyes. 'I know. I'm dealing with it. I am. It's just that seeing him again . . .' She took a deep breath and let it go. 'If I had gotten there on time . . .'

'Feeling guilty won't change anything, kiddo. He made his own choices, and you did the best you could.'

She nodded. 'It's just frustrating, that's all. But I'll handle it.'

'I know you will. And you know I'm here when you need me.'

She looked at him with fondness and appreciation and a sheen of tears in her eyes. 'Thanks.'

'That's what partners do. We back each other up.'

'Don't make me cry, Kovac,' she said with a phony scowl. 'I'll have to hurt you.'

'Careful,' he warned. 'I might like it. I'm a lonely guy.' He paused. 'So, what's the word on the case? Are you in?'

'I have to talk to Leonard,' she said, and made a face. 'Ibsen was my informant. I was on the scene. I'm the one who got the call to leave it alone.'

'That call says dumb and dumber all over it. If it was a random assault, you never would have gotten a call after the fact.'

Liska agreed. 'Dumb as dirt. Now I've got something I can take to IA and use to get access to the files on the Curtis investigation. Why would anyone warn me off a closed case unless there was a damn good reason to open it back up?'

'Anything on the caller ID?'

'The number came back to a pay phone on the backside of nothing. So Deep Throat gets credit for having a couple of brain cells. I have no hope for witnesses of the call being placed.'

'And Ogden and Rubel – their alibi holds up?'

Liska made a sound of contempt. 'What alibi? They were shooting pool in Rubel's basement. And guess who was with them? Cal Springer.'

'That's cozy.'

'He'd probably swear they'd all been on the moon at the time if that was what the other two said, he's such a chickenshit. They must have pictures of him doing a goat,' Liska said with disgust. 'Anyway, Castleton was up for Ibsen's assault. He and the shift supervisor both said I'm welcome as second if Leonard clears it.'

'Leonard's gonna have your ass for digging around in IA business.'

Liska shrugged. 'Can I help it if the guy would only talk to me? According to what I've heard, the rest of the department had tuned him out. Nobody wanted to hear about his AIDS conspiracy theories.'

'Who has AIDS?'

'Eric Curtis was HIV-positive. Puts a new wrinkle into it, huh? What homophobe would beat a gay man to death and run the risk of coming into contact with contaminated blood?'

Kovac frowned, recalling his visit with the man credited with the Curtis homicide. 'Twenty says Verma has it.'

'But if Verma did it, then who's warning me off? He's in jail.'

They stared at each other for a moment, Kovac swiveling his chair.

'I still like Ogden for that,' he said.

'Me too. That's the way I'm playing it.'

'Be careful.'

She nodded. 'How'd Mike's autopsy go?'

'No big revelations so far. Nothing under his fingernails but dirt. He had some bruising on the back of his hands, but not conclusively defense wounds. The skin wasn't freshly broken, and we know he had taken a fall recently, which could explain any marks. For that matter, Stone couldn't swear the discoloration was genuine bruising. There was a lot of lividity in the hands because of the position of the body.'

'What about gunpowder residue?'

'Both hands. Doesn't mean somebody didn't force him to put the gun in his mouth, but we can't prove someone did either.'

'So we're nowhere with that,' Liska said. 'Stone will rule it a suicide.'

'She won't do anything till all the lab work comes back, and she promised me everything is backed up – to say nothing of the fact that paperwork regularly gets *mislaid*, if you know what I mean.'

Liska grinned. 'I think Doc Stone wouldn't mind getting *mislaid* by you, if you know what I mean.'

Kovac felt heat rise in his cheeks. In his mind's eye he flashed on Amanda Savard, not Maggie Stone. The look in her eyes when he'd cupped her chin in his hand: vulnerability. He forced a scowl. 'I'm not going to bed with any woman who dissects people for a living. Anyway, she'll buy us a little time, but we could do with a miracle about now. I also asked her to go back and look over Andy Fallon's autopsy. In case Upshaw doesn't know his ass.'

'Need a miracle?' Elwood asked, walking over to the cubicle. He wore a thick mohair sweater over a shirt and tie. It made him look like a woolly mammoth.

'I'd sell my soul,' Kovac said.

'That would be something of a contradiction, as miracles are associated with positive higher powers,' Elwood pointed out. 'You sell your soul to the devil.'

'You can give him my regards if you don't spill what you've got.'

'A neighbor saw Neil Fallon's truck parked in front of Mike's house late Wednesday night. One oh–nine, to be precise. I checked the reports on the neighbors the uniforms canvassed yesterday. They hit this house, but the owner was out. The cleaning lady answered the door. So I called, and bingo.'

Kovac vaulted up out of his chair.

'That's more like it.'

'They saw this truck pull up, but they didn't hear the gunshot?' Liska asked, dubious.

'An insomniac with hearing aids,' Elwood said. 'She's eighty-three. But she's sharp as a tack.'

'How's her eyesight?'

'Great with the Bausch and Lomb binoculars she keeps on her coffee table.'

'Light?'

'Floodlights on the corners of her home. She's a

neighborhood watch commander. She didn't recognize the truck, but she got the license number.'

'Would she like my job after Leonard fires me?'

'Did she see him leave?' Kovac asked.

'One thirty-two.'

'That's earlier than the estimated TOD, but I'll take it.'

Kovac scooped the Mike Fallon Polaroids into a drawer and, looking into his blank computer monitor, tried to straighten his tie.

'Have Neil Fallon picked up for questioning,' he said to Elwood. 'I'll break the news to Leonard.'

'What the hell is this about?' Neil Fallon demanded.

A pair of uniforms had pulled him out of his shop to bring him in. His filthy coveralls looked like the same ones he wore the day Kovac had told him about his brother. His hands were dark with dirt and grease.

'Jesus Christ, my brother and my father are dead and – and – you drag me down here like a fucking criminal!' Fallon ranted as he paced hard in the tight confines of the interview room. The same room where Jamal Jackson had cracked Kovac in the head. 'No explanation. No apology –'

'You *are* a fucking criminal,' Kovac said, matter-of-fact. 'We know about the assault conviction, Neil. Did you think we wouldn't check? Now, how about you give *me* an explanation and an apology?'

He stood with his arms crossed and his back against the wall beside the two-way mirror, watching Fallon's reaction. Liska stood opposite him, against the other wall. Elwood had the door. No one availed themselves of the chairs at the friendly little round table. The red light glowed on the video camera.

Fallon glared at him. 'That was a long time ago, and it was bullshit besides. It was an accident.'

'You accidentally beat some guy into a coma in a bar fight?' Liska said. 'How does that work?'

'There was a fight. He fell and hit his head.'

Kovac looked over at Elwood. 'Isn't that what Cain said about Abel?'

'I believe so.'

'How about you apologize for lying to me yesterday, Neil?' Kovac said. 'How about you explain to me what you were doing at your father's house at one A.M. the same morning he died?'

Fallon ran out of gas abruptly. He tried to hold on to some of the anger in his expression. Beneath it was a layer of confusion, then suspicion, then fear. 'What are you talking about? I-I don't know what you're talking about.'

'Save it,' Liska advised. 'A neighbor of your father's put your truck in his driveway at one A.M.'

'You told me yesterday the last time you spoke with him was on the phone that night.' Kovac paused.

Fallon's eyes darted around the room as if he might see an explanation somewhere.

'Why would you lie to me like that, Neil? Were you embarrassed you couldn't convince your old man to fork over the money you need to pay off your ex? If that's what you talked about in the twenty-three-minute phone call placed from your bar at eleven oh-seven P.M.'

Fallon sucked in a short breath and then another, like an asthmatic on the verge of an attack. He rubbed the side of his neck with his thick, filthy hand.

Kovac shifted his weight lazily. 'You're getting that "oh, shit" look, Neil. Don't you think so, Tinks?'

'Oh, shit,' she said. 'It's sphincter spasm time, Neil.'

'Did you think I wouldn't call the phone company and request the local usage records on your phone?' Kovac asked. 'You must think I'm pretty fucking stupid, Neil.'

'Why would you do that?' Fallon asked, nervous. 'I'm not a suspect for anything. Jesus, my father just killed himself –'

'And I'm sick of hearing you remind me. I'm the one

found him with his head blown half off. You think you need to keep reminding me of that? That's not an effective strategy, Neil.

'Someone dies a violent death like Mike did, it gets investigated,' Kovac said. 'You know the first people who get looked at? Family. 'Cause no one's got better motive to croak a person than a relative. You told me yourself: You hated Mike. Add to that the fact that you need money to pay off your soon-to-be ex, and that Mike wouldn't give it to you. That's called *motive*.'

The fear began to rise to the surface. Fallon's movements became jerky. Sweat misted his upper lip. He moved backward toward the corner with the built-in bookcase. All the shelves had been removed. 'But he was my old man. I wouldn't do that to him. He was my father.'

'And he spent thirty-some years telling you you weren't as good as your fag brother. That's what we call a *festering wound*.'

'He was a bastard,' Fallon declared. 'I won't say otherwise, but I didn't kill him. As for that bitch Cheryl, it's none of her goddamn business where I get the money. I'll pay her off.'

'Or you'll lose the business you've busted your hump for,' Liska said. 'Hell hath no fury like a bitter, vindictive woman. I should know, I am one.'

'I spoke with your ex,' Kovac said. 'She sounded like she's losing patience, ready to put the squeeze on you. Did you ask your brother for the money?'

He shook his head as if he'd taken a sharp smack in the ear, incredulous at this sudden downturn in his life. He looked from Liska to Kovac. 'You gonna say I killed him too?'

'We're not saying you killed anybody, Neil. We're just asking you questions pertinent to our case, that's all. That and pointing out how things look from the police perspective.'

'Stick your perspective up your ass, Kovac. Andy's not your case. That's over. Dead and buried. Ashes to ashes and dust to dust. The brass signed off.'

Kovac arched a brow. 'And you're trying to rub my face in that for what reason?'

'I'm just saying it's over.'

'But see, we have to look at an established pattern of behavior here, Neil. One member of the family offs himself, that's one thing. Two in a week? That's something else. You hated them both. You're going through a rough time emotionally and financially. We call those factors *precipitating stressors*. Stressors that might be enough to push a guy over the line. You have a record of violent behavior −'

'I didn't kill anybody.'

'What were you doing at Mike's house at that time of night?'

'I went to check on him,' Fallon said, his gaze sliding away. Absently, he touched his face just below the bruise on the crest of his cheek. 'We'd talked earlier. I didn't like the way he sounded.'

'The way he sounded or what he had to say?' Kovac asked. 'We know you'd been drinking. You told me so. You told me you were tanked enough to mix it up with a customer, the guy you made for a cop. Did your old man say something to piss you off?'

'It wasn't like that.'

'How wasn't it like that? You're gonna try to tell me now your family was like something out of *Ozzie and Harriet*?'

'No, but −'

'You told me Mike was always chewing your ass. How was this different? What did you talk about?'

'I told you yesterday − what time he wanted to be at the funeral home.'

'Yeah, you told me yesterday. Why didn't you tell me then you hadn't liked the way he sounded? You didn't say anything about having been concerned. In fact, if memory serves, you called him an old prick. Why didn't you tell me you'd been to the house to check on him?'

Fallon turned around in a slow circle, left hand massaging his forehead, right hand on his hip. 'He killed himself after I left,' he said, lowering his voice. 'I didn't do a very good job seeing to his needs, did I? His only living son . . .'

'What did he need? What did he say?'

Kovac waited and watched as Neil Fallon paced his little circle. His bull shoulders curled in as if he were fighting a pain in his stomach. His face was flushed. He held a shallow breath, then puffed it out, held it, puffed it out. He dug into the pocket of his coveralls and came out with a pack of Marlboros.

'Sorry, Mr Fallon,' Elwood said. 'We keep a smoke-free environment.'

Fallon glared at him and shook one out of the pack. 'So throw me out.'

Kovac moved toward him slowly. 'I don't think that conversation was about what Mike needed, Neil,' he said softly, shifting gears. 'I think it was more likely about what you need. I think you were drunk and pissed off when you called him, and you argued about the cash you need. And after that conversation, you got angrier and angrier, thinking about what you need and how your old man wouldn't give it to you, how he doted on Andy and shit all over you. And you got so mad, you got in your truck and you went to give it to him in his face.'

'He was half drunk, half wasted on pills,' Fallon muttered. 'I might as well have been talking to a turnip. He didn't give a shit what I had to say about anything. He never did.'

'He wouldn't give you the money.'

He shook his head and laughed. 'He wouldn't listen to the question. All he wanted to talk about was Andy. How

267

much he loved Andy. How Andy let him down. How Andy couldn't let sleeping dogs lie.'

Kovac looked at Liska, who had straightened abruptly.

'He used those words?' she asked. ' "Let sleeping dogs lie"? Why would he say that?'

'I don't know,' he snapped. 'Because of Andy coming out of the closet, I suppose. If he'd kept it to himself he was queer, then the old man wouldn't have had to deal with it. "After all these years," he kept saying. Like it wasn't fair telling him now. Like either he should have told when he was ten or waited for the old man to die. Jesus.'

'That must have made you crazy,' Kovac said. 'You'd had a few. You'd mixed it up with that customer. You're there in the flesh and Andy's dead, but he's going on about Andy this and Andy that.'

'That's what I said to him. "Andy's dead. Can we bury him and move on?" '

He took a pull on his cigarette and blew the smoke out hard. His face had turned a deep red. He squinted to better picture the memory . . . or to keep tears at bay. He stared at the two-way mirror, not seeing it. 'I got right down in his face and I screamed at him – "Andy was a butt-fucking fag and I'm glad he's dead!" '

He shouted the words past the emotions that swelled in his throat. He covered his eyes with his left hand, the cigarette smoldering between his fingers.

'What'd he do?'

Fallon was crying, the tears sliding under his hand, tortured, broken sounds cracking from his mouth.

'What'd Mike do when you said that, Neil?'

'H-he h-hit m-me.'

'And what did you do then?'

'Oh, God . . .'

'What'd you do then, Neil?' Kovac prodded gently, stepping close.

'I h-hit h-him b-back. Oh, Christ!' He sobbed and bent

over, putting both hands over his face. 'And now he's dead. They're both dead! Oh, God!'

Kovac took the cigarette from him, breathing in the smoke, craving one of his own. With regret, he put it out on the table, burning a black mark in the woodgrain surface.

'Did you kill him, Neil?' he asked softly. 'Did you kill Mike?'

Fallon shook his head, hands still over his face. 'No.'

'We can test your hands for gunpowder residue,' Liska said.

'We'll do what's called a neutron activation analysis,' Kovac explained. 'It won't matter how many times you've washed your hands since. Microscopic particles become embedded in your skin from the blowback. It shows up for weeks after.'

He was bluffing, playing the card as a scare tactic. The test could only show whether the person had come in contact with barium and antimony – components of gunpowder – and a million other mixtures, natural and man-made. Practically speaking, even a positive result would have little forensic value and less validity in a courtroom. Too much time had elapsed between the incident and the test. Defense attorneys made a living at arguing that time equaled contamination of evidence. Paid forensic expert witnesses would have a field day disputing the results. But Neil Fallon probably didn't know that.

A knock sounded at the door, and Elwood moved away from it. Lieutenant Leonard stuck his head in. A constipated expression hardened his face. 'Sergeant. Can I have a word?'

'I'm kind of in the middle of something here,' Kovac said impatiently.

Leonard just looked at him, eloquent in his silence. Kovac looked back at Neil Fallon and stifled a sigh. If he was going to confess to anything, this was the time to get it:

while he was emotionally weak, before he had a chance to pull up the shields and regroup, before he could utter the L word.

Kovac felt like a pitcher being taken out of the game while he was still throwing heat.

He turned to Liska. 'Guess you're the closer,' he said under his breath.

'Sergeant . . .' Leonard said.

Kovac stepped out the door and followed him into the next room, where Leonard had been watching through the glass. The room was dark. A theater with a window for a movie screen. Ace Wyatt stood at the window with his arms crossed, looking through the murky pane at Neil Fallon. Wyatt gave Kovac the profile for another few seconds, then the heavy-things-on-my-mind look. It was the same expression plastered on billboards around the Twin Cities advertising his television show.

'Why are you doing this, Sam?' Wyatt asked. 'Hasn't this family suffered enough?'

'That depends. If it turns out this one killed the other two, then the answer would be no.'

'Did something happen at the autopsy I don't know about?'

'Why should you know anything about it?' Kovac challenged. 'Maggie Stone isn't in the habit of passing that kind of information around.'

Wyatt ignored the question, above the curiosity of the common street cop. 'You're treating him like you know for a fact Mike was murdered.'

'We've got good reasons,' Kovac said. He pulled the Polaroids out of his inside coat pocket and spread them out on the window ledge. 'First, he did it in the can. Lots of people do, but it had to be a hassle for him to get in there with the chair – backward, no less. Liska picked up on that. I thought maybe he wanted to leave us a neat death scene, but it makes more sense that somebody else wanted to leave us a neat death scene. When was the last time old Mike gave a shit about anyone else? The gun came out of the closet in his bedroom. Why wouldn't he just do it there? It's not like he was worried about making a mess. The place was a pigsty.

'Plus there's Neil Fallon's record, his history of problems with the old man, the fact that he lied about being at the house.'

'But the time he was there and the time of death don't line up,' Leonard pointed out.

'Other factors might have skewed the TOD,' Kovac said. 'Stone will tell you that.'

'But there wasn't anything conclusive in the autopsy to say murder, was there?' Wyatt asked.

Kovac lifted a shoulder, his eyes moving from the Polaroids to the interview room and back. Neil Fallon was sitting, both elbows on the table, his head in his hands. Liska stood beside him, leaning down.

'If something happened that night, you'd be better off telling us now, Neil,' she said quietly, like a friend. 'Get it off your chest. You're carrying a lot of weight there.'

Fallon shook his head. 'I didn't kill him.' His voice sounded tinny and far away as it came out of the television that was mounted on a wall bracket near the window. The camera in the interview room looked down on the parties involved, making them appear small and distorted.

'I hit him,' he said. 'I did that. I hit him in the face. My own father. And him in that goddamn chair. And now he's dead.'

'We'll do the neutron activation,' Kovac told Leonard and Wyatt. 'See if we can't scare something out of him.'

'And if you can't?' Leonard asked.

'Then I apologize for the inconvenience and we try something else.'

Wyatt frowned. 'Why not wait until you get word from

Stone? There's no sense tormenting the man unnecessarily. Mike was one of ours –'.

'And he deserves to have us do more than go through the motions,' Kovac said, his temper rising. 'You want I should just wave this one through, Ace? You want to go to Maggie Stone and try to get her to sign this one off as an accident too? Keep it all quiet so Iron Mike's legend isn't tarnished? Jesus. What if this hump capped him?'

'Kovac,' Leonard snapped.

Kovac shot him a glare. 'What? This is the homicide squad. We investigate violent deaths. Mike Fallon died a violent death, and we want to look the other way because we think he killed himself, because that could be us in the Polaroids in five years. Suicide makes too much sense to us, because we know what the job can do to a man, how it can leave him with nothing.'

'And maybe that's why you want to think it's something else, Sam,' Wyatt said. 'Because if Mike Fallon didn't kill himself, maybe you won't either.'

'No. I didn't want to see it. Liska put it in my face. I might have walked away from it. But she was right to dig at it, to look at it like any other shooting. There's too much going on here to just say what a shame.'

'I'm just thinking of showing due respect for his only remaining family,' Wyatt said. 'At least until the ME gives us something concrete.'

'Well, that's fine. And if you had any say in the matter, maybe I'd listen to you. But unless I had a dream, I was at your retirement party, Ace. What you think about my investigation doesn't amount to a hill of rat shit.'

Ace Wyatt's face went purple.

Leonard stepped up. 'You're out of line, Kovac.'

'What line is that? The ass-kissing line?' Kovac muttered as he walked away from the pair. Wyatt's toady, Gaines, stood in the back corner of the room, staring at him with the smug smirk of a classroom tattletale. Kovac gave him a look of distaste and turned back toward the window.

'If I was out of line, I'm sorry,' he said without sincerity. 'It's been a hell of a week.'

'No,' Wyatt said on a tight sigh. 'You're right, Sam. I don't have any say here. It's your investigation. If you want to punish Neil Fallon and invite a lawsuit against the department because you need some time on the shrink's couch, it's not my place to do anything about it. That *is* a shame, and I wish it didn't have to be that way.'

'Yeah, well, I wish for world peace and for the Vikings to win the Super Bowl before I die,' Kovac said. 'You know how it is, Ace. Murder's an ugly business.'

'If that's what this is.'

'If that's what this is. And if that's what this is, then I'll nail the turd that did it. I don't care who it is.'

He went back to the window and stood watching.

'Are you right- or left-handed, Mr Fallon?' Elwood asked.

'Left.'

Elwood set a small kit of containers and cotton swabs on the table. Fallon stared at the test kit, straightening in his chair.

'We'll swab the back of your index finger and thumb with a five percent nitric acid solution,' Liska explained. 'It doesn't hurt.'

Kovac jerked his gaze to the photos of Mike Fallon's death scene.

'Jesus,' he whispered, picking up one Polaroid and then another, looking at them, then setting them aside. One after another. His pulse kicked up a notch.

'What?' Wyatt demanded.

The thing he had known was there but hadn't been able to see. He looked at the last of the photographs.

'Please hold out your left hand, Mr Fallon,' Elwood said, preparing a swab.

Neil Fallon started to reach out, his hand trembling visibly.

Kovac held the Polaroid up against the window. A split-screen image of father and son. Mike Fallon, a dead husk, bloody, half-beheaded; the gun that had killed him lying on the floor on the right side of his chair, apparently having fallen from his hand as life rushed out of him.

'Mr Fallon?'

The question mark in Elwood's voice caught Kovac's ear.

'Mr Fallon, I need you to hold out your hand.'

'No.'

Neil Fallon pushed his chair back from the table and stood up. 'No. I'm not doing it. I don't have to do it. I won't.'

'It's not a big deal, Neil,' Liska said. 'If you didn't shoot him.'

He moved back, shoving the chair aside, tipping it over. 'I didn't kill anybody. You think I did, then charge me or go fuck yourselves. I'm outta here.'

Elwood turned toward the window.

Kovac stared at the photograph as Neil Fallon stormed out of the interview room.

'Mike Fallon was left-handed,' he said, looking at Wyatt. 'Mike Fallon was murdered.'

26

'Mike Fallon was left-handed,' Kovac said. 'He's gonna kill himself, he takes the gun in his left hand.'

He pantomimed the action for the people assembled in Leonard's office: Leonard, Liska, Elwood, and Chris Logan from the county attorney's office. 'He supports the left hand with the right, sticks the barrel in his mouth, pulls the trigger. Bang! That's it. He's dead. The recoil pulls the arms away from the body. So maybe the gun is flung away from him. Or maybe it stays in the gun hand – the left hand – as that arm swings to the side. But there's no way it falls to the right side of the chair.'

'You're sure he was left-handed?' Logan asked. The prosecutor looked as if he'd been blown across the street from the government center by an arctic wind: dark hair mussed, cheeks red. The monobrow formed a dark V above his eyes.

'I'm sure,' Kovac said. 'I don't know why it didn't hit me at the scene. I guess because it made too much sense that Mike offed himself.'

'But his son would know he was left-handed.'

'Neil's left-handed too,' Kovac argued. 'So he helps the old man along to the next life, pulls back, sets the gun down with his left hand. That puts it on Mike's right.'

Logan's frown deepened. 'That's too thin. You have anything else? Fingerprints on the gun?'

'No. Mike's prints on the gun, but they're smudged. Like maybe someone had their hands on top of his.'

'*Maybe* doesn't cut it. Maybe his hands were sweating and he changed his grip repeatedly. Maybe the prints smudged as the gun slipped from his hands after he pulled the trigger.'

'A witness puts Neil Fallon at the scene that night,' Elwood said.

'And Fallon lied about it,' Kovac added.

'But it was two or three hours before the TOD, right?' Liska took a turn. 'He didn't get along with Mike. Lots of pent-up resentment and jealousy. Mike wouldn't loan him the money he needed. Fallon admits to having argued with his father. He admits to having hit him.'

'But he doesn't admit to having killed him.'

Kovac swore. 'Is that what we have to do now? Serve every damn perp up on a platter to you guys? Dressed up like Christmas turkeys with signed confessions in their beaks?'

'You have to bring me more than what you've got. His lawyer's going to have him out of here in five minutes. You have motive, and that's it. You have opportunity that doesn't jibe with the ME's take on what happened. You've got no physical evidence, no witnesses. So the guy lied to you. Everybody lies to the cops.

'You don't have enough to hold him. I don't have enough to take to the grand jury. Put him at the scene when someone heard a gunshot. Find the old man's blood on his shoes. Something. Anything.'

'If Neil had his hands over Mike's on the gun, then he left his fingerprints on the old man's skin,' Liska pointed out.

'It'll be hard to pick up now,' Kovac said. 'Stone and Lars clipped the fingernails, examined the hands for defense wounds . . .'

'It's still worth a call,' she insisted. 'Ply her with your charm, Sam.'

Kovac rolled his eyes. 'How about a search warrant for Neil Fallon's place? So we can find the bloody shoes.'

'Type out an affidavit and go see Judge Lundquist with

my blessing,' Logan said, checking his watch. 'I'm all for nailing this bastard if he killed the old man.' He shrugged into his coat. 'But the case has to stand up. Otherwise it's another cluster fuck for the press to turn their cameras on, and I'm not going to be the guy in the spotlight stomping on the burning bag of dog shit.

'I've got to go,' he announced. 'I'm due in judge's chambers.' He was out the door and gone before anyone could object.

'The downside to drawing the politically ambitious prosecutor,' Elwood said. 'He'll take only well-calculated risks he knows he can win.'

'Logan's smart,' Leonard interjected. 'The department can't take another fiasco.'

Translation: We fuck up and the brass is up Leonard's ass with a fire hose, Kovac thought. With Ace Wyatt orchestrating the charge from behind the scenes. And the shit storm would drench him and Liska. Elwood might escape, being on the periphery of the case.

'I'll get the affidavit,' Kovac said.

Liska's pager went off and she grabbed for her belt.

'Should we get a sheriff's unit to sit on Neil Fallon's place?' Elwood asked. 'They'll want in on the search. It's their jurisdiction.'

Leonard started to say something. Kovac spoke over him, ignoring the lieutenant's authority to run the case.

'Call Tippen. See what he can do for us. If anyone from the SO is coming to the party, I want it to be him.'

'Sam, I've gotta go,' Liska said. 'Ibsen's regained consciousness. Do you need me for the search?'

'No, go ahead.'

'The night-shift supervisor called me,' Leonard said loudly, bringing her up short of the door. 'I agreed you could be Castleton's second on the Ibsen assault. In case you were wondering.'

'Thanks, Lieutenant,' she said, trying unsuccessfully not

to look sheepish. 'I meant to tell you. Ibsen is my informant.'

'Maybe when you get back, you can take five minutes to fill me in as to what he's been informing you about.'

'Sure, later.' She turned away from him, making big eyes at Kovac.

'Good luck, Tinks,' he said. 'I hope the guy has total recall and twenty-twenty night vision.'

'I'll be happy if he can do more than drool.'

'Regaining consciousness,' as it turned out, was something of an overstatement. Ibsen had cracked an eye partially open and moaned. The medical staff of the Hennepin County Medical Center ICU had responded by pumping him full of morphine.

He looked small and fragile and pathetic in the bed, swathed in bandages, wired to an array of machines. No one sat at his bedside praying for God to spare him. Not one person had come to see him, according to the ICU staff, even though his boss at *Boys Will Be Girls* had been notified, and had presumably told Ibsen's friends at the club. Apparently, he didn't have any. Then again, maybe the idea that he had been beaten to a pulp was enough to deter acquaintances from associating with him.

'Can you hear me, Mr Ibsen?' she asked for the third time.

He lay with his head turned toward her, eyes open but unfocused. Some people claimed conversation penetrated the brains of even the deeply comatose. Who was she to say it didn't?

'We'll get the people who did this to you,' she promised.

Cops. She felt sick to her stomach thinking it. Cops had done this damage. Cops had committed this crime, this sacrilege against the uniforms they wore. The damage didn't end with Ken Ibsen. It extended to the image of the department, to the trust the public was supposed to have in

278

the officers they paid to protect them. She hated Ogden and Rubel for betraying that trust, and for undermining her belief in the community of cops that had been her second family most of her life.

She wasn't naive. She knew not all cops were good cops. There were plenty of assholes walking around with badges. But murder and attempted murder? At the very core of her being she still didn't want to believe it. Ken Ibsen was barely living proof that she would have to.

'They've got a hell of a lot to answer for,' she whispered, and turned away.

A uniform sat outside the door to Ibsen's room with a fishing magazine in his lap. Hess, according to the name tag. A fat guy waiting for retirement or a heart attack, whichever came first. He gave Liska the 'Oh, it's just a girl' smirk. She wanted to kick his chair. She wanted to yank the magazine out of his hands and beat him on the head with it. She could afford to do neither.

'What precinct are you out of, Hess?'

'Third.'

'Do you know why you were pulled downtown?'

He shrugged. ''Cause I was available to watch this guy.'

He didn't seem to have an interest in knowing why someone from the downtown station house didn't get the job. He was just glad for the time to bone up on his knowledge of bait and lures for walleye. Liska had insisted on people from outside, fearing that precinct camaraderie among the uniforms could put Ibsen at risk, just as it had compromised Andy Fallon's death scene with the first responding uniform letting Ogden and Rubel into the house. She didn't know that having a lump like Hess at the door might not be just as bad.

'Has Castleton been by?' she asked.

'No.'

'Anyone else from the department?'

'No.'

279

'Anyone besides doctors and nurses goes in that room, I'm to be notified immediately.'

'Uh-huh.'

'Someone goes in that room with him – I don't care who it is – get your ass out of that chair and watch through the glass. I could have killed him five times while you were sitting here debating jigs versus minnows.'

Hess pouted a little at that, not liking being told his job by a woman, certainly not one young enough to be his daughter.

'And see about getting a personality transplant while you're here,' Liska muttered under her breath as she walked away.

She rode the elevator down to street level, thinking of Ogden and Rubel, and how far they would go, whether they would be willing to try something here, in the hospital. That seemed too great a risk, but if they'd had something to do with the murder of Eric Curtis, if they'd had something to do with the death of Andy Fallon, if they were willing to do to another human being what had been done to Ken Ibsen, then there were no limits.

Then again, maybe they didn't want Ibsen dead. He was a more horrifying symbol alive, if what they wanted was to send a message to people not to fuck with them. She wondered why they had waited till now to do it. Why not when the investigation had been hot? Maybe Ibsen didn't worry them so much as did her interest in reopening the case. After all, no one had given Ibsen much credit to this point.

Great. That meant Ibsen was made an example for her, and she really was the reason he was now lying in a hospital bed.

They had to have been watching Ibsen to catch him in that alley, she thought. They were probably watching her. Omniscience seemed a tall order for that pair. But then, they weren't simply a pair, she reminded herself. Springer had corroborated their alibi. Dungen, the gay officers' liaison, had commented to her there was no shortage of anti-gay sentiment in the department. But how many cops would be willing to go so far as assault and murder? Or be willing to look the other way? She wished she didn't have to find out.

She left the elevator, head down, lost in thought, trying to prioritize the things she needed to do. She wanted to call Eric Curtis's last patrol partner. What was his name? Engle. And she had been appointed by Castleton to go to IA to get the scoop on Ibsen's conversations with them. She wanted to call Kovac to update him on Ibsen and get the latest on the search of Neil Fallon's property. He was probably in Judge Lundquist's chambers by now.

She dug her cell phone out of her pocket and glanced up, looking for a spot out of the traffic flow to stand. Rubel stood not ten feet down the hall, staring at her, blank-faced, out of uniform. The moment froze for a heartbeat, and she registered that he had something in his hand, then someone banged into her from behind. Rubel moved forward, sliding the mirrored shades in place with one hand and sliding the other into his coat pocket.

'What the hell are you doing here?' Liska blurted, stepping into his path.

'Flu shot.'

'Ibsen's under guard.'

'Why should I care about that? He doesn't have anything to do with me.'

'Yeah, I guess you're right,' she said. 'It was your partner he had plenty to talk about.'

Rubel shrugged. 'Ogden's clear. I guess IA didn't think the guy had anything worth hearing.'

'Somebody thought so. He'll be talking through what teeth he has left for a couple of months.'

'Like I told Castleton,' Rubel said, 'I wouldn't know

anything about that. Ogden and Springer and I were playing pool in my basement.'

'That ranks right up there with "The dog ate my homework."'

'Innocent people don't live their lives having an alibi in mind,' he said, glancing over his shoulder back the way he'd come. 'If you'll excuse me, Sergeant –'

'Yeah, you and Ogden and your homophobic pals are a regular bunch of choirboys.' Liska wished she were tall enough to truly get in his face. As it was, he was looking over the top of her head.

'You know, it's not the Eric Curtises and Andy Fallons who bring shame on the department,' she said. 'It's no-neck thugs like you guys, thinking you should have free rein to crush out anyone who doesn't fit your narrow ideal of human perfection. You're the ones who ought to be run out of the department. And if I can find one shred of evidence against you, I'll burn your asses like a blowtorch.'

'That sounds like a threat, Sergeant.'

'Yeah? Call IA,' she said, and walked away down the hall Rubel had come from. She felt his eyes on her back until she turned the corner.

'Can I help you, miss?' a desk attendant asked.

Liska looked around. There was a small area of chairs with people waiting and looking miserable. The sign above the desk said LAB.

'Is this where I get my flu shot?'

'No, ma'am. Blood tests. You can get a flu shot in the ER. Go back down the hall the way you came and . . .'

Liska murmured a thank-you, tuned the woman out, and walked away.

'I'm suing the police department!' Neil Fallon ranted, his heavy boots screeching on the hard-packed snow as he paced a line back and forth to Kovac's left. He wore nothing on his head, and the wind howling across the lake had swept his hair into a frantic mess. Wild-eyed, veins bulging in his neck, he looked like a madman.

Kovac lit a cigarette, inhaled deeply, and exhaled a thin ribbon of smoke that was quickly dispatched. The windchill factor had to be fifteen below. 'You do that, Neil,' he said. 'It's a waste of money you already don't have, but hey, what do I care?'

'False arrest –'

'You're not under arrest.'

'Harassment –'

'We have a warrant. You're basically fucked here, Neil,' he said calmly.

The sun shone weak yellow light through a haze of blowing snow. The ice fishing houses that dotted the near end of the lake seemed to huddle together for warmth.

Fallon stopped, huffing and puffing, watching through the wide door as cops combed through the stuff in the cluttered workshop. The house had yielded nothing but proof that there was no woman living on the premises.

'I didn't kill anyone,' Fallon said emphatically.

Kovac watched him from the corner of his eye. 'Then you got nothing to worry about, Sport. Go have a beer.'

Tippen from the SO detectives unit stood to Kovac's right, also smoking, also staring into the cavernous mouth of the shed. The collar of his parka was up around his ears, a snowboarder's red-and-white-striped stocking cap perched on his head.

'I thought you quit smoking,' he said to Kovac.

'I did.'

'You're in serious denial, Sam.'

'Yeah, well . . . Anybody tell you you look like something out of Dr Seuss with that friggin' hat?'

'I do not like green eggs and ham, Sam I Am,' Tippen said, deadpan. 'Where's Liska?'

'You've got the hots for her.'

'I beg to differ. I was merely inquiring after a colleague.'

'Begging. Tinks'll like that. She's someplace warmer than here, working another angle.'

'Point Barrow, Alaska, is warmer than here.'

'What angle?' Fallon demanded.

'It doesn't concern you, Neil. She's got other cases.'

'I didn't kill my father.'

'So you've said.' Kovac kept his attention on the shed. Elwood was coming out, holding a pair of brown twill coveralls by the shoulders.

Fallon's whole body gave a jerk, as if he'd been given an electrical shock. 'That's not what you think.'

'And what am I gonna think, Neil?'

'I can explain that.'

'What do you think, Sam?' Elwood asked. 'It looks like blood to me.'

The coveralls were filthy. Spattered over the filth was what appeared to be dried blood and tissue.

Kovac turned to Neil Fallon. 'Here's what I think, Neil. I think you're under arrest. You have the right to remain silent. . . .'

Cal Springer had called in sick. Liska pulled into his driveway and stared at his house for a moment before turning off the engine. Cal and the missus lived in one of a multitude of cul-de-sacs in suburban Eden Prairie. The house was what realtors would call 'soft contemporary,' meaning without style. Anyone coming home to this neighborhood from a night of barhopping would run the risk of walking into a neighbor's house and never knowing the difference until the alarm went off in the morning.

Still and all, it was a nice place, and Liska would have been happy to have something on a par with it. She wondered how Cal afforded it. He made good money at his grade and with the years he'd put in, but not this good. And she knew for a fact he had a daughter at St Olaf, a pricey private college down the road in Northfield. Maybe Mrs

Cal brought home the big bacon. There was a thought: Cal Springer, kept man.

She went to the front door and rang the bell, then put her finger over the peephole.

'Who's there?' Springer's voice came through the door. He sounded as if the IRS was waiting to drag him away in chains for living above his means.

'Elana from Elite Escorts,' Liska called loudly. 'I'm here for your four o'clock spanking, Mr Springer!'

'Damn it, Liska!' The door swung open and Springer glared at her, then scanned for neighbors. 'Could you have a little consideration? I live here.'

'Well, duh. Why would I try to embarrass you in front of strangers?'

She ducked under Springer's arm and into the foyer, a place of colorless tile, colorless paint, and a colorless wood banister leading up the staircase to the second floor.

'Did you know you shouldn't have a staircase lead right to a door like this?' she asked. 'Your *feng shui* is thrown all to hell. All your good *chi* goes right out the door.'

'I'm sick,' Springer announced.

'That could be why. Lack of *chi*. They say that might have been what killed Bruce Lee. I read it in *In Style* magazine.' She gave him the cop once-over from head to toe, taking in the mussed hair, the gray skin, the bags sagging under bloodshot eyes. He looked like hell. 'Or that could just be what you get for running with the likes of Rubel and Ogden. Strange company for you, Cal, don't you think?'

'My friends are none of your business.'

'They are when I'm pretty sure they beat a man into a coma while you were allegedly playing pool with them.'

'They couldn't have done that,' he said, but he wasn't looking at her. 'We were at Rubel's.'

'Is that what Mrs Cal is going to tell me when I ask her?'

'She's not home.'

'She will be eventually.'

Liska tried to get in front of him. Springer kept turning. He was wearing baggy brown dress pants that had seen better days, and an ill-fitting gray St Olaf sweatshirt with sleeves shrunk halfway up his forearms. He couldn't even get dressing casually right.

'What's this got to do with you anyway?' he asked irritably.

'I'm Castleton's second on this assault. The vic was supposed to be meeting me. He had something interesting to tell me about the Curtis murder. And you know, now that someone went to all the trouble to shut him up, I'm all the more anxious to find out what it was he had to say. You know how I am with something like this, Cal. I'm like a terrier after a rat. I don't quit till I get it.'

Springer made a sound in the back of his throat and put his hand on his stomach. His gaze strayed to the open door of the half-bath that was tucked under the staircase.

'What are you doing, hanging with uniforms, Cal? You're a detective, for god's sake. And you must have – what? – fifteen years on them? No offense, but why would they want to hang with you?'

'Look, I told you – I'm not feeling well, Liska,' he said, glancing at the bathroom again. 'Could we have this conversation some other time?'

'After I drove way the hell out here?' she said, offended. 'You're some host. Nice house, though.'

She wandered to the edge of the foyer and looked into a living room with a stone fireplace and overstuffed couches. A tall Christmas tree was overly decorated with artsy-craftsy ornaments and too much tinsel. 'Taxes out here must be a killer, huh?'

'Why would you care?' Springer asked, exasperated.

'I wouldn't. I couldn't afford a place like this. How do you?'

She looked right at him, catching him unguarded for a

second, seeing something bleak in his eyes. It struck her very clearly at that moment that Cal Springer was probably always playing catch-up in one way or another, and probably always falling a little short of expectations.

The sound of the garage door opening caught his attention and he looked a little sicker than he had a moment ago.

'That's my wife. Home from work.'

'Yeah? What's she do? Brain surgery? Oh, silly me,' Liska said. 'If she was a brain surgeon, she would have done something about your lack of good sense.'

'She's a teacher,' Springer said, hand worrying his belly.

'Oh, well, that explains the extravagant lifestyle. Those schoolteachers just rake in the dough.'

'We do well enough between us,' Springer said defensively.

Well enough to be up to his ass in debt, Liska thought. 'But a promotion wouldn't hurt, huh? 'Course, after the fuckup on Curtis, that's looking pretty dim. So you think to run for delegate and show the brass maybe you're management material. Right?'

'Calvin? I'm home.' The soft, sweet voice came from the kitchen. 'I got the Imodium.'

'We're in here, Patsy.'

'We?'

There was a rustle of grocery bags being set down, then a moment later Mrs Cal came into the foyer, looking like a stereotype of a middle-aged schoolteacher. A little plump, a little frumpy, big glasses, mousy hair.

'Nikki Liska, Mrs Springer.' Liska held her hand out.

'From work,' Cal specified.

'I think we met at a function once,' Liska said.

Mrs Cal looked confused. Or maybe apprehensive. 'Did you come out to check on Calvin? His stomach has just been a mess.'

'Yeah, well, actually, I had to ask him a couple of questions.'

Springer had moved behind his wife. His flat face looked made of wax. His focus seemed to be on some other dimension, one where he could see his life crumbling like so much old cheese.

Mrs Cal's brows knitted. 'Questions about what?'

'Do you know where Cal was last night around eleven, eleven-thirty?'

Mrs Cal's eyes filled with tears behind the too-big glasses. She glanced over her shoulder at her husband. 'What's this about?'

'Just answer her, Patsy,' Springer said impatiently. 'It's nothing.'

Liska waited, a weight in her chest, thinking of her own mother when IA had come to the house and asked questions. She knew that feeling of vulnerability; that sense of betrayal, of being turned on by your own kind.

'Calvin was out last night,' Patsy Springer said softly. 'With friends.'

Behind her, Springer rubbed a hand over his face and tried to stifle a sigh.

'No,' Liska said, her eyes on him. 'Those people Cal claims he was out with? They're not his friends, Mrs Springer. I hope for his sake you just told me a lie.'

'That's enough, Liska,' Springer said, stepping between them. 'You can't come into my home and call my wife a liar.'

Liska held her ground, took her gloves out of her coat pocket, and pulled them on, one and then the other.

'You weren't listening, Cal,' she said quietly. 'Get out in front of this before you get caught in the wheels. Nothing they've got on you is as bad as what they've done.'

'What's she talking about, Calvin?' There was fear in Mrs Cal's voice now.

Springer glared at Liska. 'Leave my house.'

Liska nodded, taking a final glance at the too-nice house, and a final look at Cal Springer, a man being eaten alive from the inside out.

'Think about it, Calvin,' she said. 'You know what they did to him. You probably know more than that. They wear the same badge you and I do, and that's just wrong. Be a man and stop them.'

Springer looked away, hand pressed to his belly, sweat misting his pale, ashen skin. He said nothing.

Liska walked out into the cold of the fading afternoon, got into the car, and headed east for Minneapolis, wanting nothing more than to be in her modest home with her sons.

27

'What are the odds that blood is Iron Mike's?' Tippen asked over a glass of beer.

They sat in Patrick's with the diehards who always gathered after first shift, and the Friday night get-loose-once-a-week bunch.

'Slim to none,' Kovac said. He took a handful of party mix from the bowl on the table and sorted out the peanuts and pretzels. He had long suspected the hard things masquerading as corn chips were, in fact, toenail clippings. 'He had to be in front of the old man when the gun went off. The mess went in the other direction. I think the blood on the coveralls is just what Neil Fallon says it's from – gutting fish. But that doesn't mean he didn't kill the old man. And now we've got him sitting in jail, where he can sweat and fret and decide to spill the story.'

'Being the weekend, we won't get lab results on the blood until Tuesday or Wednesday,' Elwood interjected. 'If he's got something to tell, I believe he'll let it go by Sunday night.'

'Confession on the Sabbath.' Tippen nodded with the wisdom of experience. 'Very symbolic.'

'Very Catholic,' Kovac corrected. 'That's how he was raised. Neil Fallon's no hard-case killer. If he did the old man, he won't be able to live with the guilt for long.'

'I don't know, Sam,' Tippen said. 'Don't we all harbor guilt for something? We carry it around our whole lives like ballast. Something to weigh us down and keep us from reaching for true happiness. It reminds us we're not worthy, gives us an excuse to underachieve.'

'Most of us didn't clip our own fathers. That kind of guilt rolls out,' Kovac said. 'Eventually.'

He rose from the booth, wishing he didn't have to.

'Where are you going?' Tippen demanded. 'It's your turn to buy.'

Kovac dug out his wallet and dropped some bills on the table. 'To see if I can't hasten the process along for someone.'

Someone down the block from Steve Pierce was having a Christmas party. Music and conversation and laughter escaped the town house as a fresh batch of guests arrived. Kovac leaned back against his car for a moment and watched as he finished his cigarette, then dropped the butt in the gutter and went to the door.

Lights shone in the windows of Pierce's duplex. His Lexus was in the drive. He might have walked down to the neighbor's party, but Kovac doubted it. Steve Pierce wouldn't join in the holiday festivities this year. It was damn hard to be merry and bright with the weight of loss and grief and guilt hanging around your neck. Kovac's hope was that the fiancée would be absent, leaving Pierce alone and vulnerable.

'Kick 'em when they're down,' he muttered, and rang the bell.

Time passed, and he rang it again. More guests arrived down the block. One of them, a guy wearing a red muffler, ran into the yard, threw an arm around a snowman, and began to sing 'Holly Jolly Christmas.'

'Jesus, you again,' Pierce muttered as he pulled the door open. 'Have you ever heard of a telephone?'

'I prefer that personal touch, Steve. Shows how much I care.'

Pierce looked worse than he had the night after he'd found Andy Fallon's body. He was wearing the same clothes. He stank of cigarettes and scotch and sweat – the kind of sweat from emotional upset. The smell of it was different from the smell of physical work, more sour and sharp. He had a short glass half-full of scotch in one hand and a cigarette hanging from his lip. He looked as if he hadn't shaved since the funeral.

'You care to throw my ass in jail,' he said.

'Only if you've committed a crime.'

Pierce laughed. He was close to drunk, but he probably wouldn't allow himself to cross over, to deaden the pain completely. Kovac suspected he wanted to hurt, and the scotch allowed him to maintain it at a tolerable level.

'Neil Fallon's in jail,' Kovac said. 'It looks like he might have killed the old man. I'd like to hear your take on that.'

'Well.' Pierce raised his glass. 'That calls for a toast. Come on in, Sergeant,' he invited as he walked away from the open door.

Kovac followed. 'A toast that Neil's in jail or that Mike's dead?'

'Two for one. They deserved each other.'

They went into the den with the dark blue walls. Kovac pulled the door shut behind him, to buy an extra minute or two if the girlfriend showed up.

'How well do you know Neil?'

Pierce took another glass from the small cupboard above the bar and splashed in some of the Macallan, then topped off his own glass.

'Well enough to know he's a thug. Angry, jealous, petty, mean. A chip off the old block.' He held the new glass out to Kovac. 'I used to tell Andy he must have gotten sent home from the hospital with the wrong family when he was a baby. I could never see how he came out of that pack of pit bulls. He was so decent, so good, so kind.'

His eyes reddened around the rims, and he went to the narrow window that looked out on the side of the house. The place next door was dark.

'He was so much better than they were,' he said, the

sense of injustice and frustration thickening his voice. 'And yet he couldn't stop trying to win them over.'

Kovac sipped the scotch, realizing at first taste there was valid reason it cost fifty bucks a bottle. Molten gold might taste this smooth.

'He was his father's favorite for a long time,' he said, his eyes steady on Pierce. He eased around to the side of one of the leather armchairs for a better angle. 'I imagine it was pretty hard for him to take rejection from the old man.'

'He kept trying to make it up to him. As if he had something to be sorry for. He wanted the old man to understand something a guy like that will never grasp in a million years. I told Andy to let it go, that he couldn't change someone else's mind, but he wouldn't listen.'

'How was he going to make it up to him? What could be the trade-off?'

Pierce shrugged. 'There isn't one. That's just it. Andy thought maybe they could do something together. Write the old man's memoirs or something. He used to talk about that sometimes, that maybe if he knew more about the old man, he could understand him better, find some common ground with him. He wanted to know more about the shooting that put him in the chair, that being a defining moment in Mike's life. But the old man didn't appreciate the effort. He didn't want to talk about what happened. He didn't want to talk about his feelings. I doubt he had the right vocabulary for it. Personal enlightenment isn't high on the list for guys like Mike Fallon, or Neil.'

'And what about Neil?' Kovac asked. 'He claims it didn't have any impact on him when Andy came out.'

Pierce laughed. 'Sure. Smug asshole. He hated Andy already. He thought being the straight one gave him an advantage with the old man. He wasn't such a black sheep anymore. Homosexuality trumps being a felon in the redneck scheme of things.'

'Did Andy see much of him?'

'He tried to do macho, brotherly things with Neil from time to time. Hunting, fishing, that kind of thing. A complete waste of time. Neil didn't want to understand Andy or like Andy. Neil didn't want anything from Andy but money.'

'He'd asked Andy for money?'

'Sure. First he put it to him as an investment opportunity. I told Andy to forget it. Give Neil the money if he didn't care if he ever saw it again. As an investment? What a crock. Might as well flush the money down the john.'

'What did Andy do?'

'Put him off. Kept saying maybe later, hoping Neil would take the hint.' He drank some more of the scotch and muttered, 'Investment opportunity.'

'Did they ever fight, that you knew of?'

Pierce shook his head. He sucked the cigarette down to the filter and put the butt out against a corner of the windowpane. 'No. Andy wouldn't fight with him. He felt too guilty about being better than the average Fallon. Why? Do you think Neil killed him?'

'That door's still open.'

'I don't see it. Neil's not that clever. You would have caught him by now.'

'We have,' Kovac reminded him.

'Still . . . you know what I mean.' He went back to the bar and freshened his drink for the umpteenth time. 'Neil's the messy type, don't you think? Shooting, stabbing, blood and gore, devastation at the scene, fingerprints everywhere.'

'Maybe so.'

'He sure as hell wouldn't be sorry. Christ, he probably couldn't *spell* sorry. He's the one who should have died,' Pierce said bitterly, and drank more of the scotch, stirring up his anger, pouring fuel on the flames. 'Worthless excuse for a human being. It doesn't make sense that someone as good as Andy –'

Tears rushed up on him like a flash flood, and he choked

294

on them and fought against them, and lost. He swore and threw his drink. The glass shattered against the bar top, spraying the immediate area with liquor and shards of crystal.

'God!' he cried, covering his head with his arms, as if fending off the blows of a higher power punishing him for his sins. He staggered from side to side, sobbing; dry, raw sounds tearing at his throat. 'Oh, God!'

Kovac waited, let him feel his pain, gave him time to look the demon in the face.

After a time, he said, 'You loved him.'

It sounded strange saying it to a man. But as he witnessed the depth of Steve Pierce's pain, he thought he should be so lucky to have another human being – male or female – care that deeply about him. Then again, maybe all he was seeing was guilt.

'Yes,' Pierce admitted in a tortured whisper.

Kovac put a hand on his shoulder, and Pierce shrank away.

'You had a relationship with him.'

'He wanted me to admit it, to come out. But I couldn't. People don't understand. They don't. Even when they say they do, they don't. I've seen it. I know what's said behind the back. The jokes, the snickering, the lack of respect. I know what happens. My career . . . everything I've worked for . . . I – I –' He choked himself off, as if the argument wasn't convincing even to his own ears. He sank down in one of the leather chairs, his face in his hands. 'He didn't understand. I couldn't . . .'

Kovac set his own drink aside. 'Were you there, Steve? The night Andy died?'

He shook his head and kept on shaking it, wagging it back and forth as he tried to collect himself.

'No,' he said at last. 'I told you, I saw him Friday night. Jocelyn's girlfriends had a wedding shower for her. I hadn't seen him in a month. We had fought about his coming out,

295

and . . . We hadn't been together in a long time. Hadn't even spoken.'

'Was he seeing someone else?'

'I don't know. Maybe. I saw him at a bar one night with someone, but I don't know if there was anything to it.'

'Did you know him? This other guy?'

'No.'

'What'd he look like?'

'Like an actor. Dark hair, great smile. I don't know that they were really together.'

'What happened when you went to see him Friday night?'

'We fought again. He wanted me to tell Joss the truth.'

'You got angry.'

'Frustrated.'

'How long had you and Andy been involved?'

He made a vague motion with one hand. 'Off and on since college. At first, I thought it was just . . . experimentation . . . curiosity. But I kept . . . needing . . . and living this other life . . . and I couldn't see a way out of it. I'm engaged to Douglas Daring's daughter, for god's sake. We're getting married in a month. How could I . . . ?'

'You'd had that argument before.'

'Fifty times. We'd have that fight, break it off for a while, get back together, ignore the issue, he'd get depressed . . .'

He let the sentence trail off and sat there, slumped over like an old man, his expression bleak with pain and regret.

'Would he have told Jocelyn?' Kovac asked.

'No. He wasn't like that. It was up to me, my responsibility. And I wouldn't accept it.'

'Was he angry?'

'He was hurt,' he said, then fell silent for a moment. 'I don't want to believe he might have killed himself, because I don't want to believe I might have caused him to.'

His eyes filled again, and he closed them tight, squeezing the tears out between the lashes.

'But I'm afraid I did,' he whispered. 'I couldn't be man enough to admit what I am, and now maybe the person I loved most in the world is dead because of that. Then I *did* kill him. I loved him and I killed him.'

Silence hung between them for a moment, only the murmur of the stereo in the distant background. One of those soft pseudo-jazz stations that seem to play the same song continuously; same beat, same wimpy saxophone, same lazy trumpet. Kovac sighed and thought about what to do next. Nothing, he guessed. There was no point in pushing Pierce further. This was his secret, the weight around his neck. His punishment was to carry it around for the rest of his life.

'Will you tell Jocelyn?' Kovac asked.

'No.'

'That's a hell of a big lie to live, Steve.'

'It doesn't matter.'

'Maybe not to you, but don't you think she deserves something more?'

'I'll be a good husband, a good father, even. We make a stunning couple, don't you think? That's what Joss wants – her own life-size Ken doll to dress up and take out and play make-believe with. I'm very good at make-believe. I've played it most of my life.'

'And you'll get your partnership at Daring-Landis, and everyone will live miserably ever after.'

'No one will even notice.'

'It's the American way.'

'Are you married, Kovac?'

'Twice.'

'So you're an expert.'

'On the misery part. I finally figured out it was cheaper and easier to be miserable alone.'

They were silent again for a moment.

'You should tell her, Steve. For both your sakes.'

'No.'

Kovac saw the door to the hall swing open slowly, and a ripple of dread went through him. Jocelyn Daring stood in the doorway, still in her coat. He didn't know how long she had been standing there, but by the look on her face it had been long enough. Tears and mascara striped her cheeks. All the color had drained from her lips. Pierce looked at her and said nothing. Slowly her mouth pulled back into a trembling snarl.

'You stupid son of a bitch!' She spat the words out like so many bullets, then flew across the room, shrieking like a banshee, eyes wild with fury.

Kovac caught her around the waist as she launched herself at Pierce. She screamed and flailed, fists swinging, connecting with his forehead and splitting open the cut that had begun to heal. She kicked him and twisted out of his grasp, grabbing a pewter candlestick off the end table.

'You stupid son of a bitch!' she screamed again, swinging and hitting Pierce – who hadn't moved – a glancing blow off the side of his head. 'I told you not to talk to him! I told you! I told you!'

Kovac grabbed her again from behind and struggled, dragging her backward. Her body was taut and strong, and she was tall, and her fury was superhuman.

Pierce did nothing to defend himself. Blood ran in bright rivulets down the side of his head. He wiped at it with his fingertips and smeared some onto his cheek.

'I loved you! I loved you!' Jocelyn shouted, nearly incoherent. 'Why did you have to tell? I could have made it right.'

The fury ran out of her then, and she collapsed, sobbing. Kovac maneuvered her to a chair and eased her down into it. Body limp, she slipped down to the floor and curled into a ball, pounding her fist against the chair. 'I could have made it right. I could have . . .'

Kovac leaned down and pried the candlestick from her

hand. Blood dripped from his own wound onto her sweater. Baby-blue cashmere.

'I think you're right, Sergeant,' Pierce said dimly, staring at his bloody hand. 'It probably is easier to be miserable alone.'

The neighbor had managed to find three square feet of yard not already occupied, and had added a new display to the montage: a lighted scoreboard counting down the hours and minutes to Santa's arrival.

Kovac stared at it for an indeterminate length of time, mesmerized by the ever-changing numbers, and wondered how bad the suspension would be if he were to be arrested for destruction of private property. How many glowing, garish icons to the overcommercialization of the holiday could he destroy before the damage toll took him over the line from petty misdemeanor to something worse? Could he plead a felony down and still keep his badge?

In the end, he didn't have the energy for vandalism, and simply went into his house. It was as empty as before, except for the stench of garbage that should have been left at the curb that morning.

Home sweet home.

He took off his coat, threw it over the back of the couch, and went into the half-bath off the hall to wash up and assess the damage. The gash above his left eye was angry-looking, crusted and smeared with dried blood. He should have gone to the ER to get it repaired, but he hadn't. He dabbed at it with a washcloth, wincing, then gave up and washed his hands and took three Tylenol.

In the kitchen, he opened the fridge, pulled out a half-eaten meatball sandwich, and sniffed at it. Better than the garbage . . .

Sandwich in hand, he leaned back against the counter and listened to the silence, the scene at Pierce's house

299

replaying through his head. Jocelyn Daring, insane with rage and pain and jealousy, flying across the room.

I told you not to talk to him. . . . Why did you have to tell? . . . I loved you. I loved you.

Why did you have to tell? Strange wording, he thought. As if Pierce's homosexuality was a secret she had already known, even though Pierce hadn't told her and had had no intention of telling her.

He thought back to the night he'd first met her, the way she behaved toward Pierce – possessive, protective; the carefully blank look in her eyes when he'd asked her if she'd known Andy Fallon.

That's what Joss wants – her own life-size Ken doll to dress up and take out and play make-believe with. . . .

She was amazingly strong. Even now, Kovac's biceps ached from the effort to restrain her.

Pensive, he raised the sandwich to take an absent bite. His pager went off before he could taste-test for salmonella. The display showed Liska's cell phone number. He dialed her back and waited.

She answered the phone: 'House of Pain. We deliver.'

'Yeah. I'll take another smack in the head, and a kick in the teeth for dessert.'

'Sorry. No time for fun. But this'll make your day. Deene Combs just reached out and touched someone. One of Chamiqua Jones's kids is dead.'

28

'What happened to you?' Liska asked, frowning at Kovac as he climbed out of the car.

'A woman scorned.'

'You don't have a woman to scorn.'

'Why should that limit my chances at suffering?' he asked, taking in the scene.

Chamiqua Jones's neighborhood was shabby, the houses sagging old monsters built in the early part of the century and later cut up into apartments. But it was by no means a slum. The families who lived here were poor, but for the most part did their best to look out for one another. The gangs and the crack dealers were far worse enemies to them than to white suburbia.

And this was why, Kovac thought as they walked toward the gathering of cops and crime scene techs.

A small body lay in the street near a pile of snow. The body had been covered. The mound of dirty snow was splashed with blood. Chamiqua Jones stood off to one side, wailing, screaming, rocking, friends and neighbors trying to comfort and restrain her.

'The kids were playing on the snowbank,' Liska said. 'According to one of them, a car with three or four gangbangers pulled up, one stuck his head out the window and called the name Jones. When he saw which child reacted, he shot her. Caught her once in the face, two to the torso.'

'Aw, jeez.'

'Not exactly a subtle message.'

'Whose case?'

'Tom Michaels.'

At the mention of his name, Michaels looked up from a conversation with one of the uniforms, and immediately came toward them. Stocky and full of nervous energy, he wore his hair slicked straight back with a ton of goo to combat the fact that he looked about seventeen. It didn't work. He was a good cop.

'Sam, I knew you and Liska were on the Nixon assault,' he said. 'I figured you'd want a heads-up on this.'

'Thanks, I guess,' Kovac said. 'Any ID on the shooter?'

Michaels made a face.

Answer: no. And there wouldn't be. The Jones girl was dead because her mother had been asked to testify against one of Deene Combs's thugs. The neighborhood's leaders would make an angry show of demanding justice and daring citizens to stand up and fight back, but no one would. Not after this. And who the hell could blame them?

'I told you!'

The shout turned all their heads. Chamiqua Jones stormed toward them, her focus on Kovac, her eyes full of tears and pain and anger. She thrust a gloved finger at him.

'I told you you was gonna get me killed! Look what they did! Look what they did! They killed my child! They killed my Chantal! What you gonna do for me now, Kovac?'

'I'm sorry, Chamiqua,' Kovac said, knowing how horribly inadequate the apology was.

She glared at him and at Liska. 'You're sorry? My child is dead! I told you to leave me be, but you had to keep on. Testify, Chamiqua, you said. Tell what you saw or we'll put your black ass in jail, you said. I told you what would happen. I *told* you!'

She hit Kovac in the chest with both fists as hard as she could. He let her have her shot. Then she stepped back, glaring at him because it hadn't helped.

'I hate you!' she shouted.

Kovac said nothing. Chamiqua Jones didn't want to hear how rotten he felt, or how badly he wished this hadn't happened. She wouldn't forgive him or absolve him for doing his job, for following orders. It wouldn't impress her that he had become a cop because he wanted to help people, to try to do his little part to make the world a better, safer place. Chamiqua Jones didn't give a shit about him, except to hate him.

'Ms Jones, if there's anything we can do –' Liska began.

'You've done enough,' Jones said bitterly. 'Do you have children, Detective?'

'I have two boys.'

'Then you pray to God you don't ever have to feel what I'm feeling. That's what you can do.'

She turned away and went to where her daughter's body lay. No one tried to stop her.

'It's a pisser,' Michaels said quietly, watching as Jones pulled the cover back and touched her child's bloody head. 'If people could stand up and give us thugs like Combs, this wouldn't happen. But because this kind of thing happens, nobody wants to stand up.'

'We tried to tell Leonard to back off,' Kovac said. 'Come up with some other angle to get Combs. But Sabin thought if we could nail the guy from the Nixon assault, he could turn him for Combs.'

Michaels sniffed. 'Bullshit. No banger's gonna beat a guy's head in with a tire iron, then give up his boss.'

'You know it and I know it.'

'And Chamiqua Jones pays for it,' Liska said, not able to take her eyes away from the grieving mother.

'Whatever you need from us relating to the Nixon case, just ask,' Kovac said.

'And vice versa,' Michaels said.

Kovac put a hand on Liska's shoulder as Michaels went back to work. 'Life sucks, and the night's still young,' he said. 'Come on, Tinks. I'll buy you a cup of coffee. We can cry on each other's shoulders.'

'No, thanks,' she said absently, still watching Chamiqua

Jones even as they started to walk away. 'I need to get home to my boys.'

Kovac put her in her car and watched her drive away, wishing he had someone to get home to.

A terrible sense of urgency chased Liska home. A feeling of dread, of impending doom. She couldn't escape the idea that while she had been paying her respects to the mother of a dead child, something horrible had happened to her own children. She drove fast, ignoring traffic laws and speed limits, feeling almost as if Chamiqua Jones's words to her had been a curse. That was stupid, she knew, but it didn't matter.

As a homicide detective, she encountered death on a regular basis. Like most cops, she had hardened herself to it long ago. That was the necessary route to maintain sanity. But there was no immunity to the effects of seeing a dead child. There was no escaping the emotions – the anger and sadness at how brief that young life had been, at the things that child would never experience; the heavy sense of guilt that the death could have been prevented somehow, some way. Adults could look out for themselves. Oftentimes an adult victim's life choices put the person in the situation that ended his life. But children never chose to be put at risk. Children were dependent on the adults in their lives to keep them safe.

Liska felt that burden now, as she turned off Grand Avenue and spotted her home. It was still standing. That was a good start. It hadn't been burned to the ground in her absence. It didn't matter that the sitter had told her so just ten minutes prior when she'd called home on her cell phone.

She pulled in the driveway, abandoned the car, and hurried to the house, fumbling with her keys.

The boys were in their pajamas, stretched out on their bellies in front of the television, mesmerized by the video game they were playing. Liska dropped her purse, toed her shoes off, and hurried across the room to them, ignoring the sitter's greeting. She fell down on her knees between them and scooped a boy into each arm, earning howls of protest.

'Hey!'

'You ruined my chance!'

'I was winning!'

'You were not!'

'Was so!'

Liska pulled them close and breathed deep the smell of clean hair and microwave popcorn. 'I love you guys. I love you so much!'

'You're cold!' R.J. exclaimed.

Kyle gave her a speculative look. 'Do you love me enough to let me stay over at Jason's house tonight? He called and asked.'

'Tonight?' Liska said, hugging him tighter. She closed her eyes against silly, sudden tears of relief and joy. 'Not a chance, Sport. Tomorrow, maybe. Not tonight. Not tonight.'

The sitter saw herself home. Liska played with the boys until they couldn't keep their eyes open anymore, then shepherded them off to their beds and lingered at the door, watching them sleep.

Calmer, reassured they were safe and sound, she checked all the locks, then drew a bubble bath – a rare, feminine treat. The warmth penetrated muscle, easing out the tension, the anxiety, the feeling of toxicity that always lingered after working a murder scene, as if evil hung in the air. She closed her eyes and rested her head on a rolled-up towel, a steaming cup of tea on the edge of the tub. She tried to clear her mind of everything and just drift, just *be* for a few minutes. What a luxury.

When she was completely relaxed, she opened her eyes, dried her hands, and reached for the stack of mail she'd piled on the edge of the vanity. No bills. No junk mail. Just a small stack of what looked to be Christmas cards. Once again, she wasn't going to get her cards out until God knew what holiday.

There was a card from her Aunt Cici in Milwaukee. A photo card of cousin Phil the dairy farmer and his family all in matching 'Got Milk?' T-shirts. Hallmark's finest from a college friend who had otherwise lost touch so long ago she still addressed the envelope to Mr and Mrs; why did people like that bother? Was it really so much trouble to cull out the database?

The last of the envelopes was addressed only to her. Another computer label, no return address. Odd. Obviously a card. The envelope was red. She slipped the letter opener under the flap. A simple business-type card with 'Season's Greetings' on the front. Something fell from it as Liska opened the card, and she swore and grabbed the dark square as it hit the surface of the bathwater.

A Polaroid snapshot. No. Three photographs stuck together.

Photographs of her children.

Liska's blood ran cold. Goose bumps pebbled every inch of her skin. Her hands began to tremble. One photograph had been taken as the boys stood in line to get on the bus at school. The second showed them playing with a friend as the school bus drove away from the stop down the block. The third showed them walking up the sidewalk to the house. On each photograph, someone had drawn a circle around each of the boys' heads with a black marker.

Inside the card, the only message was a phone number typed in black.

Setting the card and photos aside, Liska hauled herself out of the tub, wrapped her dripping body in a towel, and grabbed the portable phone. She was shaking so badly, she misdialed the number twice. On the third try, the call went through, and she waited. A machine answered on the fourth ring, the recorded voice sending a bolt of fear straight through her.

'Hi. This is Ken. I'm out doing something *so* exciting, I can't take your call right now. . . .'

Yeah. He was lying in a bed in a surgical intensive care unit. Ken Ibsen.

29

Famous last words: *It seemed like a good idea at the time.*

Kovac rang the bell before he could change his mind. He knew the minute she looked out the peephole in the front door. He could feel her presence, could feel her scrutiny, her indecision. Finally, the door opened and she looked out at him.

'Yes, I do have a phone,' he said. 'I have several, and I do know how to use them.'

'Then why don't you?' Savard asked.

'You might have said no.'

'I *would* have said no.'

'See?'

She didn't invite him in. Her eyes narrowed as she stared at his forehead. 'Were you in a fight?'

Kovac touched his fingers to the spot, remembering that he'd never finished washing the blood off. 'An innocent casualty of someone else's war.'

'I don't understand.'

'No. Neither did I,' he said, recalling the scene at Steve Pierce's house. 'It doesn't matter.'

'Why did you come here?'

'Mike Fallon was murdered.'

Her eyes widened. 'What?'

'Someone killed him. I've got his son, Neil, sitting in the pokey now, reflecting on the cleansing power of confession.'

'My God,' Savard murmured, opening the door a little wider. 'What have you got on him?'

'Nothing, really. We did it with mirrors. If it weren't the weekend and if he had a clever lawyer, he'd be sitting in his bar by now,' he admitted. 'On the other hand, he had opportunity, motive, and a bad attitude.'

'You think he did it.'

'I think Neil is proof there should be a lifeguard at the gene pool. He's a small, mean, angry person, bitter over the fact that people don't love him in spite of himself. His father's son,' he added, an ironic twist to his mouth.

'I thought Mike Fallon was your friend.'

'I respected what Mike represented on the job. He was an old-time cop.'

He looked back out toward the street, where a car was going by slowly. A couple checking house numbers. Normal people looking for another Christmas party. They probably hadn't come to this neighborhood from a murder scene.

'Maybe I had a soft spot for him because I want someone to have a soft spot for me when I'm that old and that resentful.'

'Is that what you came here looking for?' Savard asked. 'Sympathy?'

He shrugged. 'I'd even settle for pity tonight.'

'I don't keep much of that around.'

He thought she was almost allowing herself to smile. There was something softer in her eyes than he'd seen before.

'How about scotch?'

'I don't keep that either.'

'Neither do I. I drink it,' he said.

'That's right, you're a stereotype. The tragic hero.'

'The twice-divorced, smoking, drinking workaholic. I don't know what's heroic about that. It reeks of failure to me, but maybe I have unrealistic standards.'

'Why *did* you come here, Sergeant? I don't see what the news about Mike Fallon has to do with me.'

'Apparently so you could make me stand in the cold

while you chip away at my self-esteem with your blunt indifference.'

Almost-amusement to go with the almost-smile. 'Laying it on a little thick, aren't you?'

'I find subtlety is a waste of time. Especially when I've been drinking. I've already been indulging in that scotch we were talking about.'

'Drinking and driving? I guess I'd be doing a public service if I invited you in for a cup of coffee.'

'You'd be doing *me* a service. The only thing that overheats in my car is the radiator.'

Savard sighed and opened the door wider.

Kovac took advantage of the opportunity before she could change her mind. Winning the war of attrition. The house was warm and smelled of a wood fire and the aforementioned coffee. Homey. His house was cold and smelled of garbage.

'I think maybe *you're* developing a soft spot for me, Lieutenant.'

'Mmm . . . in my head,' she said, and walked away.

Kovac toed off his shoes and followed her through a small formal dining room to a country kitchen. She was dressed for lounging in a loose, flowing outfit the color of sage. Like something an old-time Hollywood star would wear, he thought. Her hair tumbled around her head in soft, silver-blond waves. A very alluring picture, except that there was a stiffness in her back and neck as she moved that hinted of pain. He wondered again about her story of a fall. Obviously, there was no one living with her, no boyfriend hanging around on a Friday night.

'How are you feeling?' he asked.

'I'm fine.'

She took a stoneware mug from a cupboard and filled it from the pot simmering on the coffee machine. The room was lit softly by small yellow lights mounted under the cupboards and on the ceiling.

'I take it Neil Fallon doesn't have an alibi.'

'Not that stands up in court,' Kovac said, leaning against the island. 'People never believe anyone else was home alone in bed. They always suspect everyone in the world is having sex or committing crimes but them.'

'Milk? Sugar?'

'Black, thanks.'

'No physical evidence?'

'None I believe will hold up past the lab.'

'He didn't leave any prints on the gun?'

'No.'

'What made you decide it was murder, then? Something the ME came up with?'

'The scene. The position of the gun. It shouldn't have fallen where it did. Couldn't have, if Mike pulled the trigger.'

She handed him his coffee, sipped her own, and made a thoughtful sound. 'That's sad his life had to end that way. His own son . . . imagine . . .' she said, staring at the floor. 'I'm sorry.'

'Yeah. You know, he had a chance to make things right with Andy and he didn't take it. Then everything went to hell on a sled.' He tasted the coffee, a little surprised there was no exotic flavor to it. It was just coffee. 'Apparently, Andy wanted to do something with Mike in relation to the Thorne homicide. Write down Mike's story or something.'

'Really? Did Mike tell you that?'

'No. A friend of Andy's mentioned it. Mike didn't want to do it. I guess stewing in the memories and sharing them were two different things. Did Andy ever say anything about it to you?'

Savard set her cup aside and crossed her arms as she leaned back against the counter. 'Not that I recall. Why would he?'

'No reason. I thought he might have mentioned it in passing, you being friends with Ace Wyatt. That's all.'

'We're not friends. He's an acquaintance. We have people in common.'

'Whatever. I guess he must have dropped it, anyway,' Kovac said. 'I didn't see anything in his office relating to it. No file, no clippings or anything like that. Unless all that stuff is in the same place as his copy of the Curtis-Ogden file. The same place as his laptop. Wherever that might be.'

'What do you think he hoped to gain by looking into his father's past?'

Kovac shrugged. 'Understanding, I guess. What Mike was these last twenty years started the night of that shooting. Or maybe he was just a brownnoser, trying to win the old man over by pretending interest in his father's life. You could say better than I – was Andy a kiss-ass?'

She thought about it a moment. 'He needed to please. He needed to succeed. That's why he took it so hard when the Curtis-Ogden case closed. He wanted to be the one to say it was over, not just have it end because Verma copped a plea.'

'I guess I know what that's like,' Kovac said with a sheepish smile. 'I'm not supposed to be spending time asking questions about Andy Fallon's death – or his life, for that matter – but I want to know. I want to feel satisfied. It ain't over till I say it's over. That's the way I am.'

'It makes you a good cop.'

'It makes me a pain in the ass. I once had a captain tell me that I'm paid to investigate crimes, not solve them.'

'What did you say to that?'

He laughed. 'To his face? "Yes, sir." My bank account couldn't handle a suspension. Behind his back? I called him something I shouldn't say in front of a lady.'

Savard picked up her coffee again and took a sip, looking at him from under her lashes. The almost-amusement, a shade of speculation. *Sexy*, he thought, *for a lady with a beat-up eye. Beautiful, bruises or no.*

She glanced away. 'I went over the case file, by the way.

Ogden was verbally abusive to Andy several times during the investigation, but that's not unusual. He made a couple of vague threats – also not unusual. Then Verma made his deal and it was over. There were no addendums to the file after the case closed. Ogden had no reason to continue contact.'

'What about Ogden's partner? Rubel?'

'Nothing about him. I don't think that was the name of his partner at the time of the incident. I think it was Porter. Larry Porter.

'For what it's worth,' she added, 'I personally believe Ogden was dirty. I believe he planted Curtis's watch at Verma's apartment. There just wasn't any way to prove it. We'd taken it as far as we could go based on what we had.'

'And after Verma copped, you would have had the union on you for harassing Ogden. And the brass on you for pissing off the union,' Kovac said. 'You're paid to investigate, not to solve.'

'And I have to live with the idea that Andy might have killed himself in part because of that,' she said quietly.

'Maybe,' Kovac conceded. 'Or maybe he killed himself because his lover wouldn't come out of the closet. Or because he thought his father might never love him again because he *had* come out of the closet. Or maybe he didn't kill himself at all.

'See, maybe it wasn't your fault at all. But you'll let the idea hurt you anyway,' he said. 'You'll punish yourself and think of a dozen ways you might have stopped it from happening – if only you'd been quick enough, sharp enough, or able to read the future in tea leaves.'

'I guess I'm an easy read.'

'No, you're not,' he said quietly, thinking she was one of the toughest people to read he'd ever come across. So guarded, so cautious. And that made her all the more intriguing to him. He wanted to know who she really was

313

and why she had become that person. He wanted to be allowed behind the walls.

'That's just what I'd do, that's all,' he said. 'It's what my partner would do too. I try to tell myself it's proof we haven't entirely detached from the human race. Though sometimes I think I'd be better off if I did.'

The weight of the evening rolled up against him, the emotions pressing against his own walls. He had successfully kept it at bay for a little while: the image of the street full of emergency vehicles; of the child's small body and the bloodstained snow.

He wandered to a set of French doors that looked out on a deck. A security light illuminated a wedge of backyard. The moon brightened what lay beyond, reflecting off the snow in a way that gave the landscape a blue cast. Dreamscape. Trees edged the property, keeping the neighbors from looking in.

'I lost one tonight,' he confessed. 'The child of a witness to an assault I was working. A little girl shot to death just to send a message to the neighborhood.'

'How is that your fault?'

He could see her edging closer. The filtered light from outside fell across her face, a gossamer veil that made her skin look pearly. *Softness*, he thought. Soft skin, soft hair in soft waves, lips that looked as soft as satin. He didn't try to see the walls and sharp edges; he wanted to pretend they didn't exist.

He shook his head. 'It's not. Not really. You look at a situation like that, an innocent child shot dead in the street. The shooter's probably fourteen and got the job handed to him on account of he's a juvenile, and he took it because a kill makes him with the gang. They shoot the little girl to scare people who are already on the edge of thinking life's too damn hard to care about anything but their own hide. They do it to scare the mother who didn't want to see a drug dealer getting his head beat in and wouldn't have testified anyway 'cause her first concern is to stay alive long enough to raise her children not to be sociopaths.

'You look at all that and there's plenty of blame to go around. But I'm a part of that picture too. I'm supposed to protect people, not get them killed. And I had to stand there tonight and look in that woman's face and offer an apology, like that would make it all right.'

'Blaming yourself won't make it right either,' Savard said.

She stood just to his right. She could have taken his hand in hers. He held his breath as if she were some wild creature who would bolt at his slightest movement.

'We do the best we can,' she said softly, looking inward. 'And punish ourselves for it. I've tried to make my choices with the idea that I've made those choices for the greatest good. Sometimes someone suffers in the process, but I made the decision for the right reason. That should count for something, shouldn't it?'

Kovac turned slowly to face her, a part of him still afraid she might run away. The need for reassurance was so clear in her eyes, it hurt him to see. A glimpse over the wall.

'It should,' he said. 'What is it inside us that doesn't let it?'

'I'm afraid to know,' she confessed, eyes bright with tears.

'Me too, I guess.'

She stared at him for a moment, then whispered, 'You're a good man, Sam Kovac.'

Half a smile curved his mouth. 'Would you say that again?'

'You're –'

He touched a forefinger to her lips. They felt exactly as he had imagined. 'No. My name. Say it again. Just so I can hear how it sounds.'

He moved his hand to cup her face. A single tear slid

315

down her face, silvered by the light. The word slipped from her lips on a trembling breath. 'Sam . . .'

He bent his head and captured the word in his mouth as he touched his lips to hers. Hesitantly. Asking. Holding his own breath tight in his lungs, even as desire swept through his veins in a warm rush.

Her hands came up slowly and rested on his forearms, not to push him away but to connect. Her mouth trembled beneath his, not out of fear but out of need. Accepting. Wanting. Her tongue touched his.

The kiss went on. Time suspended. He lifted his mouth a scant inch from hers and whispered her name. He took her into his arms as carefully as if she were made of glass. When he raised his head again and looked into her eyes, she said one word:

'Stay.'

Except for the pounding of his heart, Kovac went absolutely still. 'Are you sure?'

She leaned up and touched her lips to his again. 'Stay . . . Sam . . . Please . . .'

He didn't ask again. Maybe her life was as empty as his. Maybe their souls recognized the same pain in each other. Maybe she just needed to be held, and he needed to hold, to care for. Maybe it didn't matter why.

She led him up the stairs to a bedroom that carried a ghost of her perfume in the air and on the sheets. Pieces of her lay scattered on the dresser: earrings, a watch, a black velvet hair band. The lamp on the nightstand glowed amber, the light bathing her skin as he undressed her. He'd never seen anything so exquisite, had never been so moved by a woman's gift of herself to him.

She handed him a condom from a drawer in the nightstand; he tore open the package and offered it back to her. They didn't speak. Everything was said with a touch, with a look, a shuddering breath, a trembling sigh. She guided him to her. He entered her and thought his heart had stopped. They moved together, and it beat like a drum.

Need. Heat. Passion. Immersion. Languor. Urgency. One melded into the next and back again. The tastes of salt on skin, coffee on tongues. The feel of warm and wet, hard and soft. When she came, it was on a crescendo of hard-caught breaths and the wordless, desperate sounds of need. Release for him came like a bolt of lightning. His body jumped and jerked, and he thought he cried out but he wasn't sure.

He never stopped kissing her. Even after. Even as she fell asleep in his arms, his lips moved over hers, against her cheek, on her hair. In his heart was the fear the chance might not come again and he had to get his fill now, tonight. Then exhaustion swept over him like a blanket, and he closed his eyes and fell asleep.

When Kovac came around, he thought he'd had one hell of a dream. Then he opened his eyes.

Amanda.

She lay on her side, curled toward him, sleeping quietly. He pulled the covers up over her bare shoulder, and she sighed. The lamplight fell across her face, drawing his attention to the raw burns and bruises around her eye and cheekbone. His stomach clutched at the thought that he might have – must have – touched those places as they'd made love, and caused her pain. The idea of hurting her made him sick. If he ever found out a man had made those marks on her, he would track the guy down and beat him.

He rubbed a hand against his sternum, feeling as if he'd been kicked. Jesus, he'd slept with a lieutenant.

He'd fallen for a lieutenant.

You sure know how to pick 'em, Kovac.

What was she going to think when she opened her eyes? That she'd made a mistake? That she'd lost her mind? Would she be embarrassed or angry? He didn't know.

What he did know was that what they had shared was pretty damn special and he wouldn't regret it.

He slipped from the bed carefully, pulled on his pants, and went down the hall in search of a bathroom, not wanting the sound of running water to wake Amanda. He found a guest bath with fancy towels and decorative soaps that were probably not intended for use. He used them anyway. The reflection that stared back at him in the mirror looked tough, beat-up, showing age and the effects of a life with more disappointment than fulfillment. What the hell would a woman see in that and want? he wondered.

He washed up and went back into the hall, catching the smell of burning coffee wafting up from downstairs. They'd left the pot on.

He went down to the kitchen and turned it off, pouring himself half a cup of what was left. Sipping at the coffee, he began to wander through the house, turning off lights as he passed through the rooms.

Amanda Savard had created a nice retreat for herself. The furniture looked comfortable, inviting. The colors were soothing and quiet. Odd, though, that there was nothing of her – no family photos, no snapshots of friends or of herself. A lot of framed black-and-white photographs of empty places. He remembered seeing some of those in her office, and he wondered what they meant to her. He wanted to see something that spoke about her life. But maybe that *was* what he was seeing. God knew there wasn't much evidence of who he was in his house. A stranger would have learned more about him in his cubicle at work.

In the living room, he took a poker and stabbed at the dying embers of the fire, breaking them up, pushing them apart. He closed the glass doors and went to turn out the ginger jar lamp on the end table by the sofa. A book lay on the table. Stress management.

Beyond the living room, beyond a pair of open French doors was another room with lights on and a stereo playing softly. It sounded like the same light jazz station Steve Pierce had been listening to.

Kovac went in to turn it off. Her office. Another lovely oasis of cherry furnishings and photographs of nothing. He'd seen a desk this neat once in an office supply store. That kind of fastidiousness spoke of a need for order and control. No big surprise there. The cubbyholes of the shelves above the desk held a few mementos that made him smile. A small carving of a mother tiger and her cub rolling together. A collection of colored glass paperweights that were more works of art than tools. A stress relief toy that was a little rubber creature whose eyes popped out when squeezed. A badge.

Curious, he picked up the badge and looked at it. It was an old style. One he recognized from when he had first come on the force half a million years ago. Certainly before Amanda's time, which meant it had to have belonged to someone who meant something to her.

City of Minneapolis. Badge number 1428.

The first thing he'd seen in her home that hinted at her past, and it had to do with the job. Maybe her life really was as empty as his.

He put the badge back in its place, turned off the lights and stereo, and left the room, the light falling from the second story guiding his way. He climbed the stairs, thinking of sliding back under the covers with her, feeling her warm, soft body next to his. It had been so long since he'd known that kind of comfort, he'd forgotten what it was like.

'No!'

The cry came as he was halfway up the stairs. Kovac bolted up the rest and ran for the bedroom.

'No! No!'

'Amanda!'

She sat upright in the middle of the bed, eyes wide open,

arms swinging at nothing, engaged in a battle with something only she could see inside her mind.

'No! No! Stop it!'

'Amanda?'

Kovac stood beside the bed, not knowing what to do. It was an eerie sight. She appeared to be awake, but she didn't seem to see him standing there. Slowly, carefully, he eased a hand out to touch her shoulder.

'Amanda? Honey, wake up.'

She jerked at his touch, shying toward the other side of the bed, wild-eyed. Kovac caught hold of her arm as gently as he could and still hold on to her.

'Amanda, it's me, Sam. Are you awake?'

She blinked at him then, whatever horrible spell she had been under shattering. She tipped her face up and looked at him, seeing him, and the confusion in her face was enough to break his heart.

'It's all right, honey,' he said softly, sitting down on the edge of the bed. 'It's all right, sweetheart, you had a bad dream. You're all right now. It's all right.'

He drew her to him and she curled against him like a child. Her whole body was shaking. Kovac held her with one arm and pulled a blanket up around her with the other hand.

'I'm sorry,' she whispered. 'I'm sorry.'

'Shhh . . . There's nothing to be sorry about. You had a bad dream. You're all right now. I won't let anything hurt you.'

'Oh, God,' she whispered, miserable, embarrassed.

Kovac just held her. 'It's okay.'

'No,' she said, pulling away. Head down, not looking at him. 'No, it's not. I'm sorry.'

She got up from the bed, finding a silk robe among the covers and pulling it on, covering herself as if she were ashamed to have him see her.

'I'm very sorry,' she said, still not looking at him.

Kovac said nothing as she hurried across the room and disappeared into the bathroom. There came that feeling again: that there wouldn't be a second chance with her, that tonight was it. He had seen her at her most vulnerable. Amanda Savard would have a very hard time dealing with that.

He sighed heavily and got up, finding his shirt and pulling it on. Knowing exactly how little good it was going to do, he went to the door of the bathroom and knocked.

'Amanda? Are you all right?'

'Yes, thank you. I'm fine.'

He winced at the formality in her tone, recognizing it as one of her favorite defenses, a way to keep people at arm's length. He deliberately took the other route.

'Honey, you don't have to be embarrassed. The line of work we're in, we all have bad dreams. You ought to catch some of mine.'

The water ran, then shut off. There was no other sound. He could imagine her staring at herself in the mirror, the way he had done earlier. She wouldn't like what she was seeing: the marks on her face, the pallor of her skin, the look in her eyes.

He stepped back as the doorknob turned. She came out and stopped, arms wrapped around herself, her gaze just missing him.

'This really wasn't a very good idea –'

'Don't say that,' Kovac said.

She closed her eyes for a second and went on. 'I think we both just needed something tonight, and that was fine, but now –'

'It was better than fine,' he said, moving into her space, willing her to look at him. She wouldn't.

'I want you to leave now.'

'No.'

'Please don't make this more awkward than it already is.'

'It doesn't have to be awkward at all.'

321

'I don't see people from work.'

'Oh, really? Who do you see?'

'That's none of your business.'

'Uh – yes, I think it is,' he argued.

She sighed and looked away. 'I don't want a relationship. It's best I say that now, so we can just let this go and move on.'

'I don't want to let this go,' Kovac said, putting his hands on her, taking gentle hold of her upper arms. 'Amanda, don't do this.'

She turned her face away and stared at the floor. 'Please leave.'

She couldn't hide the emotion that trembled in her voice. He heard it plainly: pain, sadness. He felt the same things for her in his own heart.

'Please . . . Sam . . .' she whispered.

He bent his head and touched his lips to her cheek. He brought up a hand to stroke her hair. 'I'm sorry.'

She closed her eyes tight against the threat of tears. 'Please . . .'

'All right,' he murmured. 'All right.'

He stepped away from her, seeking out the rest of his clothes. She didn't move. When he was ready, he went to her again and touched her cheek with the back of his hand.

'Come lock up behind me. I need to know you're safe.'

She nodded and went with him.

In the entry hall, he pulled on his shoes and coat, and hunted his gloves up out of the pockets. She never met his eyes once. He tried to wait her out, just standing there by the door like a dope, but she wouldn't look up and she wouldn't say anything. He wanted to shake her and pull her into his arms and kiss her. But men weren't allowed to make a point that way anymore, and it probably wasn't the way to play Amanda anyway. She needed care and time; enough space not to feel threatened, but not so much that she could retreat.

Like you really think you can pull this off.

'Whatever you decide,' he said at last, 'this wasn't a mistake, Amanda.'

She said nothing and he let himself out, the cold slapping him in the face.

Here's your reality, Kovac, he thought as the door shut and locked behind him. *Out in the cold, alone.*

It wasn't anything less than he'd had before, but it was worse now because he'd had a taste of what could be.

He drove back into the city on empty roads, went back to an empty house and an empty bed, and lay awake the rest of the night staring inward at the emptiness of his life.

30

Liska pulled into the driveway, barely sparing a glance at the dashboard clock. Saturday morning in her house meant youth hockey. Kyle and R.J. started the day on the ice at six A.M. She had left them under the watchful charge of a buddy who worked sex crimes for the St Paul PD and had two boys of his own in the same league. No adult would come within ten feet of those children with Milo watching them.

Barely seven-thirty now, and the sun was just coming up. Most of Eden Prairie was probably still sleeping off the eggnog hangovers from the Friday night Christmas parties. Liska didn't care. She'd spent the forty-five minutes driving out here stoking her anger like a blast furnace. She didn't care if she had to kick the door in and drag his hairy ass out of bed. She was going to speak with Cal Springer, and he was going to listen.

She stormed to the front door of the too-nice house and leaned on the bell, then stabbed at it over and over. She could hear it ringing inside, and no other sound. The cul-de-sac was still. Cars parked overnight in driveways had windows thick with frost. The toothpick-young trees in the yards were flocked with white. Liska's breath silvered the air. It was so cold, it hurt to breathe.

The door opened and Mrs Cal, dressed in a flannel nightgown, stared out at her, her little mouth a round O of surprise.

'Where is he?' Liska demanded, walking in uninvited.

Patsy Springer stepped back. 'Calvin? What? What do you want at this hour? I don't –'

Liska gave her a look that had cracked confessions out of hardened criminals. 'Where is he?'

Cal's voice came from the direction of the kitchen. 'Who is it, Pats?'

Liska moved past the wife, digging a hand down into her purse as she homed in on her target. Cal sat at the oak table in the breakfast nook wearing the same clothes he'd had on the day before, a soft-boiled egg and a bowl of Malt-O-Meal in front of him. He gaped like a fish when he saw her.

'What are you doing here?' he demanded. 'This is my home, Liska –'

She pulled the Polaroids from her purse and slapped them down on the table beside his plate. Springer started to move his chair back. She grabbed a handful of his hair and held him in place, close at her side, ignoring his howl of pain.

'These are my children, Cal,' she said, working to keep from shouting in his face. 'Do you see them? Are you looking at these?'

'What's the matter with you?'

'I'm angry. These are my boys. Do you know who sent me these pictures, Cal? I'll give you two guesses.'

'I don't know what you're doing here!' he said, trying to get up again.

Liska yanked his hair and wound her fingers into it even tighter. Mrs Cal hovered at the archway to the front hall, her hands fluttering at her chest.

'She's crazy, Calvin! She's crazy!'

'Rubel and Ogden sent me these,' Liska said, grabbing one of the snapshots with her free hand. She stuck it in Cal Springer's face. 'I can't prove it, but they did. These are the people you're dealing with, Cal. This is what shitbags they are. They would threaten little children. And you're protecting them. That makes you the same as one of them, as far as I'm concerned.'

'Calvin?' the wife shrieked. 'Should I call nine-one-one?'

'Shut up, Patsy!' he shouted.

'If anyone harms a hair on the head of one of these boys,' Liska said, 'I'll kill that person. I mean that, Cal. I'll fucking kill them, and no one will ever find all the pieces. Do you understand me?'

He tried to get away from her. Liska yanked his hair and hit him in the forehead with her knuckles.

'Owww!'

'You stupid son of a bitch!' she yelled, and hit him again. 'What's wrong with you? How can you get in bed with them?'

She shoved him away from her abruptly and he fell off the chair and scrambled backward across the floor like a crab.

'You're despicable!' Liska shouted.

She grabbed the cup with the soft-boiled egg and threw it at him. He brought his arms up to protect himself and fell backward, hitting his head on a cabinet. It sounded like a gunshot. Mrs Springer screamed.

'You go to Castleton, you spineless worm,' Liska ordered. 'Tell him where you *weren't* Thursday night. You go to IA. They don't love anything more than they love a sniveling, worthless piece of shit like you. You turn these animals in or I'll make the rest of your career a misery Job couldn't survive! Nobody. *Nobody* threatens my children and gets away with it!'

She threw the Malt-O-Meal at him as a final exclamation point, then gathered up the Polaroids and stuffed them back into her bag. Springer stayed where he was, Malt-O-Meal running down his cheek.

Liska took a couple of fast, deep breaths to compose herself, and looked at Patsy Springer. 'I'm sorry to have interrupted your breakfast,' she said, her voice still trembling with rage.

Mrs Cal made a little cry in her throat and ran into a corner of the room.

'I'll see myself out,' Liska said, and left the house, shaking so hard she felt as if she was having a seizure.

When she got in the Saturn, she let go of a sigh.

'Well,' she said aloud as she cranked the key and started the engine. 'I feel better.'

Why did you have to tell? I could have made it right. . . .

What the hell had Jocelyn Daring meant by that?

Kovac sat on a small chair in one corner of Andy Fallon's bedroom, staring at nothing. He replayed the memory of Jocelyn Daring walking into Pierce's study. The look on her face. The fury in her eyes. If he hadn't been there to stop her, what kind of damage might she have done to Pierce?

He probably should have arrested her for what she *had* done. Minnesota laws had zero tolerance for domestic abuse. Even if the victim didn't want to press charges, the state did. But he hadn't taken that step. Mitigating circumstances, a lawyer might argue. Poor Jocelyn. Upon hearing her fiancé's confession of a homosexual relationship, she lost her mind for a moment and struck out. Why add insult to her injury?

Because she might decide to finish the job.

She had left the house willingly, silently, dragging an overflowing suitcase to the waiting car of her maid of honor. Steve Pierce had gone by cab to the nearest ER to claim he'd slipped on the ice and cracked his head.

Love American style.

Love . . .

Kovac tried to shake off that thought and focus instead on the scene of Andy Fallon's death. That was part of the reason he had come here: to get his mind on something other than the big tumble he might have actually taken for a lady with lieutenant's bars and some deep dark trouble on her mind. He was trying not to wonder at the source of her nightmare, trying not to think that what had happened wasn't an isolated incident, and that was why she'd asked him to go — because she was afraid it would happen again and he would want to know why. Those were the thoughts he had come here to avoid. Those thoughts he kept thinking and then reminding himself not to.

Nor did he want to think about how it had felt to make love to her or the incredible sense of protectiveness that had come over him as he'd held her after the nightmare. He would put his mind on work, which was the only thing he was really very good at anyway. The job never told him to take a hike.

The corpse smell lingered in the room. Kovac stuck his nose over a steaming cup of Caribou dark roast and breathed deep.

I guess I'd be doing a public service if I invited you in for a cup of coffee. . . .

He blinked out the image of Amanda standing at her front door, peeking out at him. He needed to consider a different blonde.

Question: Could Jocelyn Daring have killed her fiancé's gay lover? Yes. Had she had the opportunity? He didn't know and couldn't ask her. The case was officially closed; he had no right to question anyone. Had Pierce mentioned being with her the night of Andy Fallon's death? If she'd had the opportunity and taken it, how had she pulled it off? How would she have gotten Fallon to bed? No one had suggested Andy Fallon had flipped the switch both ways. Everyone had spoken too highly of him to imagine he might go to bed with his lover's girlfriend. So, there was that problem.

He thought of the sleeping pills, of the wineglasses in the dishwasher.

Maybe . . .

Next question: If she had drugged him, knocked him out, could she have hung him? Could she have lifted a man's deadweight?

He stared at the bed, then at the beam the rope had hung from. He got up from the chair and went to sit on the edge of the bed, then rose and stood approximately where the body had been hanging. The full-length mirror was positioned exactly as it had been; the word *Sorry* appeared scrawled across his belly. The mirror had been dusted for prints but hadn't been confiscated as evidence because no crime had been committed. Kovac looked in it now and tried to picture Jocelyn Daring on the bed behind him.

It might have been possible to get the victim into a sitting position on the edge of the bed, put the noose around his neck, then hoist him up with the rope and tie the rope off on the bedpost. Maybe. What had Andy Fallon weighed? One-seventy-five? One-eighty? One hundred eighty pounds of unconscious, uncooperative weight. Jocelyn was strong, but . . .

While a woman might have struggled to accomplish what he had just imagined, a man would have been able to pull it off more easily.

Could Neil have followed that same basic plan? Killed his brother for not loaning him money, or for not being a loser like him, or because he was jealous, or because he wanted to punish their father before he did him in too?

Kovac went back to his chair and sat again. He looked at how tidy the room was, remembered how perfectly made the bed had been. It had struck him odd that Andy wouldn't have sat on the bed before he did the deed. And that there were sheets in the washing machine.

Who did their laundry, then killed themselves?

He thought of Neil Fallon's place as they had executed the search warrant. The kind of frat-house filth and disorder that gave single guys a bad name. Pierce had said it: *Neil's the messy type, don't you think? . . . devastation at the scene, fingerprints everywhere . . .*

Neil Fallon hadn't changed a sheet in his life. There was

no evidence in his own home that he had any idea how to run a dishwasher.

Who then? Who else had motive? Ogden's beef with IA was over. Unless Fallon had come up with something new. And they might never know that unless they found Fallon's personal notes on the case. And how could that ox Ogden pull off something with this much finesse? It wouldn't be his nature. Beating someone with a pipe was his nature. How would Ogden even have gotten in the front door? Fallon wouldn't have let him in the house. Maybe at gunpoint.

There was no denying Liska had stirred the hornet's nest looking at the Curtis-Ogden angle. . . .

As for Steve Pierce, Kovac felt he had done his confessing. He didn't see Pierce killing his lover in cold blood, the way Fallon had died. If he had loved Andy the way he seemed to, he couldn't have humiliated him that way. And the sex-game angle didn't play, according to Kate Conlan.

Kovac sighed. 'Speak to me, Andy.'

It didn't take Sherlock Holmes to figure out most murders. A true whodunit was the exception rather than the rule. Most people were killed by someone they knew, for a reason that was simple.

Calls to the friends in Andy's address book had turned up nothing. He hadn't been that close to that many people. Too many years of living a secret life. Only Pierce had mentioned having seen him recently with another man. Another lover?

Most people were killed by someone they knew, for a reason that was simple.

Private life: family, friends, lovers, ex-lovers.

Professional life: co-workers, enemies made on the job or because of the job.

He didn't know what other cases Andy had had in the hopper. Savard wouldn't give that out, especially since his death had been ruled something other than homicide. She didn't seem concerned that any of his current caseload might be harboring a murderer. And so Kovac came back to the only case he knew anything about: Curtis-Ogden.

No. That wasn't exactly true. According to Pierce, Andy might have been looking into the Thorne murder. But what could have come of a case closed twenty years ago – besides resentment from his father?

Which brought Kovac back to suicide. Maybe a guy like Andy – a guy who dotted all his *i*'s and crossed all his *t*'s, a guy who needed approval and control . . . Maybe a guy like that *would* change his sheets before he stretched his neck.

Most people were killed by someone they knew, for a reason that was simple. Themselves. Suicide. Depression.

Death didn't get more simple than that.

Too bad he couldn't make himself buy it.

The homicide office was quiet on Saturday. Leonard never came in on weekends. Shift detectives were primarily on call. People sometimes came into the office to catch up on paperwork. Kovac spent most of his Saturdays here because he had no life.

He hung his coat up and wondered what Amanda was doing with her Saturday. Was she thinking about him, about what had happened? Was she reliving the moment he'd walked out the door, rewriting it in her head so that she asked him to stay?

He fell into his chair and stared at the telephone.

No. No, he wouldn't call. But he snatched up the receiver to check his voice mail. On the off chance . . . There was nothing. He sighed, flipped through the Rolodex, and dialed a number.

'Records, Turvey.' The voice on the other end rattled with gravel and phlegm.

'Russell, you old mole. Why don't you get a fucking life?'

'Ha! What the hell would I want with that? J. Christ. If I had to interact with regular people . . .' The old man made a gargling noise. 'Argh. I'd sooner hump a monkey.'

'Yeah, there's an image.' Russell Turvey: sixty-whatever years old with a face like Popeye, a cigarette hanging on his lip, a stomach like a basketball, doing it with a monkey.

Turvey laughed and coughed and hacked. His lungs sounded like a couple of plastic bags half-full of Jell-O.

Kovac picked up the pack of Salems he'd bought on the way in and threw it in the garbage.

'What'd you need, Sam? Is it legal?'

'Sure.'

'Well, shit. You're no fun. Getting dull in your old age. Hey, that was too bad about Iron Mike, huh? I heard it was you found him. It's always those hard-ass guys that eat their guns.'

'Yeah, well, he might not have. I'm looking into it.'

'J. Christ! You're shittin' me! Who'd waste a bullet on a moldy old turd like him?'

'I'll keep you posted,' Kovac promised. 'Listen, Russ, I came across an old badge the other day in a junk shop. I'm curious who might have worn it. Can you find something like that?'

'Sure. If I don't have it, I know who does. I got nothing else to do here but sit around with my thumb up my ass.'

'You're killing me with the visuals here, Russell.'

'Argh. Come on down and take a picture for your scrapbook. What's the badge number?'

'Fourteen twenty-eight. Looked like a seventies issue. I was just curious.'

'I'll dig it up.'

'Thanks. I owe you one.'

'Catch the bastard that capped Mike. We'll call it even.'

'I'll do what I can.'

'I know you, Sam. You'll do nine times more than that, and some brass cocksucker'll take all the credit.'

'The way of the world, Russ.'

'Argh. Fuck 'em.' He hacked into the phone and hung up.

Kovac dug the cigarettes out of the garbage, bent the pack in two, and tossed it back in.

He turned the computer on and spent the next hour getting to know Jocelyn Daring. Through one source, he found out she had graduated cum laude from Northwestern, where she had been a standout field hockey player. Athletic. Strong – he already knew that. Aggressive – he'd seen that for himself. She was fourth in her class at the University of Minnesota law school. Ambitious. Hardworking. Through DMV records he discovered she had a lead foot and did a poor job feeding parking meters. That could suggest a certain disregard for rules . . . or so would say John Quinn and his profiler pals.

But he discovered no criminal record, no newspaper stories about her flipping out in a restaurant or anything of the sort. He hadn't really expected to. Even if Jocelyn had a history of irrational behavior, her family had the bucks to cover it up.

Not so the Fallon clan, Kovac could see as he went through the file Elwood had put together on Neil. Neil's life foibles were a matter of public record. The assault conviction, a couple of DUIs, tax problems, health code violations at the bar, run-ins with agents of the Department of Natural Resources for taking more than his legal limit of damn near every living creature that had a season on it.

The pattern was one of wanting more than what he was entitled to. A man with resentment for authority. The complete opposite of his brother – something Neil undoubtedly blamed Andy for, though it had most likely happened the other way around. Andy had watched Neil screw up and cause trouble, and he had gone a hundred eighty degrees in the other direction to please his father. And he'd done it right up to the end, with the unforgivable exception of telling the old man the truth about his sexuality.

Poor kid. Even going so far as to try to understand Mike through his life experiences. What was to understand? There weren't that many layers to guys like Mike Fallon. That was where Neil had the edge on Andy: he had understood Mike perfectly.

'I've got nothing to say to you, Kovac. Not without having my lawyer present.'

Neil Fallon glared at him and paced by the door to the interview room. He looked natural in the orange jailhouse jumpsuit, except it should have had dirt and grease on it. He had had to cuff the pants legs to keep from tripping over them.

'This isn't about you, Neil,' Kovac said, sitting in the plastic chair and squaring an ankle over a knee. Mr Relaxation.

'Then why are you here? I got nothing to say to you.'

'So you've said. So I guess you don't want a chance to help yourself out.'

'How can I help myself out if it isn't about me?'

'Good faith.'

Fallon's eyebrows climbed his forehead. 'Good faith? Stick it up your ass.'

'For a guy who claims to be straight, you're awful big on wanting me to stick something up my ass,' Kovac observed.

'Fuck you!' Fallon snapped, catching himself too late. He growled and paced some more. 'I'm suing you, Kovac. Suing this rotten police department.'

Kovac sighed his boredom. 'Look, Neil, you tell me you're innocent. You tell me you wouldn't kill your old man.'

'I didn't.'

'So help me understand some things. That's all I'm asking. Understanding is the key to enlightenment. You know, the policeman is your friend,' he said as if he were talking to a four-year-old. 'And if he's not, you're fucked. Make me like you here, Neil.'

Fallon leaned against the wall beside the door and crossed his arms, thinking.

'My lawyer says not to talk to you without him present.'

'Once you've engaged counsel, nothing you say without him present can be used against you. You can't get hurt here. You can only help yourself. I never wanted us to be enemies, Neil. Hell, we shared a bottle. You're a decent, hardworking guy. So am I.'

Fallon waited, lower lip sticking out.

'I brought you some cigarettes,' Kovac said, holding up the pack.

Fallon came over and took it, making a face. 'They're all bent!'

'Hey, they still burn.'

'Jesus,' he grumbled, but took one out and tried to straighten it. Kovac handed him a lighter.

'I'm just curious about some things with Andy – and no, I don't think you killed him. I don't know if anybody did. Everybody says he was depressed. I just want a clearer picture of that, that's all.'

Behind the haze of smoke, Fallon narrowed his eyes, thinking: *trick question.*

'See, I'm a homicide cop,' Kovac went on. 'I look sideways at everybody when somebody's suddenly dead. It's nothing personal. If my old man turned up dead, I'd look at my mother, for chrissake. But there's another picture here to look at. Say, what if Andy wanted to get close with your dad again. He wanted a chance to win him back, so to speak. So he tries to do some things with Mike, talk to him, spend time with him. Maybe he buys him that big-ass TV in the living room –'

'Wyatt bought that,' Fallon said, matter-of-fact. He took a seat and considered the crooked cigarette.

'What?'

'Ace Wyatt. The old man's guardian angel,' Fallon said sarcastically. 'It was always that way since the shooting. Wyatt helped with hospital bills, bought stuff for the house, for Andy and me. Mike always said that's how it was – cops looking out for cops. That's what it's all about, he said, obligation. And that's what it was. Wyatt never wanted to spend any time with the old man, or with any of us. He'd come into the house and act like he thought he was getting fleas. Big asshole.'

'Yeah, that's pretty rotten, buying you stuff like that.'

'I always figured he felt guilty 'cause Mike caught that bullet. Wyatt living right across the street from Thorne and all. Him being the one that Thorne called for help. It should have been him in that wheelchair. But Mike beat him to it.'

Kovac digested the theory, thinking Fallon probably had a pretty good handle on it. Mike had caught that bullet instead of Ace Wyatt, and he'd never let Wyatt forget it. The fading image of the noble legend washed away by the acid rain of reality.

'Mike needed something, he'd call Wyatt,' Neil went on, puffing on the L-shaped cigarette. 'And don't think he didn't throw that up in my face every chance he got. I should have been taking care of him. The oldest son and all that bullshit. Like he ever did shit for me.'

'How old was Andy at the time of the shooting?'

'Seven or eight, I guess. Why?'

'Someone told me he had wanted to sit down with Mike and talk about what happened. To try to get a better understanding of your father.'

Fallon laughed and coughed and puffed on the crooked cigarette. 'Yeah, that was Andy. Mr Sensitivity. What's to understand? Mike was a bitter old son of a bitch, that's all.'

'I guess Mike didn't want to talk about what happened. Had Andy said anything to you?'

He thought about it for a moment, looking as if he was trying to remember. 'I guess he said something about it one of those last times I saw him. Mentioned it in relation to Mike not wanting him poking at old wounds. I didn't pay much attention. What was the point digging all that up?' He studied Kovac for a moment. 'Why do you care?'

Kovac turned the information over in his mind, mixing it into what he already had, trying to recall something he thought Mike had said in the last few days of his life.

'I'm just thinking,' he said, just to fill airtime. 'Andy had some problems with depression. If it meant a lot to him to get back with the old man, and Mike wouldn't cooperate, then maybe he really did hit bottom and check out. And maybe Mike blamed himself. . . .'

'Well, that would be a first.' Fallon finished the cigarette and crushed the butt out on the sole of his shoe. 'Never blame yourself when you can blame someone else. That was Mike.'

Kovac checked his watch.

'So if you're on the suicide angle now, how long before I get outta here?'

'It's out of my hands, Neil,' Kovac said, pushing to his feet. He went to the door and pushed the buzzer for the jailer. 'Not my fault. It's those rotten lawyers. I'd help you if I could. Keep the cigarettes. It's the least I can do.'

31

The *Minneapolis Star Tribune* printed Ace Wyatt's shooting schedule for *Crime Time* in the entertainment news every Thursday. Part of the show's gimmick was Wyatt's interaction with the audience. It was like a fucking infomercial, Kovac had thought the few times he'd watched it. Or something from the Food Channel. Ace Wyatt: the Emeril Lagasse of law enforcement.

The crime du jour was being reenacted in a hockey rink in the suburb of St Louis Park. Murder by curling stone: a cautionary tale of poor sportsmanship. Kovac badged the security bruiser standing at the roped-off section of bleachers and walked into the thick of Ace Mania.

A twelve-by-twelve red carpet had been spread on a section of the ice. The camera stood at one corner of it, along with a bored videographer who looked like Gandhi in a down jacket. Another videographer, this one on skates and with a handheld camera, leaned against the frame of the hockey goalie's net. Four lucky fans had been chosen to sit in the penalty boxes. Another hundred sat behind them. Lots of large women and wimpy-looking older men in red *PRO*Active! sweatshirts.

'We need quiet now, people!' shouted a thin, rawboned woman in black-rimmed glasses and a coat that looked as if it had been made from olive-green shag carpeting. She clapped her hands precisely three times and the crowd obediently went silent.

The director, a fat guy gnawing on a Slim-Fast bar, shouted at the two actors: 'Places! Let's get it right this time!'

One of the actors, a fiftyish guy in a Nordic patterned

sweater and what looked like blue tights, slipped and slid across the ice, arms working like spastic propellers at his sides.

'It's bothering me, Donald,' he complained. 'How can I think like a curler when there's a hockey goal sitting there?'

'Tight shots, Keith. No one's going to see the net. Think small. If you have to think at all.'

The actor went to find his mark. The director gave the God-spare-me-from-actors shake of the head.

Kovac spotted Wyatt sitting away from the audience, having his makeup retouched. Hugging themselves against the cold of the arena, a couple of Hollywood mover-shaker types stood behind him, smiling gamely while Gaines snapped a Polaroid. An anorexic young woman with brilliant red hair sculpted into a hedge on top of her head, and a twenty-something guy in a black leather coat and tiny rectangular spectacles.

'One more for the scrapbook,' Gaines said. The flash burst, and the camera spat out its product.

'The audience doesn't seem to mind the cold,' the guy said.

Gaines gave them the engaging grin. 'They love Captain Wyatt. We turn away droves at every taping. They're so excited to be here. What's a little chill?'

The girl bounced up and down and rubbed her hands over her arms. 'I've never been so cold in my life! I haven't been warm one minute since I got off the plane. How do people live here?'

'You think this is cold?' Kovac said, and huffed his disgust. 'Come back in January. You'll think you died and went to Siberia. Colder than a grave-digger's ass.'

The girl looked at him the way she might look at some odd creature in the zoo. Gaines lost the grin.

'Sergeant Kovac. What a pleasure,' he said flatly.

'For me too,' Kovac said, giving the scene the disdainful

once-over again. 'I don't get to the circus every day. I have a real job.'

'Yvette Halston,' the redhead introduced herself. 'Vice president, creative development, Warner Brothers television.'

The guy stuck his hand out. 'Kelsey Vroman, vice president, reality programming.'

Reality programming.

'Kovac. Sergeant. Homicide.'

'Sam!' Wyatt came up out of his chair, shooing the makeup woman away. He pulled the paper-towel bib out of the neck of his double-breasted navy Italian suit and tossed it aside. 'What brings you here? Did you get the lab results back on the Fallon evidence?'

The WB VPs pricked up their ears at the sound of real cop talk.

'Not yet.'

'I made a couple of phone calls. They're on it today.'

'Yeah, thanks, Ace,' he said without appreciation. 'Actually, I came to ask you about something else. Have you got a minute?'

Gaines came to Wyatt's side, clipboard in hand, and tried to show him a schedule. 'Captain, Donald wants to get through this section before one. The rest of the curling people were told to be here no later than one-thirty for the interview portion. We'll be cutting lunch by thirty minutes as it is. The union people will have a fit.'

'Then break for lunch now,' Wyatt ordered.

'But they're ready for the shot.'

'Then they'll be ready after lunch, won't they?'

'Yes, but –'

'Then what's the problem, Gavin?'

'Yeah, Gavin,' Kovac goaded. 'What's the problem?'

Gaines gave Kovac a cold look. 'I believe you're the one who pointed out that Captain Wyatt is retired from the force,' he said. 'He has other obligations than to solve your case for you, but he's too decent a man to tell you to go away.'

'Gavin . . .' Wyatt chided. 'I don't have any obligations more important than a murder investigation.'

The VPs both got wet on that one.

'Ace,' the redhead purred, 'you're consulting on a case? You didn't tell us! That could be very exciting! What do you think, Kelsey?'

'We could get something set up with various law enforcement agencies for a weekly segment. Police, DEA, FBI. Have the consultation at the end of the show. Five minutes, *mano a mano*, detective to detective. Ace offers the benefit of his no-nonsense wisdom. I like it. It adds a sense of immediacy and vitality. Don't you think so, Gavin?'

'It could work very well,' Gaines said diplomatically. 'I'm just concerned about our schedule today.'

'We'll deal with it, Gavin,' Wyatt said dismissively, then turned to Kovac again. 'Let's go upstairs, Sam. You can have a bite while we talk. Our caterer is fabulous. Gavin found him. Makes the best little quiches.'

Wyatt led the way up the concrete steps to a room overlooking the rink through a long window. Food had been artistically arranged on a long table draped in red with the *Crime Time* scrapbook as a centerpiece. Wyatt didn't go near the spread, but gestured Kovac to.

'I don't like to eat when we're shooting,' he explained, opening a bottle of water. 'I stay sharper that way.'

'Gotta stay on your toes for this.' *And not bust the girdle*, Kovac thought. Wyatt looked as if he hadn't taken a full breath in five hours.

'I know you don't think much of it, Sam,' he said, 'but we're serving a real purpose here. Helping solve crimes, helping people stand up for themselves and prevent crime.'

'Making a bundle.'

'That's *not* a crime.'

'No. Never mind me,' Kovac said, paging idly through

the scrapbook, slowing at the pages from Wyatt's retirement party. Posed and candid – if there could be such a thing as a candid shot of Ace – Polaroid shots of the great man in his glory. A shot of Wyatt pumping Kovac's hand, Kovac looking as if he'd just grabbed hold of an eel. A posed shot with a Channel Five reporter. A candid of Wyatt speaking to Amanda Savard. His gaze lingered.

'I don't like game shows either,' Kovac said, trying to remember having seen her there that night, but he'd been too busy feeling sorry for himself. 'I'm told I'm getting cranky in my old age, but that's bullshit. I've always been cranky.'

'You're not old, Sam,' Wyatt pointed out. 'You're younger than me, and look where I am now. A great second career. On top of the world.'

'I'll probably just stick with the one career until someone shoots me,' Kovac said. 'Which reminds me why I'm here.'

'Mike.' Wyatt nodded. 'Do you have anything more on the son, on Neil?'

'I'm more here about Andy, actually.'

Wyatt's brow furrowed. 'Andy? I don't understand.'

'I'm curious as to the why of it all,' he said in vague explanation. 'I know he'd been looking into the Thorne murder, thinking maybe Mike would want to reminisce, maybe they could get closer through it.'

'Ah . . .'

'He talked to you.' He put it as if it were a statement of fact, as if he'd seen the notes, leaving little room for denial, even though he knew no such thing.

'Yes,' Wyatt said. 'He mentioned it to me. I know Mike didn't want any part of it. Painful memories.'

'For you too.'

Wyatt nodded. 'It was a terrible night. Forever changed the lives of everyone involved.'

'Tied you to the Fallons like you were family.'

'In a way, yes. You don't go through something like that with another officer and not come away with a bond.'

'Especially with the circumstances.'

'What do you mean?'

'With you living right across the street. With the Thornes calling you for help, but Mike getting there ahead of you. You had to feel a little like Mike took that bullet instead of you, huh? Mike probably felt that too.'

'The tricks of fate,' Wyatt said with a dramatic sigh. 'My number wasn't up. Mike's was.'

'There must have been a little guilt though. You went above and beyond the call helping Mike out all these years.'

Wyatt stood silent for a moment. Kovac waited, wondering what the makeup was hiding. Surprise? Anger?

'Where are you going with this, Sam?'

Kovac shrugged a little and picked a baby carrot from a tray on the table. 'I know Mike took advantage all these years, Ace,' he said, snapping the carrot in two. 'I'm just wondering . . . With you making the big move to Hollywood . . . Making big dough . . . I'm just wondering if he might have tried to squeeze you for a little more.'

Kovac could see the color rise in Wyatt's face now.

'I don't like the direction you're taking,' he said quietly. 'I tried to do right by Mike and his family. And maybe he did take advantage and play on my guilt for not being the one in the chair. But that was between Mike and me, and that's how it should stay. We both deserve better than what you're thinking.'

'I'm not thinking anything, Ace. I don't get paid to think. I'm just wondering, that's all. You know me, I've gotta take things apart and see how they work.'

'The job's made you too cynical, Sam. Maybe it's time you got out.'

Kovac narrowed his eyes a little, studying Wyatt, trying to decide if that was a threat. Wyatt could make a couple of his famous phone calls, and that'd be it. Kiss the career good-bye or spend eternity down in Records listening to Russell Turvey hawk up lugies. And for what? To reveal the awful truth that Ace Wyatt felt guilty for being alive and whole? Even if Mike had tried to squeeze a little extra something out of him, the notion of Wyatt killing over that was ludicrous.

Unless the reason he had paid Mike Fallon off all these years had to do with some other kind of guilt altogether.

'How well did you know the Thornes?'

Gaines rapped on the open door and came into the room then, eyebrows raised at Wyatt. 'Excuse me, Captain. Kelsey and Yvette have gone to buy parkas. Everyone is breaking for lunch. Will you be joining the audience, or is this going to take longer?' he asked, emphasizing the word *this* with a look at Kovac. He pulled a small lint brush from a jacket pocket and gave Wyatt's lapels a quick swipe.

'No,' Wyatt said. 'We're finished here.'

Kovac popped the carrot in his mouth and chewed thoughtfully as Wyatt walked away. He followed at a distance and watched as Ace Wyatt worked the crowd of people who had so little going on in their lives they would waste a Saturday watching this bullshit.

Like me, he thought with a smirk, and walked out.

The on-line archives of the *Minneapolis Star Tribune* went back only to 1990. Kovac spent the afternoon in a room in the Hennepin County library, straining his eyes looking at microfiche, reading and rereading the articles written about the Thorne murder and Mike Fallon's shooting. They laid out the story as he remembered it.

The drifter-cum-handyman, Kenneth Weagle, had done some work for Officer Bill Thorne's wife and had apparently taken a shine to her. He had come to the house that night knowing Bill Thorne was on patrol. He'd been in the neighborhood long enough to scope out the comings and goings of residents. He had attacked Evelyn Thorne in

344

her bedroom, raped her, slapped her around, then started looting the house. By chance, Bill Thorne had stopped back home and walked into the house, unsuspecting. Weagle shot him with a gun of Thorne's he had found in the house. At some point Mrs Thorne had phoned Ace Wyatt across the street. But before Wyatt could arrive, Mike Fallon did.

Bill Thorne was given a hero's funeral with all the trimmings. There were photographs with that article. The long motorcade of police vehicles. A grainy shot of the widow in dark glasses, being consoled by friends and family.

According to the article, Thorne had been survived by his wife, Evelyn, and an unnamed seventeen-year-old daughter. In the photo, Evelyn Thorne looked a little like Grace Kelly, Kovac thought. He wondered if either of them was still in the area. He wondered if any of Bill Thorne's old cronies would know. Evelyn Thorne had been a relatively young woman at the time of the incident. Chances were she had remarried. She would be fifty-eight now, the daughter thirty-seven.

If Andy Fallon had been looking into the case, wanting to come to some kind of understanding, he might already have done the legwork. But there was no file. Kovac wondered if Amanda could be talked into letting him look around Fallon's office, check out his work computer. The Thorne murder wasn't an active IA case. She might not care.

You don't even know if she'll ever speak to you again, Kovac.

There was that.

'Sir?' The librarian's voice startled him. He jerked around to find her standing too close.

'The library is closing,' she said apologetically. 'I'm afraid you'll have to leave.'

Kovac gathered the copies of articles he'd run off, and went back out into the cold. Afternoon had surrendered to night, though it was barely five. The homeless who had spent their day in the warmth of the library had been shooed out along with him. They milled around on the sidewalk, instinctively shying away from Kovac, smelling cop. The librarian had probably thought he was one of them. He hadn't shaved, had spent the afternoon pulling at his hair and rubbing his eyes. He felt like one of them, standing on the cold street in this bleak, gray part of town. Alone, disconnected.

He tried to call Liska on his cell phone and got her voice mail; debated paging her, then let it go. He drove home so he could feel alone and disconnected in a warmer setting.

The neighbor had added to his lawn display a painted plywood cutout of Santa bending over, showing three inches of butt crack. Hilarious. It was positioned directly toward Kovac's living room window. Such class.

Kovac contemplated taking out his gun and blasting Santa an asshole. *See the humor in that, cocksucker?*

The house still smelled of garbage, even though he had taken it out. Like the corpse smell at Andy Fallon's. He tossed the copies of the Thorne murder articles on the coffee table and went into the kitchen. He burned some coffee grounds on the stove to get rid of the odor – a trick he'd learned at death scenes. See if Heloise put that in her helpful hints column. *What to do in the event of putrid corpse decay.*

He went upstairs, took a shower, pulled on some jeans and wool socks and an old sweatshirt, and went back down in search of supper, even though he had no appetite to speak of. He needed calories to keep the mind going. If keeping his mind going was what he really wanted tonight.

The only edible food in the house was a box of Frosted Flakes. He ate a handful, dry, and poured some of the scotch he'd picked up on the way home. Macallan. What the hell.

On the stereo, he found the faux jazz station playing a faux jazz tune, and he stood at the window listening to it and sipping the Macallan and staring at Santa's ass.

This is my life.

He didn't know how long he'd been standing there when the doorbell rang. The sound was so unfamiliar, it took three rings before he responded.

Amanda Savard stood on the front step, the black velvet scarf swathing her head, hiding her wounds. Some of them anyway.

'Well,' Kovac said, 'you must be a detective too. I'm unlisted.'

'May I come in?'

He stood back and waved her in with the scotch glass. 'Don't expect much. I get so many tips from the Home and Garden channel, but I just don't have the time.'

She went to the middle of the living room, pushed the scarf off her head, but didn't remove her gloves or the long black coat. She didn't take a seat.

'I came to apologize,' she said, looking just past his right shoulder. Kovac wondered if she could see Santa's moon, but if she did, she didn't react.

'For what?' he asked. 'Sleeping with me? Or throwing me out after?'

She looked as if she wanted to be anywhere but there. She held her hands together, then brought one up to touch her hair near the burns. 'I – I wasn't – I didn't mean –' She stopped and pressed her lips together and closed her eyes for a moment. 'I'm not – I don't easily . . . share my life . . . with other people. And I'm sorry if I . . .'

Kovac set his glass on the coffee table as he stepped close. He touched her cheek, his thumb brushing just below the wound. Her skin was cold to the touch, as if she must have been sitting out front for a long time before she worked up the courage to come to the door.

'You don't have to be sorry, Amanda,' he said softly. 'Don't be sorry about me, or for me.'

She met his gaze. Her lower lip was quivering ever so slightly.

'I'm not good at this,' she said.

'Hush.' He bent his head and touched his mouth to hers. Not with passion, but with something gentler. Her lips warmed, and softened, and opened to him.

'I can't stay,' she whispered, her voice tight with whatever conflict she was battling internally.

'Shh . . .'

He kissed her again. The scarf fell to the floor. He trailed the kiss down her neck and slipped her coat off her shoulders.

'Sam . . .'

'Amanda . . .' His lips brushed the shell of her ear. 'I want you.'

A delicate shiver ran through her. He felt it pass beneath his hands as he slid them down her back. She turned her head and her mouth found his. A trembling kiss. Hesitant, but anxious. Needing, but afraid. She opened her eyes and looked at him through tears.

'I don't know what we can have,' she said. 'I don't know what I can give you.'

'It doesn't matter,' he answered, the truth of the moment. 'We can have this. We can have now.'

He could feel her heart beat against his chest, marking the passing of time. Even now he couldn't read her, didn't know what questions she asked or answered within herself. He could feel the sadness in her, the emptiness, the loneliness, the conflict. He recognized those qualities, responded to them, lost himself in them as they sank down onto the sofa.

They could have this. They could have now. Even if that was all they ever had, he didn't have anything else that was worth a damn by comparison.

'I can't stay,' Savard said softly.

She lay in Kovac's arms, the pair of them on his sofa, covered by her coat. His skin was warm against hers. She liked the feel of his body pressed to hers, of her legs tangled with his; the feeling of being wrapped up with him, the suggestion of being inseparable. But it was a suggestion she couldn't fulfill. That knowledge left her feeling empty, hollow, isolated.

He touched the back of her head and pressed his lips to her forehead. 'You don't have to, but you can . . . if you want. I might even have clean sheets.'

'No,' she said, forcing herself to move, to sit up. She pulled her clothes together and covered herself. 'I can't.'

Kovac levered himself up on one arm and gently combed out the tangles he'd put in her hair. 'Amanda, I don't care where the nightmares come from. Do you understand what I mean by that? It doesn't matter. It doesn't scare me that you have them.'

It matters to me. It scares me, she wanted to say, but she didn't.

'You can share them with me if you need to,' he said. 'Believe me, there's nothing I haven't heard.'

Of course, that wasn't true, but she didn't point that out to him either. She had learned long ago when to argue and when to be silent.

Kovac sighed behind her. 'The bathroom's down the hall on the right.'

Kovac watched as she walked out of the room, half dressed. If this was all he could have of her, it was better than anything he'd ever dared hope for. Let her keep her secrets. He was oh-for-two with deep relationships, why try again? But he knew better. Amanda was a mystery, a puzzle. He would never rest until he got to the heart of her. As guarded as she was, she would resent the intrusion, and he would ultimately destroy what they did have.

He pulled his clothes on, rubbed a hand over his hair, and sat on the arm of the couch, sipping at his scotch while he waited for her to emerge. She came back into the room looking just as she had when she arrived. Beautiful, reserved, disguised.

'I don't know what to tell you,' she said, addressing the empty aquarium.

'Then don't tell me anything. You brass types,' he said, making a face. 'There doesn't have to be a master plan.'

She looked worried about that.

He went to her and touched her face with the back of his hand.

'Sometimes we just need to follow a trail and see where it goes,' he said. Sam Kovac, sage. 'Listen to me. Like I know what I'm talking about. I'm a two-time loser. Every trail I take ends up in a dark tunnel with a train coming my way. I should stick to just being a cop. I'm good at that.'

She found half a smile for him. It faded as her gaze fell on the coffee table. Her brows drew together.

'What's this?'

'The Thorne murder. Mike Fallon's shooting. Andy was looking at it. I'm just turning over rocks, see what crawls out.'

'Follow the trail and see where it goes,' she said absently. She spread out some of the pages, not picking them up, just looking at them.

'Sad story. You're too young to remember.'

'Sad,' she murmured, staring at the bad copy of the photograph of Bill Thorne's widow being consoled by her family.

'Life turns on a dime,' Kovac said.

'Yes, it does.'

She straightened and adjusted the velvet scarf, took a deep breath, looking past his shoulder again.

'Just say, "I'll see you around, Sam," ' he told her. 'It beats the hell out of good-bye.'

She tried to smile but failed, then rose up on her toes and kissed his cheek, her hands tightening on his shoulders. 'I'm sorry,' she whispered.

Then she was gone, and all he had left to keep him warm was a fifty-dollar bottle of scotch.

'You're not as sorry as me,' he said as he stood in the open door and watched her drive away.

Next door, the Saint-O-Meter was counting down the minutes.

The phone rang, and he actually hurried to pick it up. It didn't even matter who it was.

'Lonely Hearts Club,' he said. 'Join now. Misery loves company.'

'Do you take masochists?' Liska.

'Two for one if you join with a sadist.'

'What are you doing, Kojak? Sitting home feeling sorry for yourself?'

'I don't have anyone else to feel sorry for. My life is an empty shell.'

'Get a dog,' she said without sympathy. 'Guess who partnered with Eric Curtis until about a year before he was murdered?'

Kovac took a sip of the Macallan. 'If you tell me Bruce Ogden, I'm walking out of this movie, Jodie.'

'Derek Rubel,' she said. 'And guess who was at HCMC yesterday having a blood test, then lying about it?'

'Derek Rubel.'

'Give the man a cigar.'

'I'll be damned,' Kovac murmured.

'No,' Liska said. 'But I have a feeling Derek Rubel will be.'

32

Steele's was the kind of gym where sweating and grunting were required. There were no jazz dance aerobic classes, no yoga. It was all iron, hard-bodied hard-asses, heavy metal blasting from the stereo. It had the ambience of a machine shop, and the stench of people with too much testosterone was enough to make a normal person's eyes water.

Liska badged the bored biker chick working the desk and went into the main weight room. She stood at the edge of the action for a moment, scanning the small crowd, secretly awestruck by the male bodies. Amazing to think what an ordinary human could become through well-applied obsessive behavior and, in some cases, the miracles of modern chemistry. Every third guy in the gym was built like the Incredible Hulk.

Rubel stood in a corner, spotting someone on a bench. He wore a black T-shirt with the sleeves cut off to accommodate upper arms as thick as Virginia hams. The muscles were so perfectly defined, he could have been used as a live model for a human anatomy class.

Liska wove her way through the maze of people pumping iron, knowing the instant Rubel became aware of her, even though he didn't look right at her. She could sense the energy change in the air. She walked up to the bench and looked down into Bruce Ogden's ugly face. He was straining beneath a barbell loaded with iron plates the size of truck wheels, red in the face, squawling.

She cut a look at Rubel. 'Does he make this much noise in bed?'

'I wouldn't know.'

'I'd ask his girfriend, but he's never had one as far as I've been able to find out.' She leaned over Ogden again and made a face of apology. 'Whores don't count. Sorry.'

Ogden let out a roar and shoved the barbell up.

'What do you want, Sergeant?' Rubel asked. 'We're in the middle of something here.'

'I'll say you are,' Liska said, deadly serious, showing some of her hatred for these two men. 'You're up to your necks in it. And note how I came here in person to tell you to your faces. No anonymous call from a pay phone. No photographs in the mail. I've got bigger balls than both of you put together.'

Ogden racked the barbell and sat up, grunting, sweat running off his face like rainwater. 'Yeah? We heard that about you.'

Liska rolled her eyes. 'Now with the lesbian innuendo. You're too much, Ox. Maybe if you stopped trying to make yourself look like a big bad heterosexual male animal and exercised your brain instead, you wouldn't be in this shit. But it's too late for you to get smart now. You crossed the line when you decided to involve my children. There's no going back from that. And, since it's not legal for me to rip your beating hearts from your chests and show them to you while you die, I'm going to see you both in prison.'

'I don't know what you're talking about,' Rubel said without emotion.

Liska looked him in the eye and made him wait. 'I've got Cal Springer. He's mine. I turned him. And now the fun begins,' she said with malicious relish. 'First one to the prosecutor gets the deal. Cal and I are sitting down with someone in Sabin's office tomorrow at noon.'

Ogden's mouth curved in a pout. 'You're full of shit, Liska. You don't have anything or you'd be pulling out cuffs.'

'There's nothing to have,' Rubel said, still cool. 'There's no case.'

Liska smiled up at him. 'You keep thinking that,

sweetheart. And why don't you also spend some time thinking about what happens in prison to good-looking boys like you? I hear it gets rough. Then again, maybe you like it that way.'

She reached up and patted his cheek. 'Too bad Eric's not alive to fill us in.'

Bang! Right between the eyes. Rubel didn't flinch, didn't change his expression, but he felt the hit as surely as if he'd taken a bullet. Liska felt the shock wave roll off him, and he knew she knew. She savored the moment. Maybe a thousand moments like that would make up for what she'd felt when she'd seen those photographs of Kyle and R.J.

Maybe not.

She turned to go and pulled up short. Just for a heartbeat. Rubel and Ogden probably didn't even notice. She doubted she faltered longer than a split second. But in that split second, eye contact was made. Standing ten feet away, taking a break from squats on the Smith machine, was Speed.

'Are you sure the voice activation thing works?' Springer whined. 'What if it doesn't turn on?'

Barry Castleton knelt on the floor in front of him, duct-taping the microcassette recorder to Springer's squishy midsection. As the lead on the Ibsen case, Castleton had deserved a heads-up when Springer broke. Liska wanted the collar herself – for personal reasons more than for what it would put in her jacket – but she couldn't cut him out and live with herself. Castleton – forty-something, African American, a tendency to dress like an English professor – was a good cop and a good guy. If she had to share, she didn't mind sharing with him.

'Don't worry about it,' he said to Springer. 'It's foolproof.'

Kovac snorted. 'Nothing is foolproof to a talented fool.'

They occupied Springer's kitchen. Springer, Castleton,

Tippen from the SO – because they were out of their jurisdiction and wanted to cover their asses with the county people – Liska, and Kovac. Mrs Springer had gone to stay with a sister. Liska wondered if she would come back after this was all over. Probably. Then again, it remained to be seen if Cal would escape jail time and be here for Mrs Cal to come back to.

Springer's first part in the drama had been to look the other way when Ogden planted evidence in Renaldo Verma's house. In doing that, Ogden had him on the hook. It was one thing for a uniform to do something stupid, but the lead detective on a homicide investigation was a much bigger target and stood to lose much more. Cal Springer, with the high waters of his lifestyle already coming up around his head, couldn't afford to lose.

'I'm not feeling well,' Springer complained.

'Yeah, we can all smell that, Cal,' Castleton grumbled, getting to his feet.

Liska broke the pattern of her pacing, went over to Springer, and kicked him.

'Ouch!' He bent over and grabbed his shin.

'A man might die because of you, and you're complaining you don't *feel well*?' she said with utter disgust. 'My children were threatened because you weren't man enough to say no to Bruce Ogden.'

'He could have cost me my job,' Springer defended himself.

'And now you're going to prison. Great choice, Cal.'

'You don't understand.'

She stared at him, incredulous. 'No. I don't understand. I will *never* understand. You let Ogden plant evidence so you could close a case and get a big one in your win column.'

'What was the difference with Verma?' he argued. 'The guy was a killer. We knew he did it! And – and – the vic was one of ours. We couldn't let him walk for that!'

'How dare you pretend an interest in justice!' Liska spat

355

the words at him. 'That wasn't your motivation, that's your rationalization. Your motivation to look the other way on Verma was for your own advancement.'

'Oh, and *you've* never done anything to get ahead,' Springer sneered.

'I've never contaminated an investigation. Did it ever occur to you that maybe Verma *didn't* do Curtis – an HIV-positive gay cop who'd changed patrol partners three times in five years and had lodged formal complaints of harassment.'

'When I had Verma cold on the Franz murder? No.'

'Hey, fuck that, Springer,' Castleton jumped in. 'Bobby Kerwin got Verma on Franz. You weren't even in the picture.'

Springer clenched his jaw. 'It was a figure of speech. Verma was good for an identical murder and how many robberies? Why shouldn't I take him?'

'The fact that you didn't have any physical evidence might have weighed in there,' Tippen suggested.

Springer scowled at him. 'Why should I suspect another cop, for god's sake? We spoke with all of Curtis's ex-partners. There were no red flags.'

'Then you weren't listening,' Liska said. 'Curtis's last partner, Engle, told me – and he doesn't know me from anyone – he thought something had gone on between Curtis and Rubel. He didn't tell you when you were looking into Curtis's murder?'

'It didn't pan out,' Springer said. 'I mean, look at Rubel. He's not queer. And – and why would he kill Curtis? They hadn't been partners for a long time.'

'Because of the HIV, you moron. If Curtis infected Rubel with an incurable, terminal disease, I would call that motive, wouldn't you?'

Springer inhaled and exhaled.

'And it didn't strike you odd that a couple of months after Curtis was murdered, Derek Rubel, who had been one of Curtis's partners, suddenly became partners with the guy who tampered with the evidence in the case?' Liska asked.

Springer looked ready to have a temper tantrum but was too afraid of Liska to do it. Red in the face. Shaking. 'People get reassigned all the time. Besides, the case was closed by then.'

'Oh, well, the case was closed. So what if you hung it on someone who didn't do it? He'd done something else just as bad. And you were already way on the meat hook, as far as Ogden was concerned. He could have sold you to IA in a heartbeat,' Liska said. 'Sure, it would have cost him. But it would have cost you more. So when Ogden and Rubel needed an alibi for Thursday night, all Ogden had to do was pick up the phone.'

'Ogden would have ruined me.'

'Bad cops ruin themselves,' Liska said quietly, remembering Savard telling her that when she had gone into IA after Andy Fallon's body had been discovered. It seemed like a year ago.

'It didn't matter to you what they did to Ken Ibsen?' she asked.

Springer turned his face away in shame. He hadn't cared enough to put himself on the line, and someone else had nearly paid with his life.

'I wish I could drag your sorry ass to the hospital and make you stand next to Ken Ibsen's bed when his doctors come to examine him,' she said. 'I wish I could take his memories of what those two animals did to him in that alley, and permanently implant them in your brain so that you would have to relive that attack over and over every day of your miserable life.'

'I'm sorry!' Springer shouted.

'Yes, you are.'

Kovac stepped between them and took Liska by the arm.

'Come on, Tinks. They'll be here soon. Let's go hide for the surprise party.'

He led her into the Springer pantry, a narrow closet of a room lined with shelves of canned foods and extra china. Liska leaned back against one set of shelves, Kovac the other.

'You got 'em, Tinks,' Kovac said quietly.

'They're on the hook, not in the net. I want them bludgeoned and on my stringer.'

'Then maybe you shouldn't chew the shit out of the one person who's going to get them there for you.'

'He deserves worse.'

'He deserves exactly what you said – to relive Ken Ibsen's attack every day of his life. But we'll have to settle for his career being ruined and his sorry butt in jail.'

'They threatened my boys, Sam,' she said, trembling again at the thought. 'You know, I kept thinking all week, what homophobe would beat a gay man to death in a manner that exposed him to so much blood? It didn't follow. Every guy I know like that is terrified of AIDS. They think they can get it from toilet seats, a handshake, breathing the air. It had to be someone who was either completely ignorant of the risk, or someone who was already infected. Then I saw Rubel at HCMC. . . .'

'Rubel didn't hate Curtis because he was gay,' Kovac said. 'He killed him because Curtis infected him. Revenge.'

'And Ogden put the evidence on Verma to protect Rubel because they're lovers.'

'They're bad guys, Tinks. And you got 'em.' He reached across and touched her shoulder. 'I'm proud of you, kiddo.'

'Thanks.' She looked away and chewed on her lip. 'You think Springer can get them to cop to Andy Fallon?'

'Maybe. If they did it.'

Tippen stuck his head in the pantry. 'The party guests have arrived. Places, everybody.'

Liska drew her weapon and checked it. Kovac did the

same. The game faces went on. They would stay where they were while Cal Springer tried to get Ogden and Rubel to incriminate themselves on tape. When they'd heard enough, the trap would be sprung with Ogden and Rubel in the kitchen. Meanwhile, radio cars from the SO would roll in as backup.

The doorbell rang. There was the sound of voices, though Liska couldn't make out the words. She visualized Springer greeting his guests, inviting them in, assuring them he was on their side. But the tone of the voices changed abruptly, and Cal Springer started to shout *no!* The word was cut short by a gunshot.

'Shit!' Kovac yelled and bolted from the pantry.

Liska was right behind him.

'Freeze, police!' Castleton shouted.

Three more shots.

Kovac dashed for the living room, crouching low.

Liska went out the service door to the garage, and to the door that opened onto the driveway.

Rubel and Ogden were running for Rubel's truck, a dozen feet in front of Liska, guns out.

'Rubel!' Liska shouted, and discharged her weapon, then ducked back behind the door.

Two quick shots answered her, one splintering the door frame at the top. Three shots came from somewhere, and a man screamed.

The truck engine roared to life and spun backward out of Springer's driveway. Liska swung the door open to see Rubel sticking an arm out the truck window, and fire flashed from the end of his gun.

Lights and sirens running, a pair of radio cars were screaming toward the bottleneck of the cul-de-sac. Rubel never slowed down, splitting the space between the noses of the cars. One clipped the rear passenger side of his truck with a *bang!* Rubel kept going, speeding away as one of the sheriff's cars swung around to give chase.

Bruce Ogden lay sobbing on the driveway, rolling like a beached seal, trying in vain to grab at his back.

Liska ran toward him, leading with her weapon, and kicked his gun out of reach. Kovac ran up from the sidewalk, cursing a blue streak.

'Springer's dead!'

'Help me! Help me!' Ogden squealed. A dark stain spread on the ice-packed driveway beneath him. Liska stared down at him, thinking of Ken Ibsen.

A radio car from the Eden Prairie PD roared up, and two uniforms bailed out and came running.

'Don't touch him without gloves,' Liska ordered, stepping back. 'He's a health risk.'

'Whose bright idea was this?' Leonard asked, looking right at Kovac.

'We had to move fast, Lieutenant,' Liska said. 'We wanted Ogden and Rubel on tape before they had a chance to lawyer up.'

They stood in Cal Springer's living room with the cold fireplace and unlit Christmas tree. Cal was at that very moment being zipped into his own personal gift bag to be delivered to the morgue. He had taken a shot point-blank in the middle of the chest.

'We sure as hell never thought this would happen,' Kovac said.

'I could see Rubel and Ogden trying to get him out the door,' Castleton said. 'Probably to take him somewhere and make him disappear. Springer knew it. He tried to pull back. Rubel shot him before I could do anything.'

'Jesus H.' Leonard stared in disgust at the body bag on the gurney as the ME's people wheeled it out the front door. 'The press is going to have a field day with this.'

And, oh yeah, Mrs Springer, sorry for your loss, Liska thought.

'Every cop in the metro area and surrounding counties has the BOLO on Rubel,' Castleton said.

'He'll probably ditch his truck and steal some wheels,' Kovac said. 'He's got nothing to lose now. We catch him and he goes down for two murders and an aggravated assault. He'll never see the light of day.'

The Eden Prairie police chief stepped into the foyer from outside. 'Lieutenant Leonard? We have members of the press waiting.'

Leonard cursed under his breath and went away.

Liska went into the Springers' kitchen, pulling out her phone to call and check on the boys. Speed came in through the laundry room, stopped in the doorway, and stared at her.

'Are you okay?' he asked.

'No.'

Liska dropped her head and punched in Milo Foreman's phone number. Speed waited, listening as she explained the situation briefly and asked if the boys could stay until Sunday. She closed the phone and dropped it in her coat pocket.

'I'd ask what you're doing here,' she said, 'but –'

'I heard it on the scanner.'

'Really? You didn't just follow Ogden and Rubel out here from that gym you don't belong to?'

He rubbed the stubble on his jaw and looked away.

'What were you doing there, Speed?'

The big sigh. 'I've been on loan to Minneapolis narcotics. They were aware of a steroid problem within the department. They needed an unfamiliar face.'

'How long?' she asked, feeling the anger, the hurt, the frustration building inside her.

He hesitated again before confessing. 'The last two months.'

Liska laughed and shook her head. *Why should it hurt this much?* she asked herself. She shouldn't have even been surprised. Maybe she wasn't surprised. But she had to admit, there had been that sliver of hope, that tiny little spark. . . . After all these years, he still hadn't managed to kill it. She couldn't understand how it hadn't died of its own accord.

'So your sudden renewed interest in my life and the boys –'

'Is genuine, Nikki.'

'Oh, please.'

He moved toward her. 'I knew you had run into Ogden and Rubel. They were at the gym that afternoon you caught the Fallon thing.'

'And what was your purpose in watching me deal with that?' she asked. 'And you never saying one fucking word to me –'

'I can't talk about a case, Nikki. You know that.'

'Oh, but it's fine for you to pump me for information about my case,' she said. Every question he'd asked her this week bubbled up in her memory. 'You are such an asshole.'

He came toward her again, backing her toward the counter, trying to look sad and concerned and hurt by her low opinion of him. Liska ducked away, cringing away from any contact with him.

'Nikki, I was looking out for you, for the boys –'

'How were you looking out for us?' she demanded. 'By not filling me in? By not letting me know you were there for us?'

'You didn't exactly ask me to stick around.'

'Don't try to put this on me!'

He spread his hands and took a step back. 'I thought I could keep an eye on you without compromising my investigation or yours.'

'So that I wouldn't blow your collar if mine didn't pan out,' Liska said. 'Or were you planning to swoop in at the end, like Superman, and save the day for everyone? That would have been a nice feather in your cap, wouldn't it? Get the bad guys, get the girl –'

Speed was losing patience, as he always did when charm and false sincerity failed him. 'If that's what you really think, Nikki . . .'

Liska took a deep breath and willed her own emotions down. 'I think you need to go. I have a job to do.'

He bit back another sigh, regrouped mentally, tried to come again with the concerned-friend routine. 'Look, I know this isn't the time or the place. I just wanted to make sure you were okay. Maybe I'll stop by the house later –'

'Don't do that.'

'I can take the boys for the afternoon tomorrow if you want.'

'What I want,' Liska said, pointing her gaze toward the laundry room because it was hurting her to look at him, 'is not to see you for a while, Speed.'

It finally sunk into him that he wasn't going to win this one. Charm and looks could take him a long way in his day-to-day world, but he had run out of disguises with her. At least until the next time she felt weak enough to believe in him.

'Take the boys tomorrow if what you want is to be with them. But don't do it to get to me.'

He hesitated for a moment, as if he had something more to say, but he didn't say it. He went back out the way he'd come.

Liska stood there, staring at the floor, trying to clear her mind, get back to work mode, shake it off, suck it up, be tough. Again. She could see Kovac standing in the archway to the main part of the house.

'Why do I never learn?' she asked.

''Cause you're a hardhead.'

'Thanks.'

'Takes one to know one.' He came in and hooked an arm around her shoulders. 'Come on, Tinks. Unless you decide to run out and put a couple in that asshole's head, our work here is done. Call it a night. Go home. I'll put a radio car in front of your house.'

She made a face. 'I don't need –'

'You *do* need. You're the one who found Rubel out, kiddo. And he knows where you live.'

A chill went down her back like an icy finger.

'You know,' she said, putting her head on his shoulder, 'some days I wish I was a waitress.'

33

By six A.M. news of the manhunt for Officer Derek Rubel had brought in reporters from every major network. Minneapolis was crawling with camera crews. Kovac, Liska, Tippen, and Castleton had all been ordered to speak to no one regarding the murder of Cal Springer. Interviews were being handled by Leonard, the Hennepin County sheriff, and the Eden Prairie chief.

The FBI had been called in on the case, along with the Minnesota Bureau of Criminal Apprehension. The Minnesota and Wisconsin State Highway Patrols both had helicopters in the air, doing a grid search for Rubel's black Explorer, a tedious job sparking one false alarm after another. Minnesota was full of black Ford Explorers. None of the ones stopped and searched belonged to Rubel.

Neighbors and known associates of his were questioned as to his habits in order to try to come up with a list of likely hiding places. Deputies were dispatched to eighty acres of hunting land in the scrub near Zimmerman, property owned jointly by half a dozen officers. There was no sign Rubel had been to the crude cabin.

Ogden, who had taken two bullets in the shoot-out, had been airlifted by chopper to the Hennepin County Medical Center, where he was listed as stable after three hours of surgery. He had yet to be questioned, and already the union had staked out a lawyer at the door to his hospital room.

Kovac worked KOD duty all night, preferring knocking on the doors of perfect strangers to spending the night in his empty house. By morning, his social skills were running on empty. He passed the baton to Elwood and went home.

The neighbor was out in the frigid sunshine wearing his

plaid bomber cap, digging bits of snow from his yard with a spade.

'Goddamn dogs,' Kovac heard him grumble as he got out of the car. At the slam of the door, the old man's head came up and he drew a bead on Kovac through his cockeyed glasses.

'Hey, we heard about that manhunt!' he called, his excitement overriding his dislike for Kovac. 'A killer cop, huh? Are you in on that?'

'I'm the guy they're looking for,' Kovac said. 'Driven mad from sleep deprivation caused by my neighbor's garish light display.'

The neighbor couldn't decide whether to show offense or pretend good humor.

'Quite a story, this guy,' he said. 'It's all over the television. They're even doing a special *Crime Time* on it.'

'Another good reason to read a book,' Kovac grumbled.

The neighbor paid no attention. 'Best goddamn show on television.'

'Reality programming.'

'You know that guy? Ace? He's something. He's a *real* cop.'

'He used to be a woman,' Kovac said, unlocking his door.

The neighbor gave a little jolt of surprise. He narrowed his beady eyes to the size of BBs. 'You're sick!' he announced, and went back to the other side of his yard to hunt for dog shit and yellow snow.

Kovac went into the house. His gaze went directly to the couch, and he stood there for a moment before it hit him.

Someone had been there.

The articles he'd brought home from the library were strewn all over the coffee table. His briefcase had been pried open and now lay on the floor, half hidden behind a chair. The television screen had been kicked in.

The air in the room seemed to thicken and crackle with

electricity. Kovac could feel it on his skin. His pulse jumped. He opened his coat and discreetly reached inside, slipping his gun from the holster. With his other hand, he dug his cell phone out of his pocket and hit 911.

He reported the break-in as he crept through the house, room by room, taking in the damage, looking to see if the perpetrator was still in the building. The drawers had been pulled from his desk. His dresser had been gone through. Cash he had left on top of the dresser was gone, along with an expensive watch he'd won in a raffle at a law enforcement conference. That said burglary. Probably a junkie looking for stuff to pawn.

He checked his bedroom closet, relieved to find his old .38 in its shoe box on the shelf.

Back downstairs, he found that the intruder had broken in through the kitchen door. A task that looked to have been embarrassingly easy. He would take some ribbing for his lack of home maintenance, Kovac thought as he turned and saw the basement door ajar.

He flipped the light switch and listened. Nothing. He descended the first few steps, then crouched down to look, still fairly well concealed by wall.

The basement wasn't finished space. He kept a dehumidifier going to fight the damp of the concrete walls and floor. There was no furniture, nothing that would be of any interest to a thief; only half-empty paint cans and boxes and boxes of old case files.

Boxes that had been pulled from the shelves and dumped all over the floor.

His cell phone trilled in his pocket.

'Kovac.'

'Liska. They've found Rubel's truck. In Lake Minnetonka. Went off the road, down an embankment and through the ice.'

'So he's dead?'

'I said they found the truck. Rubel wasn't in it.'

The atmosphere on the banks of Lake Minnetonka was not unlike that on the first day of fishing season. Cars and news vans lined the narrow strip of road. People wandered up and down, waiting for something to happen. Deputies had established a perimeter beyond which only law enforcement personnel were allowed. Just before that line, various representatives of the media had staked out their territories. The largest of the sideshows, by far, was *Crime Time*. The same crew from the ice rink had set up as near to the yellow crime scene tape as possible.

Kovac stared. Ace Wyatt, bundled into a heavy parka, stood on his trademark red carpet before a crowd of spectators. Beyond him, beyond the yellow tape, Derek Rubel's Explorer had been pulled ashore by a tow truck and stood with all doors open as the crime scene unit from the Minnesota Bureau of Criminal Apprehension went over every inch of it. They would look it over here, at the scene, then the vehicle would be transported to their garage in St Paul and every piece of hair and lint in the thing would be cataloged and held under a microscope.

Kovac took a moment to assess the scene, trying to imagine it without the crowd. They were on a narrow finger of the lake that had been deemed beneath the efforts of development. A couple of small houses were within sight, near enough to walk to on a cold night, but not so near for a witness to see a man leaping from a vehicle as it ran into the lake.

Tippen came over in his Dr Seuss hat, hands stuffed in the pockets of a fat parka.

'They checked the houses. One is vacant. The other isn't, but nobody's home and there's no vehicle. They're trying to track down somebody who might know where the owner is – or rather, where the owner is supposed to be. No luck so far.'

'Rubel's probably riding around with the owner's body

in the trunk of the owner's Buick,' Kovac said. 'What a nightmare.'

'It's that. Minnesota hasn't gotten this kind of attention since Andrew Cunanan.'

'Andrew Cunanan wasn't a cop. This has Hollywood written all over it.'

Kovac spotted the WB VPs just at the corner of Wyatt's carpet, right behind Fat Donald, the director. The redhead had bought herself a parka that looked made from aluminum foil. Gaines came over to them and seemed to be explaining something, pointing one arm toward the lake, where, in the distance, ice fishing houses dotted the snowscape.

Kovac looked around again, trying to get his bearings – hard to do for a city boy tossed out into the maze around Minnetonka. But he didn't think they were far from Neil Fallon's place. Where Gaines was pointing might have been it, though one ice fishing hut looked pretty much like the next to Kovac.

Wyatt was having his makeup done again while some toady held a light meter next to his head and called out numbers.

'Can you believe this guy?' Kovac said.

'His people were here staking out that spot practically before we were,' Tippen said. 'It pays to have friends in high places, even at a freak show like this.'

'Especially at a freak show like this. Reality programming.'

A gust of wind came up off the lake, blowing Wyatt's red muffler across his face. The director swore, then turned and swore again at the woman in the shag carpet coat, then announced everyone should take ten, and stalked off toward the official *Crime Time* motor home parked on the road.

The videographers dug out cigarettes. Shag Coat went onto the carpet to adjust Wyatt's scarf, the WB VPs right behind her. Gaines paused en route to accept a steaming cup of coffee from another minion.

Kovac joined the cadre, giving the eye to the bouncer who stepped toward him at the edge of the carpet. The bouncer stepped back.

'Johnny-on-the-spot here, aren't you, Ace?' Kovac said.

'Too bad we can't say the same for you, Sam.' Wyatt stood perfectly still while Shag Coat arranged the offending scarf in an artful and clever way. 'I understand you and your partner were in on the fiasco last night.'

'Yeah, well, I'm a real cop, I don't just play one on TV. As you know, in the real world, with real bad guys, shit happens.'

'And you step in it?' Gaines suggested as he put the coffee cup into Wyatt's hand.

'I swim through it, Slick. If that's what I have to do to get what I'm after. You should know how that tastes, you being a professional kiss-ass. Do they give college degrees for that now?'

'We're very busy here, Sergeant,' Gaines said tightly.

'I understand, and I'll let you get back to finding the cure for cancer in a minute. I just have a question for Captain America here.'

Wyatt huffed a sigh. 'You're starting to get on my nerves, Sam.'

'Yeah, I have a talent,' Kovac said. 'After our chat yesterday, I was curious, so I went back and read over the articles from the Thorne murder. That's a hell of a dramatic story, Ace. I'd forgotten. You ought to do a special on that. A movie of the week maybe. The network could run it to hype the new show.'

'The show will succeed on its own merits,' Wyatt said tightly. 'I have no intention of capitalizing on that night.'

Kovac laughed. 'You've done it your whole career. Why stop now?'

'No!' Wyatt barked. 'That was *never* my intent. What happened with my career at the time was out of my hands.'

He turned and snapped at the shag coat woman, who was still fussing with his clothes. 'Leave the goddamn scarf alone!'

The WB VPs looked at Wyatt, then at each other, then at Gaines, panicked at having been left out of the loop.

'It's a tragic story,' Kovac explained.

'Which is precisely why the captain doesn't want to bring it up,' Gaines said, putting himself between Kovac and Wyatt. He spoke to the VPs. 'A friend of the captain's was killed, another was left a paraplegic. You can understand why he wouldn't want to dredge up the trauma.'

'No, they can't,' Kovac said. 'That night made the Ace here a hero. He saved another cop's life. It's a story made for Hollywood. Ace makes it big with the show, everybody in America's gonna want to hear it.

'I'm just wondering, Ace,' he continued, cocking his head to look around Gaines. 'Have you kept in touch with Bill Thorne's widow over the years? It occurred to me she might appreciate hearing about Mike's passing.'

'No,' he said. 'We lost touch.'

Kovac raised his brows. 'As close as you stayed with Mike, you lost touch with Evelyn Thorne? After all you went through?'

'Because of all we went through,' Wyatt murmured.

'When Andy Fallon talked with you about the case, did he mention if he'd spoken with her? Or with Thorne's daughter?'

'I don't recall.'

'Well, I'm sure it's in his notes,' Kovac said. 'I just haven't found them yet. I'll let you know. In case you want to reach out.'

'We need to clear the set, Sergeant,' Gaines said, trying to back him away. 'We're airing this tonight. Trying to help bring this mess to a conclusion for you.'

'That's big of you, Junior,' Kovac said. 'Frees me up to concentrate on something else. Thanks.'

Kovac walked away, shooting a glance up at the bouncer. 'You should have gone into wrestling. Better class of people.'

34

'Once again, citizens, this is a photograph of the known *murderer* at the heart of this manhunt tonight.'

Wyatt had what was often described as 'the look of eagles.' Steely-eyed. Hard-jawed. A face that inspired fear and trust.

'This is the face of Officer Derek Rubel. Known to have *murdered* a fellow police officer. Suspected in several more *brutal* crimes. This man is at large in our country tonight, and it's going to take the courage and diligence of citizens to bring this *animal* to justice.

'If you see Derek Rubel, do *not* under *any* circumstances approach him. This man is *extremely* dangerous. What *do* you do, Citizen Jane?'

'*Do* go to the nearest telephone and call the police,' the woman says.

Another member of the audience is called on.

'*Do* write down a license number!'

On cue, the audience shouts in unison, '*Be PROActive!*'

The hot-line number and Web site address appear on the screen.

The television goes black.

Admirable.

A testament to the powers of redemption and penance.

A service to the community. Empowering to the powerless.

The agitation returns.

A fear burning in the pit of the stomach and radiating outward.

Fear of discovery.

Fear of death.

Fear of the inner knowledge of one's own capabilities when threatened.

There is the sense that the world is turning faster and faster, growing smaller and smaller, making discovery inevitable.

It is only a matter of time.

The thought repeats endlessly as the gaze scans the photographs of death.

It is only a matter of time.

Kovac must die.

35

'I love that show,' Liska said as she hung up the phone.

Across the cubicle, Kovac scowled. He had his computer on and the telephone receiver wedged between his shoulder and ear.

'The hot-line phones rang off the hook after the show ran last night.'

'With how many legitimate leads?' he asked.

'All it takes is one. What's your problem with it, anyway?' she asked.

'I hate —'

'Besides that you hate Ace Wyatt.'

Kovac pouted. 'That'd pretty much be it.'

'Look what that show does. It teaches people who feel they have no power to stand up and make something happen. If Cal Springer had paid attention to that message, Derek Rubel wouldn't be running loose now.'

'It's the whole reality programming thing.'

'You love *America's Most Wanted*.'

'That's different. What Wyatt has is a game show. What's next? Interactive court trials? People can log on and vote guilty or not guilty?'

'They've already got that on *Dateline*.'

'Great. And next season they can televise the executions from Texas. Maybe they can get Regis Philbin to host,' he crabbed.

'Who are you on the line with?' Liska asked, finally noticing that he had yet to speak into the receiver.

'Frank Sinatra.'

'Kojak, he's dead.'

'I'm on hold. Donna at the phone company. Anyway,

what if the show gives someone a false sense of power, and they do something stupid and end up dead?'

'What if someone ends up dead because they're spineless and stupid and they don't watch the show?'

'I hate Ace Wyatt.'

'The WB is promoting him as Captain America.'

Disgust made a strangled sound in his throat. 'Aw, jeez, those fucking VPs. They stole that from me!'

'Call your agent, Hollywood.'

'You're the one who wants that, Tinker Bell, not me.'

'Just so I get my fame for catching Rubel, not for being killed by him.'

Kovac drew breath to ask her how she was doing – really doing – when, finally, a human being picked up on the other end of the line.

'Sorry to keep you on hold, Sam. What can I do you for?'

'Hey, Donna. I need the LUDS on a Minneapolis number.'

'You have the paperwork?'

'Not exactly.'

'That would mean no.'

'Well . . . yes. But the guy's dead. Who will care?'

'How about his family?'

'Dead and in jail.'

'How about the county attorney?'

'I just need to shake something loose here, Donna. It doesn't have to stand up in court.'

'Mmm . . . You didn't get it from me.'

'I never have, but I live in hope.'

Donna cracked up at that. Classy broad. Kovac gave her Andy Fallon's phone number and hung up.

'What are you after?' Liska asked.

'I'm not exactly sure,' he admitted. 'I want to go through Andy's phone records and see if something jumps out. Andy was poking around in the Thorne murder, trying to connect to Mike through his experiences. When I did some of that same poking, I got a rise out of Wyatt. I want to see –'

'You're obsessed, Sam,' Liska said. 'You don't like Rubel for Andy's murder? If it *was* a murder.'

'No. It doesn't fit. Andy's scene was too neat. Look what Rubel did – beat a guy to death with a ball bat, beat a guy near to death with a pipe, shot a guy point-blank in the chest. Where's the finesse?'

'But you said Pierce told you he'd seen Andy with another guy. What if it was Rubel? That might track. Andy was looking at Ogden for being dirty. No one knew Ogden and Rubel were an item. Through his connection to Curtis – having once been a patrol partner – Rubel gets close to Andy to keep an eye on the case from the inside, so to speak. Andy gets too close to some truth. . . . See?'

'No way. Rubel was Ogden's partner –'

'Not at the beginning of the investigation. There was no connection between them at the time, none that anyone knew of. Rubel had been patrol partners with Curtis, but Curtis swore none of his former partners harassed him.'

'Until he infected one.'

'And if Andy somehow found out about Rubel's HIV status . . .' She left Kovac to finish the thought for himself, then added, 'I'm putting Rubel in a photo array and showing it to Pierce.'

'Have at it,' Kovac said. 'Meanwhile, who broke into my house? Why would Rubel? It's not like I've got the one piece of evidence that can hang him.'

'That could have been anybody, for any reason. Probably a junkie looking for your secret cash stash. Or maybe it was some other scumbag you're looking at for something else. It doesn't necessarily have anything to do with Fallon.'

The possibility had crossed Kovac's mind. He had other cases ongoing. . . . He grabbed his phone on the third ring.

'Homicide. Kovac.'

'Kovac, Maggie Stone. I looked over that case – Fallon, Andy.'

'And?'

'Is he in the ground yet?'

'I don't think so. Why?'

'I'd like to have him back for a visit. I think he might have been murdered.'

Maggie Stone's office at the Hennepin County morgue always made Kovac think of those news stories about crazy old people whose bodies were found mummified among the stacks of newspapers and magazines and garbage they had not thrown out in nine years. The room was a maze of papers and professional journals and books on forensic medicine and motorcycle magazines. Stone rode a Harley Hog in good weather.

She waved Kovac into the office with one hand, holding a sugared jelly doughnut in the other. The doughnut was oozing red from its center, and bore a little too much resemblance to some of the stuff in the photographs spread out on the desk.

'Do you ever read any of this?' Kovac asked.

She peered down at a photo through a pair of funky reading glasses and an illuminated magnifying glass. 'Read what?'

Her hair was a peculiar toffee shade this month, cut in a pixie style and slicked to her head with goo. Most days she looked as if she hadn't remembered to use a comb since the eighties.

'What did you find?'

'Okay.' She swung the magnifying glass on its swivel arm so that Kovac could look through it from the other side of the desk. 'What I look for on the neck in a hanging death is a V-shaped bruising or abrasions, obviously following the angles of the noose. We see that clearly here,' she said, pointing out the marks. 'And you found him hanging. We

378

know he was hung. However, I also see what looks to be some shadows of a straight-line bruise around the neck here.'

'You think he was strangled, then hung?'

'The bruising isn't clear. Anyone looking at this case with a foregone conclusion of suicide wouldn't even notice it. But I feel that it's there. If I'm right, I suspect the killer might have put protective padding between the ligature and the victim's neck. If we're lucky and the funeral home did a poor job of preparing the body, I may still be able to get some fibers off the throat. And, if the bruising *is* there, I'll bet there's more at the back of the neck.'

She sat back, made two fists, and held them out in front of her to demonstrate. 'If the killer tightens the ligature with his hands, the knuckles press into the back of the neck, leaving several bruises. If you're looking at a garrote, then the pressure at the point where the ligature crosses and tightens creates a significant single bruise.'

'There aren't any photographs of the back of his neck?'

'No. I admit this wasn't the most thorough of autopsies. But it came in looking like a slam-dunk suicide, and apparently there were calls from your end of things to move it through quickly for the family's sake.'

'Didn't come from me,' Kovac corrected her, frowning as he looked at the photographs. He stared at the barely discernible bruises on Andy Fallon's throat, just below the vivid marks the noose had made. The nerves in his stomach came to life like a tangled pile of worms. 'I'm on the ass-end on my end of things. That pressure came from higher up the food chain.'

That pressure had come from Ace Wyatt.

Kovac leaned over the counter and caught Russell Turvey sitting back in the corner paging through *Hustler*.

'Jesus, Russell. Do me a favor and don't offer to shake my hand.'

Turvey barked and growled, his chest sounding like thunder in the distance. 'Kojak! J. Christ! You'd be back here too, if you got the chance.'

'Not with you.'

Turvey laughed again, tossing the magazine under his chair. He grabbed hold of the counter and rolled himself into position without getting up.

'I hear Springer bought it,' he said, fixing his squint eye on Kovac. The other one looked off to the left. 'I never liked him.'

Like that had made Cal Springer's demise inevitable.

'You were there too,' Turvey said.

'I swear I didn't pull the trigger. Liska can vouch for me.'

'Ha! Argh . . . Liska,' he purred, his expression a postcard for the word *lascivious*. 'Is she a dyke?'

'No!'

'Not even . . .' He waggled a hand.

'No,' Kovac said emphatically. 'Can we move on, please? I came down here for a reason.'

Turvey waved a hand at him. 'What?'

'I need to look at an old file. The Thorne murder. I don't have a case number but I've got the dates –'

'Don't matter,' Turvey said. 'It's not here.'

'You're sure?'

'I'm here every goddamn day. You think I don't know the place?'

'But –'

'I know it's gone because someone from IA came down and asked for it a couple of months ago. Mike Fallon's kid. It wasn't here then. It ain't here now.'

'And you don't know where it is?'

'Nope.'

Kovac sighed and started to turn away, wondering who might have it or have a copy.

'Funny you should ask for that one,' Turvey said.

'Why is that?'

''Cause I found that badge number you asked for the other day. It belonged to Bill Thorne.'

Amanda Savard had Bill Thorne's badge sitting on her desk in her home.

Kovac just stood there, trying to get his brain around that idea.

'I remember Bill Thorne,' Turvey said, rubbing his knobby chin. 'I rode patrol in the Third Precinct back then. He was the meanest son of a bitch I ever knew.'

'You're sure?' Kovac asked.

Turvey's brows went up. 'Sure? I once saw him knock a prostitute's teeth out for lying to him.'

'You're sure it's Thorne's badge?'

'Yeah. I'm sure.'

Kovac walked away, Russell Turvey's words blurring into white noise.

Amanda Savard had Bill Thorne's badge on her desk.

He went into the men's room, ran the cold water and splashed his face, then stood there with his hands braced on the sink, staring into the mirror.

His mind scanned back over the days, flashing on images of her, of the two of them. He thought back to Saturday night. They'd made love on his couch. And when she was getting ready to leave, she'd looked down at the coffee table and had seen the articles he had gathered at the library.

What's this?

The Thorne murder. Mike Fallon's shooting. Andy was looking at it. I'm just turning over rocks, see what crawls out.

Life turns on a dime, he'd said.

And gives back change.

He went to the first floor, where traffic was heavier than usual, the hall busy with cops and with reporters looking for scraps on the Rubel manhunt. No one seemed to see him. He stood at the edge of the scene, looking past the crowd, toward Room 126.

She was likely in her office. IA would be busy digging up dirt on Rubel and Ogden, going through any reports of prior problems with either of them. Savard would likely be called on the carpet by a captain who would demand to know why the investigation into Ogden and the Curtis murder had died out. Why hadn't any mention been made of Rubel at the time?

If he went down there right now, he might catch her between calls. And ... what? Confront her like some cheated husband? He could see the scene in his mind. He could feel the humiliation. No.

One of the reporters spotted him, and life snapped back into fast-forward mode.

'Hey, Kovac,' the guy said, coming over, trying to keep his voice down so as not to tip off his competition. 'I hear you were on the scene Saturday night. What happened?'

Kovac held up a hand and turned away. 'No comment.'

He ducked into the anteroom, pushed past the crowd trying to circumvent the receptionist, and keyed his way into the main office. Liska was gone. Donna from the phone company had come through with Andy Fallon's phone records for the past three months. Distraction. He could do this while his brain tripped and stumbled over the subject of Amanda. He turned on his computer, brought a reverse phone directory up on-line, and started in.

Too many of the numbers were unlisted. Nowadays, everyone wanted anonymity – and to avoid telemarketers. Those numbers that were listed were not of much interest. Mike, Neil, take-out restaurants. There were several calls to something called the Hazelwood Home. Kovac looked it up in the on-line Yellow Pages and found the place discreetly described as a 'care facility.' Care of what? A rest home for Mike, maybe? Though Mike Fallon hadn't really seemed in need of anything like that. A housekeeper, yes. A nursing home? No.

When he had gone through the list with the reverse

directory, Kovac started with the cold calls, dialing the unlisted numbers and, for the most part, getting answering machines.

One of the machines belonged to Amanda Savard. Fallon had called her at home several times in the last few days of his life.

Andy Fallon had been looking into the Thorne murder. Amanda Savard had Bill Thorne's badge on her desk.

She had very coolly denied Andy's mentioning his private investigation into the Thorne case.

God *damn*! If only he had Fallon's notes. There had to be files somewhere . . . and his laptop . . .

Or he could walk down the hall and ask Amanda point-blank about Thorne's badge.

His gut told him not to ask.

Or maybe it wasn't his gut at all.

She had Bill Thorne's badge. She had seen Andy Fallon on the night of his death. She had been to his house. Andy had phoned her house frequently just before he died.

I love a puzzle, he thought, a vicious feeling cracking through him like a whip.

Amanda Savard had gone to bed with him. Twice. He was poking around in the death of Andy Fallon. Andy Fallon had been poking around in the death of Bill Thorne. Amanda had Bill Thorne's badge.

He grabbed the telephone receiver and punched in the number for the Hazelwood Home.

The Hazelwood Home was a psychiatric care facility.

Kovac grabbed his coat and hat and bolted.

The wind skimmed over the snow, lifting a fine powder into the air so that, from the end of the driveway, the Hazelwood Home appeared shrouded in mist. A former private residence, the home was a sprawling, overdone homage to Frank Lloyd Wright. Long, low, horizontal lines gave the impression that the building was crouching into the ground. Huge old trees studded the snow-covered lawn. Beyond the grounds, the landscape looked open and marshy, which was much of the landscape west of Minneapolis.

Kovac parked under the carport at the entrance and went in past dueling holiday displays. Christmas on one side of the foyer, Hanukkah on the other. The overwhelming impression of the entry hall was darkness. A low beamed ceiling seemed too close overhead.

He looked for the youngest, least-experienced staff member working around the front desk, and homed in on her. A cherubic girl with natural blond curls clipped like a poodle's. Her name tag read 'Amber.' Amber's eyes went wide as Kovac showed her his badge, using it to lure her away from the older woman answering the phone.

'Is he near *here*?' the girl asked, worried.

'Excuse me?'

'That guy,' she answered in a hushed whisper. 'That *killer*. Are you here looking for him?'

Kovac leaned toward her. 'I'm not at liberty to say,' he whispered back.

'Oh, my gosh.'

'I need to ask you a couple of questions, Amber,' Kovac said, pulling out a snapshot of Andy Fallon he had taken from Mike's place. 'Have you seen this man around here?'

She seemed disappointed the photograph wasn't of Derek Rubel, but she recovered gamely.

'Yes. I've seen him. He's been here a couple of times.'

'Lately?'

'In the past few weeks. He's a police officer too,' she said, narrowing her eyes. 'At least, he *claimed* to be.'

'What was he doing here? Who did he speak to?' Kovac kept one eye on the older woman at the other end of the desk. At a place like Hazelwood, discretion would be the rule. Amber looked too innocent of sin to understand the meaning of the word.

'He came to visit Mrs Thorne,' she said simply, eyes blinking.

'You have to understand, Sergeant, Evelyn lives in her own world,' the doctor said as they walked down the long hall toward Evelyn Thorne's room. 'She'll acknowledge your presence. She'll interact with you. But the conversation will be her own.'

The psychiatrist was a large, soft-looking woman with a thick mane of long blond hair.

'I just want to ask her a couple of questions about the cop who came to see her a couple of times,' Kovac said. 'Sergeant Fallon. Did he speak with you?'

The doctor looked troubled. 'I spoke briefly with Mr Fallon. I wasn't aware he was here on police business. He told me he was Evelyn's nephew. He asked me if she ever speaks about her husband's murder.'

'Does she?'

'No. Never. She had her breakdown shortly after his death.'

'And she's been like this ever since?'

'Yes. Some days she's better than others, but she pretty much stays in hiding in her mind. She feels safe there.'

The doctor looked in the glass set in the center of Evelyn Thorne's door, then rapped twice before going in.

'Evelyn, you have a visitor. This is Mr Kovac.'

Kovac stopped just inside the room, feeling as if he'd taken a fist in the belly. Evelyn Thorne sat in an upholstered armchair, looking out her window, dressed in a blue track suit. She was thin, the kind of thinness that came from nerves. Her hair had gone gray. She wore it swept back from her face with a velvet headband. In the newspaper photograph he'd thought she looked a little like Grace Kelly. In reality she looked too much like someone else.

She turned her head to see him, her eyes a little vacant but her mouth curved in a pleasant smile.

'I know you!'

'No, ma'am, you don't,' he said, walking toward her.

'Mr Kovac needs to ask you some questions about the young man who came to see you, Evelyn,' the doctor said.

She paid no attention to the doctor. 'You were a friend of my husband,' she said to Kovac.

The doctor gave him the I-told-you-so look and left them.

The room was spacious, with normal-looking furniture except for the hospital bed, which was draped with a pretty flowered spread. *Not a bad place to while away the hours locked inside your own reality*, Kovac thought. It had to cost some major bucks. He wondered if Wyatt was footing the bill for this as well. No wonder he needed to go Hollywood.

'So nice of you to come,' Evelyn Thorne said with formality. 'Please have a seat.'

Kovac took the chair across from her and held out the photograph he'd shown Amber. 'Mrs Thorne, do you remember Andy Fallon? He came to see you recently.'

She took the photograph, still smiling. 'Oh, isn't he handsome? Your boy?'

'No, ma'am. He's Mike Fallon's boy. Do you remember Mike Fallon? He was a police officer. He came to your house the night your husband died.'

He didn't know if she heard a word he said. She seemed not to.

'They grow up so fast,' she said, getting up from her chair and going to a little bookcase that held a lot of magazines and a Bible.

'I have pictures too,' she said, digging for a magazine at the bottom. *Redbook*. 'She thinks she took them all. She doesn't like having photographs out, not of family. But I had to keep a few.'

She pulled a manila envelope from the magazine and extracted a couple of snapshots.

'My daughter,' she said proudly, holding them out to

Kovac. He didn't want to touch them, as if not touching them, not looking at them, would keep their truth at bay. But Evelyn Thorne pushed them into his hands.

She was younger in the photograph. A little thinner. Her hair was different. But there was no mistaking Evelyn and Bill Thorne's daughter: Amanda Savard.

36

Amanda Savard was Bill Thorne's daughter.

He remembered the only hint in the newspaper articles from all those years ago: *Thorne is survived by his wife and one daughter.* That was it. No name, no photo.

Savard was Evelyn's maiden name. He had been able to get that much out of her. Amanda must have taken the name for her own after the murder. Otherwise, she never could have come on the job without people making something of it.

Andy Fallon worked for Amanda Savard, Bill Thorne's daughter. He'd been looking into Bill Thorne's murder, the night Mike Fallon was shot, the night Ace Wyatt became a hero. Ace Wyatt had been paying off Mike Fallon for years. Andy Fallon was dead. Mike Fallon was dead. . . .

Kovac sat in the dark parking lot of the building that housed the Wyatt Productions offices. On his third cigarette in two hours, his head was pounding. Hell of a day. He felt beat up. He felt old. He felt hollow. Funny, he'd thought he was too cynical to be disillusioned or disappointed. *The joke's on you, Kovac.*

The building was nondescript. A brick two-story like a thousand others in the western suburbs. The parking lot had emptied in the last hour as the business day had come to a close and the CPAs and attorneys and orthodontist who shared the building had climbed into their cold vehicles and rolled down the street in a fog of exhaust to edge their way into the rush-hour crawl on 494.

Wyatt was expecting him. Had expected him ten minutes ago. Kovac let him wait, let the office staff leave. The Lincoln was parked in a reserved spot near the front of the building. Kovac had parked three rows back, alone. His pager trilled and he checked the display. Leonard. Fuck 'em.

He turned off the car and walked across the lot and into the building, tossing his cigarette just outside the door, not caring where it landed. The circular reception desk was deserted, the telephone ringing. A directory board on the wall showed Wyatt Productions to be on the second floor.

Kovac walked past the elevator, went up the stairs, and slipped into the outer office unnoticed. Like the rest of the building, everything was gray – the carpet, the walls, the upholstery on the square furniture. The walls were covered mainly with photographs of the great man being given commendations for this and that remarkable feat, being honored for his selfless service to the community. Photographs of him with local celebrities, with legends in law enforcement, with movie stars buttonholed on the sets of pictures being shot in the metro area.

The man had never met a camera he wouldn't turn his good side to. Evelyn Thorne's included.

Kovac sniffed and shook his head.

The knob turned on the door to Wyatt's office and the sound of voices spilled out in dribs and drabs, the volume rising and falling.

'. . . that kind of publicity . . . unacceptable, Gavin.' Wyatt.

'. . . situation can be defused . . . denials . . .' Gaines.

'Goddammit, you have to . . . image . . . my audience is Middle America, for god's sake.'

'I'm sorry –'

The door closed tight again. Kovac moved closer, straining to hear. Then Gaines came out, looking flushed and angry.

'What's the matter, Slick?' Kovac asked. 'Hard day on your knees?'

'I realize you have no appreciation for what I do,

Sergeant,' he said. 'There's really no need for you to make the point every time we meet.'

'But I like the way it makes your nostrils flare, Gavin.'

Gaines looked ready to bend an iron bar with his teeth. 'Captain Wyatt has been waiting for you.'

'Good. I'm a busy man.' Kovac went to the door, then looked back at Wyatt's right hand. 'You can go, Gaines. The captain won't be needing you. We're just going to talk about old times.'

Wyatt stood looking out a window at nothing. Darkness had fallen like an anvil an hour before. He watched Kovac's reflection in the window.

'No word yet on Rubel,' he said. A statement of fact.

'You'll hear it before I will.'

'Shouldn't you be out on the search?'

'With all your citizens beating the bushes? They'll bring him to you hog-tied. He can be the special guest on your next show.'

Wyatt went for the straight line. 'Maybe. I like the idea of the occasional interview with a bad guy. Let the public see how twisted minds work.'

He'd been spending too much time with the WB VPs.

'I have other cases ongoing,' Kovac said. 'Mike's murder. Andy's murder . . .'

Wyatt looked straight at him then.

'No one called you?' Kovac said, feigning shock. 'Stone believes Andy was strangled before he was hung.'

The color drained from his face. 'What?'

'Marks on the throat,' he said, running a finger around his own to demonstrate. 'Faint but there. The doc who did the autopsy missed them. I asked Dr Stone to personally go back over the autopsy, just in case the new guy missed something – having had pressure on him from higher up. Good thing, huh? Or he might have been buried with that little secret.'

'Why . . . ?' Kovac could see Wyatt scrambling mentally,

trying to get his legs back under him, trying to sound intelligent and ignorant at once. 'Do you think it had to do with Rubel?'

'Personally, no,' Kovac said. 'I think it's a pretty damn strange coincidence that first Andy dies and it looks like suicide, then his old man buys it and it's made to look like suicide. Don't you find that strange?'

Wyatt furrowed the famous brow. 'So you like Neil for both murders?'

Kovac ignored the question, feeling too raw and wrung out emotionally to dance the mental minuet. 'I found Evelyn Thorne. Andy found her too. You think I'll end up the same as he did, or the same as Mike?'

'I don't know what you're talking about.'

'Jesus Christ, Ace,' Kovac said, the impatience burning through. 'I don't have time for this bullshit! It goes back to Thorne! Andy found something about what happened that night, something no one else saw at the time, because they didn't want to see it, or they buried it because it was all in the family. It was cops. Thorne was a cop, you, Mike. The only one dead not a cop was that poor bastard Weagle.'

'Weagle attacked Evelyn!' Wyatt said. 'He – he beat her. He raped her. He shot Bill. Killed him. He shot Mike.'

'Did he?' Kovac asked. ''Cause I'm wondering here, Ace, why people interested in that case, connected to that case, are suddenly dead if it happened the way we all heard back then.'

Wyatt walked away, went behind his desk. Retreating, or taking cover . . . Kovac never took his eyes off the man, every muscle in his body taut, ready to move. He positioned himself so he could see both Wyatt and the door.

'What did Evelyn say to you?' Wyatt asked. 'She's not a well woman. I'm sure the doctors told you she's often delusional.'

'You told me you'd lost touch with her. You told me you didn't know where she was.'

'I was trying to protect her. Evelyn never recovered from what happened. She was always ... fragile. Something broke in her mind that night. The doctors have never been able to fix it. She retreated to a safe place, a world of her own. She seems to be happy there most of the time.'

'She showed me photographs,' Kovac said. 'Pictures of the old neighborhood, barbecues, friends. You know, she didn't have one photograph of Bill. Not one photograph of her husband.'

'Painful memories.'

'How painful?' Kovac asked.

Wyatt closed his eyes and drove his hands back over his hair. 'What's the point of this, Sam? It was twenty years ago.'

Kovac stared at him, looked around the plush executive office, thought of the career Ace Wyatt had made for himself since the night someone had shot and killed Bill Thorne. What if it was all a lie? A house of cards. A legend born of blood. With Wyatt's show poised to go national, what if Andy Fallon had found the answer to that question?

'There's a body count, Ace,' he said. 'If you don't see the point of that, you're in a bad place.'

Wyatt pulled down the game face, a granite mask. 'You haven't shown me any evidence that these deaths are tied to one another, or tied to the past. I don't believe it.'

'I'll admit, at this point, I'm still fishing,' Kovac said. 'Probably the same as Andy was fishing. But I think he found something – which is why he's dead – and I think I know where he put it. If it's there, Ace, it's mine. Better for everyone to get out in front of it now. You know what I'm saying? You. Savard. I know she's Thorne's daughter.'

Wyatt looked through him. 'You're saying you think I've done something wrong,' he said flatly. 'I haven't. I didn't. There's nothing to be gained in stirring up old dust,

Sam. People, careers, reputations could be damaged. For nothing.'

'I think two people are dead because of it,' Kovac said. 'That's something, Ace. I don't give a damn about any of the rest of it.'

He went to the door and put his hand on the knob, looking back at the legend. A man he'd never liked, and still there was a place deep inside him where he felt sorry.

'Evelyn sends her love,' he said quietly, and let himself out.

She was so tired. . . .

The workday had come and gone. Savard remained sequestered in her office. Hiding. Avoiding the press, avoiding having to go home. She had turned the lights off, except for her desk lamp, and sat, letting the silence envelop her. What a relief to be still, she thought, staring at the photograph she had taken and developed and framed herself years ago. A winter landscape.

This was why she shot landscapes rather than people: the stillness. If she could find stillness in her surroundings, she could hope to achieve it within herself . . . if only for a little while. If only while she was lost in the stark beauty of the picture. For those few moments, she could successfully ease the tension that quivered at the core of her.

The stillness didn't last tonight. A cacophony of sound invaded her brain. Angry questions, blunt questions, demands, directives. All that and the message from Hazelwood on her voice mail. She was so tired.

Kovac knew.

It had been just a matter of time. In the back of her mind, she'd always known that. In her heart, she had hoped for something more: a fold in time where events could be trapped, contained, separated, isolated. What a lovely idea. If only. But the past was poisonous and difficult to restrain, seeping around the edges of the boundaries she erected.

She closed her eyes and conjured an image, the fleeting memory of feeling safe and cared for. She had wanted so badly to accept it. She didn't want to carry the weight anymore. She was so tired. . . .

When she opened her eyes again, he was standing there. Panic clenched like a fist in her chest as she wondered if this moment was real or surreal. The nightmares came so frequently lately, it was becoming more difficult to tell.

He stood there in the shadows, expressionless, silent, the collar of his coat turned up. A sense of dread began to build deep inside her.

'You're Bill Thorne's daughter,' he said, and raised a gun.

37

Kovak took his time driving, playing it all through in his mind, trying to sort into chronological order the things he had learned today, patching the gaps with educated guesses. Trying not to react to any of it in an emotional way. Trying not to feel the sense of betrayal. Trying not to remind himself that he'd been right all along: that it was better not to want something more.

Neil Fallon's bar was closed, looking abandoned. The whole place looked like a shantytown that even the bums had forsaken – the crude cabins, the ice fishing houses, the work shed, the shed where Fallon stored the boats – all dark and empty of life, save for the rats. The only lights were a couple of security lights on poles and the Coors sign buzzing in the tiny window of the bar.

Kovac parked under the light and got out. He dug his Maglite out from under a pile of junk on the floor behind the driver's seat, then went to the trunk and rummaged through paper bags and evidence kits, finally coming up with the tire iron.

The wind had not let up. The temperature had dropped. It wasn't a night for a walk in the moonlight. Kovac took one anyway, going down to the boat shed. Senses sharp, he was hyper-aware of the cold, of the way it felt in his nose, in his lungs; hyper-aware of the sound of his shoes on the packed snow. He stopped near the shed and looked down the bank and down the shoreline.

In the moonlight, he couldn't see to where Derek Rubel's truck had gone through the ice, but it wasn't far. Standing among the empty buildings in the middle of nowhere, Kovac thought this was the kind of place where a man might vanish from one dimension into another and never be seen again.

There was a secret worth knowing. He filed it away for future reference. He had a feeling escape was going to look like a fine option after this was all over.

The gun went off with a deafening *bang!*

Amanda jerked back, up and out of her chair, arms flinging out to the sides.

And then she was awake.

The office was empty.

She stood behind the desk, her heart racing, lungs pumping as if she'd run a mile. She could smell her own sweat. Her clothes were damp with it. The emotions built and built and built inside her, choking her. Crushing her. A ragged sob tore from her throat and she flung herself at the desk, swinging her arms, knocking down the lamp, sending everything scattering, tumbling, falling, crashing. She pounded her fists on the desktop, crying, fighting, furious, terrified.

When the adrenaline ebbed and the outburst died, she sat back down in her chair and forced her mind to work.

No matter how she might have deluded herself all these years, it had always been only a matter of time.

Time was up.

She pulled open the desk drawer and took out the gun.

With the tire iron, Kovac pried loose the latch plate from the old door. The latch, complete with padlock, flopped to the side, and he went into the shed. He clicked on the flashlight in order to find the light switch.

Half a dozen boats of various sizes and types had been parked for the winter. Kovac walked around them, looking at the names. *Hang Time, Miss Peach, Azure II.* He chose one called *Wiley Trout* and climbed the ladder. When he climbed back down, he held a large, heavy backpack by one padded strap.

'Put it down, Kovac.'

Kovac held the bag out to one side and breathed a sigh. 'Put it down or what?'

'Or I'll kill you where you stand.'

'As opposed to killing me later and making it look like suicide? You weren't kidding when you said you did whatever the captain needed.'

'No, I wasn't kidding,' Gaines said. 'Put the bag down.'

'I guess you think there's something in it worth having.'

'It doesn't matter what's in it. Put it down.'

'Ah,' Kovac said, turning his head, trying to see what Gaines had pointed at his back. ''Cause you see, there's nothing in it but a ream of scrap paper. But you'll kill me first and worry about the evidence later. I know this is going to sound like a cliché, but you won't get away with it, Gaines. It's too late. Too many people know too much.'

'I don't think so,' Wyatt's assistant said with confidence. 'You suspect, you don't know. You're just fishing, and you're on your own. You don't have an official investigation. You haven't spoken with Leonard about your suspicions. You don't have any evidence as of now. The only people aware of what Andy Fallon was looking into are people who stand to lose. Neil Fallon was arraigned today for his father's murder. The ME won't change the ruling on Andy's death.'

'You sound pretty damn sure of all that,' Kovac said. 'Did Wyatt tell you he'd make it happen that way?'

'Wyatt doesn't know.'

'He doesn't know you've killed for him, that you've gotten rid of the people who could ruin his image with the American public? That's selfless of you, Gavin. He should be giving you a bonus.

'Or does that come later? When he's established, when the show's a hit and the big money rolls in? Is that when you show him the pictures or the videotape or whatever evidence you've squirreled away? Show him how much you love him.'

'Shut up.'

'And how do you explain my death?' Kovac asked, shifting his feet, shifting his position subtly. He still couldn't see what Gaines had in his hands. 'I'll tell you right now, Slick, I ain't gonna let it look like no suicide. If I'm going down, I'm going down kicking.'

'I have some ideas. Put the bag down.'

'It was easy with Andy, wasn't it?' Kovac said. 'He comes to Wyatt to ask some innocent questions. You see it makes Ace nervous. Maybe you decide to dig a little yourself, try to find out what Andy's got. Maybe he doesn't even realize what he's got, so he's got no worries. You're a good-looking guy, he's a good-looking guy. You go out a couple of times. He doesn't think much of it when you drop by with a bottle of wine. . . .'

'I didn't want to kill him,' Gaines said, and Kovac could hear the emotion in his voice, a strange mix of regret and relish. 'I'm not a killer.'

'Yes, you are. You thought he had something that might ruin your future. You planned it out. You drugged him. You strangled him unconscious so he couldn't fight. Then you hung him from a beam and let the noose do the last of the job.'

'I didn't want to.'

'And I'll bet you stood there and watched while he kicked and twitched. It's amazing how fast it happens, isn't it?'

'I told him I was sorry,' Gaines said. 'I was. But he would have ruined everything. He would have ruined Captain Wyatt. I've worked too hard for this chance. It's right there, in reach. It's happening – the show, the network deal. He would have taken it away. For nothing. For something that was over twenty years ago. For something that can't be changed. I couldn't let that happen.'

'You know what happened that night?' Kovac asked.

'I know Mike Fallon knew. He'd kept his mouth shut all this time because Wyatt paid him off. Andy had figured that out. If he had gotten his father to talk . . . I couldn't let that happen.'

'Wyatt has to suspect, Gavin. You think he's gonna keep you around if he knows you're a murderer? He's a cop, for chrissake. It's a law enforcement show. If he's smart, he'll put the collar on you himself and save his own ass. Think of the network special that would make.'

'Drop the fucking bag!'

'You're a murderer,' Kovac said again. 'He finds out –'

'So is he!' Gaines screamed. 'Drop the fucking bag!'

Kovac had no time to digest the revelation. He caught the motion of Gaines's arm in his peripheral vision and dove forward. The claw hammer just grazed the back of his head, his shoulder taking the brunt of the impact. Even through the thickness of his coat, the pain was a hard, hot ball, burning into the muscle.

Kovac rolled onto his back as Gaines swung wildly for his head again, burying the head of the hammer in the dirt floor.

'Drop it, Gaines!' Liska shouted. 'You're under arrest!'

'Gun!' Kovac yelled as Gaines drew from inside his open coat and ran.

Kovac rolled to the side and half under the boat. But Gaines's purpose now was escape, and he was already running, the backpack in his left hand, gun in his right. He swung his arm back and let a shot go. Liska answered back. Gaines kept running, heading for the lake-end door of the boat shed.

Liska charged past as Kovac pushed to his feet and pulled his weapon. Gaines ducked around the side of the last boat for cover and fired two more shots. Liska ducked right, the second of the shots splintering the fiberglass hull she used for cover, the bullet coming through two inches from her head. Then Gaines was out the door.

Kovac went out a side door and crouched behind several fifty-five-gallon oil drums, straining to hear, to get some bearing on which way Gaines had run. He couldn't hear anything but the wind.

'Elwood's got his vehicle,' Liska said, dropping down behind him, breathing hard. 'Tippen'll have radio cars on the way by now.'

They had set up the trap on the fly. No time to take the plan to Leonard. No desire to. Kovac admitted there hadn't been much to use as bait, but he'd heard enough and pieced together enough to float a hunch. If they kept the plan between themselves and no one bit, nothing was lost. If they had taken it to Leonard and Leonard had nixed it, nothing could have been gained.

Kovac pulled off a glove, touched the back of his head, and came away with bloody fingers. He swore under his breath. 'Which way did he go? He gets off the property and we have another Rubel on our hands, you and I are gonna be on duty at the county landfill.'

'We'll be *in* the landfill. Leonard will have us killed.'

Kovac moved to the last of the drums and scanned as much as he could see of the yard. No sign of Gaines, which meant he could have taken refuge in any one of the buildings on the property and they could end up with a standoff situation. Then suddenly the angry buzz of a small motor split the air, and there was no time to think.

The snowmobile burst out the end door of Neil Fallon's work shed, roaring straight for Kovac. Kovac planted his feet and squeezed off a shot, hitting the nose of the machine, then dove out of the way, rolled, and came up running.

Gaines had the throttle wide-open, heading for the lake, heading for the open area to the east of the ice fishing houses. The machine bucked hard over wind-packed drifts. Kovac ran after it, hoping just to keep Gaines in sight. He squeezed off two shots on the run with no real hope of hitting anything.

The snowmobile hit the bank and flew, Gaines coming up off the seat. The machine twisted out from beneath him in midair, ass-end dropping down, Gaines still hanging on to the handlebars.

Kovac ran harder. He could see Liska coming on his left.

The snowmobile hit the ice on end, driving into it. The sound of the lake's surface breaking was like a crack of thunder. Gaines landed beside the machine and went still for an instant.

'Watch the ice! Watch the ice!' Liska shouted as Kovac ran down the length of the old boat dock.

Gaines was already shaking off the impact, struggling to get to his feet, the backpack strapped around his shoulders. The snowmobile was going down, the ice around the point of impact cracking and popping. Another *pop* and the machine was gone.

'Give it up, Gaines!' Kovac shouted. 'There's nowhere to go!'

Gaines came up with the gun and pulled off another round. Kovac dropped flat to the dock. Gaines's scream brought his head back up.

'He's in the water!' Liska yelled.

Gaines made a strangled squealing sound, one arm flailing above the surface. Kovac stepped off the dock, testing the ice.

'Hang on, Gaines! Don't move!'

But Gaines was in panic mode, bobbing down in the water, then coming up and attempting to throw himself out of the hole, only breaking more ice and sending himself under again.

Kovac got down on all fours, spreading his weight over

more of the surface, moving toward the crumbling edge inches at a time.

'Gaines! Don't fight!' he shouted.

He could hear Gaines gasping, wheezing. The water temperature would send the body into shock quickly, shutting systems down. The weight of wet clothing would pull at him like a suit of armor. The backpack would be like an anvil strapped to his shoulders. His muscles would cramp and the panic would worsen.

'Let me grab your arm!' Kovac yelled, reaching out. Beneath his body he could hear the ice cracking.

Instead of allowing Kovac to take hold of him, Gaines clawed at him wildly but couldn't catch hold, couldn't grip. Another few inches of ice gave way and an animal sound of fear wrenched out of him.

'Hold still! Goddammit! Hold still!' Kovac screamed.

He focused on Gaines's arm and lunged forward, grabbing hold. The ice beneath his chest gave way, and his upper body went face-first into the water.

The cold was so intense, it was like hitting a brick wall at full speed. Instinctively, he beat at the water with his hands, as if it were solid and he could push himself up against it. He felt Gaines's hands on him, pushing him, pulling him, trying to drag him in. Another force pulled at him from behind, anchoring his legs, pulling him backward.

Kovac jerked his head back, came up coughing, choking, kicking, trying to scuttle backward to gain safer ice.

'Sam!' Liska shouted.

She was behind him, flat on the ice, still hanging on to one of his legs. Kovac went still. His fingers were already half numb with cold. Coughing, choking on the water he'd taken in, he stared at the hole in the ice.

Gaines was gone. The water was still and black in the moonlight.

For just an instant Kovac flashed on what drowning would be like: that brief instant beneath the water, blind, trying to come up for air and feeling nothing but ice above your head.

Then he closed the door on that part of his mind and crawled back toward the dock.

38

'And you think *I'm* ambitious,' Liska said. 'I've never actually murdered anyone for career advancement.'

They sat together in Kovac's car. The SO units had made the scene and Tippen was walking them through. One of the deputies had loaned Kovac a dry sweater. He'd borrowed a filthy hunting coat from Neil Fallon's workshop to put over it. The sleeves came halfway up his forearms, and it smelled like a wet dog.

'You've talked about it,' Kovac said. Someone had brought coffee. He drank it without tasting the coffee or the scotch Tippen had come up with.

'That doesn't count.'

They were silent for a moment.

'How much do you think Wyatt knows?' Liska asked.

Kovac shook his head. 'I don't know. He has to suspect by now. It all goes back to Thorne. He sure as hell knows everything about that night.'

'And it's been a secret all these years.'

'Until Andy Fallon started digging around. That must have been what Mike was talking about when he said he couldn't forgive Andy for what he was doing, that Andy had ruined everything, that he'd told Andy just to let it go. I thought he was talking about Andy coming out. . . . Jesus, all these years.'

'You think Wyatt killed Thorne?' Liska asked.

'That's where I end up. Evelyn Thorne was in love with him.'

'But how would Gaines have found out?'

'I don't know. Maybe Andy had made the same

connection and said something to Gaines. Maybe he'd seen Andy's notes. I don't know.'

'Where does the guy who got pinned for the murder fit in?'

'I don't know.'

There was a hell of a lot of story to what happened that night all those years ago, Kovac thought. Aside from Ace Wyatt, there was one other person living who might be able to tell it. Amanda.

'You want to talk to Wyatt alone?' Liska asked. 'I'll ride along if you need me –'

'No,' he murmured. 'I need to do it. For Mike. Whatever else he was, he meant something good to me once.'

Liska nodded. 'I'll go back to the office, then get a jump on the paperwork for this adventure.'

'Why don't you go home, Tinks? It's late.'

'The boys are staying with my mother because of Rubel. I got nothing to go home to but a radio car with a couple of assholes sitting in my driveway.'

'No word on Rubel yet?'

'Lots of tips. Lots of false alarms. I hope something flushes him out, if he hasn't blown for Florida by now.'

'Are you scared?' Kovac asked, looking at her.

She met his gaze and nodded. 'Yes. For myself. For the boys. I just have to keep thinking we'll get him first.'

They fell silent again.

'I feel really old, Tinks,' Kovac said at last. 'Tired.'

'Don't think about it, Sam,' she advised. 'If you stop moving long enough to think about it, you won't get up again.'

'That's cheery.'

'Hey, I've lost my shot at a career in Hollywood,' she said with a false scowl. 'What do you want from me? Mary Fucking Sunshine?'

405

He found enough energy to chuckle, then coughed. His lungs still hurt from the cold water.

'Hey.' Liska reached across and patted his cheek. 'I'm really glad Gaines didn't kill you, partner.'

'Thanks. Thanks for saving my life, partner. I could have been under that ice with him.'

'That's what friends are for,' she said simply, and got out of the car.

Somehow, even in the middle of the night, all legal on-street parking spaces around city hall were taken. Liska pulled into the emergency zone smack in front of the building and left it there. The hell if she was parking in a ramp tonight.

She was secretly glad for the chance to come back to the office. She had always liked being here at night, while most of the city was asleep. Tonight it beat going home. If she went home, she would have too much quiet time to think about the sorry state of her personal life, too much time to miss the boys.

The hallways were quiet. The feds had set the Rubel task force in their own building on Washington Avenue. The action would be there tonight.

She paused in front of the door to the IA offices, thinking how strange the circles of life could be. A week before, she would have spat on the ground at the mention of Internal Affairs. In a matter of days she had seen enough bad cops to last her a lifetime.

No one noticed her as she went into the CID offices. Maybe she would just stay the night, she thought as she stowed her purse in the drawer, sleep in the space under her desk, like the homeless people who sought out hiding places in the skyway system after everything had closed.

She clicked the computer on, turned to take her coat off . . . and found Derek Rubel standing at the end of the cubicle, holding a gun.

'Tell the story. From the beginning.'

The room was so quiet, Savard could feel the silence as a pressure against her eardrums.

Wyatt sat behind his desk, staring at her, staring at her gun. She had placed a small tape recorder on the desk in front of him. They were in his home. Just the two of them. Wyatt had married once in the years since the night of Bill Thorne's murder. It hadn't lasted.

'Tell the story,' she insisted. 'Don't waste my tape.'

He looked hurt. 'Amanda . . . why are you doing this?'

'Andy Fallon is dead. Mike Fallon is dead.'

'I didn't kill them,' he said.

'All these years,' she whispered. 'All these years, I couldn't tell . . . because of Mother. Because of what she did that night. That man was already dead. I couldn't save him. I thought I could make it up somehow, make it right some other way . . .'

For a long time she had let herself believe that was penance enough: stopping other bad cops from hurting people. Keeping the dirty secret of her family, the dirty secret of the family of cops her father had been a part of. At the same time, she dedicated her life to breaking the secrets of the people in the MPD, not allowing the cops in her department to get away with what Bill Thorne had gotten away with, with what Ace Wyatt had done.

Wyatt had done his own penance. But it hadn't mattered. Her father was still dead . . . except in her nightmares. Weagle was still dead . . . except in her nightmares. Now Andy . . . Now Mike Fallon . . .

'I can't live with all these corpses in my head,' she said, voice quavering. She made a motion with the gun. 'You tell the story. Tell it now.'

'Amanda . . .'

His voice was like a razor on her nerves: condescending, patronizing. She shifted the gun two inches to the right and put a bullet into the wall behind his head.

'I said tell the story!' she screamed.

Wyatt went white, then red. Sweat ran down his face. The strong ammonia smell of urine burned the air.

'I . . . can't . . . take . . . this . . . any . . . more,' she said through her teeth. There was a part of her brain that recognized her behavior as irrational. But then, that was part of the problem, wasn't it? She had been too rational, too practical for too long, suppressing the horror, the fear, the knowledge that what had happened was wrong and that she could have stopped it all.

'I'll begin for you,' she offered, then announced herself and the date and the place, beginning the tape in the way she would any police interview. She introduced the subject, stated the date of the incident. Wyatt stared at her.

'I loved your mother,' he said. 'What I did, I did for her, to protect her. You know that, Amanda.'

Tears filled her eyes. 'She's protecting herself now. No one can hurt her. I can't let any more people die and not do anything about it. That's wrong. I became a cop to keep that from happening. Do you understand that? Because of that night, I am what I am. I became a cop to police the police, so what happened that night wouldn't happen to someone else. But then it did.'

'I didn't kill them, Amanda. Andy. Mike. I didn't –'

'Yes, you did. Don't you see? Tell the story.'

'They killed themselves,' he said, but there was no conviction in his voice. He couldn't even tell the lie to himself.

Tears rolled down Wyatt's face. He was shaking visibly. He looked at the tape recorder, probably wondering if she wanted the story on tape because she was planning to kill him after he had finished telling it.

'Bill Thorne was the cruellest man I ever knew,' he began, his voice trembling. 'He tormented your mother, Amanda. You knew that. Nothing she did was good

enough for him. He took his anger out on her. He beat her.
He didn't hurt you, though, did he, Amanda?'

'No,' she whispered, trembling too. 'He never hit me.
But I knew. I saw. I hated him for it. I wanted someone to
stop him, but no one ever did . . . because he was a cop.
You saw what he did to her – the black eyes, the bruises.
You saw. The other cops saw. They all looked the other
way. I could never understand that,' she said. 'The others,
maybe . . . but you. She loved you. How could you have
let that go on?'

'Your mother didn't want –'

'Don't. Don't even pay lip service to that excuse. That
she didn't want the embarrassment, that she didn't want to
make trouble. She was a battered woman.'

He looked away, ashamed.

'Because he was a cop,' she said. 'You let it all come to
what happened that night because you couldn't rat out a
rotten son of a bitch like Bill Thorne.'

Wyatt didn't answer. There was no answer.

'On the night in question . . .' she said.

'I got a call from her that something was wrong. She was
hysterical. Bill had come home unexpectedly. He'd been
drinking. Bill would do that – drink on the job. He had no
regard for any rules but his own. He –' He broke off and
started again, the emotions of that night coming back. 'He
raped her. He beat her.

'Evelyn had had enough,' he said, staring down at the
desktop, tears falling faster. 'She got hold of a gun, and she
shot Bill twice in the chest. Then she called me.

'I couldn't let her be punished for what Bill had done to
her. I couldn't trust that the courts would take her side.
What if it came out she and I had been seeing each other? A
prosecutor would have seen it as motive. She might have
gone to prison.'

'And so you found Weagle –'

'He was there. In the neighborhood. He was on the

409

street as I went to your house. I didn't know what he might have seen or heard.'

Wyatt put his head in his hands and began to sob. 'I got him to come into the house. And I shot him . . . with Bill's thirty-eight. Oh, Jesus . . . Then Mike came . . . and I was there with the body. I panicked. . . .'

'Jesus Christ,' Kovac said, pushing the office door open. He stared at Wyatt, who was crying and choking and did not look up. 'You shot Mike Fallon.'

Liska stood frozen. A thousand things went through her mind in a heartbeat. To rush him, to scream, to throw something, to try to take cover. Thank God she had called the boys earlier and told them she loved them.

'Put the gun down, Rubel,' she said in a tone that was remarkably, ridiculously conversational.

'You bitch.'

He wore the mirrored shades. She couldn't see his eyes. Not good.

'You're smart to give it up here,' Liska said. 'No one will hurt you. You're with family.'

'It was none of your fucking business.'

'You killed a man,' she said. 'That's all my business.'

Behind him, Liska could see Barry Castleton moving in slowly, his eyes huge, gun in hand.

'Put the gun down,' she said. 'You won't leave this building, Derek.'

'What do I care?' he said. 'I knew that when I came in. I'm a dead man walking. I've got nothing to lose. Better to die now, fast. And what a bonus – I get to take you with me, bitch.'

'You put Mike Fallon in that chair,' Kovac said, coming into the room. 'All these years you let everyone think you were the big hero. You put him in that fucking chair.'

Wyatt cried harder, blubbering through his hands. 'I

410

didn't mean to! I panicked. When I realized . . . I did what I could to keep him alive. Thinking all the while that my career was over, that he would tell. But still I kept him alive –'

'And became a hero because of it.'

'What could I do? I tried to make it up to him.'

'Yeah, I'm sure having a big-screen TV made all the difference,' Kovac said. 'Did he know it was you that shot him?'

'He claimed he never remembered all of it. And yet . . . there were times . . . comments he made . . . I thought maybe . . .'

'And no one ever checked the ballistics beyond seeing all the slugs were thirty-eights,' Kovac said. ''Cause you were all cops except the dead mutt with the record. And besides, you had a witness – Evelyn. Or were there two?' he asked, looking to Savard.

Savard never took her eyes off Wyatt. 'I was told to stay in my room, to say I hadn't seen anything. I did that because of Mother, because she would have taken the blame.'

'Jesus.' Kovac took a breath, feeling sick.

'Mike was the hero,' Wyatt insisted. 'Mike was the hero.'

'Mike is dead. Gaines killed him. Because of you. And he killed Andy,' Kovac said. 'You knew Andy was asking about that night. He came to you. Then he turns up dead. You had to know –'

'No! I thought he killed himself!' Wyatt insisted. 'Really –'

'You could have stopped it all,' Savard said, tears running down her face. '*I* could have stopped it. Andy had come to me too. After he found Mother. I should have stopped it then. I'm a cop.

'I could have stopped it,' she said, looking inward. The gun was in her hand, her hand was shaking badly. 'I'm sorry. I'm so sorry, Andy. . . .'

'You didn't kill him, Amanda,' Kovac said gently, his anger shifting to fear as he watched her look at the weapon in her hand. 'Let me have the gun. We'll stop it now, tonight. I'll help you.'

'It's too late,' she murmured, looking inward. 'I'm sorry. I'm so sorry.'

'Give me the gun, Amanda.'

She looked at the weapon in her hand and raised it, turning the barrel toward herself.

'Drop the gun, Rubel!' Castleton called. 'We're on you.'

Rubel pointed the nine-millimeter at Liska's chest and screamed, an animal roar, his face going red, the cords in his thick neck standing out like ropes beneath the taut skin.

'Give me the gun, Amanda,' Kovac said, stepping toward her. Everything inside him was shaking. 'It's over now, honey.'

'I could have stopped it,' she said.

Kovac took another step. 'Amanda, please . . .'

She looked into his eyes. 'You don't understand.'

'Amanda.'

'It's all my fault.'

'No,' Kovac whispered, reaching out slowly. His hand was shaking like a drunk's.

'Yes,' she said softly, nodding her head. Her finger stroked the trigger. 'They're all dead because of me.'

Castleton roared back, screaming, moving on Rubel.

Liska jammed her hand into her coat pocket.

Rubel turned his head, just for a second. A second was all she needed.

The tactical baton snapped to full length, and Liska moved in and to the side, swinging it overhand as hard as she could. The bones in Rubel's forearm snapped as the gun went off, and the shot went into a wall. Then Rubel crumpled to the floor, screaming, writhing.

Liska dropped the baton and walked out of the cubicle.

'Amanda . . .' Kovac whispered. He would later look back on that single instant in time, and know that what he'd seen in her eyes at that moment was a reflection of his own dying hope.

'Amanda . . . give me the gun.'

'No,' she said softly. 'No, Sam. Don't you see? I could have stopped it twenty years ago. My mother didn't shoot Bill Thorne. I did.'

Kovac would never have any memory of the sound the gun made when it went off. He would never remember the screams – Ace Wyatt's, his own. The memory would forever be in images only:

The spray of blood and bone and brain matter.

The split second of surprise in Amanda's eyes before they went blank.

Himself, sitting on the floor, holding her body, as if his consciousness had detached from his own body and pulled away to try to escape the horror.

But there was no escape. There never would be.

39

'Tippen called,' Liska said.

She looked like hell. Tinker Bell on heroin. Pale, purple smudges under her eyes, hair sticking up in all directions. Who knew the last time she'd slept. Kovac could barely remember the last time *he'd* slept. Yet, exhausted as he was, the last thing he wanted to do was go home. The job was his refuge. Liska's too.

And so they had gone on instead of going home. A new day had dawned, bright and cold. They stood on the front steps of Gavin Gaines's town house for the execution of the search warrant, looking for whatever they could find to tie him to the murders of Andy and Mike Fallon. Looking for anything that might suggest Ace Wyatt had knowledge of those murders.

Kovac looked at the sun, a pale orange ball in the palest of blue skies, a halo around it. Sundog. Meant it was cold.

No fucking lie.

'He said they found Andy's files,' Liska said. 'In his boat. Good hunch.'

'Neil told me Andy had been out there Sunday afternoon,' Kovac said. 'The files weren't anywhere else. Gaines didn't have them, or he wouldn't have followed me out there last night. Though I'll bet he grabbed the laptop and got rid of that the night he killed him.'

'Why do you think Andy hid the files and then let Gaines into his house?'

'I don't know. Maybe he just didn't want Gaines to get a look at them. I'm sure he didn't think Gaines would kill for them.'

'What's going to happen to Wyatt?'

Kovac shrugged. 'There's no statute of limitations on murder. We've got the tape with his confession to killing Weagle and shooting Mike.'

'And his lawyer will say it was given under duress, and he hadn't been Mirandized, and blah, blah, blah.'

'Yeah. I'd say there's no justice,' he said. 'But there is. Sometimes it just takes a while to come around. And sometimes when it does, it's not quite what we had in mind.'

They said nothing for a moment, just stood there watching the street.

'I'm sorry about Savard,' Liska said.

Kovac hadn't told her about his feelings for Amanda. What was the point in anyone hearing that? Bad enough that he had to deal with it at all. Worse to have sympathy. Worse yet, pity. But he'd told her the tale of what had happened in Wyatt's house. He'd told her what he knew, what he'd pieced together, what Wyatt had told him in the aftermath.

He could too easily picture Amanda, seventeen and vulnerable and afraid; in need of justice, not getting it from the people she should have been able to rely on. She'd done the only thing she thought would save her mother: she'd shot her father dead. Then Evelyn Thorne had done the only thing she believed would save her daughter: assumed culpability. Then Wyatt had come into the picture, and the tragedy spiraled on.

He remembered now what Amanda had said to him Friday night as they stood in her kitchen. *I've tried to make my choices with the idea that I've made those choices for the greatest good. Sometimes someone suffers in the process, but I made the decision for the right reason. That should count for something, shouldn't it?*

'I'm sorry too,' he murmured at last, glad for the sunglasses that hid his eyes and the emotions in them.

'There's nothing left for Wyatt,' he said, digging a

415

cigarette out of his pocket and hanging it on his lip. 'He's over. There's nothing left . . .'

For me, he thought, but he didn't say it.

He had the job, the only thing he'd ever been any good at.

Somehow it didn't feel like enough now. He didn't think it would fill the hole inside him. Maybe nothing ever would.

'How are you doing?' he asked.

Liska shrugged and put on her shades. 'Okay for having stared into the face of death. I wouldn't want to do that every day.' She gave him the elbow and a smirk. 'See? That Hollywood job would have been the way to go. Money for nothing.'

They were quiet again for a moment, then she said, 'I was scared. I'm still scared. I don't want to think about the boys growing up without me. Someone sticks a gun in my face and I make a joke of it. But it's not funny.'

'You're not gonna leave me, are you, Tinks?'

She didn't answer him right away, and when she did, it wasn't really an answer at all. 'I'm gonna take a vacation. Take the boys somewhere fun. Get a tan.'

Elwood came to the door and stuck his head out. 'You'll want to see this.'

They went into the town house and followed him through a maze of cops, up the stairs to the master bedroom and into a walk-in closet.

Gaines had been a clotheshorse. The closet was hung with rods of suits and shirts. Shelves were stacked with sweaters and shoes. Someone had pushed aside the clothes on the rod that extended across the back of the closet to reveal a secret work of art.

'Jesus,' was all Kovac could say.

Gaines had filled the wall with photographs and news clippings of Wyatt. Articles about the man, about the show, about the deal with the WB network. Polaroids of Wyatt in fifty different settings, shaking hands, posing with officials and fans. Photographs of the two of them in various social settings. In the center: Wyatt's eight-by-ten glossy. A shrine.

'Eew,' Liska said, wrinkling her nose. 'Does anyone besides me want to go take a shower?'

'I found these in an envelope on the shelf,' Elwood said, handing Kovac a stack of Polaroids.

Andy Fallon hanging from the beam in his bedroom. Full body shot. Naked. Freshly dead. A close-up of his face. Mike Fallon sitting dead in his chair.

'Something for the scrapbook,' Kovac said, echoing Gaines's own words as he had shot pictures at Wyatt's party and at the ice rink with the WB VPs.

'You think he took them to blackmail Wyatt later on?' Elwood said.

Kovac looked from the Polaroids to the collage and back.

'No,' he said, handing the photographs back. 'I don't.'

EPILOGUE

Amanda Savard's funeral was Thursday. A week to the day after Andy Fallon's. Kovac attended alone, one of two dozen people in the small chapel at the funeral home. She had lived a confined, controlled life within the walls of her defenses. Kovac suspected he was one of the few people who had ever had a glimpse inside those walls.

Evelyn Thorne was there with her doctor. Whether or not she knew what was happening was anyone's guess. She sat quietly through the service, staring at the photograph she had brought with her. Amanda at the age of five. Bright-eyed and very serious. Her hair in a ponytail with a blue velvet bow. She showed it to Kovac three times. A part of him wanted to ask to keep it, but he didn't.

The service was simple, the basic closing on earthly existence. Ashes to ashes and dust to dust. Such an inadequate distillation of life: you're born, you live, you die. There were no eulogies. There was no service graveside. She was not buried next to her father.

The details of Amanda's involvement in Bill Thorne's death had been kept from the press. Her funeral was not considered newsworthy. Mike Fallon's funeral drew a thousand law enforcement professionals from all over the upper Midwest, and made the front page of the *Star Tribune*. Kovac did not attend.

He slipped back into the chapel after the service had ended, after the rest of the mourners had gone. He sat for a long time, staring at the closed casket, not quite allowing himself to wonder what might have been. The funeral home director came in and gave him that same hopeful look as waitstaff in a bar at closing.

'Take your time,' the man said with a polite smile, backing away toward the potted palms along the side of the room.

Kovac stood and dug a hand into his coat pocket. 'Can I leave something with her? Is it too late for that?'

'Certainly.' He came forward again, his eyes kind. 'I can take care of that for you.'

Kovac pulled out the badge he had carried as a patrolman when he'd first come on the job too many years ago. He looked at it, ran his thumb over it, then handed it to the funeral director.

'I'd like her to have this.'

The man took it, nodded, and offered a gentle smile. 'I'll see that she gets it.'

'Thanks.'

There were just two cars left in the side lot. His and Liska's. She stood leaning against his driver's side door, arms crossed.

'You okay?' she asked, eyes narrowed.

Kovac looked back at the building. 'Naw, not really . . . I broke one of my own rules. Expected too much.'

Liska nodded. 'I broke that one too. . . . So, I guess we can be morose together.'

He shoved his hands into his pockets and hunched his shoulders against the cold. One corner of his mouth twitched up. 'I'm not morose, I'm bitter.'

For a moment she just looked at him, not with the cop eyes, but with the eyes of a friend. Then she came away from the car and put her arms around him and held him. Kovac hugged her back, eyes squeezed tightly against the need to cry. They held each other that way for a minute, maybe two.

When she stepped back, Liska popped him on the arm and tried to grin. 'Hey, we've got each other, huh? Come on, partner, I'll buy you a cup of joe.'

Kovac smiled softly. 'You're on . . . friend.'

available from
THE ORION PUBLISHING GROUP

☐ **Cry Wolf** £6.99
TAMI HOAG
978-1-8579-7478-2

☐ **Dark Paradise** £6.99
TAMI HOAG
978-1-8579-7359-4

☐ **Night Sins** £6.99
TAMI HOAG
978-0-7528-0353-1

☐ **Guilty as Sin** £6.99
TAMI HOAG
978-0-7528-1539-8

☐ **A Thin Dark Line** £6.99
TAMI HOAG
978-0-7528-1617-3

☐ **Lucky's Lady** £6.99
TAMI HOAG
978-0-7528-1718-7

☐ **Dead Sky** £6.99
TAMI HOAG
978-0-7528-7813-3

☐ **Magic** £6.99
TAMI HOAG
978-0-7528-1716-3

☐ **Ashes to Ashes** £6.99
TAMI HOAG
978-0-7528-2691-2

☐ **Still Waters** £6.99
TAMI HOAG
978-0-7528-3768-0

☐ **Dust to Dust** £6.99
TAMI HOAG
978-0-7528-4333-9

☐ **Dark Horse** £6.99
TAMI HOAG
978-0-7528-4960-7

☐ **Kill the Messenger** £6.99
TAMI HOAG
978-0-7528-5922-4

All Orion/Phoenix titles are available at your local bookshop or from the following address:

Mail Order Department
Littlehampton Book Services
FREEPOST BR535
Worthing, West Sussex, BN13 3BR
telephone 01903 828503, *facsimile* 01903 828802
e-mail MailOrders@lbsltd.co.uk
(Please ensure that you include full postal address details)

Payment can be made either by credit/debit card (Visa, Mastercard, Access and Switch accepted) or by sending a £ Sterling cheque or postal order made payable to *Littlehampton Book Services*.
DO NOT SEND CASH OR CURRENCY

Please add the following to cover postage and packing

UK and BFPO:
£1.50 for the first book, and 50p for each additional book to a maximum of £3.50

Overseas and Eire:
£2.50 for the first book plus £1.00 for the second book and 50p for each additional book ordered

---

BLOCK CAPITALS PLEASE

name of cardholder .... *delivery address*
                      .... *(if different from cardholder)*
address of cardholder ....
....
....
....
        postcode ....   *postcode* ....

☐ I enclose my remittance for £ ....

☐ please debit my Mastercard/Visa/Access/Switch (delete as appropriate)

card number ☐☐☐☐☐☐☐☐☐☐☐☐☐☐☐☐☐☐

expiry date ☐☐☐☐   Switch issue no. ☐☐

signature ....

prices and availability are subject to change without notice